TO SAVE THE CHILDREN

At that instant heavy things began to be shoved or carried to the door and, Caroline thought, were left there. "This is only for you darlings," Mama called, grunting from exertion. "I've called the police and they'll come and let you out—don't worry." Her laugh wasn't quite Mama's. "He's strong, but it would take a while for him to move everything—and I'll tell him he has no time to waste!" She laughed again as things thudded and creaked, clanged and rattled, cracked and tinkled and rumbled into chaotic place on the other side of Caroline's bedroom door. "He *won't* do it to you, Caroline—and he won't do it to you *again,* Thaddie!" The noises and Mama's increasingly garbled distant ramblings continued for minutes along with frightening sounds of her labored breathing.

"Now I lay me down to sleep," Caroline prayed bolt upright, saying the one prayer she knew, "I pray the Lord—"

BLOODLINES

J. N. WILLIAMSON

LEISURE BOOKS   NEW YORK CITY

A LEISURE BOOK®

December 1998

Published by

Dorchester Publishing Co., Inc.
276 Fifth Avenue
New York, NY 10001

ISBN 0-8439-4468-4

Printed in the United States of America.

For some of the understanding women in my life, starting (always) with Mary, then moving along to my sister Marylynn; my daughter Mary; my good friend, Mona Keller; and for my editor Pamela Pia; the great teacher Jean Grubb; plus my granddaughters Joy, Alaina, Stephani, B.J., Michelle, Natasha, and the distaff twin, brilliant Amber.

Death is a pebble tossed into placid water
Rings of agitation rush outward, a myriad of lives
Disturbed . . .
          —t. winter-damon, *The Magick Mirror*

Prologue

"We are pilgrims here,
with a dwelling place elsewhere."
　　　　—Malcolm Muggeridge, *The Green Stick*

So small any shadows they cast were consumed instantly by insignificance and twilight, two unnoticed children stared at two adults. They hated them on sight.

A third adult sat in the dimly lit parlor with the visiting Tinsdales but she was merely old Enid Godby, who ran the guardian home. Miss Godby was of no importance to them.

Mr. and Mrs. Tinsdale were the young adults who might take them away.

More specifically, though neither brother nor sister could have quite explained the details of their automatic hatred to anyone but each other, these "Tinsdales" were the latest grown-ups who might take them even farther from Father. So far away even he might not be able to find them.

So, because they were just children who had already

learned there was a need to justify fear of the unknown even when it was disguised as hatred, five-year-old Caroline told her big brother Rhonda Tinsdale's hair wasn't really red like that and that her legs were skinnier'n the legs of a dead cat they'd seen once. Six-year-old Thaddie replied that Thurman Tinsdale's mustache was one he'd drawn on his lip, and he was even uglier'n the dead cat had been. Then they muffled giggles.

Neither child had the slightest need to point out that Mrs. Tinsdale wasn't half as pretty as their dead mama, Deborah, or that Mr. Tinsdale wasn't half as neat as Marshall Madison, their father who had run off into the night—left them without even saying why, or good-bye.

Because if they *had* mentioned Father, they would then have needed to open up their months-old wounds and try to understand why the bravest and smartest and best grown-up in the world had not wanted them any longer and hadn't even contacted them since he left.

While the three adults down in the parlor discussed the children's immediate future as quietly and calmly as if the topic was the weather, Thad and Care spoke in whispers like verbal feathers on a flight of stairs leading to the two dormitories. Both brother and sister had been asleep when the Tinsdales arrived from Queens, yet neither had been awakened by the closing door, the grown-up chatter, or the hectic autumn weather swarming all over SoHo like small wild things attacking. They didn't know why or how they had awakened. Perhaps it had been something about the locket Caroline wore on a chain around her neck, with a picture of Mama inside. She liked believing that a part of Deborah Madison still lived in the photo on the right side of the locket. Alas, there was no likeness of Father occupying the left side.

Regardless of the real explanation, fair-haired Caroline had come to consciousness immediately and then crept out of the gender-separated dorm and gone to awaken her brother in the boys' section. None of the other boys awoke because no conversation between Care and Thaddie had been needed; this was the enactment of a pact the siblings shared—an understanding that one would let the other know when outsiders came to inspect and bargain for them.

They'd begun a soundless descent to the first floor when it occurred to the year-older, black-haired, and dark-skinned Thad that prospective foster parents always came to the guardian home by day—at least that was how it was since Caroline and he had been brought there.

But Thaddie hadn't told his sister how that surely meant Rhonda and Thurman Tinsdale had *already* visited the guardian home and seen or met Care and him, and that they had come back because they'd surely decided on somebody. Caroline didn't scream or cry real loud when she got the bad news, but she got a sad look like Mama'd had, and that was scary for Thad. It made him believe he might lose her too.

Now, perched on a step with his tiny legs thrust between the railings in the defiance of hoped-for invisibility, Thad was badly worried. He didn't for an instant believe the despised Tinsdales had returned to Miss Godby's because they had chosen some other children in her care. That wasn't because of any old locket—Thad had nothing substantial to remind him of either parent—or any other sort of magic either. It was because he knew with all his heart that he and Caroline were the best-looking kids in the crummy old house, the smartest, and the best—

Because Marshall Madison, his father, had told him so. Him and Caroline, they was special.

"We would like to know more about their birth parents," Thurman Tinsdale said quietly to Enid Godby, glancing toward his pretty wife.

Rhonda followed his lead as if they had rehearsed it.

11

"Yes, friends of ours who already took a couple of foster children insisted we inquire." She uncrossed, then re-crossed, long and silken legs. "Many children these days are born . . . well, addicted." She glanced at Thurman. "We're new to the program, so—

"Thad and Caroline are addicted to nothing," Miss Godby said, interrupting. She was a single woman of sixty-four who had begun to dream of retirement, seemed older than her years, and the hope of finding homes for a few more children before she gave it up gave her the demeanor of a beardless female Santa Claus. "Besides, they're *not* newborns, infants. I've already told you everything on record about these children, and there's positively no evidence of any emotional or physiological burden."

"Not *everything*," Rhonda said smoothly, lifting fine auburn brows.

"The parents"—Thurman took the thread—"we know nothing about them at all."

"They're *wonderful*!" Caroline Madison answered, her whisper getting loud enough at the end that her brother Thad clapped his palm over her mouth. She got pale, even whiter-faced, when she was mad. Thad couldn't remember when even the skin of her neck and her arms had looked so pale. He raised two or three fingers tentatively away from her mouth, and Caroline's chin dropped to her chest. "Better'n *you*!" she said to the adults, but once more softly enough that Thad could relax.

He stuck the front of his face between the railings with his spindly legs and brooded. He shared that trait with Care, he knew deep inside (without having words for it); he and she both got super-still a whole lot, and he did it sometimes when he wasn't really mad or unhappy. Caroline got silly when she was happy, he remembered, but it was a distant memory now and he probably wouldn't remember it much longer.

Unless he remembered how Mama once had been happy—and silly—too.

"I will not go into any detail about the birth parents," Miss Godby said after a pause. "You may take my word for it that there is no reason to hesitate in accepting Caroline and Thad involving genetics or any aspect of heredity, including known diseases or addictions. No defects, no biochemical inheritance. Each birth was one-hundred-percent normal, and there is no evidence of any form of abuse. You've both seen their medical records since they were put in my care, and they're clear."

Neither Tinsdale glanced toward the other, not visibly. Thurman, however, clearing his throat, was obviously going to insist on asking their prearranged questions. "Social Services explained to us that what you're talking about is entirely correct, Ms. Godby—"

"Miss," the white-haired woman interjected. She smiled. "Or Enid."

"Enid," said Rhonda Tinsdale as if she were making up her mind, "we're prepared to provide an inducement." Seeing something in the older woman's expression change, she threw up her hands, begged Miss Godby to wait. "But that's just because we *have* reached a favorable decision. About the children." Rhonda flushed and Thurman nodded. "We've heard that you have a marvelous record of service here—and that you'll be retiring soon." Rhonda grasped Thurman's hand, squeezed it. "We'll be wonderful foster parents, and—"

"And eventual adoption isn't entirely out of the question," Thurman finished.

Little Caroline turned to gaze at Thad, and his expression informed her that they were remembering the same information. Others at the guardian home—older kids who might now remain until they were grown and simply permitted to leave—had taught the Madison children how the system worked. Grown-ups could sort of *sample* girls and boys for maybe entire *years*, then send 'em back to this big old place as if the adults might be able to find a better buy, a new and improved product, somewhere else.

But it wasn't *like* that for them, this was all so awful and dumb! Caroline hoped Father would come and get her and Thad *any day now*—'cause they wasn't real orphans at *all*!

Thad said nothing. He just stared glumly down at the adults, the railings of the stairs before his face like jail bars. *I hate 'em*, he thought. Ol' nerdy fake-mustache man, skinny fake-red-haired woman, askin' about *his parents*—like they had some *right*!

"If you intend to continue insulting me with monetary offers for my cooperation in your obtaining these children," Miss Godby said, "I'll have no choice but to report it to the county." She spoke in the most pleasant and Christmasy of voices, even smiled. "I doubt it would do any harm, though, to give you two pieces of information concerning their parents. First, the mother is deceased. There's no chance of her reentering the picture at some later date."

The Tinsdales smiled, appeared to be pleased by the information—Thad and Caroline noted that, their fear and ardent dislike deepening—and settled back against their chairs. Rhonda said, "Thank you. That would make ultimate adoption more appealing, of course. And what is the other fact, Enid?"

Miss Godby didn't reply at once, though she drew in a breath to speak. When she did, her voice was so hushed, the words she uttered so much on a toneless, single line that the sister and brother had to strain to hear her. "It would be best if *those people*—the parents—are forgotten as soon as possible." She paused minutely. "Especially by Thad and Caroline."

We won't forget them, thought the two eavesdropping

kids on the steps in unspoken unison. *We won't ever forget 'em!*

"That's the last information we'll get from you about the birth parents?" asked Thurman. Miss Godby didn't even bother to nod. "But both children seem—normal? Healthy?" Godby's head moved up and down. "Thank you," he said, then glanced at his wife. They said it in unison:

"We want the boy, then. We'll take Thad."

When the first time in his six years of life came that Thaddeus Madison fully knew he was male, he reacted to a crisis in a masculine fashion. He held both his hands over his sister Caroline's opening mouth until he was pretty sure she wasn't going to shout at the three grown-ups. Then he sort-of wrestled her up the second floor and a place far enough up the hall that they wouldn't be overheard.

The first time in her five years of life that Caroline Madison fully knew that she was female and wanted to react to outrage in a feminine manner was when she started to let the grown-ups deciding their fate know that she and Thaddie were not going to be separated like two slices of sticky Kraft cheese. 'Cause she and him loved each other very much and they'd *already* been separated both from Mama and from Father. She went on practicing being feminine by trusting her year-older brother, however, allowing him to lead her away from these newest people who were breaking their hearts.

But she went on making her point clear. "We can't let 'em do it to us!" she insisted outside a fire exit on the almost-dark second floor. "How could Father *find* us, then?"

Thad couldn't give her a direct answer and didn't know what to say. Boylike, he put his face against his sister's cheek and shoulder, simultaneously seeking the opportunity to think; Caroline's untapped maternal instinct; and a place to hide. "I don't know, Care," he admitted. Then he jerked his head back, his dark eyes flashing. "But he would, though, Father *will* find us. 'Cause he can do just about anything he wants!"

Avoiding Thaddie's intent expression, Caroline considered that, instinctively groping through his male intensity and usual exaggeration for an evidence of hard fact. Father was the one they'd seen most on a daily basis because Mother had a job, and he'd always made them smile, never minded if they bothered him when he was writing, kissed their booboos and bandaged them. He'd sung little songs in words neither Caroline nor Thaddie ever heard anywhere else, then fixed dinner for the whole family before Mama got home from work.

And Caroline knew she loved Father a lot even if it was her mother she missed most—so much that it hurt her deep in her chest and in the farthest part of her throat whenever she had to say her name. It was okay for Thaddie to look forward to their bein' saved by Father 'cause she did, too, and it was okay that he thought Father was the smartest and strongest man in the world 'cause boys prob'ly believed more in their daddies. But it had been Mama who went to work for them all, and who came home with big hugs and kisses every night, and Caroline would never see Mama again.

She supposed it was okay for Thaddie almost never to even mention Mama. "I only know those people downstairs are breakin' us up," she said. Seeing tears in his eyes, too, released her own—copiously. "An' I just c-can't *stand* it!"

He scanned her face with a longing to help, to make her stop crying, but felt so helpless. "I'd stop 'em if I could, Caroline," he swore, "b-but I don't know *how*." Slumping against the red fire door, he suddenly seemed the younger child. "We're *small*, Care—that's all. They can do whatever they wanta do—any of 'em—'cause we're not big enough yet.'' Thaddie's familiar temper flared in his moist eyes, creating a flush of crimson just above his high cheek-bones and sweeping up through his temples. "*Damn* 'em! I got to be grown-up *real* soon so I can—can *kill* 'em all. So I can tear the heads offa all the adults who pick on us, and make Halloween *pumpkins* outta them!''

Nearly laughing, Caroline tried to sniff her tears away. The image of Miss Godby with candles where her eyes were and her big face kind-of orange was a funny one.

But Thad said, "I mean it, Care!'' and turned his tiny hands into white-knuckled fists. "I *do*! Bein' little is the worst thing a person can be!'' He startled Caroline by striking the door behind him, then trying not to show the pain when the heel of his hand smarted. "I'll grow up fast, become *really* big—a giant maybe! Then they'll never even *try* to break us up again!''

She tugged the bottom of her pajama top up to dry her own eyes on. "Thad, you know it'll take a while to get big.'' She said it like that to make him listen, to be serious. He got ree-diculous sometimes, like Mama'd said. Mama had even asked Father to talk to him about bad ideas he got, but Father'd laughed, sort-of, and said Thaddie was just like him. Now it seemed so awful that it had been Mama who did the bad thing. "T'morror or the next day, them Tinsdales are gonna take you home with 'em, and there's nothing you or me can do about it.'' She nodded her head with solemnity, trying to make Thad accept things the way they were—like Mama'd always used to do. "An' after that we won't see each other anymore and we won't see Father or Mama either.''

"It's not true!'' He took Caroline by the shoulders and slammed her back against the wall, not hard enough to hurt but enough to make her stare into his wounded, furious black eyes. "Don't ever say that, not *ever*—you *mustn't*!'' From downstairs there were the sounds of Mr. and Mrs.

17

Tinsdale leaving and their voices were soft but friendly with Miss Godby now, like somebody who knew they'd be back real soon. "Father's gonna come find us *wherever* we are, and put the family back together." Thaddie was so insistent that she believed him. He was letting his voice rise, and they were supposed to be asleep in bed. "He is! I *know* it!"

Caroline glanced down the length of the hallway, back at her brother. She was trying with her whole heart not to doubt him and, if she couldn't keep from it, not to let Thad see her doubt and a sudden fear that turned her cold all over. For a moment she didn't know what the fear was there for, and then she did. It was that she was afraid Thaddie couldn't make it without her or Father around.

"I swear it to you," Thad was going on, "cross my heart and hope to die!" He was nodding to make Care nod, trying to pump his own conviction of the eventual reunion into her head and heart. She didn't remember ever hearing him sound that way, nearly . . . well, *powerful*. Kind of like Father could sound. Thaddie had a certainty to him (though Caroline did not know the word) that made him appear bigger than he was. "Father *will* find me—and then we'll come for *you*!"

Miss Godby's slow, heavy footstep on the stairs sent them skittering and, when Caroline was back in the girls' dorm, her heart thudding in her chest, she began to believe Thaddie—not a lot, but some. Hopping into her bed among children she scarcely knew called Candy and Ada and Carlotta and Lydia and Claudette, she was already separated some from Thaddeus so she *wanted* to believe what he'd told her, Caroline realized that.

Lying back in the darkness, she fingered the locket that had been Mama's. Why had Thad been so sure Father could find them (or him)? Was it just a hope? Was it like the faith of Mama's religion which Mama sometimes men-

18

tioned but Father said was "sheer superstitious nonsense"?
Or was it only 'cause Thad was kind-of a daddy's boy like
she'd always believed she was kind-of a mama's girl?

Sometimes, alone in the guardian home—alone even
with the other girls around—she felt that she might be forgetting . . . things. Things and stuff Mama or Father had
done or said. And she also felt that she might remember
that stuff sometime, except she wasn't sure she wanted to.

She did know part of what her mind told her to forget
concerned the night Mama . . . died . . . and Father ran off
without sayin' good-bye. She supposed she might be a little
mad at him for that—or for something. What she remembered real easy was the way strangers came to the house
the next morning, unlocked the door where Mama had put
Thaddie and her, and took 'em to stay at Miss Godby's.
Whether Thad had heard the awful noises that came from
their folks' bedroom right before Mama died, she couldn't
be sure. Thaddie had a way of lyin' perfectly still in bed
and sleeping with his eyelids halfway open, so she could
never be sure he was asleep. An' he didn't even get mad a
whole lot, "ree-diculous" like Mama'd said he got, till
much later.

Caroline turned on her side, simultaneously craving sleep
and fighting to remain awake. She could see some of them
skinny ol' girls in the dorm and some was snorin'. Candy
and Lydia'd claimed parents "got funny" now and then
and hated their children, even did terrible things which Caroline promptly tuned out when piggy ol' Lydia went into
detail. But she knew Father and Mama had never done any
of that stuff to her, Caroline positively *knew* it.

A big problem was whether or not Care could keep her
promise to Thaddie that she wouldn't ever forget their
folks. When she'd whispered that secret to Carlotta, Carlotta said she was too little to understand *any*thing, and Ada
added that all men were monsters, that none of 'em could

be trusted. Well, who cared what they said? Carlotta had stringy hair and she was a little snot, and Ada just said whatever Carlotta or fat Lydia said anyway, then made it sound even worse, so what did they know?

And there was also the fact that Candy, Lydia, and Carlotta were *double* orphans. They wasn't *single-parent orphans* like Thaddie and her, who still had Father, so that made them skinny ol' girls just a bunch of jealous-pots!

Care finally fell asleep in an anxiety that she was somehow forgetting too many things about Mama and Father, and with the acute, guilt-provoking concern that she might even forget what they looked like as she got bigger. Not Mama, maybe, 'cause there was a picture of Deborah Madison in Caroline's locket, but her daddy. She slipped into sleep only when she realized again she and Thaddie were nothing but kids and she couldn't really help it if she *did* forget Father, or Mama. Sometimes it was prob'ly easier to let stuff fall out of your memory about the things grownups did or said than try to figure out why they said or did it.

But Thad was a different proposition entirely, Caroline knew. Thaddie was like the sun or moon to her. When Mama had gone to work and Father tried to write things in his room—she'd never got to learn what he was writing— her bro was always around. Thad was like air, or food and water. He was the one she would *always* be able to talk with even if they didn't see each other for years and years. Care would remember Thaddie forever.

And she also knew that her big brother of six forgot absolutely *nothing*.

Thurman Tinsdale of Queens half dreamed and half reflected that night about the intriguing possibilities that automatically developed by taking a six-year-old boy into his life for a while. They included:

Making it through his days at work with less awareness of the rumors he imagined were whispered around about his apparent sterility (and the much worse stories related to the *reasons* for infertility, i.e., his suspect masculinity);

The likelihood of advancement in his job, long denied him (Thurman thought) because his family demographics just didn't "measure up";

Rhonda being more the redheaded pepperpot he believed he had married, once she could mentally append the word "mother" to her private résumé and once more discover there was a reason for sexual intercourse beyond the desire to have children;

Taking the dark-haired kid—Thad, *that* was it—to ball games Rhonda found boring (though Rhonda could tag along too if she wanted);

Finding out if he had any interest in fatherhood and, if Thurman found that he had, having somebody to work for who would someday get the fortune Thurman still imagined he might accrue from his dazzling business ideas.

Mustache twitching in the dark, he heard himself think, *It mightn't be all bad*, and then he was fast asleep.

Beside him, Rhonda Tinsdale dreamed glorious rainbows. Her unconscious mind knew that one arcing strand of color would lead to a pot of golden love—son for mother, mother for son. She was so thrilled by what was about to happen in her life—in *theirs*, hers and Thurman's—that she began to toss and turn, and her nightgown hitched itself up to the vicinity of her waist. Even if she ultimately proved to be infertile and never succeeded in getting pregnant, Mom would get off Rhonda's back; the mother would soon come to accept such a handsome little boy as her grandson. Rhonda might even *keep* him, might get permission to *rename* Thad—call him "Rondell," her beloved dead daddy's name! Still sleeping, she forced the nightgown back down to cover herself, and washed herself in the illumination of her internal aurora till morning.

It was a night for dreams.

A child in SoHo, New York City, dreamed of a pale, beautiful woman and a somber, kind but distant man who took their places at a dining room table with two small children. Tonight the woman had brought home wonderfully fragrant white boxes containing pizza, and the serious man, whose dinner preparations for his family had awaited only his final touches, was trying to conceal his hurt feelings. Father did that so well most of the time. Father rarely went out because of his literary work, but he neither drank too much nor had friends of either sex, and he prided himself on tending to the two children, keeping them clean and sometimes telling them exciting stories just so they'd be content until Mama came home. Each of the children knew he hated pizza. Father's tastes, he'd sometimes said, were "rarefied," "refined," and he disliked what he called "the crass and coarse."

Mama, though, was all merriment—she'd won a promotion in her job and wanted to celebrate with the family—and each of the others, including Father, soon entered into her spirit of enthusiasm.

Then the child's dream became ominous; in the way of dreams, there was no undercurrent of throbbing music, and no dimming of the light from the dining room chandelier to warn the boy and girl. There was just the mood, the *sense*, that all was not well in their house . . . at that point when Mama mentioned that it might be necessary for them to think about moving.

In the sleeping child's dream there were faint tears in Father's eyes, and sadness spread across his somber, familiar face. The child, then and now, was instantly empathetic; they'd *always* lived in that house, the children; it was *home*.

But brave, quiet Father said nothing. And when the tears

in his eyes went unnoticed by his wife, he consumed the rest of his portion of pizza without protest. His cheek muscles worked and worked. He swallowed it all, hard.

A child in the same Manhattan building dreamed a different dream, but there were no rainbows, no recitation of dim possibilities in the future, no radiant smiles, and no lights gleaming from a crystal chandelier.

There was thunder that walked. Bleak, black, ominous thunder that enveloped the child as if transforming the quaking little human being into a frail lightning bolt that could never dart across the sky and live its normal life.

The walking thunder had many names in addition to those by which it was known, and its power was absolute, there was no getting away. It rumbled of love, of needs that were both eternal and all but infinite; of desire that gave it all its blackness and beat passionately at the nucleus of its contrived and terrible affection. "Shhh," it said, "you'll get used to this, you'll come to *want* it, to *expect* it from me. You're mine; I'm yours. *Shhh*. Be still. This will make us family more than anything else." And "You *know* I *love* you." And "It'll hurt only for a few moments. *See?*"

The dreaming child, terrified once more in sleep, made no sound because—in the dream as in life—there was a hand of thunder covering its mouth. And now a hand that smothered all protest because, in the sharing, it was the child's own hand.

A door opened, and the mate of thunder stood in the aperture, aghast.

Aghast, but silent.

The door closed behind the horrified mate, leaving the child with It.

"More," the child called, not then but now, obedient and true. Tears fell in the darkness and went unseen. The child's hands worked, clawed, made motions as if there were a real desire to embrace the blackness of thunder again. "Come back. *Come back!*"

There was nothing about the departure of little Thad with the young Tinsdales that failed to surprise Miss Enid Godby.

Instead of understandable hysterics on the part of both children—a dreadful time when Thurman Tinsdale might have had to tear the boy away from his sister, while Caroline screamed and then wept inconsolably for hours—Thad and Caroline merely embraced, gave each other a hasty peck on the cheek, and Thaddeus Marshall was off on his first placement with foster parents.

It was done with almost adult dignity, Enid realized. In all her years of running the SoHo guardian home, all the painful partings not only of siblings but of little lost human beings who had somehow made friendships in such an environment, Enid had never witnessed such an outwardly calm and poised leavetaking.

Perhaps—just as she was finally on the verge of retirement, that *would* be the irony of it!—she'd gotten the hang of preparing the children for their loss!

Or maybe everyone in authority, including me, just plain misread the relationship these two kids had with their father and their mother, Enid thought as she peered out the window, holding the drapes back so Caroline could watch too. For the first time it occurred to her that the suicidal mother of the two darlings could have had some reason that was less selfish and neurotic than it had looked, because she seemed to have done a very good job with the fair-haired little Care.

Or maybe, although the police only wanted him for questioning, Marshall Madison had murdered his wife before leaving, humanely sparing his children a similar fate.

Just at the moment she released her grip on the draper-

24

ies—the Tinsdale car was out of sight—and let them drop back into position, the silence of little Caroline caused Miss Godby to stare down at her again.

A line of blood straight as a red arrow in flight had formed just under Care's tightly compressed lips.

The girl had bitten all the way through her lower lip. As Miss Godby finally realized what she'd done, blood began to seep down Caroline's defiant little chin like so many scarlet ribbons.

Reaching in a pocket for her own hankie, shocked badly, Enid stooped to the child with maternal concern and an urge to soothe. It passed through her mind too—with an intuition arising from her efforts toward placing hundreds of deserving youngsters—that Thaddeus Madison, seated in style between Rhonda and Thurman Tinsdale on the way to Queens, was almost surely expressing his own grief in just the same silent, courageous fashion. Pressing the handkerchief to Caroline's mouth broke her iron resolve, however; Care's lips parted—

Then the most soulful and soul-clutching sound Enid Godby had ever heard produced by a human throat wailed and reverberated through the parlor of the old guardian home. Her fair head raised as she peered directly ahead of her while seeming to recognize no one present in the house, Caroline's sound of sorrow was quite nearly a howl. Yet she did not resist when Enid pulled her against her side; the single wail simply turned into a plaintive, noiseless weeping.

And after that, for the many weeks it took to reach Caroline emotionally and evoke a smiling manner pleasing enough for Care to meet prospective foster parents, the child alternated between moods of uncommunicative withdrawal and what Miss Godby had always called "being a double handful." There was no further display of tears, none—but there was an effort made toward independence, or isolation (Enid knew there were times with little ones when the difference between them was slim)—and there were events that aging Miss Godby found inexplicable. Two of them stayed with her after she retired.

The first event, surfacely, was one with which Enid had had considerable experience. More than fifty percent of the youngsters she'd housed in her career had been young girls. And it was always the older children who were difficult to place, always the girls and boys in their teens who tended to develop neurotic problems created by the absence of real mothers and fathers to prepare them for life.

A child called Candy had entered puberty and then awakened one morning to discover she'd begun her first menstrual period during the night, while she slept.

But it wasn't Candy who was the first to see what had happened; indeed, Candy coped with the eternal problem well enough considering subsequent developments. It was five-year-old Caroline who saw.

Candy, apparently, had climbed out of bed right after hearing the recorded music that awoke all the children for the day, didn't know she had left a trail of blood down her nightgown, and merely happened to turn in little Caroline's direction.

Anybody who hadn't arisen for the day until then was instantly awake as a result of Care's reaction.

She pointed for a moment, mutely, then began to scream as if the hounds of hell were pursuing her. An instant later, her screams becoming a series of staccato squeals that seemed to turn her fair skin increasingly pale as she emitted them, Caroline ran forward, *charged* at poor Candy, and struck her with both tiny fists, knocking Candy sprawling.

Then she'd spun and sprinted barefoot in the direction of the boys' dorm as if in search of her brother Thaddie's protection before just stopping in the hallway, freezing herself in place, and staring at Enid and the other children with an unforgettable expression comprised of multiple emotions.

As nearly as Miss Godby could see little Care was terrified, ready to try to fight everybody in the building, and filled with a realization of personal loss so profound that even the older girls such as Lydia and Carlotta were hesitant to approach or to tease her after seeing her face clearly.

For awhile, oddly enough, Care seemed better after that. Still gloomy and inclined to keep to herself, she was more responsive when Miss Godby or other children attempted to cheer her up and get her involved in their activities.

In fact, when two more weeks passed and Caroline finally gave her the impression of having grown more accustomed to her brother's departure, Enid was contacted by a young couple who she felt would be ideal for the girl and whom she believed Caroline would like. Additionally, Camille and Jake Spencer preferred a foster child who was no longer a toddler and one who was ready to start school. Desiring to make magic one more time before she retired, Miss Godby decided to use her own money to buy Caroline a new dress, something that would bring out the color in her cheeks and show her off to the best possible advantage.

It turned out to be a simple frock with enormous red polka dots against a white background, with a red sash. It was easy for Enid to imagine how sweet and pretty Care would look in it.

The child's complex reaction to her gift was one Miss Godby hadn't ever observed before and certainly hadn't expected.

Initially—though it was clear Care did not truly like the dress—it appeared all would go well. After poking the present hastily back in its sack as if hoping it might just disappear, Caroline tiptoed across the parlor floor and threw her arms around Enid's neck, bestowing a giant hug. The embrace was brief, but the old woman knew many aban-

27

doned children found it hard to give up all their memories of their first homes; they often clung to them as long as they possibly could, and then—if they were as young as Caroline or Thaddie—they awoke one sunny morning in total harmony with a new environment. Therefore, any warm response from an unfortunate child like Caroline was a heartening sign, so Enid decided to go ahead with arrangements for Caroline to get acquainted with the childless couple.

But right before the Spencers were due to arrive at the home the next afternoon, Enid sent chubby little Lydia up to the girls' quarters to remind Caroline to get dressed, and Lydia returned as out of breath as if she had been running—or frightened. "I think you better go up 'n see Caroline yourself, ma'am," Lydia reported.

Enid did, and found Care on the floor in front of her bed, clad only in her underwear, with something silvery flashing in her busy little hands.

The "something" was a pair of shears from Miss Godby's room. Caroline was obsessively cutting the pretty new polka-dot dress to pieces!

Enid rushed to the girl to take the scissors away but stopped a yard or so from where Caroline sat, not in fear but because she suddenly saw what Care was doing.

She was trying to cut all the red polka-dots out of the little gown without harming the white background!

"Why, Caroline?" Miss Godby asked, removing the shears from the child's hands without encountering the slightest protest. "Why are you doing this to your new dress?"

The tears welling up into Caroline's eyes did not spill over. She stared up at Enid in obvious despair and mumbled an answer that was as enigmatic and seemingly meaningless as any the elderly woman had heard in her career. "The reds and whites," Caroline mumbled. She used both hands to point at the pile of polka-dots she had already excised, and what remained of the dress. Then she shrugged. "The reds," she said—"and the whites . . ."

Remarkably all went well with Caroline's interview once Miss Godby got her into one of her old dresses, long since brought there from her own home. Months had passed and the girl was growing normally so all that clothing was beginning to be too small for her. Perhaps it was a matter of how badly Camille and Jake Spencer wanted a child to take in, at least for a while; perhaps it was just the wan smile Caroline mustered for them, and some familiar chord the young couple managed to strike in her own lonely heart. Whatever the explanation for it, Caroline and the Spencers took to one another virtually on sight and Enid Godby was able to make one final placement of a child in a good, temporary home at the end of her career.

When Miss Godby herself left the guardian home to move into retirement—and as time passed and her own needs began to take precedence over the many memories she'd accumulated over the long years—even the recollection of a five-year-old squatting on the floor, cutting a nice new dress to shreds and trying to explain it with the enigmatic use of five little words—*the reds and the whites*—eventually receded from the forefront of her thoughts.

It took awhile.

It surely wasn't possible, but the old woman believed she was awakened by the sound of snow pattering down on her house. Soft, gentle snow, as persistent and usually as cooperatively unobtrusive as the mounting weight of years on her equally white head.

Had there ever been a winter with so much snowfall in New York? It wasn't a case of several inches falling in a day (or some other short period of time), it was a case of it falling *daily*, with the regularity of a metronome. The constant snow seemed to Miss Godby exactly the way all other extremes of climate had come to seem to her this past number of years, like a relentlessly repeatedly delivered message of God. These days there was something to the unbroken days of heat or humidity, to cascades of rain that turned the old skyscrapers Niagaras, and to the mercilessly mounting mounds of ghost-sheet snow that made Enid imagine she was supposed to be listening intently to the cosmic communiqué.

What made the weather excesses so hard to tolerate was the impersonality of the message, the fact that it appeared to be meant for the majority of people of a certain age— and up—not the unsubtle communication itself. All it said, Enid believed, was "This may be the *last* hot spell/thunderstorm/cold snap for *you*"—as if she should somehow begin to enjoy heat that baked her brains out!—Or, more directly, "Get ready! Prepare yourself! This is *it*!"

Enid supposed a person in her so-called "golden years" might interpret the persistence of the ceaseless snowfall and the message it seemed to convey as a test designed for old people which if she passed again this season qualified her for another year or so of life. Forgetting something had awakened her, amused by the idea, she rolled over on the other side, hoping to be lulled back to a sleep that banished the half-formed nightmares with which she had been haunted for a week or more now.

The dreams appeared to be linked to newspaper stories Miss Godby had read lately concerning perfectly dreadful things that were happening to children. These weren't even horror stories limited to the mean streets of Manhattan and other large cities, they were happening almost everywhere in America. They ran an evil gamut from infants being born with addictions inherited from their parents, to youngsters selling their bodies, to child sexual abuse committed by fathers, mothers, foster- and stepparents—even people with the kind of responsible positions Miss Godby herself had filled for so long! And suddenly, as though completely out of some horrible nowhere, there were reports of children raping *other* children!

Now Enid knew she wouldn't go back to sleep. Even before retiring from her job she'd realized that matters were getting worse across the nation, that there would probably be more girls and boys abandoned—obliged to fend for themselves—as the century ran itself out of breath and died. It wasn't political or economical now, she thought; it was a question of what she had always called "me-firsting." Even the folks who tried to say the right things these days always placed their own needs and desires first, and no, it *hadn't* always been that way, regardless of what anyone claimed. In the past people frequently put their own *needs* ahead of everything else except their loved ones, but *not* their desires.

The big problem was that nobody paid any attention to the differences between those words—and others—any longer.

There, that *sound* again . . .

And it wasn't snow falling on the roof or blowing against the windows.

Good heavens, Enid thought, it was the sound of knocking on the front door of her house! Tapping, actually; soft, sporadic tapping, as if the person standing outside in the darkness and the unraveled white blanket of snow were tiring out (*or a phantom waiting may have decided to come for me another night*, Enid added to herself).

Even with the scary notion, though, she was rising, slipping her feet into house slippers, and reaching for her robe. As an afterthought, she switched on her reading lamp and then, passing from room to hallway and to stairs, every other light she passed. It didn't make any sense that a Western Union messenger (did they even *have* telegrams any longer?) was bringing her tragic news, because Enid hadn't married and all the relatives she'd genuinely considered "family" were gone, so she didn't worry about that. Once, she had imagined there were friendships she'd formed in her working years, but she was no longer a part of that world, and as time passed (*that* again!) she'd lost touch with all those people. She was truly alone—

So *who*, Enid wondered as she padded in her slippers across the front room to a door that suddenly seemed forbidding, would want to see her (*come for me*) at such a late and ungodly hour? The caller rapped again, but this time so softly she would not have heard the noise if she had been in her bed.

Miss Godby, six feet away, stared at the door, noticing whorls and splintering places in the varnished wood—seeing even the hinges which held the door in place (*against the outside*)—she hadn't observed in the twenty-two years she had called the building "home." Then, squinting to be certain the two chains were securely in place, she edged the door open a couple of scant inches.

For a second she saw no one through the crack and was too busy inwardly recoiling from a savage winter's blast to think of anything but her relief that the quiet rapping was seemingly only in her imagination.

But then she lowered her gaze and started, instantly remembering the child who waited on the other side of the door, making the identification in spite of how heavy the snowfall seemed to have constructed and animated a half-frozen creature of its own.

Enid demanded, "What in heaven's name are you doing here?" possibly more sharply than she'd intended. There'd been real anger that a youngster she herself had placed in a warm, presumably safe environment had been permitted to go out—at night too!—in such bitterly cold weather. "Well, come inside quickly!" Enid said, removing the chains and throwing the front door wide. Despite the furious ice-wind rushing in, she nudged the door shut with her toe and began stripping away a frigid coat and unwinding a stiffening muffler. The youthful skin at the neck felt corpse-cold to her touch.

Then she led her midnight caller into the warmer regions of the living room, deeply perturbed by the carelessness of the foster parents—and something more she couldn't quite name as yet. Enid had recognized this little one at once; she'd made it her business to memorize the faces of all the children left in her charge for any length of time and still believed she could identify most of them, even today, from their photographs.

When it occurred to her that this *wasn't* the guardian home where the children had stayed, but her home, her visitor appeared to read her thoughts. "I looked you up in the phone book, Miss Godby."

"*I* see," she murmured cheerily as she hung the frozen coat and muffler above a register. Yet she did not see at all. Something very bad—brutal, perhaps—must have happened for the poor thing to have run away in the dead of winter. It wasn't safe for any tyke to wander the streets by day, let alone at night, and her neighborhood wasn't what it once was. "Do sit down, for goodness' sakes," she added with a gesture in the direction of her most comfortable easy chair. She waited till her guest was perched on it, short legs dangling and the sopping feet scarcely touching the floor, before taking her seat on a sofa nearby. "I wish I had some children's clothing here, but I—I never had children of my own." *Or a husband,* Miss Godby thought with ancient wistfulness.

"It's okay." The child's shivering had stopped. Enid was surprised by the composure she saw in the serious little face, and she realized she had expected signs of fright, even terror—or certainly relief to be safe with her. Instead, her small caller was slowly and steadily gazing around the front room, pausing at the photographs of her long-deceased parents and older sister on the mantel, and then halting with startling poise on Enid's own eyes. "It didn't work out with them." The most minute emphasis put on the pronoun, but her ears did not detect any trace of fear, regret, even hatred. "It's not your fault. I been in two other foster homes since, but it didn't work out there either."

"I'm so sorry." Enid spoke with sincerity, but the odd dread that had bothered her when she was leading the way to their seats was pushing forward in her mind, preventing her from asking questions she felt she ought to ask. The main one got through: "Are you back at the home now, then? Where are you staying?" *That* was it, because this child with the disconcertingly calm eyes should not be out in a snowstorm at night!

The gaze they'd shared was broken. Something like evasiveness—a clear hesitation to provide all the details, at least—was evident as the Madison child glanced away. "I'm . . . *out there*," came the answer. Then the gaze, the eyes, were back on Miss Godby's. A grandfather clock that had been her father's tolled once, solemnly, from deep in the house. "I want you to help me find my family."

Enid heard neither the clock nor the youngster's last remark, however. The "something else" she'd sensed was wrong had become crystal clear in her mind.

The shockingly poised and totally unfearful child who had come to her out of the blue and sat nonchalantly in her favorite chair, barely even making an impression in the cushion, looked literally *no different* than back when the placement with two foster parents occurred. Enid's astonished stare could not be concealed. *This simply isn't possible*, she told herself, searching for evidence of growth, of change, in her visitor and seeing none. It could not be, because—

Seven years had passed since Enid Godby's retirement from the home. Yet *this* little person had not changed . . . *at all*.

Part One

Flesh
&
Blood

"Settle in, don't struggle so.
The winding-sheet will loosen,
Soon. Rest easy until then."

—Lin Stein, *R.I.P., Temporarily*

Chapter One

He had walked much of the night away when it was done, when most of what he had lived and toiled for lay in ruins and the centerpiece of his existence was beyond his help as well as his harm, getting reacquainted with loneliness.

Because he was the kind of man he was, he believed no one had ever experienced the degree of isolation, agonizing loss, and apartness from all others he knew that night. It was even worse than the previous times he'd been obliged to dine on shadows, attempt to survive without a kind word from the lips of anyone familiar—safe—to him and he felt that he could have proved it: After leaving his present home forever, he'd sat fully dressed in a rest-room stall to scan his old journal, a weighty tome he had kept most of his adult life. On occasion he had inserted all of it in new binders, simply to preserve the record. And over the years he'd periodically reread parts of the journal, not from nostalgia—sentiment for an existence of unparalleled anguish would have been mad—but to remind himself of the wisdom to continue *controlling* himself, his urges, and even his needs, so he would not jeopardize the improvement he'd accomplished, progress attained through infinitely small steps culminating in his marriage to Deborah, celebrated and cemented by the births of his son and his daughter.

One moment, only days before, he'd dared to dream of a future that would delight *him*, would include the soul comfort of knowing his later years would not be devoid of companionship, and everything was suddenly lost— especially Deborah.

The earlier periods of being cut adrift, forced to begin life anew, had not been like this, no.

For Deborah, Thaddeus, and pretty Caroline had not been part of that past, his past.

As now they would be.

And so he strode the two-mile width of what was known as the original New York City, started back again across West Thirty-fourth, finally wandered down Seventh Avenue toward the Village, absolutely without destination, objective, plan, or purpose. Remembering it would never be prudent to be caught by the authorities for even the most minute violation or indiscretion, Marshall Madison had obeyed every sign intended to order the pedestrian's passage. Whenever he caught sight of another person approaching, he turtled his head down into his coat or stopped walking and pretended to be looking into the windows of shops closed for the night, or stooped to retie a shoestring. When he waited for traffic lights to change, and another post-midnight walker dawdled next to him or across a street, he averted his face to the best of his ability—because that, above all, was what he did not want now: For anyone to see his naked face and possibly make a scene.

It was why he'd rarely left his home and Deborah's through the years of their marvelous marriage, and then, when he had had to go out, he'd tried to do so only by night.

Just as he'd felt impelled to do since the hideous pivotal evening when Deborah'd caught him with their child. And as he had done virtually every night until—the last.

Refraining from compelling others to see his ugliness was just the courteous, considerate thing. But if circumstances gave him and them no other choice, Marshall knew what to do. He had not left home too fast to remember to slip his . . . other identity . . . into a pocket.

And when his lonely all-night walk brought him within range of someone slower afoot than he—or departing a building after working quite late, obliged to lock up before proceeding—Marshall refused to break his own effortless stride with so much as a pause, even if that might have sounded inconsistent to another person. He had nothing to fear from them, after all, and he had as much right on the streets after dark as any other citizen of New York. He'd done nothing wrong—or at any rate, nothing that could not be explained to a man capable of pure logic.

It wasn't his fault if no such human being existed.

So instead of retarding his pace or peering into store windows as he'd done when others merely approached him, Marshall let the people ahead of him believe, if they felt like it, that he might be stalking them.

Even if he probably wasn't doing that at all.

Some—the sick or aged, especially those who struggled to survive on the streets, others with money or illegal substances in their pockets—soon heard his footfall behind them, and glanced over their shoulders. This tended to amuse Marshall in spite of his new grief and loneliness, since they couldn't see his face, at night, at any distance. He knew that if they quickened their paces or turned down a different street, each would be perfectly safe from him. They did not know that. Their fear and guilt alike enlivened him, provided a tiny ray of hope. Life after Deborah might not be entirely absent of interest and amusement.

Of course, it wouldn't be at *all* absent (he knew that night of parting) once he had Thaddie and Caroline with him in a place of their own.

It was getting quite late, there weren't many people sharing the darkness with Marshall now, and almost all of those he caught up with got out of his unwavering path after they saw the well-built figure in the black coat bearing down on them. A few caught a glimpse of the stalker's eyes. When they did, an emotion akin to survival-drive let them register the fact that Marshall's eyes did not seem to blink (among other things about them) and they turned corners or crossed streets with alacrity.

One person a few blocks west of Tompkins Square had allowed the survival instinct to wither, partly because he had his own antisocial agenda.

He deliberately slowed down so that Marshall Madison could easily catch up.

Then, while Marshall was looking slowly around to see if prowl cars that might prove obtrusive were in the vicinity, and taking half a step past the second man, the young thug came lithely up behind Marshall and locked one arm around his neck. In his other hand was a knife with a switchblade that reflected dully but convincingly from a streetlight several yards away.

And the youth held his weapon so that his victim would be coaxed into seeing two things clearly—the point of the knife, and the way he'd thoughtfully allowed approximately two inches of Marshall's throat to be exposed as an unmistakable target.

"I want whatever bread you got on you—and the coat," he said as menacingly as he could. While taller than Marshall and considerably younger, his voice was high-pitched and light. *Frightened, actually*, Marshall thought as he stood quite still. "Hear me, man? I'm gonna step back a step an' let you go, so you can get your bucks and take the coat off—but I'll have the blade ready, and I *will* cut you! You *hear* me, man?"

"Clearly," Marshall said, waiting.

There was a sort of pause he had heard before when his inflection failed to convey the proper note of apprehension or terror, but, as usual, this thug did what he'd said he was going to do.

Of course, he hadn't said what *else* he'd probably do once he had taken the coat and Marshall's money, and the chance of getting blood on the former was reduced to a minimum.

"Well, *go ahead*, man!" the boy said from behind him. "Do it!" That was incipient hysteria showing in his voice now; obviously he was high on something and hoped to sustain the level indefinitely. "Maaaan, I'll *do* you—don't you *believe* me?"

Sighing and dropping his shoulders, Marshall unbuttoned his black coat. He used the fingers of one hand for that. He used the other five to draw something out of his pocket and carefully, almost tenderly, mold it to his face. "Yes, I believe you," he replied, turning very slowly to confront his attacker. "I most certainly do—though it really matters little one way or the other."

Without looking at Marshall, the younger man tried to snatch the coat away. After all, the victim had his arm out, he was extending it to him.

But Marshall tugged, harder, at the same second the young thug tried to take it, and found himself sailing the few feet between them until he carommed off his mark's hard and unyielding chest.

Squealing, the youth jabbed the point of the blade into the side of Marshall's neck. But his body was badly off balance and it entered not quite half an inch, cleanly missing the jugular vein.

Making no sound whatever, seemingly reacting without pain or fury, Marshall pinioned the mugger's wrist, preventing any secondary thrust. With the knife still in his own neck, he reached out with his other hand and arm. The fingertips sank nearly as far into the soft places of the assailant's throat as the blade penetrating Marshall's, but his aim was truer. The boy tried to cry out again but settled for making a hissing sound between his teeth. Gradually his eyes turned down in their sockets as he realized bones were starting to fracture in his wrist at an almost microscopically increasing rate. That was when he let go of the knife hilt.

"Were you going to 'do' me this way?" Marshall asked, and it was the same instant the younger man finally saw his face—or what he believed was it. When Marshall reversed the knife and whisked its point in a horizontal motion over the front of the mugger's throat—just piercing the skin—it was impossible to tell whether the expression of horror on the terrified face was put there by the sudden and shocking pain, the faint spray of blood—no longer that of his intended victim—or the way the older man looked to him. "Or was *this* it, perhaps?" Marshall asked.

His second pass sliced off most of one ear, the outer rim completely severed. Before it reached the pavement, the blade was excavating a definite hole in his neck, at just the place Marshall had been wounded. This cut, though, was deeper, not life-threateningly so if the thug received medical help soon, but a cavity carved with surgical precision. Blood rushed from it, his neck, and from his maimed ear, and he slipped slowly to his knees, wanting not to vomit and striving to find out how he could cover the three awful wounds with his two trembling hands.

Marshall had squatted on his haunches then, doing so

unhurriedly, with care not to touch the knee of his trousers to the dirty pavement. Bad enough that this creature had held and sullied his coat, however briefly. He looked deeply at the youth, cowering now, with his dark, terrible, infrequently blinking eyes. "I am so damned lonely," he confided. "So damned and so lonely." Marshall had not put down the knife. "But you are unfit company even for the smaller vermin infesting the streets. At least they have the decency to scurry away when I approach."

Then he had rested the switchblade on the sidewalk, careful only to be sure the thug made no effort to rise and run.

And he put his hands around those areas of the young man's neck where the blood was unlikely to spurt and get on his clothes. He didn't relinquish his hold while life pumped in his victim's veins, but watched the inevitable departure with undimmed interest—and several tears of regret washed his sallow cheeks.

When it was done, Marshall found that his own spilled blood was just on his shirt beneath the collar, drying already. He was unsurprised to find that he felt regenerated but was pleased to see that action had given him a new direction. His first step was establishing new quarters, and he imagined that might be interesting too. But that was merely the number one priority, because the result of everything he did now would be finding and taking Thaddeus and Caroline—taking them with him. Wherever he went, forever.

Chapter Two

The taxi wended its way briskly through Prospect Park even though it wasn't the quickest way the driver knew to reach his destination. Years ago, it had been one of the prettiest spots in all of Brooklyn and Jake still held that it wasn't bad. Sometimes he knew that he saw it with the eyes of a thirty-five-year-old man who'd grown up not many squares from Fulton Street and remembered how he'd wanted to live near the park someday, but that didn't matter. The first really hard frost hadn't yet come, there were still brilliant flowers to inhale as he drove along Ocean Parkway, the wide boulevard also leading to old Coney Island, and still a few kids who went to Prospect just to play. It wasn't all bad.

What he'd never dreamed of doing when he was a kid was living over in Brooklyn Heights. He probably never would, but there were late afternoons like this, with his flag down, when he nearly had to pinch himself to realize his Gamille grew up in the Heights—back in the days when that was something. Why, till they got really lucky thanks to Miss Godby and became Caroline's foster folks, Cammy's upper-crust past had pretty much been Jake Spencer's primary source of pride—to think that a bum like him had ever married a classy dame like her!—and his primary source of irritation.

Cammy herself (gawd, she hated that nickname!) hadn't ever rubbed it in; but there had been the holidays when her old lady and old man came over and Jake had seen the fish-eye "Daddy" gave their dump. First had been the unloading of so many packages for poor underfuckingnourished Princess Camille that Jake had had to resist the urge to make a joke about a sixteen wheeler being parked at the curb. *Then* had come the fish-eye. And questions like "How's the can industry, Jacob? Better or worse during a Republican administration?" Sheesh.

After they got sweet Caroline, things got different. Jake's pop, who'd put almost forty years in at the navy yard on Wallabout Channel, had himself a new neighbor in the Greenwood Cemetery, and he was Cammy's old man. Perfectly amazing the way a graveyard leveled everything out.

The cemetery was about midway between the Heights and Jake's house, a half mile southeast of Prospect Park, another good reason for swinging up the parkway after work.

The other thing Jake liked about living out on Lefferts Avenue was that some of the trees in Prospect totally blocked any glimpse Camille could possibly have of the goddamn Heights. Her mother didn't even live there now and you couldn't see anything that far west except the New York skyline anyhow, but it was like a symbol, maybe a metaphysical thing, to Jake. Cammy'd never once said she was homesick in ten years of marriage, and *he* sure as hell didn't want to go back to Fulton Street to hang out; but this way they really had their own home.

Or at least they had since Care came to live with them.

He slowed down once he was on Lefferts and across Nostrand Avenue because it was residential and this wasn't the City, where he hacked, this was where People lived. None of the other cabbies he worked with had ever understood why he didn't mind driving into the City every day or why he wanted to keep his roots in Brooklyn, much less why Caroline's coming had meant so much to him that he and Camille adopted her as soon as they could. Jake smiled, loosened his day-long tight grip on the steering wheel. Probably the shmucks didn't understand it in part because he'd never figured it out entirely himself. Sometimes he wanted to believe it was how much happier Camille was with a little girl to raise, but that was your basic cop-out. Mainly, it had to do with, well, *completion*; that was the term for how close Care and he himself had become, even if it hadn't been overnight.

No, it had taken every hour and every minute of the seven years all three Spencers had spent together now. Because it *hadn't* been together-time for most of those wonderful and difficult, fulfilling and maddeningly frustrating years—not with Caroline's mind spinning off now and then to her memories of other parents, a brother she'd been crazy about and lived God-knows-where today, and not with Cammy sometimes getting wistful about her father and how it had been easier when he was alive and spreading the loot around.

And not with him, Jake Spencer, occasionally brooding that they might've made a big damn sorry mistake because of heartache caused by Care's recurring nightmares, the far-away look in the eyes so otherwise full of magic they let you believe things you hadn't been able to believe since you were eight, her birth mother's locket that the New York Giants couldn't pry away from her even when it was bath time, and the moments when she'd reminded them with ice-rink coldness that they weren't her "real" pop and mom.

And who could ever forget Caroline's weird aversion to anything with the colors red and white. Hell, even Camille had thought for awhile that the kid needed to see a shrink and there'd been no way they could afford *that*. As recently as only a couple of years ago, Care had ripped the covers off magazines using red and white together, even gotten bent out of shape over a box of Valentine's Day candy Jake brought her! It was a good thing he didn't root for any basketball or football teams that had the two shades as their team colors, Jake had told himself back then. If he'd been eyeballing cheerleaders on TV, Caroline would've howled till he turned the set off!

Then, though—there was no hint it was comin', no goddamn *clue*, he would positively have sworn to it!—Care had knocked all that crap off. Just like that—right out of the blue—she'd turned into Jacob and Camille Spencer's daughter. And it was enough to make a man believe his prayers were being answered. It took Cammy and him around a month to see what a huge change had taken place in their kid. Suddenly, without warning, there were absolutely no signs of Caroline yearning for a past she surely couldn't remember much by then anyway, not a tear or sob, not even one objection to stuff with red and white on it. Best of all, there were no more freeze-you-where-you-stood arguments filled with the sort of strange, sneering animosity that somehow blamed them for "stealing" Care from her wonderfulterrificsimply *MAH*velous birth parents.

Whoever the fuck they'd been other than total assholes who'd let an incredibly sweet, smart, and beautiful child like Jake's Caroline wind up in a hole like that guardian home.

So it was seven years in the house on Lefferts Avenue, the last two really and finally "together." In the past year, he and his wife had saved their nickels and dimes and adopted Caroline Spencer, given her their last name (which

49

the kid said she wanted real bad). So now she was Caroline Spencer, and she would always be. Hang the past, Brooklyn Heights and Fulton Street, "real" parents who didn't give a damn, and guardian homes!

Jake stopped the cab with only the faint breath of a squeak before an older frame house with a brick façade and a great front porch. Shortly after he and Cammy got hitched, the porch had sold the place to Jake on sight. Camille of the Heights in a house with a hack husband and a twelve-year-old daughter who had made it a genuine family.

It wasn't all bad.

Not for the first time, Jake remained in his cab several minutes before getting out. He was just breathing in the nice life he, Cammy, Caroline, and God had made, a stone's throw from Prospect Park. It was for real, all of it, and it always would be.

This was forever.

2

The twelve-year-old sat on a chair just inside the house, looking through a window and over the porch with the swing she loved to curl up in on pleasant summer days, and watched her Pop.

Beyond him and the taxi and the park, Caroline could detect the hulking big-city skyline on clear days when the upper stories of the taller buildings were like shadows that shimmered, instead of being black. Once, she had come to this rocking chair anytime her homework was done and no one was watching to stare into the distance, trying to see through the shimmer and to scan both the great monoliths and the smaller buildings that were like burial mounds by comparison. She'd hoped in some way to find Thaddie and

Father—not by actually *seeing* either of them, because she had given up such childish ideas before Pop and Mom took her from the home. By sensing their whereabouts. Father had been such a giant to her when she was tiny, always so able to convey the impression that he could do almost anything, that she had almost been able to imagine him atop a skyscraper, waving his arms above his head to signal to her, staring back at just the instant she was peering out the window in Brooklyn.

And she'd thought for a long time that Father would come and save her, that he'd have Thaddie with him, that the two of them might positively burst into the house where she lived with the Spencers and simply take her away.

Until Caroline was about ten, and it occurred to her, once when she was perched on the rocker just as she was now, to ask herself: Save me from *what*?

And then, a very long, troubled moment later: Take me away from . . . *home*?

And one day when she had her allowance in her hand, and she was in a drugstore, and a candy bar looked delicious even if it was wrapped up in red and white paper, Caroline had discovered a few more questioning words were living in her mind but that they'd somehow never gotten to her inner ear where she could listen to them: *Take me away from Pop and Mom?* But she didn't *want* that, Care knew, picking up the candy bar and hurrying to pay for it before she might change her mind. She really wanted her new parents and the real home, where each of them sometimes went somewhere else whenever it made sense to do it, and everyone knew it wasn't really Terrible Out There, and that they'd go home again and be together. It hadn't been like that when she and Thad were little.

That night at supper was the first time she'd ever really *looked* at either her Mom or her Pop. That night was the first time Care stopped seeing Mama, Father, and Thad much more clearly than she'd ever been able to see Camille and Jake Spencer; and she *liked* the way her "folks" were; what they had; how they tried hard to make her happy. And Caroline knew then that she *could* be happy if she just let herself. Because Father lied, he'd never come for her the way he had said—but her Mama's face was there to see, inside her locket, whenever Care needed to see it.

Which was when she'd run to her room after helping wash dishes and *bolted* the candy bar down all by herself, and decided just to miss Thaddie. But more like she missed Mama.

Then she had carried the red and white wrapper from the candy in her own hand, as carefully as if it were a live bomb—*but she touched it!*—all the way down to the kitchen wastebasket.

And started to get happy, sort of.

She waited for Pop every chance she could lately, sitting in the same rocker, because she liked everything about the way he looked and it was kind of fun to see him or Mom be real *natural*, the way people were when they didn't think anyone was watching.

Pop had light brown hair that went nearly to his shoulders, but he tied it behind his head with a rubber band when he went to work in the morning. He'd told her how he had cut it real short when he and Mom were trying to get her for their little girl, but now she was his daughter "for sure" so he'd wear it any damn way he wanted. Pop was the handsomest man there was (though she didn't quite admit that to herself, remembering how nice Father had been). He had blue eyes that were usually opened all the way and truly *looked* at a person, and a small nose he said was "pugged" (Pop didn't like it much but Caroline thought he should), and a just-right mouth that told a daughter every mood he was ever in. He wasn't very tall but he'd done a lot of stuff in sports when he was younger and had good muscles. One knee was a mess (poor Pop) 'cause he played football in the streets over around Fulton as a little boy, and sometimes he had to pop it back into place—the grossest thing Care'd ever seen, but she thought it was fascinating to watch him do. She figured it made him sort of a self-doctor and felt these days that he could probably fix just about anything if he really wanted to.

Mom was great too. It was only that Pop seemed more exciting, in a way. 'Cause he got mad sometimes—'specially if he was drinking beer when Mom didn't want him to—really a lot more than Father ever had. (But Father hadn't wanted her. Not really . . .)

If it wasn't for the dreams she was still having—just not talking about anymore—real happiness might have been possible.

Caroline continued to dream of the evening that had ruined everything, when Mama brought pizza home—'cause she was excited about a promotion in her job—and spoiled Father's dinner. Seven years ago Care hadn't known just what a "job" was, certainly not what "promotion" meant. Now, though her new Mom didn't have a job outside the house, Caroline had learned from seeing Jake rise for work every day what that was, and both her adoptive parents spoke of friends who sometimes earned more money. (Pop occasionally liked bragging that he was "one of the *self-employed* set," but the company whose name was on his taxi belonged to some people in the Bronx. It said so right under "Garden Street Cab.") Mom baby-sat sometimes for other ladies on Lefferts or the streets nearby like East New York or Sterling.

Father had been a writer and never went out more often than he had to. He'd spent a whole lot of time in a room of the apartment he called his "study" when he wasn't tending to her or Thad, he cooked and kept everything spotless; but Care knew now she should have seen *something*

Father wrote in print—and she never had. Her gathering knowledge served both to clarify and confuse elements of the old dream. Knowing how Pop—Jake—yearned to work for a different company so he'd have a territory less dangerous, better paying, and closer, enabled her to understand why Mama had been willing to move elsewhere if it was a fine promotion. Jake Spencer worked hard, as Mama had, while Father had stayed home most of the time but always acted like he was boss. None of that seemed fair to poor dead Mama now.

And it shed a bewildering but brighter light on part of the dream that turned into a nightmare—the part Care had never fully understood. First she saw tears in Father's eyes, then the sadness *that now appeared, as well, to have been fear*! Why would he have been afraid to go live *elsewhere*, a father Thad and she believed somehow to have been almost magically powerful or confident?

As though merely posing the question let Caroline go on, remember more, her nightmare had begun during the previous year to proceed—to *continue*—though it was nearly impossible to tell how much of it was real, or exactly when things had happened.

But it was trying to take her to the question of *why* Mama killed herself; and Caroline, finally, was starting to want to know. . . .

Screams, she remembered them. No, not screams exactly, more like one long-drawn-out cry—a *wail*, that was what they called it—Mama wailing as though she might make the awful, scary sound forever. Wailing from the *bathroom*—not the night she did it, *before* that. A glimpse of Mama's face in Caroline's nightmare, the beauty drained away along with what color Mama'd had, an expression so *terrible* that seeing Deborah Madison's face in Care's sleeping mind was nearly like truly seeing it again, in life. Something more, about Father coming out of the bathroom and looking just the way Father always did except *worried*, maybe—

And a *single nightmarish glance* at her brother Thaddie as he slipped into their bedroom, climbed into bed real fast; and Care knew then as she knew now that he was the same old Big Bro he had always been—

But wasn't. Because—she could not make the dream explain this part even when she felt she was really, truly trying to do it—Thaddie was . . . *different*, then.

Caroline watched Pop get out and slam the cab door, head up the walk with his funny kind of serious grin, reminded so powerfully she couldn't evade the truth how unlike Father or even Mama he was—and Mom, too—and how happy she was that that was so.

She was jumping from the old rocker to greet Pop, when she realized she couldn't ever forget her bro no matter what, and knew she couldn't even want the nightmare-dream to leave her forever till she'd gotten everything she could get from it.

She also realized that most of her happiness was gone. Again.

3

Nothing about the entire day had gone well for Harwell, and he was relieved to find an acceptable excuse for departing his midtown office slightly ahead of quitting time. It was always a bitch to get a decent seat for the commute to White Plains, where Beverly had insisted he meet her for drinks before dinner, so every second counted. *Enduring one bitch in order to bed another one*, Harwell thought as he hurried from the elevator and bustled toward the front doors. Yet he heard the weary monotone in his head and sensed it wasn't only more thematically unkind than he meant but tedious and self-boring besides. A man might bore others harmlessly—he might even enjoy the hell out of doing it—but when he began to bore himself, he was in some trouble.

Maybe he'd blame it on Beverly, or the bevy of Bevs he'd known in recent years, for a while, even if the complete and purposive summoning of self-pity was a trifle indulgent. He kept himself in reasonable trim without getting obsessive about it, there were still others for a man like him. If he could see through to a not-graceless means of shucking and then speedily replacing Bev, then find another mistress without too many miles on her, he might conceivably make it to retirement with no more than a single woman after the new mistress. Fuck and shuck, that was the way to cook—and keep fresh.

But for now, Harwell thought as he shoved himself out onto the sidewalk, shuddering at the first nip of autumn breezes, there was White Plains and nothing else for it.

He took two steps and was starting to thrust one leg forward for a third before realizing that the small boy in his path was not getting out of the way. With a grunt, Harwell broke stride like a three-year leased car with sluggish brakes and glared down at the child.

Some six or seven years old—probably not Latino—this was surely the grubbiest street urchin he'd seen all year. Scruffy, underfed, feverish of eye. It was also staring at him with the kind of aplomb and insight one expected from an adult. Perhaps it was just familiarity and they'd met, however improbable that was. "Do I know you?"

"Only if you know me in your heart, sir," the urchin said—or Harwell thought so.

"How's that?" Maybe he'd misunderstood. Such words drifting upward from a dark-haired boy with strangely stunning dark eyes didn't want to register for a moment. They also demanded more focus than Harwell believed he could give just then. "What do you want?"

"Want? Well, somewhere to live." Thad said it as if he might think he'd met Santa Claus but he held his eyes wide and maintained contact by dint of willpower and experience. "And something to eat, every day. But I sure wouldn't ask them things of a stranger, sir—'cause I'm not your reasonal—responda—"

"Responsibility. Well, you got that part right at least." The little kindness of helping the urchin to complete his sentence brought a tentative smile to Harwell's razor-blade lips, but he tried to forestall it by beginning to break the gaze they shared.

"It's my mom who talks about what's in people's hearts. She and my little brother"—Thad Madison swiveled his head, held the well-dressed man's eyes as he indicated the general direction of Central Park—"well, he's too sick for Mom to leave and he needs his medicine." This was where Thaddie's instincts told him tears or a sniffle would be effective, yet they hadn't been back when Thad was really about seven and polishing his act. This afternoon he straightened his back, brushed at the hopeless dirt staining his small jacket more deeply than dye had, and kept his head proudly erect. "I didn't have enough money t-to get his prescription filled so the drugstore man w-wouldn't give it to me." He dipped a hand into one pocket of the tattered jeans, withdrew an always eye-catching big handful of change along with a slip of paper with printing on it. And scribbling.

"What do you have there?" Harwell asked on cue. "You have more loose change than I do."

"But it don't add up to how much little Marsh's medicine costs—eleven dollars 'n' seventy-nine cents." Swallowing hard, head raised to reveal a bobbling emotional Adam's apple, Thaddie pointed at the apparent doctor's prescription. "See, I don't want more than that, sir—and I got *change* for you here if you have a ten and two dollar bills! I know there's at least eighteen cents for you." He barely recaptured an escaping sob.

"Twenty-one," Harwell said quickly. Being the comptroller for a publishing house taught one to perform subtraction swiftly, even without the computer. The boy, he would be cute if washed and decently clad. He seemed intelligent too, rare in homeless types. What was the matter with men—fathers—these days? The child's mother couldn't be much older than thirty, might only be little more than a child herself. Maybe he should meet her. . . . "It's '*doesn't* add up to eleven seventy-nine.' " Harwell withdrew his billfold. "Don't those people of yours even make you go to school?"

"No," Thaddie said honestly, "but they used to." His dark eyes were dilating looking at the sheaf of bills and the compartment in which the man probably kept his credit cards. When he saw the adult was squinting at the "prescription" sheet he had, Thad made himself stop staring at the billfold and begin counting out change. "I sure 'preciate your help and Mom will too, 'cause it'll keep my little brother going for a whole—"

A few nickels and dimes, several pennies and one quarter slipped through Thaddie's slim, short fingers and collided with the pavement where they immediately began to roll.

Swiftly, Harwell clapped his foot down on the quarter heading toward him. Then he jerked his head around to follow the journeys of the other coins—

And his customarily firm grip on his billfold was broken. Harwell felt it positively *ripped* from his fingers, yet it was done with such surprise and cleverness that over a second passed before he remembered to stare down at his hand. His *empty* hand.

"Thank *you*, sir," called the boy of the streets, sprinting away at a speed Harwell knew he had never reached during his own childhood. And the miserable little thief had the gall to even sound grateful!

Then the boy's other words floated back to the grown-up on a note of seeming sincerity that sounded at least as genuine—implausible as that was—as his expression of thanks. "I'm real sorry, mister—I really am."

But what actually ended up remaining in Harwell's thoughts in the annoying days ahead of him, when he had managed to replace some identification and to alert people about his plastic, was a keen, offputting recollection of the strength such a small person had displayed in tearing the billfold out of his hand.

Maybe he had been wrong about the little bastard's age.

And possibly Beverly would eventually forgive him for not getting to White Plains for drinks that night, even if she had said she was beginning to find him boring.

4

Thaddie should be starting back to school, the old woman thought, above her needlecraft. She shoved back the red yarn she was working with at her table in the dining room and told herself she was pausing because of the arthritis that ballooned her knuckles and made it hard to work her fingers. Then Enid raised her head to gaze out the window next to her hutch—once, it had been Mother's—and realized the time of year had come when one could not remotely guess the time of day from the look of the sullen light. Autumn, Miss Godby thought with a completely internalized shudder. An astrology buff, she liked knowing when famous people were born and said, just with her lips, "Only someone born in September or October could consider April the cruelest month." T. S. Eliot was wonderful but fall was the start of winter's waste land. It simply took a while.

Last winter, when Thad Madison gave Enid the shock of her life, she had decided to tell him the name of the foster parents with whom his sister, Caroline, had been successfully placed, but her memory failed her utterly. Then, when the boy had refused her offer to let him stay overnight until she'd learned the name of the family from which he had clearly run away to look for Caroline—when he'd gone back into that awful night—she hadn't quite known what to do. She might have taken more action than she did, but he hadn't believed her, Enid had sensed that. He'd thought she wouldn't tell him how to go see his sister again, and he immediately lost all trust in her.

Miss Godby looked down again at the pattern in the book by her elbow and picked her needle up again, but some blurriness of vision was preventing her from seeing the rabbit in the pattern with the necessary clarity. The poor boy had been sadly mistaken. She yearned with her whole heart to see *her* sister, her *family*, again, but there was exactly one way that could be possible now and she had not wanted to die in the waste land. . . .

Then when Thad had slipped noiselessly out of the house while she was surreptitiously trying to reach the police, eager to get more help for him than she could give, it suddenly had seemed to Miss Godby that it was an act of terrible betrayal to summon the authorities after a tiny boy had come innocently to her for help. A note from Thaddie she found in her chair—"Im OK dont worry"—had momentarily confirmed her suspicions to herself: What good were police in a situation like that? He had done nothing wrong. Wouldn't the authorities just frighten him, and wasn't it possible he might refuse to go with them? Then what would they do?

Thaddeus Madison was so *small*. He did not appear to have grown at *all*!

By the time morning rolled around and Enid had been sure Thad was miles away, she had decided not even to inform the guardian home where she'd worked for so many years. She didn't like or even trust the person who'd replaced her—a man—and this occasion was the first in which she could face the fact that one of her children had been abjectly miserable in a placement without the need to bear in mind who was paying her salary. Always before, unless there was evidence of some mistreatment on the part of the fosters, she hadn't truly stood up for the child.

Now, however, nine months later, there was already a chill on the air, all American boys and girls should be resuming their educations, and there was a chance that the Madison boy might be facing another winter on his own.

Enid could not conceive of how a child so small could make it through another one.

Nine months. She repeated the time period in her worried thoughts. What could her indecision and inaction have brought into Thad Madison's life since then?

She pushed back from the dining room table and went to the phone to call the home, raising the instrument to her ear and hearing the dial tone before it dawned on her that she no longer remembered the number.

The Madison children's mother was a suicide, Miss Godby recalled while she squinted through the autumnal gloom into her personal phone book. The father just ran off. Disappeared as if he cared nothing for any of them—or had something to conceal. Yet she'd gained enough information on the case to know that neither parent had a criminal or psychiatric record—in the father's instance, he had almost no record whatever. Which was presumably why, during Enid's remaining workdays at the home, the authorities hadn't even located the dreadful man for questioning. And if you couldn't find a grown man, with his need for employment and to pay taxes and all, how in the world would they have been able to find a clever and resourceful boy who lived on the streets? She knew a great deal about the young, even if she'd never had children herself. They didn't hesitate to climb or crawl anywhere because it was dirty or germ-laden, they could hide where adults would never think to look, they knew no danger, and they could become fearless to the extent of recklessness.

But it was still past time to endeavor to do what she could for Thaddeus's own good, Enid assured herself when she had dialed. And, if the conceited boor who'd taken her place at the home didn't know what to do about it, she'd eventually remember the name of the people who'd taken Caroline in. Why, it wasn't inconceivable the sister might know her brother's last whereabouts.

Why didn't they pick up? The red yarn she was using for a border around the needlework rabbit lay beside another skein, of white yarn. The image of a little girl frenziedly cutting the red colors out of a beautiful new dress filled Miss Godby's memory for a moment. Ordinarily, she never got to see the children again if a placement was permanent. That was so wonderful and so heartbreaking it was like a symbol of all life.

He answered the phone with the same words she'd used so often. Drawing herself erect, Enid identified herself, then launched into the purpose of her call.

It took her a moment to realize Hector Crossland had interrupted her. *"Who?"* was what he had asked.

And that took Miss Godby's presence of mind away, made her begin to stammer, and, in referring to events that had transpired during the winter—nearly a year ago—she found herself leaving out salient points.

It was during the ensuing minutes of the telephone discussion that Enid learned that regardless of how much you yearned to do the right thing, however belatedly, pressures bearing on your own well-being might become so hard to stand that one only wished to be doing something else, elsewhere. That was especially the case when a person realized both that she was an unwelcome caller, much too late (and the other party relished the fact), and getting older in a manner that had less to do with the passage of time than the accumulation of strife, and regret.

Still, feeling clammy at the temples and breast, Miss Godby went on trying.

And Hector Crossland said shortly, "We put all those ancient records in the computer and it's down. Can't help you."

Ancient? "They're *thirteen* and *twelve* now," Enid protested. "The children." She almost added that it was "only seven years ago," but realized that wouldn't help her, or Thaddie.

"Look, Edith," her replacement said, "times have changed since you were here. There's a new kind of kid; there're new methods, restrictions—"

"Restrictions?" she interposed. "Restrictions on finding a missing boy, whom we placed? It's a simple matter, to begin, of getting the names of the foster parents to whom he was sent, contacting them, learning if they *did* something to him, and when they last saw—"

"Restrictions on giving out information over the phone to persons who have no official ties to this institution," Crossland said bluntly. He chuckled then, as though showing his willingness to overlook an old woman's foolishness. "I'll pull the boy's file up when I can, all right! Keep it handy in case somebody else brings him in. Now, why don't you enjoy your retirement, Edith? Anybody who puts a year in on this job, dealing with these brats, has it coming."

"It's 'Enid,' *Herman*," Miss Godby snapped, "my name

63

is Enid Godby—and you haven't heard the last of this!''
And she slammed the phone down, had to stoop to pick it
up when she saw she'd missed and placed it, belatedly, in
its cradle.

Then she sat at her phone table for some time, unwilling
to trust her legs and back, her heart, to stand.

"But he has," she said to herself, the house, all. He
almost certainly *had* heard the last of it.

And she of Thaddeus and Caroline Madison.

When able, she put the red and white yarn away in a
shoebox she kept it in, then found a different pattern.

She told herself it was the arthritis acting up in her hands
that kept her from beginning it instead of the way they, and
her heart, were trembling.

5

Living on the street, Thad Madison knew by now, was at
once easier for a child and a whole lot harder.

The easy part came from just the kind of mind game he
had played on D. D. Harwell (Thaddie knew that had been
the man's name because it was typed or printed all over
his identification and his credit cards), because almost no
one flinched in alarm when they saw a boy who looked six
or seven years old coming up to them. They might very
well walk on, even shoulder him out of their way (Thad
had worked very hard to refrain from jumping on their
backs and hitting them with his tiny fists because that just
made policemen see, and remember his face); they might
very well tell him to "beat it" or "fuck off," and refuse
to fall for any of his carefully contrived scams.

But he had seen how some grown-up street people operated and how seldom they scored. Part of it was the way
boozers and cokeheads reached the point sooner or later

that they looked like just what they were and nothing they tried to tell other grown-ups worked, unless the mark was feeling very generous or very liberal, or from out of town. It was the same thing with street hos, which was the only name Thaddie had for them—a gift of jargon from one of the few fellow con artists who had ever been friendly with him. Even when a ho was a girl or boy no older than he was, they got that special *look* to 'em—and they always seemed surprised and disappointed when they'd been either as cute or dirty as possible and the man or woman they propositioned wouldn't have sex with them no matter how much they lowered their prices. Sooner or later—and it was becoming sooner for girls on the street recently with ordinary folks laid off or wanting safe sex—the hos and the scam artists and the regular panhandlers alike couldn't keep need, envy, sin, or hatred out of their expressions until, one day, Thaddeus didn't see them around any longer.

Sooner or later for everyone but Thad, that is, the boy thought while he counted the money in Mr. Harwell's billfold (to the best of his limited ability). Thad, the Unchanging. An acquaintance in his twenties who'd almost become his friend—but he got arrested, and never came back—had asked if he was a dwarf, and Thaddie'd beat him up till the guy got a good hold on him and then sat on Thad's chest.

Alone in the broken-down lobby of a condemned hotel in the Bowery district, Thaddie told himself he wouldn't think about his size anymore, even the lack of it! So what if he could scrunch down into this old sofa so's no one on the streets knew he was there, he was damn *cute*, everybody said so—and he made a living from it! Some of the girl hos had felt sorry enough for him that they let him see 'em bare-ass, *even watch*, even if they wouldn't do it with him yet. And he was pretty strong too, and fast, though he didn't know if he could lick guys much bigger than he was because they wouldn't believe he was really twelve or because he just could. And if he didn't have any buddies, screw 'em, it was 'cause they was jealous, 'cause they not only got older and bigger, they got all . . . all *used up*. Sometimes he thought he didn't change the way they did because he just did what he had to do, he didn't really like lyin' to people and stealin'.

And what he had to do was refuse to get caught and put in some damn foster home again where Father couldn't find him, he had to *stay* out on the *streets*, so Father would see him someday.

"I wonder where Caroline got put," Thad said aloud, and two of the rats across the lobby lifted their sleek heads that were almost like the nozzles of much larger animals, except rat eyes were kind-of like two more nostrils stuck up on top of their heads.

A few times when he'd run away from foster homes—not Thurman and Rhonda Tinsdale's, 'cause it was too far to go when he was *really* a little kid—Thaddie had made his way to the old guardian home in SoHo, then hung around till he was fairly sure he'd seen all the kids there and realized Care had been placed. ("Placed" was a funny word; the Tinsdales had had place settings, they'd said, for dinner, but him and Caroline wasn't just a knife and fork.)

"I don't wanta think about them," Thad informed rats both seen and unseen. "What happened there or any of the other foster homes." Recently reminded he was among them, the rats continued grayly about their business.

What was *hard* about being a kid on the streets was like now, when Thaddie had a lap full of cash and credit cards. 'Cause he couldn't just spend it and buy things any old place. This wasn't the first good score he'd made, and Thad knew from experience that stuck-up stores rarely believed he had plastic of his own and that real hotels, unlike the old dump he lived in free now, wouldn't have given him a room if he had put a million bucks down on the front desk!

So half of what Thaddeus Madison used the money and cards for was food; everything he wanted to eat (on nights like this) at fast food restaurants, and perishables—plus a few cans of vegetables—he could bring back to the fleabag hotel from markets and delis.

He got up from the lobby sofa (he had a real pillow there, too, 'cause he knew better than to sleep in any rooms in a place that might cave in any minute) and crossed the floor to a little room where the hotel people used to hang and stack bags. On the way, he listened to his only friends stir like a ton of fallen autumn leaves, careful never to trust all rats, and poked one credit card and most of Mr. Harwell's cash into his jeans pockets.

The anteroom contained the other half of the things Thad had bought the past couple of years. Before that, his earlier possessions had been lost when a building he'd lived in was razed before the sign said it would be, and he was on the street.

Dozens of shirts and name-brand jeans hung from the abandoned racks, all of them new and never worn. New underwear, socks, and shoes were piled across the top—in case a given rat became desperately hungry, the stuff was too high up to reach without going to considerable trouble—and a few dozen comics and books were atop the clothing. The majority of the latter had been leafed through repeatedly, if only laboriously read; Thaddie's education consisted of portions of the first two years of schooling, and two weeks of a third, the whole experience of learning having occurred in more schools than he could recall.

And the encyclopedic knowledge he'd gained on the streets.

Not that that had been the Tinsdales' fault or any of the other foster homes, like he had told Miss Godby in her home last winter. They'd all been shitty make-believe parents, and one couple Thad had spent only a few weeks with had been far worse than shitty, but they'd been happy to stick him away in schools.

He skinned down, paused to sniff his armpits. Robby and Rodge, two rats Thaddie knew pretty well, raised their own heads to inhale and Thad giggled. Donning new underwear—even a T-shirt since he was goin' to McDonald's and have all the Big Macs he wanted—he thought about how nice Miss Godby had been really, and wished he and Care had understood her job. It was clear now that she'd just wanted 'em to have a real house to live in, with real folks to like 'em, so it wasn't her fault that she'd broke him and Caroline up.

She just hadn't known how the way she and Care had treated him was a whole lot better than bein' with people who couldn't even pretend good and thought you were some sort of toy or who didn't really want anything 'cept the money they got for bein' foster parents. They'd all had nice places to live (once you was "placed"), but a house with two people like his sister and Miss Godby who didn't tear you up inside, was much better, even if it was old.

Thad buttoned his new red shirt, then balanced himself awkwardly against the lobby wall as he crammed his short legs into the tight new jeans legs. Thurman and Rhonda came to within about twelve feet of him while his head was turned, but he called Robby's name and he and Rodge half-heartedly chased the rats Thaddie hated away. He made a mental note to bring back a sack of regular burgers for his "sort-of friends," which was how Thaddie thought of the leaders, and the other rats he halfway trusted. Not that he would make the mistake of trying to single them out, or throw bites to them like he'd heard you could do with dogs. The one time he had ever attempted to feed the beasts individually, at some other hole he'd lived at awhile, they had ganged up on him and chased him all the way out of the building and about a zillion miles toward the South Bronx!

Still caked with dirt except for smears where Thaddie got spit on his fingers and wiped them on his forehead and cheeks, he paused to look around before crawling through the broken window. (When he was outside, he'd press the boards back in place over it.) Maybe he should climb up the fire escape to the roof tonight, when he returned. It was just a four-story building, but he hadn't gotten up high to see if he might spot Father out looking for him in a few days. The city wasn't really as big as folks liked to think it was, but it would take real good luck, Thaddie knew now, to be somewhere at exactly the time Father was searching for him and Care in the right neighborhood. There were so *many* buildings, so *many* people—and you had to keep one eye open for the rats, another for the police (some of whom might possibly ask you questions), another eye for the perverts who wanted to hit on you. With one eye out for Father, that made four you needed—and Thaddie didn't even wear glasses!

"See you guys later," he promised, bracing himself for the New York night.

6

She had removed all her clothing before going into the bedroom because her nakedness still seemed to have a way of shocking Jake. She knew he would want to make love tonight, a Friday, and she had lost track of how many nighties and how much underwear her husband had all but wrecked over the years. Not that he had ever *hurt* her— that wasn't in Jake, she knew she was one of the fortunate wives—and not that his recurring excitement after their long marriage was not, in a way, high praise.

J. N. Williamson

Looking at (but not quite examining) herself in the full-length bathroom mirror, Camille was tempted to wonder anew at both the differences between Jake and her and between the modern breed of woman she kept hearing about and Camille Spencer. She was almost always happy when her husband desired her—knew for a fact how blessed she was that he actively desired no other—but usually preferred all the accoutrements of lovemaking to the actual sex. After more than a decade of marriage, she felt she had a choice between believing that the newer kind of woman was simply a better actress—or endowed with a better imagination—or that she herself had never gotten the hang of it. Camille patted cologne where it was supposed to do the most good, smiled privately. Jake would certainly have made a joke about her "getting the hang" of sex!

Camille's smoky eyes returned restively, nervously, to those of the woman in the mirror. Time to remove her glasses and go in to Jake before he yelled to her, wanted to know if "everything was okay." And it was, it was *definitely* more okay than it had ever been before they found Caroline. (She thought of it sometimes like that, of "finding" their adopted child, as if other female and male flesh had not brought Care into the world.) But the real difference between the sexes was that men had a knack for being temporarily satisfied by steps of progress, and contentment, then coasting on their laurels until some unavoidable problem developed. ("I'll rest on your laurels anytime, Cammy," Jacob would say.) Women—Camille Spencer, anyway—operated on a different clock and found completion only in completion, if they recognized it then. Jake knew the past, and today—no, this *hour* of today. She lived in the past, present—and Caroline's future.

And Caroline was trying to dwell in the present but, born to be a woman one day, couldn't really look forward to the future of anyone or anything—and could not be fully content one hour—till she dealt with the past and made a new, better one with them. The child—twelve years old and beginning suddenly to blossom, for goodness' sakes, but only half her life spent with Jake and her—had made *fantastic* progress, more than they had once imagined possible. Yet she continued to have the bad dreams, continued to peek into that old locket with her birth mother's picture, even while she appeared to believe she was absolutely happy with them.

And Care didn't know that she had heard her *whispering* to the poor, dead woman, and heard Care crying out her brother Thaddie's name in her sleep. What in the world had *happened*, what had the monstrous father of those children *done* to them and to his wife?

"Yo, Cammy," Jake called from bed, "everything okay in there?"

Fine, Camille thought. Then she remembered to say it aloud, more or less. "Be there in a sec."

Softly, in the hope he wouldn't hear her, she flipped off the lights over the washbasin. Practical concerns ruined sex for him, she knew, though it had been impossible for Camille to detect in what fashion that might be true.

She was turning toward the door connecting the two rooms, when she saw the moonlight coming through the bathroom window and the way it looked on her upraised bare arm and equally bare abdomen. Camille turned back to the nearby mirror to contemplate this different, wholly nocturnal edition of Camille Spencer (*the moon is full and it bathes everything in beauty but full moons are supposed to make people hysterical or crazy so maybe it's because the light is alien or maybe we can't live with much beauty*).

Her blond hair, ordinarily so light of hue it looked peroxided, girls had said that when she was growing up in the Heights. It was because Dad always said to stand up straight and "look regal," but any impression of good breeding was replaced at ten or twelve feet by the notion that she was just pretentious, or artificial. Lori'd told her that once. But she'd also said that when someone got within a yard or so of her, they got another impression, a surprise—because she really was modest, even shy. And so there'd never been many close women friends; they'd never gotten close, as Jake had.

But up close Camille also appeared suddenly shorter, even Jake had admitted it! Her rounder lines showed up, then, when she had a tendency to stare down—out of shyness—which made other people look down too, and see what dreadful legs she had! It was all such a vicious circle, far too complicated—until Jake whispered on the third date they had that he'd just found out you had to get as close as anybody *could* to tell that her legs and her figure were really just as pretty as her smoky eyes and her pale blond hair. "But I'm gonna be the only one who ever finds that out," he'd added, "because I'll be the only one who ever *gets* that close!"

She opened the bedroom door and padded barefoot inside, knowing just how she would find her husband and not encountering any surprises: He kept a sheet up to his middle even if she was supposed to be nude, because he felt his penis was terrible until it was up. Camille hadn't tried to find out if it was her fault or his that they couldn't have children, because she'd been afraid she might learn it was his, and it would have hurt him badly. Having forgotten to remove her glasses, she paused a few feet from where Jake lay with his back turned, reading a magazine, and smiled inside. Everything about the way he looked was fine with her and she hadn't seen that for a while since she usually took her glasses off. Lori'd told Camille once that because her lenses were so thin and clear, some of the girls believed she didn't really need glasses and wore them to be snooty. She was blind as two or three bats without them, and she'd worn them so long they were as natural to her as her slow-to-smile, rather-too-wide mouth. "Yo, Jake," she called.

He glanced up, around, grinning. He liked it when she used the sort of language he enjoyed, and she assumed he knew she didn't mean it condescendingly. Snootily. "You got your specs on," he said, rolling over and raising the sheet for her.

"And I'm going to leave them on awhile," Camille said, climbing in. "So I can see what I'm doing for a change."

"Screw the sheet, then," he answered, kicking it to the foot of the bed.

Camille raised almost colorless brows. "Why would I want to do that when I have *this*?"

Caroline's scream—part of it was mumbled words, incomprehensible at their distance from her room—sent Camille back to her feet and running through the bathroom. En route, she snatched up her robe, heard Jake muttering sounds no more understandable than Care's as she poked her arms into it; then both of them were in the second floor hallway, rushing toward Caroline's bedroom.

The twelve-year-old was sitting up in bed, her fair-skinned face trapped in the ambivalence between sleep and reality—perhaps, Camille thought, or sensed, between the reality of the past and the future to which she was richly entitled. Even as they entered the room, they saw how hard she was struggling—fighting—to push the memories of her early years back into her mind to keep them from counting so much.

"I r-remembered what Thaddie told me that night," Caroline stammered—"but I don't know what it meant!" She stared straight ahead of her as Camille sat on the mattress beside her and took her hand. It lay curled in Camille's palm as if Caroline weren't aware it was there. "After he came out of the b-bathroom, while Mama—Mama Deborah—was crying."

"Hey, Care," Jake told her from the foot of the bed, bedsheet wrapped around his waist. "You don't have to remember any of that shit. You don't—"

"Jake, be quiet," Camille said sharply without raising her voice. She took Caroline's fingers, clasped them over her own hand, squeezed gently. "Just remember it might have been a nightmare, sweetheart—not real. Tell us whatever you want us to know, all right?"

Abruptly, Caroline offered her a rare hug. "Th-Thaddie said Father chose *him*. He was crying, a *lot*, and he wouldn't let me come s-sit next to him—but he was still happy in a way. Happy, or—*p-proud*."

"Well," Jake put in, "maybe everything was just a mis-understanding then, if your brother was okay. Maybe your . . . first mom was—well, jealous or something. Of some little secret your old man told Thaddie. Maybe—"

"*No*, Pop!" Caroline interrupted, blond hair swirling with the fierce shake of her head, " 'cause I remember there was red on Thad. R-red on his white pjs."

Camille glanced at her husband with evident disgust. *She can't say "blood,"* her lips told him noiselessly. *The damned molester.* Abruptly, Caroline startled them by hurling herself back into the bed, sobbing. "He said he l-loved me, but he chose *Thaddie*!" Care choked the words out. "I dunno j-just what he *did*, but he picked my bro *instead*." She'd buried her face in her pillow and a numbed Camille and Jake had to strain to hear what else she gasped. "My father *r-rejected me*!"

Chapter Three

Alone in the loft he took for momentary sanctuary, Marshall Madison stared down through the murk of memory and midnight at the always-traveled city streets.

Each memory grew brighter, as if illumined by the shield of stars above the building until it burned freshly in his reddened eyes like the glow of hot cinders.

Because each memory—each in its own way—was tied to that which Marshall had hated most in a lifetime of hating: Dying. Not death, of necessity; dying. He hadn't yet experienced the former, so he was hesitant to condemn it out of hand. Some there were who spoke of death as an oasis of peace and rest, as a new land Columbus might have yearned to explore, and claim as his own or his queen's. Many saw it as a chance to sum up, and begin anew refreshed. Marshall did not like to be rude, and prejudgments were the mark of an ignorant man.

But he *knew dying*, he'd known it since he was a small boy, and a person of advanced years who boasted of his wisdom informed Marshall that—already, in youth—he was starting to die and that everyone born began instantly to experience the dying process. Healthy people, unhealthy people, it was all the same. Each had been born to die, perhaps literally so—perhaps all of life was an act of patience on the part of some divinity who waited only to watch the individual exit from life.

Marshall hadn't forgotten the man's careless remarks for so long as a day in his entire life and knew that his own final regret, before expiring, would be that he hadn't been able to have a hand in that venerable personage's *own* unpleasant demise.

So it was dying he detested, whether the cessation of a sentient life or the awful finality of a treasured emotion, or a situation. Dying was his enemy, and so it had been Marshall Madison who was last to leave a good party, last to fall asleep instead of attempting to make love one more time, Marshall, who was both the first and last to weep during a sad movie or at the dying of any human being whom he had met, however unpleasantly or fleetingly.

Yet he'd been obliged to witness the arrival of the dying process within his own family, to observe its remorseless and fatal permeation. Starting with Deborah.

The images of the night when she'd discovered the truth about him were suddenly so clear that even the stars of distant evening seared Marshal's brow and eyes and prevented him from looking up and away. Beneath this loft he had recently seized, the vehicles in the street froze in position; they seemed to melt into the shadows of another night.

For he had had to see his wife's absolute trust in him die at the instant she caught him completing an intimate act with one of their two children.

And it was as though he had struck her, stabbed her, yet worse than that—worse because Deborah did not understand *why* he had desired so powerfully to do what he had done, and was incapable of listening when he strove to explain. Instead of reeling away from the nearly incomprehensible sight before her eyes with her faith and her love already simply annihilated, Deborah had reacted as if a doctor had bestowed a sentence of death upon *her* . . . *him* . . . *all* of them! Deborah, beautiful and compassionate Deborah, could not permit her soul itself even to hear his explanation, nor could she turn her love and trust—*their future*—to the dust of abandonment in one instant. The dying process was only initiated that night in her heart, not fulfilled.

So Marshall had had to watch.

And in the short time left to the family, he had seen his exquisite wife go without sleep, food, water, sustenance of any sort. It was like she immediately lost her tenuous grip on the delicate mechanism meshing the physical with the spiritual and forgotten how to nourish herself. It was as if nothing more *mattered* in the world, the universe, to her, to Deborah Madison.

And *Marshall understood her*, that was another dreadful part of the dying—he *really* did! He knew just how she felt, and why; he knew how awful it had looked, and he didn't *blame* her!

· But even if he'd tried for one thousand years to do it, he would never have been able to share those emotions of hers, only understand them, because he had his *own*, his own intransmittable needs and desires—his own (what was that high-toned word?) imperative. It was also impossible for him to *agree* with his wife in a manner of integrity for the reason that he could not possibly be sure in his own mind and heart that what he had done was wrong.

Marshall's own rising emotional drives were too powerful to cheapen them with emotional arguments based on the conventions of others. He could not even persuade himself now that it was too late for Deborah and their family, that he should *consider* if he was as evil a man as the rest of the world would have believed. Because he'd played that intellectual game so many times in the past that it had come to seem to him more an inexcusable self-indulgence than a genuine effort to learn the truth about himself. Cross-examining a stilled conscience wasn't mental masturbation. It was necrophilia.

And as sweet Deborah had starved her spirit and left Marshall to watch, she mustered her fragile energies to hover above the still-unharmed child of their marriage like a warrior whose arms had long since been stripped away. Nothing but courage and her remembered will had remained with her in those final days; yet she had nearly *dared* Marshall to attack again, she had barricaded the child's bedroom door against his tenderest desire to whisper "good night" or to brush a straying lock of hair—as though his powerful and special drive was all that would ever define him now in Deborah's eyes.

So he had reasoned with her through the door he might have caved in at any instant, striven again (but in quiet and covert tones in order not to disturb the sleeping child) to tell her the truth about himself—to swear that he'd never wanted to harm any of them.

—Until, in a split second of impulsiveness Marshall could not recall, he'd said the first of two things that were true and almost as unforgivable as what he had done to the one child: "The three of you are the only ones I've ever *not* wanted to hurt and the only ones *I* swore never to harm. Not, at any rate, according to my own definition of hurting."

Of course, that had been a mistake. A big one. Admitting that he did intend to harm other people (even when it made him unhappy), with an honest implication that he had already destroyed so many.

So he had taken to leaving at night when he could despite

the misery he experienced on the streets, hoping his absence would somehow temper his wife's feelings toward him, cause her to miss or to fear for him.

But all that had done was let him see in her face, when he returned before morning, the terror for her children (and his)—and the way she was continuing, adamantly, to perish, to will herself to *die*. At that point he'd realized without question that their marriage was nearly dead, and Deborah with it. The family itself was moribund yet he could not go for help; he could not phone anyone for guidance or assistance. If his own wife was unable to understand his inner drives, no stranger would do so—and none ever had. The ruination Deborah was capable of bringing upon him just by bringing an outsider to the apartment then was unthinkable, particularly when the bond between Deborah and him was destroyed, and one of their two children was forever changed.

Deborah grew wan, exhausted. The all-but-complete absence of sleep and food would do that. Increasingly, Marshall believed without being obliged to see it happen, she passed out beside the unscathed child Marshall had not yet reached when his drives had been at their peak. He knew that an element of Deborah's terrible loss was linked to the fact that what he had done to their other child was the one act she would never agree to share with him. Indeed, when he'd been discovered, or shortly afterward, Marshall had asked.

And she had called him disgusting, monstrous, and badly disturbed.

One evening when the four of them had dined at home and even the relatively normal behavior of their children hadn't brought warmth to the indigestible meal, Marshall made the second remark of truth and unarguable fact that then pushed Deborah over the edge. Perhaps (he mused now before the long loft window, slipping back from it till

79

all he could see was the narrow, naked corpse of another New York building, lit from within by fireflies that winked and vanished as the night lengthened) . . . perhaps he'd known his remark would make Deborah kill herself. Perhaps he'd believed that was the most merciful ending for her now. "I can get the *other one* anytime I choose," he had said quietly, amiably. "You're too bright not to know that. When I'm ready—when I *must* . . . I *will*."

Why hadn't she let herself believe it was possible he *wasn't* hurting them, instead of choosing only to believe that he would have his *way!* Were all people today so hidebound by convention?

Marshall spun all the way around from the window, staggered two tortured steps, and tripped on the still-twitching body of the man from whom he had seized the loft.

Man on floor stared at man erect, terror rising and met by diffidence, near disinterest. The legal subletting tenant of the place possessed no especially interesting characteristics—which is to say that just as he was not young, athletic, and formidably large, he wasn't old, lame, or a tiny man either. He was just a man who'd answered a well-timed knock at his door and found himself quickly overpowered by a masked man on the landing. After that, it had gotten considerably worse for him. Not being a sociable person but a family man by preference, Marshall had reckoned that he would be exposed to less chitchat and interference in equal proportion to the amount of damage he expended up front.

There was a bloody trail on the white carpet from where the unfortunate resident had painstakingly hauled his extensively broken body across the room. The trail ran from the area of the loft including his bed, an end table, and a bookshelf bearing a vase with an improbable plastic flower to the long window just a few yards from the front door. It had taken the man the better part of two days and nights to progress this far, Marshall knew, the awareness engaging his attention sufficiently for him to pause and consider an equation of passing interest: Could this fellow, hungry and untended, reach the door and hammer on it for help before perishing of his wounds?

The answer, he saw, was no. It wouldn't have mattered if he *did* make it to the door, in any case. He was much too weak to haul himself up and rap on it, but, if he did, residents in the flats below the loft would only assume he had another caller; and besides, this was New York City.

What next drew Marshall's attention was an abrupt realization that the man was dying now. Tears formed in Marshall's eyes. Most of the time they were never squeezed out, never descended to his cheeks; but they *were* tears. Marshall detested dying.

"I'll put you out of your misery in a very short while," he promised the tenant when he was fairly sure he could speak without his voice breaking with emotion. That was always so embarrassing. Worse, another person with good vision could see his tearful red eyes through the holes in his mask.

Earlier in his marriage, he had attempted to explain some of his views about existence on earth, and the matter of eternity, to her. How he had grown inclined to believe that when a person was fortunate enough to get things the way he wanted them to be, he had the obligation to see any kind of sharp or sweeping change as a kind of dying. Of course then, at that point, it made good sense to take steps to oppose such threats, such changes. Because eternity was more than a long period of time, it was something one could *aspire* to, *pursue*, even to some extent *arrange*. And anything that important really required one's full attention and commitment.

Marshall had also explained to his attentive wife the nature of *one* of his seemingly perverse obsessions, hoping that she would not scoff as the few others had done over the years, longing for her not to *challenge* his belief by feeding him false praise but to *accept* his conclusions wholeheartedly—admit that she had been drawn to the inner man—for that was what had made Deborah special to him, his belief that that was the case.

And if she had only done as he wished—not scoffed or told him he was silly—he might then have been able to explain the great drive of his life. And permit her alone to perceive just how his convictions, or obsessions, fed off one another.

But ultimately, alas, she had only proved to be a good wife with a peasant woman's mentality, not unlike the mother Marshall dimly recalled these days, trapped in her narrow, provincial beliefs.

He glanced at the broken man on the floor, sighed for what might have been. Because in all their excellent years together, Deborah had never allowed him to set the stage for him to explain how he spent his accursed and tormented boyhood:

In the day-to-day, always growing realization of the unbearable fact that he was indescribably, unbelievably, and grotesquely . . . *ugly.*

Why, that was why he had never formed a friendship as a boy or, later, as a youth; why he had kept to his parent's house whenever he wasn't obliged to be at school, in agony, or working for his father. It was why he strove to remain in his room when his *grandparenti* or other relatives stopped by; why he buried his head in books, giving the impression to casual onlookers of becoming a little bookworm; why he had begun his journal; why he had never once participated in athletics; and why he'd left school as soon as he could (though his marks were consistently excellent)—and had resisted every effort on his parents' part to force him to return and finish.

It was why he'd never had a woman before the feminine "stray cat" weakness within beautiful Deborah had made her ask him to marry her. And though he stubbornly stayed at home after their marriage began, attempting to become a writer, thereby obliging her to earn their entire income—though she simply issued her merry laugh whenever he said casually how physically unattractive he regarded himself, kissing and reassuring him—Deborah had never given him a chance to describe the *depths* of his personal repugnance and self-horror.

Or the effect that had on his *other* needs. Those that society itself viewed with horror and revulsion.

Today there was a term for the knowledge that one was inexpressibly, profoundly ugly. Marshall stood at the mantel in the commandeered loft, drinking a beer that belonged to the man on the floor, and said the words aloud: "*Body Dismorphic Disorder.*" Like most psychiatric names, it changed nothing to know it, nothing to say it. It merely classified another group of society's unfortunates, enabled the specialists to catalogue and computerize them.

For many people who were cursed with such hideous insight into their own faces, limbs, and forms, it meant that they could not go outside and would never look into a mirror. They withdrew completely in order to avoid the stares they sensed other people were covertly making at them and the shock, the sickening reactions that polite men and women tried to keep out of their blessedly normal faces that they took so damned much for granted!

Well, Marshall Madison triumphed over "B.D.D."; Marshall Madison was a *man*, thanks to his beloved Deborah and to the children they'd had who would grow up thinking *their* father was the nice-looking gentleman—not the *other* men whom they met as they began to mature! And Marshall Madison had *often* gone out, at night—he'd even made himself peer at his image in a mirror several times during just the past decade!

And those times when either need was excessively painful to cope with, of course, he had what he'd made to wear. The mask Marshall frettingly continued to alter, and improve, over and over and over again. He did so partly in the hope that if anybody who'd already seen him had somehow gotten away, they wouldn't recognize him before he was close enough to kill them—so he would not have to carry with him the saddening knowledge that they were having bad dreams about him and his face.

After he'd initiated the dying process for each of them, he always wept.

Watching things die was terrible enough. Being observed by those who had not learned to know his inner nature of acute refinement and sensitivity, his concern for those he loved and the curses he bore with him every day of his existence, was infinitely worse.

It wasn't so bad, remaining indoors most of the time—or, until now, it hadn't been. One could always plan if he possessed a mentality that roamed freely and yearned to soar, an intelligence that could never be confined not if one lived to be a thousand years old. Imagination was the ticket; the *way!*

So how could he be blamed because he'd needed for at least one of his children to turn out as *he* had in order for him, or her, to stay with them at home—always? The reason Marshall's own obsessions and self-awareness were curses was that he had been obliged to go it alone for many years, he'd had no one to instruct him. He would never have deserted his girl and boy, *never!* He'd planned to show them all the tricks, the secret social devices nobody else alive knew except Marshall Madison. He had only *begun* to introduce them to the delights of the flesh which he had learned over the years—and in the case of only *one* child!

Marshall sighed heavily, shook his head in sadness, placed the empty beer bottle in a sack which the other man kept beside the refrigerator. He had not been wrong to fear the loneliness that would overtake him if even a single member of his family ever flew the roost, or died. Realizing she could never hope to protect her remaining, untouched offspring (for that was how she'd seen it, Marshall knew with renewed grief and comprehension; it was her old-fashioned outlook on life that had poisoned her mind against him), Deborah had somehow locked Caroline and Thaddeus in their room, telephoned the authorities, and slashed her wrists.

Then, when he returned home, he had to flee—if only to keep outsiders from *seeing* him, *interrogating* him, putting his picture in the *newspapers,* or on *television*! But there'd never been an instant when he had not intended to collect the little ones, start *anew.*

He had never imagined that the goddamned courts would not only take both his children but *separate* brother from sister, making it nearly impossible to locate them!

"Now," Marshall told the man on the floor, removing his mask.

Rather courageously, the fellow had drawn within a few feet of the front door. Now he turned his seeping red head to stare back in open horror at Marshall, and Marshall did not blame him. This man had done nothing worse than respond to a knock at his door; now he was seeing his assailant as few people had seen Marshall for years. Still, he might be able to use the fellow's amiably drooping blond mustache. For the mask.

While the head was turned back in order to stare up, Marshall stooped and clutched it between his hands. It was never easy to kill a man. It was necessary to touch them in ways and in places where heterosexual men did not customarily touch members of their own sex; the hair, the cheeks, the ears and neck. One could rumple a boy's hair without becoming suspect in one's own eyes, but this was not a boy whom he was gripping in his hands. He was certainly *not* playfully rumpling the man's hair.

He was yanking the head to the side at a decidedly unnatural angle and with such force that it seemed almost ready to come off. Instead—at the last vertebra of the neck's portion of the spinal column—it was merely snapping. Once; like the efficient and healing *pop*! produced by a practiced chiropractor.

But it *would* come off if Marshall decided to finish up that way. Probably not; it was pointless. He continued to kneel behind the other man's body for a moment, considering the full yellow mustache through pools of wetness and a regret that included the realization that he'd continue to need to be outside nights rather more often than had been necessary during the years of his and Deborah's marriage.

Still, this would be a good place to remain awhile, and search for the kids. Most things a man truly required—not all, but most—were present in the loft or could be ordered. The fellow slumped at his feet had owned numerous credit cards. And in time, people who had cared for the dead man were bound to stop by. That would be a source of entertainment and stimulation; a safe one, at that.

Yet nothing whatever would be the same without his wife.

And without little Thaddie and Caroline, whose rescue from strangers' houses would remain Marshall Madison's primary raison d'être for so long as he, or they, existed.

Marshall's forehead fell forward until it touched that of the loft's true tenant and he cried, telling himself he did so for both of them, for all the unfortunate people on the lined and hopelessly troubled face of the world.

But his weeping did not lack resolve.

Chapter Four

1

After a certain age, the human mind can learn almost anything and, if the human being is physically healthy, the informed mind can instruct the body that helps house it to do virtually anything within its own rather limited capabilities.

"It is as if the finest thinking machine ever even dreamed of by the modern dolts who are so unimaginatively involved in the manufacture of computers," Father had told Caroline and Thaddie while enjoying one of his rare expansive moods, "was obliged to be the driving force for a Model-T car. The thinking machine might be enlisted in a flight to the farthest stars, but the cranky device in which it is so unjustly encased can travel only a speed fast enough to defeat an old, decrepit horse—narrowly."

Caroline dreamed that sweeter, less-ominous dream of a time that might never come around again as October leaves came loose like brown buttons and slowly covered the yard on Leffert Avenue. Lying soft on her bed, pale as sprinkled sugar in moonlight from her window, she smiled as though "Father" and "Mama" still existed for her. Unknowing, her slender fingers with the well-munched nails of a growing child closed on the locket at her gradually flourishing breast, the tips of them seeking the face of her dead mother—and the empty space in the locket where Father's photographic image did not reside.

"However," the voice from early childhood proceeded, "you children are blessed both by brains representing the best attributes of two people possessing exceptionally high intelligence"—in her past, Care half-giggled but Father did not return her smile—"and a greater potential for physical achievement then the average moppet."

Mama's face, lovely and teasing and gently filled with protest, appeared in Caroline's mind's eye. "Marshall, how you do go on! You'll turn these children's heads."

"For how else could it be," Father'd finished, smiling for the first time and throwing his arms wide for a hug from each young child in turn, "when my Thaddeus and Caroline are the products of eternal love?"

Just for the most fleeting of wonderful moments, Caroline saw *both* Mama and Father clearly in the dream—with their expressions of love and mutual pride, the complete and completing feeling of family affection filling her heart in past and in present.

And she awoke in the home of her adoptive parents, the Spencers (*her* name now too!), sensing the foolishness of the wide, happy smile she had on her face as night bore down and shadows sprawled on her blanketed legs and feet like lead weights. *Stupid!* she called her sleeping mind for being so childish as to drag her into another state of tearfulness. Caroline wiped her previously grinning lips with the back of one hand as if something vile, contaminative, had been pressed against them.

Yet she also began—at once—to act on Father's early teachings by half-consciously forbidding herself to awaken, ever again, with loud crying and shrieks of fear that disturbed Mom's and Pop's sleep. From that moment on, Care sensed as she put her fair head back on her pillows and left her tear-dampened eyes to dry on their own, her fine thinking machine of a brain would discipline her body, down to and including any temptations to bawl like a big baby in the middle of the night.

So her nightmare returned before morning, found it was unimpeded by the dreamer's need to cry out for help, and progressed. Stalked her like a masked man whose anticipated victim does not have the sense to turn the corner and flee . . .

The bedroom door burst open, battering the wall, Deborah Madison holding Thaddeus in her arms. She looked scarcely bigger than Caroline's bro; it was like someone small and feminine struggling to carry someone small and male. Mama's eyes, like festering cuts in the center of lashed bruises. Arms like bent broomsticks about to break, claw fingers gripping tight as the woman rushed across the bedroom floor, half dropping and half throwing Thaddie down—but not in anger, not in exhaustion—in a desperate hurry. Well-lit, empty hall through the doorway, silence balanced there on tiptoe, ready to flee. *She's a ghost*, Caroline, six, thought, *but still alive*. "You must stay here and not try to get out no matter what happens!" Mama's voice was the only screamed whisper Care had heard. She nodded to it, more than Mama, not wanting to hear a whispered shout. Thad, he just stared.

"Can I have another good-night kiss?" Care asked of the woman who, already, was almost gone. But, "There's no time," Mama said at the door of the room. Her arms came up sideways slowly from her body while she kept her slumped back to the two children; the arms rose like Indian

89

smoke signals that tried to convey a message without words to people who did not yet know half her language. "No time, too much time." Mama laughed, sort of, not yet gone.

Then she tore something from around her throat, turned back long enough to toss it to Caroline. It was something the girl had wanted for a long time but had never expected to get. When she opened it and peered inside, she saw that Father's picture was missing now from the locket. And when she looked up to say thank-you, the door was closed and their mama was gone. "Thaddie," she said, turning her head to question her big brother—

At that instant heavy things began to be shoved or carried to the door and, Caroline thought, were left there. "This is only partly for you darlings," Mama called, grunting from exertion. "I've called the police and they'll come let you out—don't worry." Her laugh wasn't quite Mama's. "He's strong, but it would take a while for him to move everything—and I'll tell him he has no time to waste!" She laughed again as things thudded and creaked, clanged and rattled, cracked and tinkled and rumbled into chaotic place on the other side of Caroline's bedroom door. "He *won't* do it to you, Caroline—and he won't do it to you *again*, Thaddie!" The noises and Mama's increasingly garbled, distant ramblings continued for minutes along with frightening sounds of her labored breathing.

"Listen," Thad told Care a moment after the next brief silence. He sat on the edge of the bed so still, till then, he was like a statue to his little sister. So she listened.

The bathroom door was closing at almost the same second the front door was being unlocked, the rattling sound terrifying. What was going to happen?

"Now I lay me down to sleep," Caroline prayed bolt upright, saying the one prayer she knew, "I pray the Lord—"

"Hsssst!" Thaddie ordered her.

Care stirred, twisted her head on the pillow, began to awaken because of the way sweat was running into her eyes. What she saw with her internal vision was smoky, hazed over; time past juked on the twelve-year-old's mental track like Charles Oakley of the Knicks, whom Pop liked, backing toward the basket. Caroline thought she heard Father shouting though that was so unusual it might've been the police, later—and then saw *the red dripping off Mama's white wrists.* Saw her *Mama's dead face with only the dark bruises of her eyes* imprinting themselves upon the younger Care's memory. Heard the echo of what Mama had screamed at Father as he was trying to break the bathroom door down to get to her. "*People* are coming here to save them—*police*! Now you'll never hurt my babies!"

Did Care only want to believe Father'd said he *wouldn't* hurt them and yelled to Thaddie and her, "I'll find you, I'll be back!" before he ran out the front door? Could it be true *nobody'd* said they loved her big bro and her before life changed forever?

"But Father *didn't* just run off because of the police," Care said to Mama's picture in the locket. She sat on the edge of the bed, looking at a Mama whose eyes were young, contented, and not sad bruises. Instead, she smiled at Caroline from the locket and nearly seemed to nod. "Thaddie said he wasn't scared of anyone, not even when they had guns. He j-just couldn't let anyone find out how . . . ugly . . . he was. Or *thought* he was."

Care stood on her pale, lengthening legs, closed the memento carefully, and got ready for the school day. While she showered in water as cold as she could stand it, she told anyone who might overhear the truth through her clenched teeth, "But he *wasn't* ugly—ever!"

2

The phone jangled just as Jake had finished breakfast and was staring into the closet at the front of the house, trying to decide if his usual fake black leather jacket would be warm enough or if it was truly time to drag out his old coat. The front door stood wide because he'd wanted to get a good feel for the weather Camille had shouted at him to close it, on cue, and he was holding the bottom of the coat, thinking it oughta be condemned.

"It's for you, Pop," Care informed him as she breezed by, pausing long enough to bestow an airy kiss that nearly reached his cheek. "On the phone."

"Well, who is it, f'chrissakes?" he called. His daughter was already a dwindling figure on the lane to the sidewalk, her fair hair switching from side to side. "Hey—you aren't starting to mess up your marks again, are you?"

"You'll find out when all the parents do," Caroline caroled, ignoring his first question. But she glanced back at him and grinned before, two books tucked under her arm, she bounced out of sight.

"Well, shit," Jake grumbled, letting go of the tail of his old topcoat and shutting the door behind Care with a push just short of a slam.

He headed for the dining room in a mild grouch. Phones were for women, teenage females—thank God Caroline wasn't *there* yet—and white-collar phonies. *Phones for phonies*, he told himself with a grin that might grow during the day if anyone gave him half a chance. Bad enough to have t'listen to gee-dee company dispatchers in the cab on eight-or ten-hour shifts. But Cammy, who was supposed to handle bill collectors and phone salesmen, was still keepin' the toilet seat warm. "Yeah?" he said in the telephone mouthpiece.

"Is this Mr. Jacob Spencer of Brooklyn, the taxi driver? Married to Camille Spencer?"

Sighing hugely, Jake lifted his eyes heavenward. "Yeah, lady, you win the big prize. But I'm not buying anything or making any donations this week. I'm all bought and donated out, and I gotta get to work."

"I'm so relieved to locate you," she said in Jake's ear as if he should immediately recognize her voice.

Well, she *did* sound sort of familiar, plus relieved and old as God, but they could do anything with electronics these days. Half the New Yorkers in phone sales were out-of-work actors. But Jake was strictly a family man with no pals, male or female, and almost nobody called him on the phone, so he just wasn't having any. "Let's see," he muttered, "I love you too and I'm sure Jesus loves us all." He turned, ready to run to his cab. "And I might just buy whatever you're selling *someday*—or vote for your candidate, or make a down payment on a cemetery plot while I'm eyeballing TV for your *survey*—that cover *everything?*—so have a nice day, and go call somebody else. All right?"

"It's about *Caroline Madison*." The woman said the name distinctly before Jake could cut her off. "I placed her with you people, you may remember. My name is Enid Godby."

This was like driving a hack back into the past, Care was so much a part of their lives now. Sometimes Jake felt she really was theirs, all the way; so the white-haired woman he only dimly recalled spooked him a little and he didn't know what to say.

Enid picked up the thread and spared him any further embarrassment. "It took me a while to remember your name—and even when I came up with 'Spencer', it took me longer to remember where you live.'' Why had she called Care by her old name? ''There were a great many children I placed over the years.'' Oh, yeah, she'd said she'd be retiring soon so she hadn't kept track of Caroline. Then why was she calling now, what was wrong? ''Pardon my inquiry, but may I ask how things worked out for th-the child? I have my reasons for wanting to know.''

Now Jake was on safe, sure footing. He leaned back against the dining room wall, smiling. ''They worked out great, Miss Godby. We adopted her, and she even has our name now!'' He ran his palm over his mass of long hair, found it sweaty. ''You did a great job!''

''I wish I had done equally as well for Caroline's brother.'' The voice on the line was filled with regret. ''His name is Thaddeus—Thaddie—and he ran away from his foster home last December to visit me at my house.''

But what does that have to do with us? Jake wondered. ''Jeez, that's too bad. I don't think I should mention that to Care though.'' Feeling awkward as hell and not a little bit worrying that the kids' original old man might be coming back into the picture, Jake wished to Christ she'd get to the point.

''No, I don't think you should tell the girl either,'' Enid remarked. ''I agree.'' Her voice was becoming increasingly strained. ''I was only hoping that you might . . . somehow . . . have heard from Thaddeus too. As nearly as I can judge, Mr. Spencer, he's entirely on his own. Alone. He was trying to find the rest of his family, and he's only about a year older than—than your child.''

Jake frowned, shook his head. ''That's terrible. Kid that age, on the streets—well, it ain't safe.'' Relief suffused him from head to toe, enabled him to fret even more than he ordinarily would have cared about such a situation. ''Anything I can do to help?''

Miss Godby paused. Jake glanced toward the stairs,

hoped Camille would stay up there another few minutes. Cammy had the sort of stuff that had probably made the old lady on the phone go into her line of work, and he knew she'd worry herself sick about any brother of Care's, even if he already had been shipped out before they met Caroline. Worse, he doubted Cammy could keep from telling Caroline about the boy. What Jake really didn't need—couldn't use—was anyone or anything rocking the boat. They'd put too much in this to risk screwing it up.

"I'd like to give you Thaddie's description," Enid said finally. God, she sounded tired, maybe even guilty, if that made any sense. With women, of course, it didn't have to. "And I'd like to ask you to watch out for him. I'm not with the home any longer"—she said this as if it were important for him to remember—"but you can have my number. To tell me. I'll try to d-do something for him."

"Well, sure." Jake scowled as he located a pencil and a scrap of paper, held them to the wall. "But the city, well, it's filled with kids these days. Homeless and runaways." *And twelve-year-old whores, male as well as female.* "It'll be like lookin' for the proverbial needle, so don't get your hopes up any."

The next sound she made was like Cammy trying not to cry. "He missed his sister and his father so much, he wasn't happy where he was p-placed; and after he ran off a few times, I think they simply stopped finding him and bringing him back." She was pissed now. "They never did find his father for questioning and . . . and my experience tells me to hope the boy *never* finds *him!*"

Upstairs, the toilet flushed and water ran in the washbasin. "Give me that information, okay?" he told Enid.

She did and he scribbled it down while he wondered if he might be hearing the family boat begin to rock a little already.

Then, out of the blue: "Mr. Spencer, is Caroline—growing?"

Jake's eyebrows rose. *Yeah, whadda you think?* were the words forming in his mind. "Sure is. Gettin' real pretty, too. I mean, she's never going to be a center on any girl's basketball team, but—"

"Thaddeus *wasn't* growing," Miss Godby interrupted, "last December." She fought to compose herself, Jake could tell that. "Don't look for a twelve-or thirteen-year-old boy, Mr. Spencer," she said before she rang off. "It's a handsome, black-haired *little boy* who's missing—and I don't even know why he isn't growing."

3

Efficiency was the key, he'd always said—efficiency and *compassion* in his present position, of course. It was all a matter of creating the proper system—"lining up the ducks on the pond"—and adhering to it, remembering at every moment of the day who was paying one's salary and exactly what was expected of one.

What Hector Crossland believed but didn't say was that his motto called for *ruthless* efficiency in the pursuit of personal advancement. The word "compassion" was ornamental, and he employed it (in describing his methods) only because he believed all the way to his toes that most people were incapable of putting an entirely logical, effective system ahead of nagging little problems of a momentary nature. Like children.

It wasn't that he had lied to Elspeth Goodson, or whatever her name was, the crone whom he had replaced at the SoHo guardian home. He genuinely did not know how to access the information about the boy who had run away—*Madison, T.,* Crossland read the name he'd jotted down while the old woman was on the phone—because she had blithely ignored the computing system installed months before her retirement as if it had been nothing more than a toy. Consequently, when he'd taken over the position and pledged with all his heart to restore compassionate efficiency to the placement of young people under his care, Hector found himself asea in an ocean of paper and outmoded file folders.

And those written notes and carefully typed memos that would not speedily yield to the raw data his methods required had been crammed into tall metal containers and taken out to the curb, where they could rot with all the other garbage left in waiting for the latest workers' strike to end.

The raw data he needed was simplicity itself. Name, D.O.B., race and religion, names of birth parents and/or prior guardians, summarized health record (including results of aptitude testing, if any), and an indication of where the given girl or boy had been previously placed (if applicable). All he might put into a physical folder was a winning photograph of the child.

In Ms. Grady's files, however, Hector had encountered with a dismay that had grown for several days, notes concerning the siblings of children, their preferences in *toys* and *games*, for God's sake, things that might frighten them (amateur psychology was even worse than the real thing!), and—incredible as it might have sounded—cute *sayings* of the youngsters! Well, all that had had to go, naturally; the position was complicated enough if a person permitted it to get out of his control for an instant without forgetting the fundamental obligation one had to the City of New York:

Selling children to potential buyers—consumers, if it became necessary to adopt a truly harsh standpoint. And don't blame Hector Crossland for that, he thought while he was looking at his predecessor's permanent jacket (he was obliged to retain it for another nineteen months) and deciding whether to keep his handwritten note about *Madison, T.,* in it or simply throw it away. Three quarters of the people of the planet should immediately be sterilized and maybe as many as half of the remaining people who had already mated and produced an offspring should give them to the state for proper reassignment. Hitler had gone too far, of course, he had committed excesses—but they were the excesses of ruthless efficiency. Not all the ideas he'd had about trying to improve the human race, genetically and otherwise, should be considered intrinsically wrong just because he'd killed some—

A man standing in front of him and his desk had entered the room, so quietly Hector Crossland hadn't realized he was no longer alone in his office.

The fact startled and very nearly shocked him, as did most unscheduled appearances of his fellow man. It also made Hector wonder—just for an instant—if his expression could somehow have revealed his thoughts. Hector set about altering the expression, summoning a proximate smile of compassion that he hoped might modify the general iciness which he'd observed himself on occasions when he had been surprised by unexpected mirrors. This man might be a prospective customer—*foster parent*, he amended the thought with amusement.

But the fellow was certainly an odd-looking man, even for the sort of people who were willing to risk rearing someone else's children.

"I want to inquire about a boy." The stranger wore a respectable suit, but it appeared to have been tailored even while it didn't quite fit *him*. He didn't look straight at Hector, but slightly to one side, and a man who had not studied strangers closely (as Hector had) might have thought him shy. His face, though, was aimed directly at Crossland's—

at least, the oddly mottled nose (grayer than the rest of the fellow's complexion) was. He threw up his palm before Hector could say he had come to the right place, or something to that effect. "Not *any* boy. *This* boy."

Crossland stared at the snapshot of a very dark-haired, winsome youngster which his guest threw on the desk before him. About six, or seven; no older than eight.

"Boys this young and this appealing rarely remain at the home long." Hector slipped his smile into another gear. "However, we'll do our best to accommodate your preference. The first thing is to fill out one of our standard—"

"*This* boy," Marshall Madison said. His voice did not rise. "His name is Thaddeus Madison."

Crossland lowered to his desk the official form he'd been about to proffer, letting a line like an apostrophe form between his brows. Inwardly, he was most annoyed. "We are not permitted to give out information concerning the placement of any of our children."

The odd-appearing stranger froze in attentiveness. The acceleration of his heartbeat was clear behind the immaculate white shirt he wore with the suit that was probably not his. "You know Thad, don't you?" His eyes turned toward Hector's for the first time while the blotched and somewhat oversize nose shifted microscopically elsewhere. Beneath it was a mustache that seemed lifeless, as if many yellow hairs had been glued together, then stuck on the man's lip. It didn't twitch or rise when he moved his mouth. "You placed *my children?*"

"I cannot possibly answer such questions." Hector paused, shrugged. The fellow's expression made him rethink, speedily. "Well, I've never seen this boy, no. It was before my time when he was placed in a foster home. Or two."

"By whom? *What* homes?" the stranger demanded. Though his voice didn't become louder, it was quite nearly a demand. "I must have answers about Thaddeus and his sister Caroline Madison, and I've only now found they were brought here. Tell me where they were sent."

Hector Crossland realized how stuffy it was getting in his office. He was also aware that two or three of the children had gathered just outside his door, which the stranger had left open. They were eavesdropping and his authority was marginally at stake. "A woman who preceded me in this position handled the disposition of those cases—"

"Those *cases?*" For the first time the stranger's voice was getting louder. Peculiarly, merely parts of his face—the cheeks, most of the chin—were reddening. "Are you telling me Thaddeus and Caroline were *separated*—that this 'woman' sent them to *different foster homes*? Do you *know* how hard it will be to *locate* the *two of them?*"

One of the listening children—an older, chubby girl—emitted a startlingly adult laugh, and Crossland felt she laughed because the stranger was losing his temper and because he himself seemed to be backing down. Hector knew he was an unprepossessing man, six feet tall but innately so thin he had never needed to exercise and looked like it now, a man who also looked—accurately—as though he had never come close to marrying. His own best expression was a haughty frown that once had been meant to appear dignified but, in recent obligatory photos, merely looked like a frosty sneer. Besides, this entirely unscheduled interview was starting to interfere sharply with routine.

"Who are you to barge in here and interrogate me?" Crossland rose and tapped the desk with his knuckles. The permanent folder for Enid Godby slid an inch, tilted. "The Madisons were *never* my responsibility. I have no idea where either of them was placed, and it's not *my* fault if the boy is out there, running wild. I refuse to be badgered again about a brat whom the city was nice enough to help—

at the taxpayers' expense—after his parents didn't *want* him any longer!''

The caller stared at the ceiling. ''The parents 'didn't *want* him'? 'Running . . . *wild*'?'' Suddenly he was standing, pressed close to the desk. ''Little *Thaddeus* . . . on the *streets—alone?*'' The stranger's body exploded forward from the waist up and dislodged Hector's nameplate. Without warning, the face with the yellow mustache was fewer than twelve inches away. It brought with it a distinct and very unpleasant smell. ''Tell me who *else* is 'badgering' you about him. Then I shall explain who *I* am to 'interrogate' you.''

''I don't care who the hell you are,'' Hector said. He drew back his head, turtlelike, called imperiously across the office. ''*You*, there—children! Go back to the dormitory areas at once. This doesn't concern you.''

''Is *this* the other person inquiring about Thaddeus?'' The stranger held up both Miss Godby's permanent file and the notes Crossland had taken when she called. He opened the file to glance inside, his bloodshot eyes gleaming. He seemed to scan it—to take in the contents—with surprising quickness. Then he looked up and the visible portions of his real facial skin were almost devoid of color. ''He was at her house last December? And you haven't gone out to *bring him back? In all this time?*''

Hector grabbed for the folder, got his fingers on it, then discovered that his elbow was caught in a human bear trap. Instantly, the man's thumb was pressed so painfully into a tendon that Hector released his hold, but the stranger kept his, the four fingers on the other side of Crossland's arm seemingly determined to crush the joint. ''Children,'' he called tightly, bravely enough, ''get *help*. Get Mr. Caldwell and—''

''Be quiet.'' This was all the assailant said. But he reinforced the command.

101

He picked up Hector's staple remover—a device with four metal teeth shaped, from the side, like a canine or lupine jaw—and, while Hector's whole arm was imprisoned and his body was close to the stranger's, locked the lower two fangs of the simple tool into Crossland's upper lip. Even before the man clamped the steel jaws together, the mechanical teeth were all the way through the thin, squishy tissue, drawing copious blood.

And when the staple jaws were firmly pinched in place, the caller grasped his elbow still more tightly and—slowly raising the hand with the remover, steadily forcing Hector's mouth and head backward—peeled most of the upper lip away from the abruptly exposed and suddenly skeletal front teeth.

The watching kids had come in, curious and aware that a visitor was harming Mr. Crossland. Feeling little connection with him, they had remained.

"Your 'thinking machine' is that of an ill-constructed robot. I," said Marshall quietly in Hector's left ear, "am Thaddeus's and Caroline's father. They are my crowning achievements, the major record of my existence." His initial tears mingled with the growing flood of blood on Crossland's cheek. "I came to *fetch* them, man. Nothing on earth will prevent me from finding them—least of all, a *bureaucrat*."

Gripping the staple remover quite tightly, Marshall tore the upper part of the fellow's mouth completely free of the teeth and gums. He continued to exert both pinching and pulling pressure in a sincere effort to remove the whole nose. But, he was flexible.

When the lip came off scantly a quarter inch into the base of the nose, Marshall used the heel of his hand to drive the stubborn proboscis into Crossland's functionary brain.

"Hello, children," Marshall said to the youngsters, who, now, were edging backward to the door. He really hadn't noticed them there for a while; it was his emotional nature, the tears in his eyes. Such cutie pies, however, little sweethearts, remindful of his own darlings. "Do any of *you* know my Thaddie, my Caroline?"

Heads—as well as quavering limbs—shook.

Marshall glanced into the Godby file again, unconcerned by the spilled blood on the outside of the folder splashing onto the dead man's desk. He singled out one child in particular, who was about Thaddeus's age. Only two children remained in the office now, held there, Marshall imagined, by fear.

He turned to the child he'd chosen—a boy named Mack—and knelt, smoothed the boy's hair back. "Are you ...*sure?*" Marshall asked in his softest, most paternal voice.

4

The day's problems for Thaddie began when, after eating all his stomach could hold at McDonald's, he saw a bakery open on his way back to the condemned hotel. It was amazing the way a guy could build up a little appetite taking a stroll after supper!

Besides, Thaddie still had a pocket full of Mr. Harwell's cash, he'd promised Robby and Rodge a treat (and rats didn't have to worry about getting fat, Thad assumed), and it was nice to have breakfast handy when he woke up the next day. The hotel restaurant hadn't had any food in it for a zillion years; Robby and Rodge and the rest of their family'd made sure of *that*.

Then there was the fact that each time Thaddie didn't have to go out was one less chance for some grown-up to get him. Back when Thad had run away from the Tinsdales the first time, he'd cared about the differences between the

103

adults who might sneak up and snatch him away from the only life he had now, but distinctions such as that no longer mattered. Rhonda and Thurman as well as the foster parents he'd had after them—cops who were either parents themselves and kind of hurt for street kids, and cops who just liked hassling 'em—and the rich variety of perverts and plain crazy killers who shared the city with Thaddie, they were all the same to him now.

They might grab him and keep Thad from ever spotting Father passing by, hunting for him—or maybe seein' Care, if she happened to go shopping with her foster folks.

And since Thaddie knew he was pretty small and Caroline probably had kept growing, he figured it was his job to discover *her* if their paths *ever* did cross.

So grown-ups were just the enemy itself—or people to hit on when he needed money—even while he still remembered Mama, and Father, and he'd come to know that Miss Godby hadn't hated him and Caroline or anything. Mostly, it was just that adults lived in a different world and had different things they were s'posed to do.

Thaddeus Madison was s'posed to stay alive and find his family.

The man at Ricelli's Bakery decided at the last minute that he didn't want to sell Thad any doughnuts.

He arrived at that decision even after he had filled three sacks and set them briskly on the counter, and even after Thaddie had shown him more than enough money to pay for the pastry. He was a large, sour man with a belly like dough that kept him from maintaining his apron around his waist, and a nose so red it looked as if it might catch on fire any second, probably because it didn't like him either.

There was no good reason to dislike his small customer except Ricelli generally did not like anyone much and nobody would mind if he gave a kid a hard time.

"Where'd a brat like you get that much money?" Ricelli

demanded. He held on to the trio of snowy sacks with a hand that was red but had white sugar on it. Thaddie stared at it and the way the man didn't even bother to grip the bags tightly. "Little pricks like you got dough like that from ripping honest folks off—or blowin' 'em! Which way'd you get it, huh, kid? Huh, little prick?"

"Mom sent me to get the doughnuts." Thaddie kept his gaze focused on the red and white paw. One of the rats—Clinton, Thad had called him Clinton—had looked that way when he tried to take a piece of garbage away from Rodge. Rodge's fangs had ripped off the top of Clinton's paw, including the fur. Then the rest of the family'd eaten Clinton, most of him anyway. "We're havin' a party." Thad paused. "It's my little brother Marsh's birthday."

Ricelli came around from behind the counter. The doughnut sacks dangled from the meaty paw, well above Thad's reach. "Show me Marsh's picture. Or your old lady's. Show me some ID and do it now, prick." He used his stomach to belly-buck Thaddie back a step. "Show me somethin' that shows you're *alive* and *somebody*, little prick—or I'm gonna kick your butt all the way to the Midtown Tunnel!"

Nodding once, Thad put his handful of money in his pocket. He had things he could say or do—arguments to make, ways to plead. He'd used them all a zillion times on people like the baker. Thaddie just suddenly knew he didn't want to do any of that stuff anymore.

Turning from the waist as if shyly removing his billfold, Thad planted his feet evenly—bent his knees exactly enough—

And drove his sharp elbow into Ricelli's doughboy belly with everything he had.

Ricelli went down—hit the floor of his bakery hard and fast—as if an invisible man had borrowed his fat stomach for batting practice.

Thad had been ready to snatch the sacks away if they came loose, and he caught two of the three cleanly, already spun around to run for it—but he'd never in the world expected a grown man to fall down, squeeze his eyes together like he'd been shot, and make wheezing sounds as if he couldn't get his breath. Not a big grown-up.

It was scary. And it was also pretty neat.

The grown-up threw out one arm. It landed flat on the floor, *whap*, and now his fingers on that arm were crawling toward the third sack. The sack Thad hadn't caught.

Meanwhile, a lot of the red in Ricelli's florid face was receding. He was getting his breath. The fat and stubby fingers went on crawling after the third bag even though several of the doughnuts had spilled out. Thaddie wouldn't have eaten them from that floor if his life depended on it, unless this had been the first week after he ran away from Thurman and Rhonda. The white in the angry, hate-filled, grasping fingers now was because Mr. Ricelli was hurting, scared and a little humiliated, and he was pressing the tips of the digits on the floor hard to sort-of haul his body after them.

Thad moved right up, waited till the grown-up saw how close he was (but not at the right angle for Ricelli to grab his ankles), then lifted one foot high in the air. It wasn't a big foot, but Ricelli went *"Noooo"* anyway, like he was scared to death.

Thaddie brought his foot down and smooshed the doughnuts in the third sack into crumbs and powder.

"—Prick." Ricelli popped out the word, eyes open again and just as red and white as his nose and hands. And he hauled himself to a sitting position on the bakery floor like a movie sea monster trying to flop itself up on land.

As he whirled away, Thaddie threw a lot of money tugged from his pocket straight at the grown-up face, and—clutching the surviving two sacks of doughnuts close—

sprinted through the door into the street. Then he stopped only when he had squeezed himself through the window back into his hotel and, paying no heed to the rats that scattered like bowling pins at his approach, found himself panting inside the men's room, leaning against the door as though there might be something to be kept outside.

He hadn't been frightened for awhile but he was now, and he didn't know why.

Neither the urinals nor the toilet in the abandoned hotel worked anymore—water had apparently been shut off almost immediately—but Thad still used them. He had no interest in becoming a rat, so he'd begun in the safer-looking rooms on the upper floors, then worked his way down. Once a toilet was so filled to overflowing and stank so badly Thaddie didn't want to use it any longer, he'd taken a black marker, closed a given room, and marked a big X on the door. Now, peeing (with his head) averted into the first floor urinal, he tried to remember if there were still three rooms and a men's left on two, or just the rooms. Not all floors had rest rooms. Sooner or later he'd have to take a chance on floors that looked like they might cave in under him.

And after that, all he'd have left would be the Women's rest rooms he hadn't even entered.

It was the first time he had been in this Men's in weeks, and he automatically walked to the basin area to rinse his hands. Rhonda'd taught him that much, and well.

Not a drop of water came from the faucet; but Thad saw his image in the mirror in that unexpectedly-encountering-yourself manner that tended to be oddly surprising and forced honesty on the viewer with the authority of somebody shoving him from behind. Thad wished he had remembered not to glance up. He had told himself not to look in mirrors no more.

Because, while he wasn't ugly and, unlike Father, didn't

107

think he was, the fact was that his body didn't really rise very far above the level of the washbasin. Even Thurman Tinsdale, years back, had noticed Thaddie wasn't growing a lot; that foster dad had made chalk marks on the edge of the bathroom door for weeks, and wound up with one heavy chalk line. Since Father (Thad knew now) hadn't really been a giant but an ordinary-size man, Thaddeus's failure to grow hadn't bothered him personally a lot. Ol' Thurman told Rhonda, though, he thought they'd gotten themselves a dwarf, 'cause Tinsdale had wanted "his boy" to play sports, and Thurman had set Thaddie to thinking.

Was he a dwarf or a midget? The possibility had got to nagging at him once he was on his own, right up to the point he'd figured out how to use it to stay alive. Then, most of the time, he forgot about it—especially after he finally saw a real midget doin' handstands near Union Square with his hat turned upside down a foot away. Thaddie'd gotten up close, bent over at the middle, and found that the midget had five o'clock shadow. In addition to that, the small man had *seemed* like a *man* the way he hollered at Thad to get the fuck out of there 'cause he imagined Thaddie was gonna take the hat with the money in it.

But if you weren't going to grow hardly an inch or even less a year till you were eighteen, maybe, and you started worryin' about it when you were less than four feet high— what difference would it make if you *weren't* a real midget or dwarf?

Now—tonight—Thaddeus thought he saw some difference.

First was the way his eyes looked to him in the mirror of the men's room.

Thad shivered, and it was only partly because the old hotel had no heat.

His deep, dark eyes didn't really look like a little boy's now.

It could have been how dark it was starting to get, so all the illumination he had was from a window that opened on an unused alley, but Thad thought he saw flecks of redness in the whites of his eyes. And when he tried to open 'em wide and look as boyish and cute as he possibly could, it wasn't workin' the way it usually did, it really wasn't. And even when he had climbed up on the sink so he could stare at himself up close, Thad had the same impression—only worse.

He didn't think that his eyes looked like a grown-up man's eyes either.

Scratching sounds on the rest room door, like a dozen house cats eager to be fed, startled the boy so much he fell off the basin. The rats wanted their snacks. "Oh, yeah," Thad said, looking at the window, suddenly aware night was almost on top of them. The moon was almost full and even Robby and Rodge got rowdy and ornery when that happened. He didn't want to be caught anywhere in the building without candles or his flashlight when it was black as pitch. Even Rodge couldn't be fully trusted unless he was well fed and the room was reasonably well lit.

Thad picked up the sacks, drew in a long breath, and pulled the rest room door open.

Then he dashed across the lobby to the window he'd uncovered, calling, "Come on, guys!", and was climbing up the fire escape to the roof with the rat pack at his heels, squealing. Some that excelled in wrapping their long, toe-like appendages around things took the railings, arriving first on the roof, grinning down at Thad and hissing at him to hurry. "You're a bunch of little piggies tonight," Thad said when he was safely erect again, holding the pair of sacks with the doughnuts out in front of him while he hurried to his favorite vantage point.

The pets would have to come first before he began his rooftop vigil, however—Thaddie knew that. So he threw one doughnut each to his friends Robby and Rodge, the leaders, then quickly ripped two more to pieces and lobbed them in the direction of the old skylight. The rest of the rats scrambled after them.

After that, he stuck two more doughnuts into his jacket pockets for morning. They'd look like crap and wouldn't be fresh no more, but he could eat 'em.

With the closest thing to a future Thaddie knew taken care of, he tossed both sacks with the remaining few doughnuts in the general direction of the pack leaders and turned to gaze out over the city. The rats would work the rest of it out among them.

Would he, Thad wondered, even *know* Father if he came into view four stories below? The thought entered his mind as uninvitingly as had his face and eyes in the mirror. It scared him just as much, perhaps more. Father'd never seemed to get any older either, but that was when Caroline and he were barely school age, saw their parents as a Giant and a Good Fairy, and when Marshall Madison was seven years younger. That was how funny age was, and how fair, Thad supposed. Kids grew up and kept seeing stuff differently, but adults sort of . . . kept going too.

The terrible thing—in a way—was that Father sure could recognize *him* 'cause all that was growin' up of ol' Thad was the way his eyes suddenly looked.

And what of Caroline, what of his little sister Care—did she look like a teenager almost now? Or did she stay tiny, too?

Thaddie knuckled one eye, squinted. There weren't even a lot of good streetlights down here; the neighborhood was really a slum. Behind the boy, familiar threatening noises continued from time to time, prob'ly 'cause they all wanted to sniff the sacks. Or eat 'em. What did it *mean* that he wasn't growing if people *had* to grow up? If he wasn't a midget or dwarf which kinda made it legallike, he s'posed—wasn't he breaking a law of *God's* by not growin' up? Would God know it wasn't his fault, or, when he got t'be eighteen or twenty-one or something, did it mean he had to be killed?

No one on the streets below the hotel rooftop looked even vaguely like Father and, occasionally, Thad had to jump back from the edge to keep from being seen. There were dozens of people Thad knew who'd love to find out about the place, and, for some of them, it would've been like the Waldorf. Thad didn't want to share because he wasn't sure he knew anyone who could truly *share*; they would just have tried to kill him while he was asleep to have the whole hotel to themselves.

He remembered a bad dream he'd had the other night, and also remembered that he had already remembered it three other times. But it kept coming back even when he told it to get lost.

Before it was banished this time, Thaddeus knew in a flash that Father had done something bad to him when he and Care were little—something Mama saw, too, that made her ruin everything for them. He loved her again now, even if he hadn't been able to for a long time 'cause that was when the family started breakin' up; but shoot, she was his mother and everything, and nights like this he missed her nearly as much as he missed Father and Care. What she hadn't understood was how Father told him afterward that it wasn't *really* bad, after all—

And if Father said it wasn't—whatever it was he'd done that night—then it wasn't.

He jumped as something was nudged into his hand. For a single really scary second he'd thought he was goin' right *off* the roof!

But it was only Robby, his favorite rat of all—the one he came closest to liking, and trusting, sharing. Putting something in his palm. *Prob'ly a bite of doughnut*, Thad decided, giving Robby a smile of gratitude and holding the morsel up to the moon that was nearly full.

A blood-soaked piece of Rodge—a hind leg, part of it anyway—hung from between his thumb and index finger.

Thad stood real still. He knew eyes that reflected the rays of the moon were watching him, and not just Robby's. Sure. Robby hadn't liked sharing the pack as leader anymore. Or maybe Rodge had really been Roberta, and ol' Robby had chosen another girlfriend now. He made himself stay still and grin quite a lot. An old bo he'd known for about a week once used to share his experience with rats on tankers and other boats. The old man, Thaddie remembered, used to say that the greatest gift a man could get was when the leader of a pack came to *accept* you, when he asked you to become a member with equal rights and privileges. Thad s'posed that was what was happening to him now.

He also s'posed he knew what he had to do to go on being accepted by the rat pack.

It was only fair considering he brought them doughnuts.

5

Camille kept information she learned from that evening's newspaper to herself until Caroline was in bed and Jake was exhibiting every sign that he wished he was too. He hadn't said anything about a piece missing from the front section of the paper, even though he usually complained when she had snipped something out—a hint from Heloise, an especially good column by Ann Landers or John Rosemond about raising children, perhaps an item about the social activity of some old friend from the Heights. Sneaking a peek at Jake where he was slumping deeper and deeper into his favorite chair in front of the TV, Camille remembered he wasn't the omnivorous newspaper reader she was. The sports pages were sacrosanct, of course; maybe he had found some preseason stories about the Knicks and gotten all caught up in them.

Or maybe, she wondered somewhat apprehensively as she fitted the final piece into her week-long jigsaw puzzle, an impression she'd had at dinner—that Jake was also keeping something to himself—was valid. He hadn't been nearly as talkative as he generally was, during the meal, and he'd seemed simultaneously inclined to ignore Caroline and to cast little glances her way, as if he were trying to decide whether to broach some matter to her or not.

One thing she wouldn't wonder about—not even for a moment—was whether Jake was keeping any terrible secrets to himself, such as an unspoken unhappiness he carried with him in the cab all day. Or how he'd found someone to relieve that unhappiness. Camille believed in their marriage—in Jake, what they had together and with Care—like she had never fully managed to believe in anything else.

Restive suddenly, she swept the completed puzzle off the card table into its box. It was she who was keeping a secret, till Caroline was upstairs for the night; not Jacob. And she'd stalled telling him about it long enough.

"So I don't get to see the finished masterpiece?" he said from his chair, not glancing over. He was referring to one of their rituals, to the way he always ambled over to take a look at a jigsaw puzzle once it was assembled. He rarely worked on them because, he said, he liked to see 'em done. The truth was, he was awful at working them.

"I'm sorry," Camille said, genuinely apologetic. "I forgot."

Jake yawned, sat forward in his comfortable old chair to stretch. "Like you forgot to tell me what the big deal is. What you found in the paper to get you so stirred up."

113

She shook her head admiringly, not with awe for Jake's deductive prowess, which probably hovered around the zero mark, but admiration for how close they were. Neither of them could have kept a secret for an entire night from the other. She wondered when the last time was that a birthday gift from him had truly surprised her—and vice versa, in all likelihood.

Cammy held up the newspaper clipping. "I'm probably being silly," she began.

"Silly's okay," he said. An outsider wouldn't have noticed his change of posture or attitude. Mostly, the veil of sleepiness he'd worn was completely gone.

"Something horrible happened at the guardian home in SoHo," Camille said in a breath. "Where we—met Caroline." She waited for him to answer, but he kept perching on his chair, one leg still kneeling on his hassock, doing his own waiting. "The man who replaced our Miss Godby was murdered, hideously murdered."

Jake kept his expression pretty blank, but his heart was starting to pump like crazy. He heard the old woman tell him again, *I think they stopped going out to find the boy.* " 'Our' Miss Godby?" he teased his wife, automatically trying to defuse her anxieties, her worry.

"If you mean to criticize me for saying 'hideously murdered'," Cammy snapped, "you should read the article first. All murders aren't the same." She took off her glasses, making her eyes look dreamy, blew on each lens in turn. "The perfectly *hideous murderer* got away and the police are looking for clues."

They never did find his father for questioning. Enid Godby spoke again in Jake's ears, almost as if she'd been there. As casually as he could, he asked, "Did the bastard hurt any of the children?"

"No, thank God." Camille had her specs back on and was staring at Jake. "But it seems as though the killer was searching for information." She was holding her head absolutely level and carefully trying not to blink. "The article in the paper doesn't identify anybody by name, but he apparently questioned s-some of the kids about . . . children who were sent to *foster*—" Then Cammy clamped her jaws together, rattled the jigsaw box with a twisted expression Jake might once have thought was one of high irritation.

"Don't jump to any conclusions," Jake said evenly. He rose, did a lousy imitation of a husband yawning his eagerness to go to bed. *I hope the boy never finds him*, the old lady had said about Care's brother. But what if the son of a bitch found Thaddie, or Caroline? He motioned for Camille to come with him. "Place like that guardian home has one helluva lot of kids go through it over the years."

In bed, he went to sleep almost as soon as they switched off the little lamp on the headboard, because that was what *he* could do—almost always. Camille lay with her back to his, her myopic eyes open and staring at partly formed horrors lacking almost all detail, needing only sleep and the opportunity to become full-fleshed, vivid nightmares—because that was what *she* could do.

But around half past three that night, Jake awoke like a man replacing the previous sentry on guard duty and tried to figure out what else he could do. Cammy's, he knew, was usually an inclination to sort through the most miserable facts in a situation over and over, not with the intention to take action particularly, but to *relate* to them—to allow the facts to enter into her concept of reality. Once, she'd said it was because she needed to know what was really beyond solution and what wasn't.

For him though—maybe all men, for all he knew!—Jake had a tendency to believe everything could be solved somehow, made acceptable and bearable, if you could just figure out whom to threaten, pay off, or reason with. Or smash to smithereens. He knew that, accepted and felt no shame about it. If you were dealing with a man who was decent or one who had some weak points or something he wanted, fine, you had a place to start. If you had to deal with somebody who was dishonest or indecent and he was also a jackoff numbskull, you just figured out how to rollll over the cocksucker and that was the end of that!

Jake was less skilled and therefore less decisive and direct when the problem wasn't another guy at all but a creditor, a giant bureau or agency, a concept or an idea—

Or anything as insubstantial as the original parent of the child Jake considered his, a man who might or might *not* even be alive, who might have just *murdered*—not smashed or beat up but hideously murdered—a total stranger, *and* whom Jake Spencer had never met. So he didn't have a clue what the sumbitch looked like; why the guy's wife had taken her own life; or how the bastard could just bug out and leave two cute kids to fend for themselves—then, *maybe*, resurface seven years later, bent out of shape because some guardian home had at least *tried* to find decent places for the kids to live! What *could* he do? Jake didn't have the foggiest.

So he slipped out of bed and went to the bathroom to sit and try to think. There, on the back of the toilet, he found the newspaper clipping Cammy'd described but he had not read. He did so then, borrowing what light he could get from the moon that was nearly full beyond the single bathroom window. He hadn't wanted to switch on the overhead and risk disturbing either Cammy or, just down the hall, Caroline.

The unnamed kid whom the murderer talked to had told the cops he was really weird. All of it, actually, was, "He treated us okay but he was really weird." And *that*, Jake thought as he turned his head to see the obese moon beaming in, was strange as hell—bad enough to leave him aware that the Spencer family boat could truly be sailing into some troubled waters. (A madman who treated kids "okay" after he'd torn some guy's face off?)

I can't afford to be scared of the unknown, Jake said firmly to himself, standing and tugging his shorts into place. Besides, it was dishonest, indecent crap when you looked at it that way, it didn't *get* any substance—anything real—to it till you yourself handed it a spooky mask or cape to hide behind. A man ought to know how to roll the hell over *it* too!

He started to flush the toilet, stayed his hand. It was just pee, hell with it. He'd phone old lady Godby tomorrow if he still had that note he made, warn her in case she hadn't read the newspaper. He'd also take the description she gave him of Care's brother Thad and ask some of the other drivers to help him keep an eye out for the kid. If a few guys Jake knew caught the sumbitch hitting on a little boy, he could almost feel sorry for the creep!

He himself was going to have t'watch Care closely, maybe have a little chat with her about . . . her first dad. He didn't want to do that, but he wanted less to face the strong possibility staring him in the face in that damn newspaper story:

Crazy killers were for books and TV movies—but it had suddenly become entirely conceivable that both Caroline and her missing brother were the main objects of attention for a man who was exactly that.

Chapter Five

It took Marshall Madison most of the afternoon to record, in his life journal, the story of his personal visit to the guardian home and precisely what had happened there. Because he'd had as his early literary influence a number of writers from what modern critics sometimes called "the old school"—others, untutored asses that they were, employed worse terms, such as "florid" and "purple"—he was meticulous in his choice of words. He was also integrity itself in how he strung them together, never sparing himself, not permitting that first indulgence that could show his own deeds in a better light. An author whose standards were greater than his own self-serving ego and derived them from the greats whose works stood the test of time could not preen like a peacock. Far more importantly, he could not twist the facts till they were contortionistic contrivances rendered lame and ineffectually paralyzed parodies of the raw truth.

An author who expected the events, deeds, misdeeds and

experiences of a long lifetime to be read someday and admitted to libraries of the world put it *all* down—as gracefully, pertinently, and (dare he say it?) nakedly as he was able.

Thus Marshall had confessed (as evening shadows temporarily discolored the pages on which, by hand, he was bringing the great journal up-to-date) a loss of temper and therefore of control at the point when he'd punished the guardian home popinjay for his blend of tastelessness, rudeness, and—most important—his abandonment of Thaddeus to the cruel New York streets. Marshall understood now, he wrote, that separating the children in order to find temporary homes for them might have been necessary. The dictates of contemporary economics made that otherwise unthinkable parting logical, if inhumane at its essence.

But calmly announcing that Marshall Madison's *son* was "running wild," then compounding the callousness of that by asserting that Thaddeus's parents did not *want* him or sweet Caroline, exposed such unpardonable insensitivity that the bureaucratic bumpkin's obligation to experience the dying process had been a virtual mandate of all decent society. (Marshall inscribed an impeccable sentence in which he stated that Deborah's sainted memory had screamed for justice in his thoughts of the moment. Then, however, he drew a judicious line through the sentence, omitting it. The bare truth, regardless of how relatively harsh it might one day seem to Marshall's readers, was that he had lost control on this occasion in a fashion that appeared to accumulate and then reach its own pinnacle. He felt at ease with the conviction that any parent who'd read everything else he had suffered through ignorance and misunderstanding would relate to the state of his mind.)

Marshall turned languidly in his chair, weary of working, aware for the first time of hunger pangs. He strove never to be an impulsive, excitable sort and chose now to feast his eyes on the modest library of favorite writers and thinkers he'd been at pains to gather since his late wife's peasantlike outlook on life had forced him to flee their home precipitately. Barbusse. Darwin (once, he'd hoped to discover more concerning the evolution of his own kind in that thinker's works but failed). Dr. Magnus Hirschfeld's *Sexual Anomalies and Perversions. The Pearl* (quaint but not uninstructive). De Sade's life works including *Justine* and *The 120 Days of Sodom.* Swinburne, *ah,* Swinburne! *The Unforgivable Sin. Dead Souls.* And from only a few years ago, Colin Wilson's brilliant but lamentably narrow book, *The Misfits.* The contemporary Englishman correctly recognized de Sade's valuation of "forbiddenness" in the intensification of pleasure, but stated it must depend "upon a childish element in ourselves, a defiance of adult authority"—as if there were no such thing as a pleasure to be taken that was *truly* forbidden by nearly all the societies of man!

For half his life, Marshall recalled, Nikolai Gogol's novel *Dead Souls* had moved him. The Russian's protagonist, Chichikov, had discovered that a committee of bureaucrats would advance good money on serfs—"souls"—but the problem was that those serfs who had died since a certain census were considered still alive! So Chichikov had set about purchasing "dead souls" from landowners, who put a very low price on them. And *that,* Marshall believed, was how short the distance between life and death was—it was all a matter of nose counting, dates, and one's own perception!

And his own splendid fortune since commandeering this loft, Marshall mused as he arose and started across the floor toward the refrigerator, lay in the fact that modern Americans seldom remained in one place—even their own home or work station, their latest location of easy gratification and cheap thrills—for so long as a day. They had to "go *out*" for everything even while being "*in*side" or "*in* the know" would have appeared to be their favorite direction. They were nomads without a need, insatiably nosy (though they called it "sociable" or "inquiring") beings who were universally possessed by the yen to "stop by" or "drop *in*," always unannounced—

So that *keeping* count of their butt-insky noses was a virtual impossibility—particularly when they never told either their mates or their secretaries the remote truth about where they were going, when, or how long they might be away! They behaved as if *anywhere else* might be preferable to where they were at the moment!

He gravely doubted that, personally. Marshall turned his head just slightly to the refrigerator and was able without strain to see—behind a wide and ornamental Chinese screen he'd obtained just for the purpose—irrefutable evidence of the wisdom of his antisocial proclivities.

The fridge, he found when he had tugged the door open and looked inside—leaving it open rather longer than was actually necessary to make the inspection (but minor indulgences were permissible after a good day's work)—was still well stocked.

Now the idea of going out to dine that evening occurred to Marshall and instantly became a tempting one. But that was the way of self-indulgences—of the small sins— wasn't it? You gave in to one, and two more occurred to you, each more tempting than the last! He'd forgotten that over his years of immense self-discipline, of viselike personal control, spent with Deborah, Thaddeus, Caroline. He'd completely lost sight of the way darker temptations quantified, grew by leaps and bounds.

But that too—the way he'd succeeded in turning himself into a paragon of virtue, a faultless father, and truly happy, devoted husband, dutifully performing his chosen vocational duties and rearing the little ones—was logical. Marshall sidled toward the Oriental screen, paused to heighten his interest before walking around it for an unobstructed view. One committed an act of goodness (or what society might deem normality), and two more opportunities to live with propriety—to do good works—came up. Was it possible he had struck upon a new insight—something along the lines of "Goodness can become as much a force of habit as evil if one cares to make the choice."

The bodies piled neatly upon one another so that they formed an obvious pyramid had not shifted position since Marshall last regarded them. It occurred to him to wish he knew a way to learn if the tenant in the apartment beneath his had been experiencing improved health or good fortune. After all, the person was receiving any "rays" given off by dead people because of their pyramidal formation, and a great many metaphysical types believed in magic of that kind.

He counted "one, two, three, four, five, six" before giving up the task again. He had been remiss in not maintaining an ongoing tabulation as the friends, lovers, and family members of the gentleman Marshall had had to destroy so he could keep the loft began to "drop in," to "stop by." They had been "worried" about him, they'd told the man who opened the door to each of them in turn. Not one of the first dozen people had even challenged his right to be there; to each of them he'd said a hushed "Yes?" with the door open just a crack, the lights almost entirely turned off behind him.

But the fourth or fifth caller at the loft had said how "sure" he was that his friend would "be back soon," and asked if he could wait. "Of course you may," Marshall had replied politely, pulling the door wide and *stepping* back from it into *deeper* shadow. "Of course."

And he hadn't been wearing his mask.

After he took to keeping it within arm's reach, though, the occasional feelings of loneliness—of brooding over Deborah's ill-thought decision and sadly missing Thaddeus and Caroline—were assuaged. With his unforgivable ugliness concealed, seated across from people with the lighting subdued, he'd been able to play host—something he had never done before without being surrounded by his happy, normal family, and rare enough then, and rather enjoyed it. Most of the time, indeed, he had taken to *suggesting* to visitors at the loft that Buddy—most of the callers called their companion or relative that, so Marshall assumed the easy familiarity—had "only stepped out" and would soon return. To them, when they came alone, he strove to be the perfect host, offering them not just the beer "Buddy" had purchased but good brands of scotch, whiskey, and wine— soft drinks too—Marshall sent out for, just for those occasions. It became an interesting challenge to Marshall to see how long he could talk about "old Buddy," whom he'd never had the chance to know in a fully social context; and of course, since he not only had an excellent memory but jotted down notes as soon as he once again had the time to do it, he gradually became the possessor of an encyclopedic amount of knowledge—the reigning expert!—on the topic of "Buddy."

In a way, Marshall came to imagine, he'd really turned himself into a friend of the man who once lived in the loft. Belatedly, but a friend, since he never spoke ill of the "Buddy" who was, depending upon the caller, letting him hang around a few days; his brother; his employer, waiting to "talk some business"—even Buddy's lover, simply to see what happened to the expression of the rather plain young woman to whom he was speaking.

The point to chatting about "old Buddy" as long as Marshall could keep solitary visitors willing to do it was based on his private, absolutely *forbidden* knowledge that when

123

a woman or man announced they had to go, and stood, Marshall would inform them that they were wrong. They were *never* going to go out, or in, or *away from* the loft again.

And when callers arrived on the landing outside the dimly lit loft door in pairs—once, a trio of them was waiting when Marshall murmured a shadowed "yes?"—he still played the ideal host, plying them with sociable drinks, even hors d'oeuvres Marshall took to making from time to time, but he would poison one of the two drinks. That was sporting, he thought, because he unfailingly gave the killing cocktail or highball to the female. Unhappily, that made theirs a shorter visit than those Marshall came to enjoy with a solitary caller. The undrugged male tended to respond with understandable concern when the lady bent double, clutched her stomach, now and then screamed with agony. Then Marshall had no other choice but notifying the male that that he, too, was about to die, so there was really no need to talk about phoning for medical assistance. And there'd be no opportunity to do so either.

Longing intensely for his own Deborah, Marshall empathized absolutely *tremendously* with a man placed in the position of sudden loss and inexplicable fatal predicament, killing them both with greater alacrity and free-flowing tears. Though he was occasionally pleased to encounter a solitary male visitor who wished to defend himself and he certainly was not above playing with the fellow, he was painstaking in not letting it go until there was a chance of real hope building up in the other. That would've been crude, and inhumane. He allowed such men to make a good accounting of themselves, nothing more than that. After all, it seemed important to permit a person to think well of himself when he died—but not to imagine for an instant that he might ever have left the loft.

Still (Marshall enjoyed telling himself), if the loft had

had separate, actual rooms, he could very well have kept a few males and one or two females alive indefinitely. For companionship only, of course. Forcing himself romantically upon anybody was detestable and he had never attempted such a thing even before Deborah proposed to him, and he had been a virgin on their wedding night. All his beloved books were for instruction, and—private uses no true gentleman would even have recorded in his journal. So those persons who had shared the best and warmest memories of Buddy might have been his buddies too— under different circumstances, and if he had not been cursed with such a ghastly face.

However, there were compensations, now, for the need Marshall had known to curtail his momentarily lengthening horizons, and they came in the form of the sustenance with which the callers provided him. Part of that was spiritual; another part was linked to the cash and the credit cards they carried on their persons. Quite without a sense of shame or guilt—because it wasn't his fault the loft didn't have real rooms or that people came around unasked to look for old Bud, and none of them had any further use for tangibles where they were (*um*) "going" (and *was* that in, or out, Marshal sardonically reflected)—Buddy's sociable army had completely answered the question of how Marshall might continue to thrive, fundless, in the style of a gentleman.

In fact, they ultimately made him as independent a man as blessed Deborah had done by way of her job, if merely for the short term.

Alas, of course, the inevitable transpired. Weeks had passed now without a chance to exchange gossip about Buddy, the weather, New York traffic, and the like. It appeared now that Bud's whole family and everyone the fellow had ever known had tapped on the door (what a fine person he must have been!), come in to ask about him—

and unknowingly to brighten Marshall Madison's bleak existence—and unfortunately to perish.

If people today had only taken the time to develop a fondness for correspondence, to become well acquainted through a frequent and meaningful exchange of in-depth and inquiring personal letters, none of the dead husks behind Marshall's wide Chinese screen would now be stacked like oversize, water-bloated playing cards. And he would not have had to shed tears enough to drown, say, a full-sized pony!

In fact, the entire tragic procedure of seeing dozens of men and women die where he was obliged to dwell would have appeared intolerable to him in spite of the economic freedom their deaths afforded Marshall except for the *other* contributions they had made.

He returned to the refrigerator, tugged the door open.

He'd stay home tonight and not surrender to the temptation toward indulgence. It was the manly, mature thing to do.

Then he'd rest up until morning, Marshall decided, and pay a visit of his own to the retired woman who had deemed it necessary to separate his children and sent Thaddeus and Caroline off to live with strangers. If she was a more caring person than the male bureaucrat, she certainly should know where such remarkable and clearly special children as the issue of Deborah and Marshall Madison had gone. The way Enid Godby had contacted her old place of employment could almost be seen as an act of providence.

When Marshall closed the fridge, he knew whom he had to thank for the contents of the container in his hand because he had labeled each and every one as a matter of course and of ordinary human respect. Before taking his seat at the dining table on the less offensive side of the Oriental screen, he made a gesture of salutation—fingertips to temple—to the remnant of the donor. "Your brother Buddy was a fine man," he murmured quietly. "I'm so glad we all had the chance to become acquainted—however fleetingly."

Part Two

Terror Shows

"He who has given
A hostage knows
All ways of dying
Terror shows."

—Elizabeth Cutter, *Hostage*

Chapter Six

1

To Mack Kendall, at thirteen, the cop who had come back to the guardian home to question him again about the way Hector Crossland was killed looked like one of the N.B.A. players in the anti-child abuse commercials. The ones in which seven-footers like Bill Cartwright of the Bulls or Mark Eaton of the Jazz were seen while the camera panned up their enormous bodies, then Bill or Mark bent down to say this was how parents looked to kids they were hitting on.

Detective Jesse Lewis was only a few inches past the six-foot mark, but Mack was only five six and Detective Lewis was right in his hunch:

Mack Kendall hadn't told him all he knew about Mr. Crossland's awful death.

Because he'd been the boy Marshall Madison singled out for personal attention.

Besides, Detective Lewis was standing up and Mack had a seat in the very dead Mr. Crossland's office, a room he would really rather have never entered again.

Jesse was in his forties, black, and twice divorced from women who couldn't hack the hours he'd had to put in to make a series of promotions culminating in his recent, much-sought transfer from Vice to Homicide. He'd never even had the time to see the well-meaning commercials young Mack admired because he'd been far too busy looking at the all-too-real bodies of boys and girls no larger and no older than Mack. "The thing is," he told the kid in a voice so deep it might never bottom out, "I think the man who killed Mr. Crossland is looking for the child or children he ran away and left. And I also think, Mack, that anybody who'd do such things to another man may be crazy enough to blame his own kids for leaving him—and I *don't* believe either one of us wants him to get that angry at a child. Am I right?"

Mack bobbed his head but also took his time about it. The head would have looked oversize and the face fleshy except the former was oval with short-cropped dark brown hair and it came down to a chin that was proportionately much too pointed and small. When Mack grew up, he'd grow an undistinguished mustache vaguely intended to lengthen his face, but it would only make him look that much more like a ferret. He'd been born with eyes that squinted and appeared shifty, and none of the events of his thirteen years had done anything to relieve the impression they made on people. This cop, Lewis, was just the latest adult who hadn't believed one goddamn thing he said.

Mack was also staying uncommunicative because he hadn't had enough time to decide if it mattered to him that old man Madison might eat Thaddie's nose.

Detective Lewis conquered once more his old habit of

sighing at the wrong moments. At a time like this, it gave the person he was questioning confidence that he was starting to give up. He also resisted the temptation to make every law enforcement officer's hasty threat linked to the withholding of evidence. This Kendall kid was an orphan, or the next worst thing to it; he was too unattractive to have been adopted by anybody, but he wasn't a runaway, so he was probably tougher than he looked and cagey enough not to believe the authorities would arrest an orphaned teenager who'd just been a witness to a violent murder.

But Jesse'd interviewed a helluva lot tougher and cagier specimens than this brat, and he would've bet his badge on it that Kendall was—quite precisely—withholding information. "The file folder we picked up, Mack," he said quietly, "was empty. But the name on it was Enid Godby, and we've learned she was the lady who had Crossland's job until she retired." Mack's eyes bounced, jittered, but always laterally; they never came up to find Jesse's. "Mack, she has to be someone you knew, the one in charge when you came here—because I have your file."

Now Mack glanced up—but only briefly. "I knew her, yeah. She was okay."

"Do you know where she lives?" Lewis asked.

"Unh-unh." Mack messed with the few things on Crossland's desk Jesse and the other police hadn't collected for fingerprints. The staple remover was no longer on the desk. It was in a plastic sack the police took away.

"Mack," Jesse said, more quietly than before, "your file says you have . . . remained . . . your whole time at the home. Since—well, since you were brought here."

"Yeah," Mack said. Sweatered shoulders scantly shrugged. He was trying to draw with a pencil a picture on the back of one somewhat meaty hand, outwardly bored as hell.

"Mack," Jesse said again, speaking so softly no one outside the office could have heard him, "that means you *have* to have known the son or daughter of the man who murdered Mr. Crossland."

The boy's gaze rose, eyes wider than usual. If he had managed to do that more often, Lewis thought, he might've had a chance of some family wanting him. "I guess I knew him," he admitted. "A long time ago."

"Yes, you knew him. Good. Very good." Jesse pulled out the chair on the caller's side of Crossland's desk, nodding and not smiling so much at the poor little fellow that he got Mack all excited. "Poor little fellow" was what he let himself think, too. You couldn't order custom-made faces before you were born. Now Jesse knew the perpetrator was definitely the father of a boy who'd been brought there. Very good indeed. "I'm going to ask you the name of your friend, Mack, in just a moment. But I want to give you an opportunity to remember something else first."

Mack had gone on looking across the desk at the homicide detective, but he still hadn't decided how far he wanted to go with this. Even if Thaddie's dad might really kill him or something, or might not, he felt he had to decide how much to cooperate. There might be a reward for furnishing helpful information, but there could also be some penalty nobody was telling him about. "Go ahead," he said.

"The murderer talked to you, son. You told us that. He was closer than I am. I need his full name, if you remember your friend mentioning it to you—and you *must know* what he looked like: how big he was; how old; if he had a mustache or beard; if—"

"Thad Madison wasn't no friend," Mack blurted the words out. The first animation appeared in his sallow face. "We *wasn't* friends!"

And they hadn't been either—because of what Thaddie'd done to him. . . .

2

Mack, who had come to the home after the Madison children had been placed, had known Thaddeus on two occasions, the first being when Mack and Thaddie were both nine years old.

Lying on adjacent beds in the boys' dorm, Thad had said what it was like to go live in the house of strangers, and Mack, who would never otherwise find out, had listened attentively in shared shadows.

"Thurman—that's the man—was okay awhile," Thaddie'd said just loudly enough for Mack to hear, "and I thought Rhonda, the woman, was real nice. At *first*."

"What happened?"

"Well, she wanted me to call her 'Mama', and Tinsdale, he said just 'Thurman' was okay. But I didn't want to call her that 'cause I'd already had *one* mama, and she was mine—mine and my sister's." Thad's face wasn't turned toward Mack, so all Mack could see was the back of Thaddie's head. "So I called her 'Mom,' but"—Thad glanced at the boy in the other bed for a second—"well, 'Thurman and Mom' sounded real funny and I started getting 'em mixed up. Sometimes I called them 'Dad and Rhonda'."

Mack had giggled about the mistake.

"But it wasn't funny," Thad said. "See, Rhonda believed 'Mama' was just perfect, and she liked grabbin' my head to give me big hugs. And when I just *couldn't* call her that, she got to cryin' a lot—'cause she'd said to all her friends she was finally gonna *be* a mama, an she . . . expected me to love her 'cause she'd taken me *in*."

"Why didn't you just lie?" Mack had demanded, mashing his pillow under his head so he could go on looking comfortably at Thaddeus.

"Because my *real* mama killed herself," Thad answered. And his face had looked kind-of funny, screwed up like he was either mad or going to cry.

So Mack just said, "Oh."

"And when Rhonda, she got all upset," Thaddie went on, "that made Thurman real mad. 'Why are we putting ourselves through this for that ungrateful little brat?' he asked when they thought I was asleep. 'Why don't we just send him back?' And Rhonda, she answered, 'Thurman, he's not a *fish!* You can't throw him back like one.' "

Mack giggled again. He wiped it off his mouth when he saw Thad's look, though.

"Well, when he saw we was both stuck with each other, Thurman decided I had t'earn the right to call him Dad. By playin' sports with him."

Mack was always the last kid everybody chose when they picked sides for any kind of game and he wanted real bad to get into sports. Thad's foster father didn't sound really awful to Mack. "What happened next?"

That was when Thad frowned super hard, like he was trying to remember. But Mack didn't think he had any real problem remembering. "I hadn't seen any kind of games before," Thad said, even more whispery. "I hadn't even seen a baseball. So when he threw one at me, I just stood there with the bat and the ball hit me. It hurt my shoulder." A pale hand showed the place in the dormitory shadows. "Well, Thurman asked if I was stupid or something when I threw it back and he had to sort-of chase it. He told me to just go ahead and hit the baseball with the bat and quit screwing around."

Mack, increasingly curious, squirmed into a seated position on his bed. "Did you?"

Thad paused. "I tried," he said. "I swung the bat very

136

hard. And he kept pickin' up the ball, and throwing it, and I kept swinging the bat and missin', till Thurman finally sort-of threw it underhand, real easy like, exactly when he'd got disgusted and started walking up to me. He was askin' me at the same time if I was a fairy—which I thought was pretty weird,'' Thad added, ''because I don't got any wings and even I'm taller than *that*.''

Mack thought that was a joke and said excitedly, ''Well, go on—go ahead. What happened when you swung the bat that time?''

''I hit it.'' Thaddie'd swallowed, glanced away. ''The ball went straight at Thurman, hit him in the middle of his forehead, and he—he *fell down*.'' Thad was staring into the shadows of the dorm, and his expression was veiled by more than darkness. ''Mack, I was so *surprised*. Thurman, he just stayed there on the ground, and his forehead swoll up big! Well, his eyes looked all funny, so I picked up his glove and asked him if we were *supposed* to hit people with the baseball and why *he* didn't try to *catch* it instead of letting the ball hurt his head so bad.''

Mack exploded with laughter. He positively collapsed on his bed and rolled all over it in hilarity, howling—

Until little Thad Madison was sitting on him with his tiny fists drawn back. ''It isn't funny. I didn't *try* to bat the ball at Thurman and hurt him.'' Mack looked up at the much smaller child pinning him down and, though he wiggled around and couldn't get Madison off him, Mack was giggling again. *''Stop laughing!''* Thaddie said, crying now.

''Did he whip your ass then, Thad?'' Mack said between giggles. ''I bet he tore you up!''

''No, he didn't,'' Thad answered, sniffing hard. ''Not then, 'cause he was too dizzy to get up.'' Mack still remembered vividly how the Madison kid had stared down at him, then, trying not to cry anymore but sort-of eager to say what had happened at the Tinsdales'. Mack wouldn't have the words for a long, long time to describe Thad's expression. "Father—my *real* Father—he always told me to d-do what he said to do and that whatever happened, then, he'd stand up for me. I'd *hit* the old ball like Thurman wanted, s-so I asked him . . . asked him—"

"What?" Mack demanded. "What'd you ask him?"

And Thaddie'd drawn in a deep breath, even started to get off Mack. "If I should call him 'Dad' now," he said. He seemed very sad.

Which was when Mack had made the error in judgment of laughing again—harder than ever.

"Don't *laugh* at stuff like that!" the Madison kid shouted, and struck Mack on the tip of his chin.

And the truth of it was that Mack Kendall could never tell anyone, and never would, that the blow from another nine-year-old who was so little you had to look twice to see him ran through Mack's pudgy body all the way into his toes. He'd believed at the time and he believed now, with Detective Jesse Lewis waiting for him to go on, that Thad's punch would have broken his neck if he hadn't been lyin' back against the mattress when it landed.

So when a year and a half passed and Thad was returned to the home for the last time, tryin' to make friends again and explaining how both the Tinsdales and the other foster folks he'd been placed with had begun to lock him in his room and hit on him with belts and other stuff for askin' questions, Mack hadn't made up. He'd barely listened, really, 'cause he was twice the size of the Madison runt but the brat was tougher than most of the boys who were twice Mack's size. The ones who beat Mack up regularly, till he got to be one of the oldest boys at the SoHo home. And he'd seen Thad fight some big kid who made some cracks about Thaddie's sister—and Thad was *whompin' his butt* till three buddies of the big guy got Madison off him. Thaddie'd even bit the smartass, held on awhile with his teeth!

Which was the day Thad, still tryin t'make friends, showed Mack pictures of his father and the little sister, Caroline or something. His old man's photograph was trimmed around the edges in a funny shape and Madison'd said his mom took it out of some locket and tried to throw it away right before she offed herself, but Madison had saved it.

The crazy thing was that the picture of the little brat's dad was *kind of* like the man who tore Hector Crossland's face to ribbons—Mack was certain, in fact, that they *were* the same guy—but now the old man looked . . . different. Anyway, he could tell the cop pretty much what Marshall Madison was like—if he wanted to. If he understood whether he truly wanted to help the brat who'd hit him, and hurt him.

"He was really big," Mack told Jesse, somewhat surprised that he was already speaking and completely uncertain where he was going with the description. "Tall, like an N.B.A. player—*taller*, maybe—and he didn't have any hair, he was bald as a cue ball! He had this head that *kept goin'* in back, like he couldn't get through a doorway if he turned sideways—and he was so fat, I didn't think he could even—"

Detective Lewis was walking toward the office door, open disgust on his honest black face. A uniformed cop outside the room saw his expression and was already turning to leave the home.

At least it wasn't a waste of time, Jesse thought. He knew the perp was the father of a male child who had been at the guardian home; there were lots of ways—including court files—to chase people down, it was just that some of those ways took to much time.

But now he had the boy's name. Thad Madison. Now he knew where to begin.

In a way, Jesse believed, he already knew how it would end.

3

"Miss Godby," Jake said into the phone mouthpiece after identifying himself, "I don't know if you read the newspapers or not." He glanced through the glass doors of a phone booth in a hotel where he'd taken a fare. Someone in a nice suit waiting to replace him glanced back, not bothering to conceal his hostility over the presence there of a cabdriver. "I thought I should call you about—well, about a guy named Hector Crossland. At the home where you used t'work."

"Oh, did you get some information from him about the Madison boy?" The woman's voice was a rising stir of autumn leaves in Jake Spencer's ear.

But it was his task to scatter them over the chilly October landscape. "No, ma'am," he said carefully, "this Crossland died. It seems like he was killed, maybe by the father of one of the kids the home—*you*, possibly—placed with foster folks. Ma'am, the guy messed Crossland up pretty bad. And I . . . thought you should know."

Enid didn't answer Jake for a moment, and he started wondering if she'd liked the dead man or if she had even heard what he said. Then she spoke up, her tone of voice extremely different, nothing Jake could figure out. "I was an inveterate newspaper reader my whole life, Mr. Spencer. Till after I retired." She essayed a little laugh. "Now I'm afraid I just don't keep up the way I should—except for the astrology columns."

"Can't say I blame ya there," Jake commented. "All that terrible news and all."

"That's part of it," Enid murmured—"but summer's gone. I'm afraid I might accidentally read something about . . . winter . . . coming." She paused. "You're concerned that the birth father might find my name and address and try to get Thaddie and your Caroline's addresses from me. That's *very* kind of you."

"Yeah, well, the bastard's a crazy killer—pardon my French."

"I'll be fine, Mr. Spencer," Miss Godby assured him. She sounded more like the lady Jake and Cammy'd met seven years ago than she had before. "If you'll recall, I don't *know* where Thad is, and I *didn't* write down your address." Enid even laughed. "I assure you I've already forgotten what your telephone number is!"

But did you write it down, copy it on something? Jake wanted to ask but couldn't. He cleared his throat, put his hand on the glass door in preparation to leave the booth. "I just don't wanna hear that you got hurt, Miss Godby," he said. "You might want t'think about phonin' the cops or something. You have anything around there to protect yourself?"

"Not against winter coming," Enid said obliquely. "I always wondered what form the final one would take. If it's this so-called 'father,' rest assured that I won't ruin the only worthwhile work of my life by aiding him to harm your child, or Thad Madison. "Besides," she said before they broke the connection, "everything in the astrology columns cautions me against November and December—not October—and everything in my body tells me the same!"

Jake hung up an instant later and found he had something in his eye.

To make it go away, he fairly burst through the phone booth doors and told the man in the nice suit to stick the goddamn telephone where the sun didn't shine.

141

4

Caroline had felt funny all day without knowing why. She didn't think she was sick, not really, but everything her teachers were trying to convey seemed to go in her ears only a fraction of an inch, then run into some kind of block.

And about the fourth time that happened—it was during an algebra class, and Care usually struggled to get B's in it anyway—the droning voice of Mr. Milliken did something even weirder to Caroline:

It seemed to release some memory in the girl's mind—but no, Care realized, not a memory but something entirely different.

A piece of information—a fact, it certainly appeared to be—that Caroline had no way of knowing.

Adjusting her pale, pretty face so she looked like she was listening to Mr. Milliken, lacing her fingers tightly and resting the heels of her hands on her algebra book, Care let her thoughts bring in the image that was trying to come through—

And she *saw Thaddie*, she *saw* her *bro*, way up on the roof of some old building, just as clearly (well, almost) as she saw the teacher with the fluffy, graying sideburns and his cold, tight-lipped smirk! And there were a lotta animals around Thaddie, kind-of sniffing at his ankles; and bro, he was trying to see Father from the roof—he was *looking* for Father, like he might come walking down the street any second!

But what scared Caroline and made her say *"Ohh!"* aloud, as if somebody'd pinched her from behind, was her knowing that this *wasn't* the past she was seeing—

And *Thaddie hadn't grown up at all*. He was small—

142

tiny—just like he'd been when she saw him last, back at the guardian home.

Care glanced at the algebra teacher, then around at the other kids sitting nearby. Mr. Milliken hadn't heard her cry out. The only one who had was a girl Caroline's age, called B. J., and Beege was smiling nicely back, looking concerned. Care returned the smile to show she was really okay—

And realized that she would know why *her bro wasn't growing if she only let herself.*

Urgently needing comforting, suddenly wanting the algebra teacher's monotonous, sarcastic voice to get through to her—to *make* her listen to the Now, the Today, and the Real—Care instinctively lifted Mama's locket from her breast, opened it, and peered anxiously inside.

There was Mama, lovely as always, radiant with happiness as she'd almost always looked back when the old picture was taken.

And in the other side of the locket, where no photograph remained, Caroline *saw* Father. Smiling.

Smiling with lips and eyes that moved, the latter saying, Don't be afraid of anything, you *know* I love you—

And his moving lips also saying, before the image of youthful Marshall Madison faded out of sight, "I'm coming for you, Caroline. *Look* for me—I'll be there *soon*."

Caroline had her friend B. J. with her in the girl's room minutes later when she realized she had sort-of fainted and was having her first period.

5

Jake steamed out of the hotel, mad at the world, worried as hell for the planet, too. It was midafternoon so he angled north up Seventh to the taxi garage, more determined than ever to get help in finding Care's brother. If possible, he also wanted to locate Care and Thad's original old man. It was increasingly likely it had been the crazy Madison who wiped out the guy at the guardian home and that he was the kind of weird son of a bitch who wouldn't back off until he found what he was looking for—or until somebody else stopped him in his fucking tracks! Jake had been on the phone when Caroline left for school, so there'd been no chance to ask if she had Thad's picture, but Enid Godby had given him a pretty fair description of the little kid.

And cab drivers pretended better than most actors that they never saw a damn thing, even when it went down in front of their hacks, but they were the most curious people on the planet Earth—maybe the most intelligent too, if it came down to that. If they were really turned on to it, cabbies could locate a missing kid in a city the size of New York in weeks where the F.B.I. might need several years. For starters, the drivers knew where *not* to bother looking. They understood where a boy on the streets wanting to flop or score was apt to hang out. In the latter instance, those were the same areas where cabbies preferred to pick up customers anyway, so they'd be there more frequently than the authorities.

Jake's idea was to get to the company just as a shift was ending, hoping to spot a few of his buddies. True, only the rooks had to bring their hacks back every night. But some of the drivers—he really had to stop thinking of them as "guys" or even "buddies," since there'd been women around who loved this life well enough to risk their necks for years now—liked to hang around the garage. As he hopped out of his hack, Jake wondered why anybody would prefer the dump to home and supposed it was loneliness— or maybe the opposite. Maybe there were mates or lovers just waiting for the drivers to get home so they could dump on them. People needed *some* sense of family, after all. That was what he was counting on now.

Well, he knew two things about cabbies as a group: Not to ask their reasons for doing or for *not* doing any damn thing, partly because you might really hate the explanation; that was one. The second fact was that no university existed in the world where a guy could meet more people with such a wide scope of information. Nearly half of it, of course, included cock-eyed conspiracy theories covering everything from the mayor or governor to the Mafia, from the C.I.A. to right-wing fringe groups, and from the Tri-lateral Commission to the Foreign Policy Association—and George Steinbrenner, UFOs, and the Mets or Bills!

A brief glance inside the garage—after his vision adjusted to the gloomy interior—reassured Jake that fate was going to let him take his best shot. Two people he *didn't* want to be present weren't.

Neither Salty Dugan, who believed he was the supervisor of the drivers, or Dave Fogal, who actually *was*, was anywhere in view.

Instead, Timothy, Willie Crawfield, and Lou—three of the guys Jake most believed he could count on—were there. Unfortunately, they weren't grouped together but were (as Jake wandered across the oil-streaked floor) individually occupied. Timothy, he was inside his hack with his long legs dangling outside, deep into the latest edition of *Taxi Times*. Willie (who shaved his black head to look more like Michael Jordan because Willie reckoned the image made him more popular with potential fares) was coaxing a bottle of pop from a machine and probably eager to get up a game of Tonk.

Lou, probably the oldest cabbie both in point of personal longevity and years in service to the city's pedestrians, sat in Salty Dugan's office chair, pencil in hand. Pausing, Jake smiled. Old Lou was "committing poetry" (as Timothy called it), in all likelihood.

Then Sally Schindler was visible just outside the ladies', ransacking her purse. Jake figured the expression on her lined face was the same one she had used to keep a thousand and one would-be perverts at bay. Sal was very possibly the best choice he had to enlist help in search for a missing child; she was, Jake thought with amusement, technically feminine. Trouble was, she'd come over from Yellow Cab only a few months earlier and he simply didn't know her well. Then there was the scowl she wore on her Dead-Sea-Scroll kisser; Jake realized it scared him nearly as much as it did the perverts.

When an idea came to mind, Jake headed to Lou first: Because he was old enough to be Jake's own dad and was getting deafer by the day, Lou tended to bark at everybody else. To be heard, Jake would have to shout back, and everyone in the garage was bound to hear exactly what Jake wanted them to hear. And that would reduce the number of times he'd need to explain and ask for help.

Within a couple of yards of Lou, Jake found the old guy's other senses were still razor-sharp. Doubtlessly it came from decades of learning to estimate at a glance which people hailing his cab were more apt to give him a generous tip and which ones would stiff him. Lou was staring straight into Jake's eyes at the instant Jake was in range, alert as a bulldog. They were separated only by a glassless, open space above the counter forming a partial wall of Salty Dugan's office.

"Jakey," Lou said in a gruff but not unfriendly voice, "how're they hangin'?" He went on gripping a ball-point pen tightly in a fist that was starting to gnarl.

"I'd say in the right number and expected order," Jake said with a grin.

"How's that?" It was a bark, but Lou didn't care. He

was scribbling a carefully chosen word. "You know a rhyme for purple?"

"Sure. 'Burpel.' " Jake said with more volume. "As in, 'Pat the baby's back and he'll be more burpel.' "

"Jesus, Jakey," Lou replied, "that's terrible. Never lose your license." He shook his huge head with very little white hair still fringing it. Lou's eyes were evaluative as he looked up again. "You want somethin'?"

"Yeah," Jake said loudly, and drew in a breath. This was it. He sensed one or more drivers behind him, staring at the two men making such a racket. "Lou, I need a favor."

"Well, I expected *that*." The old eyes seemed smaller suddenly, shrewder. "Try me."

And Jake did. He began with Caroline's adoption, so Sally Schindler would know of it, spoke of how hard everybody'd tried to make it work as a family, told Lou (and any other attentive listeners) about the call from Enid Godby and the news about Caroline having a brother who was missing. He was careful to include the suspicions about the two children's original father before explaining that it looked like both Caroline and Thaddie might be in danger.

"I need help in finding the boy—Thad—before that murderous son of a bitch does," Jake said, getting near the end of his speech. He had noticed Lou's eyes darting a few times to either side; facing the rest of the garage, Lou could see that the other drivers were listening too. "Can you give me a hand in this, Lou? I have a good description of Thad."

Lou squirmed around in the boss's chair, sighing and grunting as if Jake's request might have mysteriously activated some ancient ailments. "I'd like to help out, Jakey, I really would. But these old eyes ain't what they was, and you're sayin' yourself the father may be some kind of crazy killer. Besides, it ain't like he's after *your girl*, and there's hundreds of kids out on the streets these days—maybe thousands.''

"He's trying to get *both children back*, dammit, Lou!" Jake argued. "See, if—"

Jake felt a hand on his arm, turned to see who was touching him. Sal Schindler, no younger, prettier, or less hard looking up close. Jake noticed she had put glasses on and had a pencil stub poised above a notebook opened to a blank sheet. "Tell me the kid's description, Jake," she said. The look she shot at Lou should by all rights have burned at least the poem he was writing.

Jake smiled his thanks and began repeating the description he had been given by Miss Godby.

But Sal interrupted him. "The unofficial taxi code is, *we're* supposed to pick up *anybody*."

Jake saw Timothy climbing out of his hack, leaving the *Taxi Times* on the seat. He folded his arms across his thin chest, ready to listen now.

"Of course," Sally said full-voice, "some of you delicate students at the little ladies finishing school would probably avoid a fare as *dangerous* as a thirteen-year-old boy. On the grounds that you just don't have the balls for such a *ter*rible risk!"

Willie Crawfield threw down his first Tonk hand and glared hard at Sally. But he had a pen and a scrap of paper, and so did Pepe and Otis, the cabbies sharing the beaten-up card table with Willie. "So deal it out, Jake," he called. "Number 23 will find the boy for you before any female transfers from Yellow Cab!" He beamed upon them his most debonair smile. "For Air Willie, man, this is a reverse slam-dunk over a point guard!"

"Nothin' wrong with a little humor in poetry now and then," Lou put in. " 'Burpel' ain't bad for a beginner." He smoothed his bald pate, turned his poem over for a clean writing space. "Which is exactly what all you people are when it comes t' findin' missing kids!"

All Jake could say for a second was a croaked, "Thanks."

And after he'd described Thaddeus Madison again to the best of his ability and shown them all pictures of Caroline, on the theory that brother resembled sister, he provided the other drivers with his home phone number. "I don't want any of you to get hurt," Jake added. "If you happen to get a line on Madison himself, tell the police or me. Don't try to tackle the bastard yourself."

Then he lost five bucks to Willie, playing Tonk, in fewer than ten minutes.

He thought it was the best five dollars he'd spent in years.

6

Father and daughter sat together quietly, watching the start of a horror movie on one of the cable networks. Actually, Care had just finished seeing another film entirely when Jake, after telling Cammy he'd like to spend some time alone with Caroline, had entered the rec room. It was just that the child had the remote in her lap and made no effort to switch to another channel or jump up to turn the TV off.

Actually, too, father and daughter were only surfacely quiet. There was an intense chord of tension so loud emanating from Jake, he'd have been surprised if Care didn't hear it. He'd decided he had no choice except to tell the girl about the phone calls he and Miss Godby had been exchanging. More daunting by far, he knew he would have to tell Caroline that her birth father might have killed a man and was probably trying to hunt down her brother and her.

And in actuality Care herself was radiating a certain emotional strain comprised of the power her emerging dream-memories continued to hold over her, and something new: a growing impression that very strange things involving her in some way were going on even as Pop sat down on the old sofa beside her—old, crazy things that absolutely were not going to leave her alone regardless of how much she prayed they would.

"Your mother told me," Jake began, "what happened to you in school today."

Caroline neither glanced up nor altered her seated position beside Jake. "She called it my 'menstrual cycle,'" she answered, rather dutifully. "They told us about it in health, but I didn't think I'd get mine for a while yet."

Whew, Jake thought. "I just figured you might be concerned about it. Something."

"The first period's called the *menarche*," Care said. On the television screen across from them, a palely elegant man with dark hair and eyes like stars no one ever sees was the guest at a fancy dinner party. Suddenly, he rose from the table and began dancing with a pretty lady in an evening gown. Care looked up at Jake. "I'm shedding stuff called *endometrium*, in the womb."

"Is that right?" Jake tried to go on meeting his daughter's gaze but found his own eyes swinging back to the TV. This actor Langella was too goddamn nice looking for a role like this. The girl he was dancing with looked like she wanted to eat him up. "Well, just as long as you know it's natural, that you're okay."

"Oh, sure," Care said. She was still sitting so erectly, so rigidly, she felt Pop's gaze return—questioningly—to her pert profile. "I'm just becoming a woman. That's all."

That's all, Jake thought, newly hurting. He let his eyes and memory drink in his little girl who, in a way, wasn't that any more. He saw her time with him and Camille then as a water color wash that made the details impossible to see separately, and momentarily felt that he saw her in a wedding gown too, holding a child aloft that grew even as Caroline somehow managed to bear it high above the floor.

Somewhere in the picture, Jake thought, *I could make me out, tucked in a corner like an old bedroom slipper, except I'm getting smaller all the time. Dwindling away.* "Dads," he said, unaware he'd decided to speak, "mean well for their kids—or we want to mean well for them." How had it happened he'd gotten stuck on the age thing and was telling the kid about "dads" being tender about it, when he was getting ready to talk about a bastard who hadn't fought to keep *his* children? "Sometimes things happen, problems come up."

Care asked Jake directly, "You're talking about him, aren't you? Father?"

"Well, yeah." Caroline was turned to face him now, one jean-clad knee resting on the old couch, her face ready to become animated, anxious. On the screen Jake briefly glimpsed, he saw a huge bat with fluttering wings trying to get in somewhere and he took the remote from Care, switched to a weather channel. "I don't know for sure it's your first old man in what I'm gonna tell you, but—I think it is." Jake patted her shoulder and gently knuckled her closest cheek. "I want to find your brother . . . Thaddie . . . before he does."

"Thaddie?" More animation lit her young face than he'd probably ever seen in it before. Her eyes gleamed with excitement. "You're going to try to find my *bro?*"

Jake nodded. "I want to know everything you can remember about him. Not just how he looked when you were both tiny, but everything. I know you have trouble with—with that part of your life." *But I have to tell you what the son of a bitch did to another man so you'll dredge it up no matter what.*

151

And while Jake was telling her about Enid's calls and the murder of Hector Crossland at the guardian home, Camille slipped into the rec room to perch on the other side of Caroline, at the end of the sofa.

Everything, Pop had told her, *everything you can remember about Thaddie*. She was listening attentively to what her dad was saying now, but his other words, his request, was playing over and over in her mind.

"He's *not growing*," Caroline said. She spoke so softly, Jake, picking his words about the man who'd fathered her with extreme caution, didn't hear. *Everything* . . . "Pop, he looks almost the same now as he did when we were tiny!"

"Now, he didn't hurt the kids at the home at *all*," Jake was saying, "just the man who took over for Miss Godby. But *she* says he's looking for you and Thad, so . . ."

"*Pop*," Caroline said insistently. She fumbled at her side for Camille's hand, and, finding it, squeezed.

Jake and Camille finally looked at her, and they saw terror and frustration sweep into her sweet face. Jake thought it appeared that she needed to cry and couldn't because it was far more important to tell them something. It also seemed, Jake realized as Care peered slowly from his face to Cammy's and back again, as if she was truly horrified—

And confronted by a problem she could not possibly solve alone.

"I *know* now what happened to Thaddie," she said on a strain of growing hysteria—that was surely the part of her returning memory that filled her with horror—"and I know *why* Thaddie isn't . . . growing—why he won't *ever* grow up. I *know*, I *remember*!"

"Okay, finish it," Jake urged her. He glanced at his wife over Caroline's head, took the child's other hand. "Go on, kid. Tell us, so we can help both you kids and maybe Miss Godby too. C'mon, Care."

Care's lips moved, but nothing audible came out. For a second it was nearly as if she were holding her breath.

Then she was rushing across the room to the door, weeping, stopping there to look back at the parents who loved her. "I can't! I just *can't* tell you!"

"*Why?*" Camille asked. She caught Jake's hand, keeping him from running after Caroline. "Honey . . . sweetheart . . . why *can't* you tell us why your brother won't grow up?"

"Because *you'd never believe me*," Care said, tears streaming from her light-colored eyes now. "You'd *never* be able to *believe* what *happened!*"

Cammy arose to walk briskly after the girl and try, mother to daughter, to learn the truth.

Jake fell back against the couch with a big sigh, and looked at the diagram he saw on the weather channel.

It was going to get a lot colder.

7

At a time that might have been latest night or earliest morning, Enid Godby responded to a persistent rapping sound at her front door. Chill air blowing through the aperture made her draw her wrap tightly around her at the bosom.

"I'm Marshall Madison, Thaddeus's father," the man at the door introduced himself. "I believe we need to talk. May I come in?"

"By all means," Enid said without a pause, stepping back and gesturing. "Come inside before you catch your death."

To Marshall's credit, his only response—except for accepting the old woman's invitation—was a subtle smile.

Chapter Seven

1

Some kinds of people don't expect to hear a visitor knocking at the door of their houses at night. Convicts, especially those on death row or otherwise isolated from the general population. Most NCOs occupying cadre rooms in the barracks of the U. S. Army. Incarcerated people in such institutions as those that housed them because they were in some way mentally or emotionally out of balance with the greater society.

And the majority of homeless persons such as Thad Madison, who found, perhaps illegally, somewhere to stay off the streets for awhile.

Thaddie was wide enough awake to sit up on the sofa in the abandoned hotel's lobby and squint into the darkness; however, he came to the gradual realization that the sound he'd heard in his sleep wasn't actually knocking—in the sense of a caller expecting him to come to the boarded-up front door—and didn't originate at any door.

Somebody or some creature had discovered his own exit from and entrance to the deserted building. As the boy listened intently, frozen into immobility, he understood that his unknown visitor was dropping lightly to the floor—

And that a second someone or something had joined the first!

Thaddie glanced around, trying to see the telltale glowing eyes of Robby and the rest of the pack with whom he shared the hotel in uneasy alliance. Even if the rats had been sleeping too, their ears were always on alert, the muscles of their bodies always tensed for flight—or a fight to the death.

Then he remembered how contentedly they'd all dined on that fat Mr. Ricelli's doughnuts a few hours earlier. On the roof. It was possible the rats had stayed up there, at least some of them. Others, reminded by the rooftop view of the city, might have scampered down the fire escape and out on the streets to scavenge. Or the entire pack could be anywhere in the old dump of a building, including places that even Thaddie was too big to squeeze himself; they were all rebels more capable of independent thought than most animals and so driven individually to look out for number one, it was probably why their kind had survived on earth when lots of others had disappeared.

All those thoughts, inwardly expressed in the untutored and undisciplined language of a boy who feared he had more in common with the pack than with other human beings, occurred as Thaddie tried to remember the location of some object with which to protect himself. He had no shadow of doubt that anyone sneaking into this place at night—especially with a partner—might be capable of killing him. To begin with, why sneak? The hotel was boarded up and no lights were on, so there'd certainly be no guards. That made the two invaders stupid, or, worse, doped up on something. And to want to get into the building meant they were desperate people for some reason, just as Thaddie had been.

An awareness of how dumb they were and he was too, when there was enough room for dozens of people in the hotel, made the twelve-year-old blink but didn't change the facts of the matter.

Not even when one of the two midnight interlopers passed through a strand of moonlight filtering into the lobby and Thaddie saw that it was a pretty girl. About seventeen or eighteen, clad in a flannel shirt and jeans. And the facts stayed just the way they were when the other newcomer became visible in the same narrow splash of moonlight, and he was a guy the same age as the girl. A *big* guy, tugging something from the waist of his pants.

A jarringly white spear of light shot out in Thad's general direction like a laser beam, and he ducked his small body down behind the sofa, pressed it to the cushions.

Not in time. The big dude came barreling across the lobby with an animallike roar, reaching over the sofa to club Thaddie with his fists. The guy had his flashlight lifted over his head, meaning to slam it down on the boy's head, then halted in that position. *"Hey!"* he called back to the girl. "C'mon over. Ain't nothin' to sweat." He glanced down at Thaddie, wide mouth smirk like a crevice in his long, plain face. Then two hands like those of a basketball player locked on Thad's shoulders and dragged him into view. "Nothin' here but a little shit run away from his mama."

"Let go of me," Thad said, trying to think but also not wanting to make the big bastard mad. He saw the girl stepping closer, but she was still in shadows around the check-in desk and the guy, plunking him down on the lobby floor and getting an arm lock on Thad, was shoving him forward to meet her. "You aren't gonna hurt a little kid, are ya?"

Neither of them bothered to answer, and then he was facing the girl in the flannel shirt and jeans. She had yellow hair neater than Thad had expected to see, but a button was missing halfway down the shirt and both it and her jeans looked recently dirty—maybe from messing around outside, then climbing through the window. Now that Thaddie thought about it, she seemed pretty close to scared and also very nice looking.

"Whyn't you let him go, Thrice?" she asked. The voice sounded maybe younger than nineteen. "I thought we were gonna party?"

The answer was a sudden vicious tug on Thaddie's arm. It caught him off guard and he yelped in pain, jerked his head around to glare at Thrice. But Thrice might be older than eighteen or nineteen, his breath reeked of beer, and he made two of Thad Madison. "We're gonna do that all right, sweet thing." The dude appeared larger because of his huge face and head and the way his sandy hair was trimmed short, like a closely mown yard. "But I ain't sharin' what we bought with no puke-shit mama's boy—and if we let him go, his old man'll be back with the aw-thorities before I even get it in you."

"Don't talk like that," Sweet Thing said petulantly, "in front of—"

"I'm not a mama's boy!" Thad interrupted, yanking to free his arm and nearly succeeding. "This is where *I* crash and I wouldn't bring cops here for a million dollars!" He kicked backward, succeeding only in knocking over a sand-filled three-foot-high ashtray when Thrice moved his leg.

The grip on Thad's arm tightened painfully, and a menace Thrice gave off as naturally as body odor and beer breath brought a moment of strained silence. All Thaddie had to look at, the way he was pinioned, was the blond girl, and he sensed how much she wanted to be anywhere else. Thad doubted she was even from the city, wondered

157

where she'd met a dude like Thrice—and why she had come with him unless it was for dope.

But all Thaddie had to hear just then were the *quick-quick!* rustling noises elsewhere in the building that these two might take for wind. What he sensed the most and did not doubt was that they wouldn't be alone in the lobby for long.

"Two of you," Thrice said very softly, "telling me what t' *do.*" His breath on the back of Thad's head and neck came quicker, hotter. He raised a knee to prod the boy closer to the girl, who automatically took a step away. "Well, boy, since you *operate* this fine establishment, I suppose we can make it a *three-way* party. Won't take more than a little shit t' put *you* beddy-bye for a nice long night's sleep. First, though, you're just gonna have to prove you're man enough t' take it."

Thrice held to Thaddie's arm with one hand, snaked the other out toward the girl. She stepped backward again but was stopped by the front desk. Thrice's fingers hooked in the gap of her shirt left by the missing button, ripped up, then down, in a motion so swift it looked like a single move. She was so startled or afraid she didn't try to stop him as he laid first one side and then the other half of the shirt wide to expose her naked breasts.

Probably Thrice didn't even intend to draw a long scratch down the center of her chest with a fingernail.

Robby and another seven or eight members of his rodent family appeared on the desk behind the blond girl, their many mean red eyes gleaming in the murky lobby like hard lumps of igniting coal—all of them instantly observed by Thrice, facing their direction—but not the girl he called Sweet Thing.

Thaddie knew the pack was there because he'd expected them. He was looking, though, at the perfect roundnesses two feet from his face, and at the way the jagged line between them was turning the color of rat eyes burning in the night.

Neither he nor the fully grown male behind him knew whether Thad broke the grip on his arm or if Thrice, frightened by the sight of so many rats, relinquished it.

But Thaddie didn't know, because he'd raised his head to sniff the air—the blood—just the way he'd been taught. It was an automatic response, and Thad had no idea why he did it or what the pungency he felt in his nostrils could convey to the rest of his body—or his mind. When he lowered his head to look again at the half-naked girl, he was making a strange sound deep in his throat.

Sweet Thing had never before seen such oddly intense curiosity on the face of a male who saw her boobs—plus something else in the male-child's expression she would never want to identify. And even though she didn't even realize a half circle of rats was ringed at her back merely a foot away, she had never seen such a peculiar glint as she saw in the eyes of Thaddeus Madison.

With a noise that was half squeal, half shriek, she started at a run for the window through which she and the boy who had picked her up had entered this dark place.

Robby and the other rats were behind her immediately, catching up.

"ROBBY!" Thaddie called. His voice sounded unfamiliar to him. It began in a reedy boy's soprano and ended in a more mature tenor that barely sounded the final syllable in anything like a human enunciation. *"NOOOO!"*

The girl scrambled through the window without ever looking back and was gone.

At once the rats, who had obediently stopped, spun around. They weren't staring at Thaddie but at Thrice. Several of them cunningly blocked his pathway to the window while Robby and his new lieutenants dropped low, peered up at the remaining intruder into their domain with unblinking lantern eyes. Stalking Thrice.

"Jesus, kid, I didn't *really* hurt you," the muscular youth told Thaddie. He was once more edging around behind the boy, palms upraised to indicate his newly peaceable intentions, never removing his terrified gaze from the approaching pack. "I mean, shit, I offered you my girl, right, shit man, we was all gonna be buddies and *party,* am I right?"

The scent of the blond girl, of her blood, lingered on the air. The proximity of her woman's flesh to him, the nearness of her exposed navel, the torso rising to the abruptly bare breasts, the scarlet line between them just beginning to trickle, her warm and pulsating throat, kept her tart scent present in Thad's mind and senses. It threatened to overwhelm him; it brought to partial life memories ordinary nature had blocked out or screened. He had a fleeting image of himself at a younger age, similarly exposed, and of a second person who had joined him in all but heart-stopping, identical nakedness—and more.

"So call off your pets like you did for her, pal." Thrice was chattering away behind Thaddie. "I'll just book on outta here, okay, shit, we'll forget I was ever *here*, okay?" He put his hands on Thaddie's shoulders, squeezing lightly. They felt clammy, and the sweat he was emitting mingled annoyingly in the twelve-year-old's olfactory senses, threatened to obliterate a sweet thing's sweet memory. "*Do* it, kid," Thrice said with a wild chemical shift of mood, his fingers on Thad's shoulder tightening. "Call off the fucking rats or they'll hafta get through *you* to get *me!*"

"No," the boy said, very softly. His voice was still breaking between its customary pitch and the shocking, deeper new level. A thought laced unbidden through his traumatized mind, *I want to be like Father,* its impact powerful. "No. They won't."

Young Madison shot his elbow joltingly into Thrice's

stomach the way he had that of Ricelli, the bakery owner. This time he didn't stop there.

He caught Thrice's left arm, quickly dipped low to pull the winded older boy up on his back, then flipped Thrice over! The toss sent him flying much farther than Thad had intended or remotely believed possible.

Stunned, hurting, Thrice stared up at Thaddie from the lobby floor. This was the first time he'd seen the child's face since Thad himself saw, and thought, what he'd experienced a few scant minutes ago.

Thrice scrambled to his knees, too late. Bristling whiskers brushed his cheek as did a cold snout. He turned to make a run for the window and escape, felt claws tear at his flesh, then found the weight of numerous furry bodies piling on his back one after another.

The terrible noises issuing not just from Thrice but the rats finally brought Thad Madison out of the astonishment he'd known when he hurled the full-grown youth toward the eager pack. Thrice was bravely approaching the window but looking back at him, begging for help. Again the sight of bloody scratches as well as bite marks—but this time on Thrice's arms and face—magnetized Thad's attention. With immense difficulty he did the only thing he could imagine doing while the rats were in such a killing frenzy.

He screamed a sound similar to what he'd heard Robby and the dead Rodge make, and hurtled himself amid the scrabbling rodents, tearing them off the older youth's back.

He saw Thrice—powered by sheer desperation—plummet through the window to safety and, relieved when he saw the pack was merely squealing its protests but slinking into the corners of the dark lobby, continued to stare at where Thrice—and the girl—had run to freedom. When he turned to vomit, he wondered why he somehow felt miserably disappointed.

2

Jesse Lewis hadn't for a second believed much of anything Mack Kendall told him about his friend-who-wasn't-a-friend at the guardian home, Thaddie Madison. The detective had believed even less of what the ferret-faced brat said about the Madison kid's father, the suspected killer of Hector Crossland.

But of course Lewis had put the description out; that was police procedure, and Jesse hadn't worked his butt off to get into Homicide to risk being busted on some point of procedure.

When it was established that Crossland had been assaulted with his own staple remover though, even Lewis privately lost some of his professional unflappability. He'd thought he had heard of damn near everything by then, seen more than he'd ever imagined when he was in Vice; but the thought of a man walking into another man's office and peeling off his lip and part of the nose with a mothering *staple remover*—!

Jesse had gone out at once and bought a few of the little implements like it from the nearest office supply store. Using a lifelike dummy, he learned right away that the gadget *was* sharp enough to hook into human skin (if you were weird enough to use it that way), but when he attempted to determine how much strength was required to wreck somebody's face that way, he was mildly surprised to find it was almost impossible for him. And, well into his forties or not, Jesse Lewis was no pushover.

For the first time the detective had a little real sympathy for Mack Kendall. No way the killer was tall as an N.B.A. player with a bald head so long in back "he couldn't get through a doorway,'' but he was definitely strong enough to intimidate the hell out of a little fat kid!

Especially, (Lewis thought just about the time he and his men's legwork started to bear some fruit), when the kid was staring down at Hector Crossland's mess and seeing everything Madison-the-Madman had just done to the guy. . . .

The fruitful work developed when Homicide responded to eleven phone calls from people who had read newspaper stories about the crime and wanted to report tenants who had left their properties under suspicious circumstances. Lewis had given an interview in which he'd mentioned that a boy of thirteen who'd stayed for awhile at the guardian home in SoHo *must* have come from some home in the city, and that some events must have transpired for a child to wind up there. Jesse hadn't yet made it an actual appeal for help from the citizens of New York because that would have resulted in a deluge of phone calls, most of them from crackpots who wanted only to get their names in the paper.

As it was, three of the incoming tips were from landlords or landladies who had been stiffed by families leaving with unpaid rent and five more wanted to report ''unnatural'' sexual acts, Cuban Communists or Libyan terrorists, or Nazi SS men who were trying to clone or revive Adolf Hitler.

That left three phone callers with, as it turned out, legitimate reasons for contacting Lewis's department: A super due south of Chinatown who believed two male tenants were engaged in child porn and managed to chase them out, a Latino lady who remembered a neighboring couple whose child was taken away by court order, and an elderly Jewish gentleman who'd been amazed when ''a really nice family with two children basically went to hell one night.'' Jesse's assistants went out on the first pair of leads, reporting to him respectively that the two males had no children of their own (and child porn or no, each man was Asiatic) and that the couple whose child was removed were black (and the child a daughter). "One thing for goddamn sure, Kerrigan," Jesse told one officer while they were driving to the building where the final caller lived, "Mack Kendall may be a kid and a liar, but he isn't blind."

"I don't follow," Kerrigan said from the driver's seat.

"Boys like Mack wouldn't hesitate to mention it if Thaddie or his father just happened to be Oriental or black." Lewis grinned out the window, mostly to himself. "And I don't think many of my race's little sisters are going in for sex change operations."

He and Kerrigan were disappointed but not surprised to find that the flat formerly occupied by the Madison family in question had been leased to other people. The place was as old as most Manhattan residential apartments but well maintained, and with the City's housing problems the people presently dwelling in the flat might be the second or third to do so since Thaddie and his parents had lived there. Judging from what the Kendall boy had told Lewis, at least half a dozen years had passed since—well, Jesse wondered while a Mr. Epstein was admitting them to his flat, *since what*?

He asked the old man with the carefully combed handful of silver strands a different question. "What did you mean that the Madison family 'went to hell one night'?"

Epstein shrugged as he took a chair opposite the two policemen. "Pardon my hyperbole, it's a rather melodramatic way to say it. But," he paused, lips pursed, "what better way considering they were model tenants as well as the best kind of neighbors until . . . well, possibly *hell* came to *them*."

Kerrigan started to ask one of his dead-on direct questions, and Lewis spoke first. "What are the 'best kind,' Mt. Epstein?" He smiled carefully to indicate he didn't mean to be too challenging. Sometimes the indirect questions worked better.

"You never knew they were there," the old man said without the slightest pause or flicker of apology. "I had many friends, many relatives, now I have one or two of each and it is enough. The Madisons understood the difference between 'friends' and 'friendly,' until the night he killed her."

"That's quite a distinction, sir," Kerrigan murmured. Jesse glared at him.

"I meant only it isn't friendly to commit an act that brings authorities in the middle of the night. Nor neighborly," Epstein added. He offered a tight smile. "Possibly I am constitutionally, even genetically, incapable of finding authorities in the middle of the night 'friendly.' I should add, gentlemen, I do not know for a fact Mr. Madison killed Deborah.

"I know *only* for a fact she died that night in a great deal of commotion uncharacteristic to the family, and the children were taken elsewhere. And that I never saw any of them again."

Lewis said one word. " 'Deborah?' " He said it politely. Gently.

Epstein sensed the intent of the detective's question. Jesse could tell it by the way the old eyes lit up. "I have been widowed decades, but I can still see. When I cannot, I shall still hear a lovely woman's voice. When I cannot hear, I'll know her touch, please God she still grants it to me—whoever she is!" He uncrossed his legs, sat with small feet beneath turquoise trouser legs flat on the floor. "Deborah was lovely and, I insist, friendly, you should read nothing into that at all. Her husband's name was Marshall if you don't know that. I daresay you may have something in your files about the—the commotion."

"I daresay," Jesse Lewis said with an appreciative smile

and nod. Kerrigan was scribbling the name on a pad; already Lewis knew he'd never forget the name. Or Mr. Epstein's lead. "Do you remember the children's names?"

"Names, faces, voices. Ages I'm not so good with, with the little ones." He turned in the direction of the note-taking Kerrigan. "A girl, Caroline; a boy, Thaddeus. Old-fashioned names in what I thought was an old-fashioned family."

Even Lewis glanced at his assistant to share the pleasure. Marshall Madison, his possibly-murdered wife Deborah, a daughter Caroline, the boy whose given name matched the one supplied by young Mack Kendall. Real progress today!

"Please keep my card if you have anything more to tell us," Jesse said, rising and finding the pasteboard in his pocket. "You've been very—"

"Madison's *appearance*," Epstein interrupted, putting the card on the coffee table before him. He blinked several times. "His face."

Embarrassed by his omitted question, Jesse avoided Kerrigan's hard stare. How could they have forgotten to ask for that? "What about his face, sir? We could use a description."

"Alas, I won't be phoning you about *that*," Epstein said. With some difficulty he got to his feet to show them out. I merely believe it's strange that I never saw the man at all.

Kerrigan asked, "Never?"

"Never." The old man headed politely for the door, reached out to turn the knob for them. "We lived in this building for years and I never met the man." Epstein made a face. "Deborah—Mrs. Madison—said he was some sort of writer. Sometimes I'd hear him go out at night, or return, and I'd want to open my door to get a look. But that wouldn't have been . . . ." His voice trailed off.

"Friendly," Lewis finished for him, smiling, and shook hands sincerely.

The report about the death of Deborah Madison wasn't in the computer, but Jesse found it in a dusty box of files all of which were marked CLOSED CASES.

Except it wasn't truly closed, since no one had ever located her husband Marshall for questioning and the cause of death—aside from the way her wrists had been slashed—had *suicide* written in, with a question mark after it.

Old Epstein had been right, Jesse thought, staring at a photograph of the woman in life. She was lovely.

There was no photo of Marshall Madison, but he found two portraits of Caroline and Thaddeus as little kids. Neither would be much use, he figured, this much later.

They'd taken fingerprints of the missing Marshall from possessions of his left in the flat, and that was good, probably very useful with prints having been found at the scene of Hector Crossland's murder.

What was neither good nor bad, maybe, was the peculiar and unarguable fact Detective Lewis found in the dusty, closed-case file.

There was no indication Marshall Madison had ever existed prior to his marriage to Deborah. No history of his origin, education, job history. What in hell, Jesse mused, did *that* suggest?

3

The only thing that made Timothy madder than people who called him "Tim" was being told what to do. He didn't know why all the men and women he was acquainted with had decided to drive hacks, though even the *Taxi Times* sometimes made it clear they were often people whose job histories—or other records—made it hard for them to find better paying, indoor jobs. He never knew why his acquaintances were in the racket, unless they volunteered the information, because he never asked.

But he drove a taxi for a living because, around the time he'd lost his fourth so-called "superior" position, Timothy had realized he couldn't *stand* taking orders. Shit, he hadn't even liked obeying his parents, as a boy; they'd gotten so much on his case about "learning to eat balanced diets" that he'd grown up with the habit of seeing how long he could go without eating *anything*. It was why he was so skinny he looked maybe four, five inches taller than he really was.

Which, Timothy thought, was cool.

So he hadn't begun to drive his cab late at night, wasting his own dough on gas, because Jake Spencer had pleaded so hard for help, it had sounded like he was ordering folks around and certainly not because Sally Schindler had put in *her* two cents worth.

He was down here on Shit Row—Timothy's term for half the neighborhoods in the city where everything was run-down, including the people—because . . . well, because he hadn't anything better to do. Or because he was curious. Maybe, Timothy admitted as he turned a corner and eased his hack up a side street, because he might wind up helping a kid like himself. Somebody independent who just wouldn't take other people's orders. Or, if it came down to that, somebody like most people Timothy had known in his life, the kind who'd *better* find someone well-meaning to tell them what to do since they sure as hell couldn't do anything on their own!

The lanky iconoclast opened his eyes wide and whipped his head to the left as someone dashed across the street—right to left—in front of his taxi. Unless the person was wearing some new-style blouse with big pink polka-dots perfectly placed to draw maximum attention, she was a girl with her shirt open at the front and trailing behind her as she ran!

Slowing the cab to a crawl and cutting off his headlights, Timothy waited for what he fully expected to be right behind the runaway female.

His expectations were fulfilled within seconds when he spotted the male, sprinting along a sidewalk and, directly behind the partly naked girl, running out into the street—not fifteen feet in front of Timothy's hack.

He angled the cab steering wheel to the left, slammed on the accelerator, and had the satisfaction of watching the young man rebound off the fender like one of cabbie Air Willie Crawfield's bad hook shots. It couldn't've done him any lasting damage, but it sure as hell had slowed him down! Timothy got out, hustled around to where the guy was half doubled over trying to get his breath, asked innocently, "Call for a taxi, buddy?"

"No-I-didn't-call-for-no-fuckin'-taxi," Thrice gasped, relieved enough that a patrol car hadn't stopped him to recover his bravado instantly. "You that desp'rate for business, man? You coulda killed me!"

Timothy's hand was in his pocket, gripping a special knife he kept there for troublemakers. "Looked to me like you might be desperate enough to kill that girl you were chasing. You going to cool it now?"

"I didn't do nothin t' that broad, man," Thrice protested, wind back in place and straightening up. He pointed to the side of his face. "You wanta talk almost gettin' *killed*, look what that fuckin' kid did t' me!"

" 'Kid'?" Timothy said, pricking up his ears. "You don't mean that *girl*, do you?" For the first time he saw not only deep scratch marks but bruises on the younger man's cheek, jaw, and arms. Some of the scratches were seeping blood. Timothy got a pack of regular Luckies from his shirt pocket, offered one.

169

Thrice took both the unfiltered Lucky and a light from the cabbie's Djeep. Worse scratches, like claw marks, were embedded in the guy's hand. "No girl. Some shrimp from hell." He jerked his head to indicate the direction he'd come from. "These marks are from his pet rats, acourse." Thrice shuddered. "All the sweet thing 'n me had in mind was a little party." He added mournfully, "I don't even know where the squeeze lives."

"What a night," Timothy said. More sarcastically than he meant, he added, "You wouldn't mind showing me just where the little fella with the pet rats lives, would ya? I don't need to be pickin' up any fares where brats from hell and their trained—"

"Fuck you!" Thrice broke in with a snarl. He turned away from cab and cabbie, fed up. "I ain't takin' any more shit from nobody tonight. I hurt." He began walking away.

Dammit. Timothy thought, *I overplayed my hand.* "Hey, I'll give you a free lift if you tell me where you saw this kid, or something about him. How old was he? What'd he look like?"

Thrice stopped a dozen feet away, looked back. "My luck, you'd turn into a goddamn vampire or somethin'." He made a face, glanced at his partly smoked cigarette before tossing it into the street. "How the fuck you smoke cigs this strong?"

"Sorry I wasted it on you." Timothy walked back to the driver's side and the door he'd left open. "Smokes like this are for men, not wusses who run away from girls, midgets, and their pet mice."

That was his last effort to elicit the information he wanted, and all Thrice did was give Timothy the finger.

But before he called it quits for the night and went home, Timothy made a note of the general location above an ad in his current edition of *Taxi Times.*

A boy like Jake Spencer described probably wouldn't

survive long on these streets unless he got pretty smart and a helluva lot tougher than most kids his age, so the "shrimp from hell" this other street-smart guy had talked about definitely could be Thaddie Madison. Or, for all a skinny iconoclast with nowhere much to go knew, the "kid" *might* have been a midget who'd trained a bunch of rats as a new kind of guard animal!

Wish I'd gone after the running girl instead, Timothy thought wryly. *If she hadn't been too frightened or cost too much, I mightn't have had to sleep alone again tonight.*

4

Alone in her own room of the Spencers' Brooklyn home, Caroline sat on her bed with two plump pillows at her back, trembling. For the first time since she'd come to live with Jake and Camille and then to become their daughter, she wished deep down they weren't so nice.

If they weren't, they wouldn't respect her right to privacy. They'd follow her upstairs and come right into the bedroom and *make* her say what she hadn't wanted to say, because they surely wouldn't be able to believe it.

But then they wouldn't really be Pop and Mom anymore and there had already been too many total changes of personality on the part of people Care had loved for the child ever to want there to be anymore.

Caroline hugged her knees to her chest, relaxing a little, and wondered at how idly seeing an old Dracula movie with Pop—added to the awful stuff her adoptive father had told her about the murder of that man at the guardian home—had liberated so many of the most spooky memories she had about the night Mama died. Those things, along with having sort of "seen" her bro up on a roof somewhere, imagining she saw Father's picture back in her locket, and her *menarche*. Nearly all of what she had blocked out was back in her conscious brain, and Caroline supposed she knew why everything from the past was being restored to her mind: Because that ugly stuff *was* the past, and with her beginning to become a woman now, Caroline Spencer had to prepare for the *future*.

In a way, Care reasoned and smiled the little only-part-of-this-I-really-believe smirk that her pal B. J. said would get her lots of boyfriends someday, it was perfectly natural to have a bunch of weird ideas going into puberty. B. J.'d explained that most poltergeists showed up and began tossing things around the house only when the family living there had children in puberty. So instead of *her* mind doing anything truly harmful like that, Care was just throwing out her old memories. To make room for all the new ones she'd be putting *in*. It made pretty good sense, probably.

And what was also starting to make just as weird a sort of sense, Caroline realized, was why her birth mother boarded Thaddie and her up, then killed herself. Because Care now *knew*, without having the slightest idea how she had gotten the details together, that bad thing Father had done. The strange and terrible thing that had made Mama so scared for her and Thaddie that she had suffered a breakdown.

The girl broke her thinking off for a second when she realized tears were running down her cheeks like somebody'd left a faucet running and she hadn't even noticed at first. Instead of getting up to get a hankie or tissue, Care dried her eyes on a corner of her sheet. From the first floor she heard Mom and Pop talking real *seriously*, and it was too bad they had to talk and worry so much about her, *for* her. But the quiet, unobtrusive tears had started to flow not because Care was feeling sorry for herself, but because of another image her changing mind had just produced of almost-unchanged Thaddie living in a place that looked like

a whole army of poltergeists had trashed it, and a sad idea
had come into Caroline's mind: Maybe, with some kids—
probably boys—they didn't conjure up any kind of brain-
ghosts when they started into puberty. Maybe what got
them into trouble was that *they* were poltergeists themselves.

Get it all worked out for when Pop asks you again, Care
ordered herself, knotting the dampened corner of the bedsheet in one hand. *Otherwise, even he or Mom can't ever
believe what you remembered:*

Father and Mama had always been nice to Thad and her,
until what happened in the bathroom. Mama was real smart,
held a job, and paid most of the bills. Father was a genius,
and a writer, but he didn't like being around people because
he believed he was ugly, even if he wasn't.

Mama got a promotion and made Father mad—or scared
him—when she talked about getting a nicer place to live.
Maybe he was afraid she didn't love him anymore or something, it was hard to understand.

Father had Thaddie in the bathroom with him and they
both got naked, and—and Mama *saw* what they were doing.

Mama thought it was so evil she wanted to take both
Thaddie and her, Caroline, to live somewhere else, but Father said he wouldn't ever let her do that. And—this was
surmise in part, but Care was fairly sure of it—Mama'd
been afraid Father would do the same thing to his daughter
he'd done to his son.

Because Mama knew Father didn't want anybody but
them to *see* him, she realized the only way to get him to
leave their home was to wall the kids in (so he couldn't
get to her and Thad and take 'em along with him), phone
the police to report what she was *going* to do, then . . . well,
to lock herself in the bathroom and cut her wrists and
throat. Just die. Because Mama believed she wasn't strong

or clever enough to keep Father from coming for everyone someday and—well, making them do what he wanted, or something.

Reds and whites, Care remembered in the tiniest little-girl corner of her mind. Blood everywhere. On the pale skin of people she loved, Mama so white when most of her blood was just . . . gone.

And now Father was searching for Thaddie and maybe for her, evidently leaving ribbons and pools of red and white behind—because, at least partly, other people had seen his face. Her poor, brilliant, crazy, handsome Father who'd loved them all so much. *Too* much.

Tears were streaming again and Care did not care about that. Watching the old movie with Pop, she'd known at last why her birth mother hadn't dared let Father take her bro and herself to raise and why, helpless to defend them directly, she had taken her life. She *knew* what Father had done in the bathroom that horrible night, even knew in a way why Thaddie would be stuck forever on the borderline between childhood and manhood—and why Father was willing to kill the people he didn't love in order to *find* Thaddie and her.

As she realized she wasn't even sure she wanted her Pop and Mom to believe what she had to tell them and help the police catch Father, Care lay down flat and pulled the covers up over her head. *"But Father will find us,"* her bro at age six insisted once more in the child's agonized memory. *"Cause he can do just about anything he wants!"*

5

Enid Godby seated Marshall Madison in the same chair she had offered to his son, Thaddeus. How long ago that seemed now! Although she had tried politely to take his coat, he had declined just as politely. "So you're the father of that adorable child," she said. "I've wondered what's happened to him."

"As have I," Marshall said. He had the most ordinary of voices, Enid noted. But in noting it she also realized both that he formed his sentences and phrases in a manner that sounded old-fashioned, even courtly, and that he possessed a slight accent—so slight a one that she imagined one of two circumstances was the case: Either he had worked very hard to eliminate it or he had left the place of his birth so long ago that the accent was merely disappearing at last. "I am hoping you will be good enough," the man went on, "to aid me in finding Thaddeus. And his sister."

Enid felt her heartbeat accelerate for the first time since she had learned her guest's identity and told herself to be calm. She had already decided her days were numbered, so the only thing she had to fear was death itself. "I'm afraid I retired some time ago from my position at the guardian home. Of course, I did not bring any of the confidential records with me." There the careful emphasis she'd given the word "confidential" would make any gentleman drop the subject. Whether or not a murderer could ever qualify for that description Enid had no idea.

"I'm certain you would never be guilty of such a crime," Marshall said reassuringly. "However, your personnel file was on the desk of Mr. Crossland at the home in SoHo. Just inside it was a dated note with the inscription 'Madison, T.' in what seemed to be a handwriting matching other notes by your successor." The caller shifted his position slightly in the chair, enough to suggest to Enid how tense and possibly impatient he was. "It would not be unreasonable, perhaps, to believe you had made contact with Mr. Crossland about my son."

That's how he found where I live, Miss Godby realized.

"Indeed, I *did* telephone him. To express my concern about the boy and to see if—"

"You too," Marshall said with an inflection of enormous sadness, "knew my Thaddeus had been living on the streets of this cruel and chaotic city." It was a flat statement.

Regret and a feeling of guilt just as great swept through Enid. There could be no way to explain to the normal father of a child taken by the state why she had not initiated some action after learning Thaddie had run away from his foster home. How much less likely were her chances of explaining to a man who had killed to locate his son! "At least I tried to interest someone in searching for Thaddeus. And"— Enid spoke these next words with as much conviction as she had ever mustered "I truly do *not* know where you can find your boy."

Marshall did not answer at once, nor move.

Then he leaned forward in the chair, spatterings of Hector Crossland's blood like bullet holes on his white shirt. Till then he had sat back, the collar of his suit jacket turned up around the lower portion of his face, and Miss Godby had not seen him clearly. Now she did, and it was instantly apparent to her that he wore some sort of mask—or parts of a mask—that kept her from knowing what he really looked like. In this room with only a floor lamp turned on for illumination, the man seemed ashen—he reminded Enid of some of the many corpses it had been her misfortune to see in her long life—and the vestige of a blond mustache was weirdly askew on his upper lip.

"But you *can* tell me where," Marshall said flatly, his tone of voice brooking no argument, "I may find my daughter. My bright, beautiful Caroline. And you *will*."

The furnace whirred back into action at the second he completed his threat, and Enid jumped at the sudden sound. Something tied to the normality of her heat coming on— the *homeness* of it—and something about the sense of invasion she had begun to feel brought the stark truth out of Miss Godby. "No, I cannot tell you," she said, "and *I will not*."

He sat watching her another moment, silently, nothing in his face alive which Enid could see. Yet for that fleeting time she thought he had responded to her candor and integrity, in some fashion understood and accepted it, and might just depart her already violated home.

Even when he rose to his feet she believed there existed a slender chance that this life-stealer might do exactly that.

Instead of moving toward the foyer and front door, however, he started drifting slowly, steadily, and almost reluctantly toward Enid. A reason must have existed why she did nothing to escape him, did not even experience a qualm of fear; Enid could not have given it.

Madison's thumb and fingers around her neck, his icy palm against her pulsing throat—it was the first time a man had touched her anywhere in many years. His touch was gentle, he did not squeeze, and she let her soft eyelids descend.

"I respect courage, I admire it," Madison said, crooning the words like a lullaby. "Once, when I thought I had lost all else to please me save—sheer sustenance—I believed it might be the one worthwhile quality of humankind." He stopped and did not begin again until she opened her eyes and saw him. "But this is not courage, Miss Godby, is it?" His hot stare and the faintest movement of his thumb at the center of her throat were like the prologues to an unsought, greater intimacy. "Can it be that I am once more—after all these years—encountering a *different* human quality?"

"Not different." It was hard to go on meeting his stare; the surprising stink of him was bad enough, but the experiences of his life were in his red-rimmed eyes, and they wanted her to participate vicariously in them. "Not different or new, I'm sure. Perhaps, these days, not many people have the beliefs I have.''

Marshall's eyes darted away. He saw what he had hoped he would see, and he held her throat with one hand while reaching out with the other. He showed her his prize. ''In this address book I will discover the information I seek concerning my daughter's whereabouts, will I not?''

Even though the man had not tightened his grip or raised his voice, Enid blinked. Just once. She hadn't been able to see what he was reaching for. But she knew that her automatic honest reaction had given him the answer he desired.

''You know, of course,'' said Marshall, ''I was obliged to end the existence of the bureaucrat who replaced you at the home. How else could I know of you and learn your address? And because we have had this conversation, madam, you have not only some impression of my appearance but would not hesitate to contact the parties fortunate enough to be in a position to avail themselves of my daughter's charms.''

Enid was finding the strange man's near-caress of her throat, and talking above his outstretched, muscular arm, extremely tiresome. ''You must kill me too. I understand that.'' Then, on impulse, she peered deeply into his eyes, wanting to contact any vagrant quality of mercy. ''I beg of you not to harm the children. In a way, I think, they aren't precisely 'yours,' that no parent possesses his children.''

Marshall relaxed his grip, smiled beneath the sprinkling of lifeless yellow hairs, ''How jolly it might be to debate the merits of your position, but fruitless, ultimately, given your choice of words. They *are* and shall *remain* mine. As for harming them, Miss Godby . . . Enid . . . that is the furthest thing from my intentions. To make myself clear, I'm so impressed with you that I am willing to offer you the *same fate* which will be Caroline's and Thaddeus'!''

"I'm old enough to be your mother," Enid snapped, "and that is a *ridiculous* insult!"

He put back his head to laugh. "Dear Enid, permit me to explain and rid ourselves of these misunderstandings for good. In exchange for the name, address, and telephone number of the people holding my daughter"—he placed his hands on her shoulders, lowered his face until their eyes were inches from each other's—"you may come with my family and me . . . through the centuries. Together, we shall glide through the years side by side, needing virtually nothing but ourselves—*almost* nothing else—to be content."

Involuntarily, Enid gasped. She had suspected the fellow was a crazy brute, but it had not occurred to her he might be mad as a hatter. Now the lunatic was stroking her jaw, the side of her neck. "Nonsense, I'm much too old to want to remain in this body all that time. My arthritis hurts badly enough now; I hate the idea of how it would feel just twenty years from now, let alone one hundred years!"

"I salute you, then, Enid," Marshall said with a smile that twitched with emotion. "Farewell!"

He used only one hand to break her neck, being as careful as possible to complete the execution unerringly and as swiftly as humanly possible.

He wept openly, unashamedly—he could not recall when he had last shed such copious tears—as he laid her body on the floor. Gently. Though it was torment for him, he stooped to kiss her lips, once, finding neither blood on them nor a final exhalation of sweet breath.

At no point did he release the address and phone book he held tightly in the other hand.

Chapter Eight

1

Heading for home, which was marginally what he had come to consider the loft he took from the man called Buddy, Marshall plumbed the depths of his emotions even while he longed to be truly alone.

The principal emotion that tormented him as he slumped on the backseat of a cab he had summoned a few blocks from Enid Godby's home was one of self-pity. He recognized it for what it was and despised himself for the weakness, but there it was. *Why* had he had no choice except to kill the first person he'd met in months whom he liked, even admired? *Why* did a woman who was independent enough to know her own mind and values and honest enough to realize she would be miserable if she compromised them have to be the next stepping-stone in his moral and diligent quest to retrieve his own children?

Possibly he did not put himself in the shoes of other

people as often as he should—Marshall decided he ought to concede that possibility, however justified he generally was for hewing to his own course—but this time he really believed destiny had treated poor Enid as shabbily as it usually did him.

For the next few minutes he indulged in an intellectual exercise of genuinely attempting to place himself in aging Miss Godby's mind, now and then quietly weeping yet more tears as he practiced his empathy: She did not know Marshall Madison from Adam—in reality, he had simply shown up at her front door, and less-direct-thinking persons of both sexes would not even have admitted him—and had in fact known of her successor's sudden death. For any gentlewoman, it would have been hard indeed to imagine how thoroughly Crossland had earned his (highly innovative, even enjoyable to behold) murder or to anticipate the logic of what Marshall had done. Dear Enid had wished only to protect Caroline as well as the fortunate swine who'd taken cold advantage of her true father's misfortune, and—well, would he not have done the same?

That thought excited Marshall, momentarily made him forget how itchy and foul the mask was becoming, how much his eyes were starting to burn. It seemed entirely reasonable that if his own early life had taken a rather different turn and a stranger with outrageous claims (and no evidence or credentials) had presented himself at the Madison home, then demanded to know the whereabouts of children Marshall had sheltered, he would instantly have killed the caller!

It wasn't dear Enid's fault that she had no defense against me, Marshall thought. *Particularly when no one does.*

The cabdriver was also a woman, would wonders never cease, and her name—S. Schindler—was printed on the taxi license she was properly displaying. He instructed her to stop within a block of his residence. One of the routine precautions, as automatic to him now as breathing or donning clothing before leaving his residence. Before alighting, Marshall patted his chest as a double check that dear Enid's phone directory hadn't been dislodged; although he had slipped it under his shirt with the assurance that his belt would prevent it from falling on down and through, Miss Godby's passing would be a tragic waste if the book were lost. He planned to study every entry, contact everyone recorded in it if that proved necessary. For Thaddeus, Marshall knew—unable to dwell on this insight—time was of the essence.

It was just at the last moment that Marshall remembered to turn up his collar again and try to duck down, turtlelike, as the taxi's interior lights came on. After the furry warmth of the darkness in the vehicle the sudden brightness hurt Marshall's eyes and he felt awkward and fumbly as he drew out the money to pay S. Schindler. "Thank you for refraining from idle chatter during the ride," he said, thrusting the bills toward the woman and getting out of the cab as quickly as he could. "So many New Yorkers drone on and on."

Sally started to make the observation that he wasn't from the city, then, and ask where he was from. Instead, she called out to the passenger whose back was already to her, "You gave me twenty dollars too much, buddy."

Marshall pretended not to hear her. *I'm not Buddy*, he thought, striding swiftly away. *Buddy was the blessedly fortunate fellow who used to occupy my loft.*

Out of sight of the cab and driver, however, Marshall knotted, unfisted, and once more knotted his hands. Clumsy not to have paid more attention to the currency he'd given her. It was sufficient to represent a true if minor risk, largely because the drab female behind the wheel would recall such a generous tip. Marshall preferred for living people to remember nothing of him. He would have killed Ms. Schindler were she still around just then.

Modern human beings, he told himself with a rising fury born in part of weariness, were indescribably *obsessed* with economics! The world was filled with moments of ecstasy for the taking; and today's people preferred accumulating scraps of paper—and the knowledge that a public institution that theoretically could collapse on any given day was *retaining* those papers ''for'' them!

Marshall walked the block to the building with his loft, his vision inclined to become uncertain and to blur as his long and busy night drew to a close and the sure premonition of daylight lay on the New York streets. Even the most well-meaning of people kept horning in, pressing him to act in ways his marriage to Deborah had all but eliminated—and half the time it was because of bureaucrats and others who protected their pusillanimous, paltry pockets of dominion like jackals, while the rest of the time it was the human mania over *money!*

An hour's rest, perhaps two, that's what I need, Marshall told himself as he started up the stairs—a respite from *people's self-induced psychoses.* Then he would find his exquisite little Caroline, and the beloved son who was so much like him. No one and nothing could stand in his way!

2

Detective Lewis's badge and service automatic were all the way across the room on a chair, and so were his clothes. Most of them, at least. Some hadn't made the chair when he tossed his pants and shorts in that direction, and the one sock he'd managed to get off was on the floor, midway between that other stuff and the bed. Where Jesse, just about as off duty as a man can get, was lying if not precisely resting.

It was very, very late at night, and Jesse finally had the lady with him just where he wanted her. And how. That was very fine indeed, because the lady also had Detective Lewis just where *she* wanted him. And how. *And* where.

Of course the phone rang.

The lady looked down the length of her body in quest of Jesse's face, though its precise location was definitely not a mystery to her. "You *aren't* going to answer that thing," she asked, running her tongue fastidiously over her lower lip, "are you?"

"Got to." He swung his legs around her, dropped his feet to the cold floor, and rose. On his way to the jangling telephone he glanced back, grinning. "Only an Irish boy named Kerrigan had my number here, case you're wondering; not my captain. You wouldn't want me to mess up Afro-American and Irish relations, would you?"

'Well, not as long as he's *black* Irish," replied the lady, rolling over on her stomach. She had already promised Lewis no one would be calling her that late at night.

Jesse kept looking at his lady while he grunted into the phone mouthpiece, knowing his adorably bifurcated view would allow him to pick up where they left off. "You better have something worth saying to me, Kerrigan," he said instead of hello.

Detective Lewis said nothing else while he listened, intently. He caught himself nodding once as if Kerrigan could see him, a notion not pleasing to Jesse. "Got you," he said at last, loathing the next thing he was going to say. "Meet you there in thirty."

Openly listening, the lady rolled back over, the sight of her this way positively guaranteeing Jesse's ability to resume their prior activity. But she appeared distinctly displeased by what she had heard. "You're meeting him in half an hour? What could be *that* important, Jess?''

"Remember the murder case we're investigating?'' the detective said, lying atop the lady again but with his hands and arms extended so he could see her face. "We have a fingerprint match. We know for a fact now who the killer is.''

"But thirty minutes,'' she argued, nevertheless raising her hips searchingly from the bed—''that means you have only another fifteen or twenty minutes for *me*!''

Jesse stopped keeping himself from her, found other uses for his arms and hands. "It isn't how much of anything there is, including time. You ought to know that.'' Pleased with several developments, he laughed from sheer exuberance. "Everything's a case of how good the matchups are, like in sports. Here, let me show you . . .''

3

It was Henry Campbell's difficult task to keep an attentive eye on the propriety of everything happening everywhere. He knew that, accepted the impossible load as his lot in life, partly because there was no one else riding herd on society's wrongdoers with quite the same vigilance he mustered, partly because Henry had no other clear-defined lot in life.

Of course there was his actual job, the handful of meager duties there in the building that provided his income along with a free apartment. For a man of Henry Campbell's abilities and high standards, however—a single man with no other people making demands on his time, a man with great sensitivity to the common outrages perpetrated by run-of-the-mill, desensitized brutes in whatever direction he looked—maintaining the building and collecting rent was not nearly enough.

That was why he expended virtually all his considerable leisure time reading newspapers and magazines, clipping the more offensive articles, and writing so many letters to the editor that his postage expense was staggering and everyone working at the closest post office knew him by face and name. That was why he belonged to all the right organizations—and knew just how to respond when others occasionally accused him of censorship—and often stayed up late to watch the talk shows and films on cable television. What Henry saw frequently shocked him to the core, obliged him to stay up later still to fire off furious warnings of boycott to sponsors, network and local program directors.

It was exhausting work, even for a man in his late thirties who stood six foot six and weighed more than two hundred pounds. *One day,* Henry thought at times, *I'll probably just collapse from the burden and they'll find my body rotting in the apartment, one limp hand still clinging to the computer keyboard.* The thought gave Henry immense joy, created a warm spot within that was nearly like that of certain erotic reactions he remembered from the time he had dated women and almost married one.

After that, after Julie informed him she "wouldn't marry a control freak like you if you were the last man on earth," Henry had fallen into the habit of believing he hated women. For a period he was generally able now to screen away from his conscious mind completely, he'd done things he came to see as horrid, deplorably animalistic. It might nearly have been the end of the Henry Campbell who had always viewed himself as the most righteous, ethically broad minded true liberal he'd ever known—

Except for the fact that he realized, at some point in the eighties, he was no longer alone! On college campuses and elsewhere a new drumbeat could be heard if one listened intently—a low, steady cadence for the march of more and more people just like Henry Campbell who intended to take a firm stand against the casual and cruel comments of confident cretins with no higher aspirations than to master their narrow interests, take positions in business (and in a society deaf to the anguished pleas of those excluded from those positions for the same old reasons!), marry, and settle down! It was a time of epiphany for Henry, a time when he began to see women in a wholly new light. Instead of being exposed as he once might have desired it, they were revealed as *society's victims*—just as he was! Both Julie and he—of *course* she had despised him, he was trying to control the way she dressed, ate, thought!—were victims of the processes and hypocritical teachings of generations that placed accomplishment and the search for power ahead of societally correct behavior, thought and fact accumulation ahead of human feelings!

He had known it the instant he began to join the brave new organizations, to read absolutely everything with keen alertness to social slights of any stripe, and to carry signs in parades with the kind of people he would once have avoided like the plague that his whole life was changed—forever! Even if he never formed a close friendship with anyone else again, and one day died in the line of duty, Henry Campbell would not be alone.

Up early this morning as he strove always to be these immoral days, Henry was preparing this month's collection of renter checks for deposit in the building owner's account, when it occurred to him that something quite odd was going on.

He raised his head to stare upward as if he might magically succeed in looking into the loft occupied by Buddy Whatever-it-was.

The oddness he had discerned stemmed from the fact that, though payments had been made with as much regu-

larity as ever, envelopes containing *cash* for the loft were
being left in his superintendent's box—

And Henry had no recollection of catching even a
glimpse of Buddy for a long, long time.

So . . . what was going on up there?

Rising, Henry reflected on the matter for a few moments.
It didn't matter in the slightest if the tenant had taken in a
gay friend, so long as Buddy wasn't subletting the loft. It
also wouldn't matter if Buddy was living with a female
companion, except it seemed Henry's duty both to know
the fact and to make sure the woman was not in any manner
being harassed or molested. Other things, too, could be happening—things of a potentially criminal nature which
might upset the owner of the building if he, instead of
Henry, learned about them.

Henry slipped on his shoes, nodding.

His duties were clear. He had no choice but discovering
what was going on.

The realization brought a warm spot to the enormous
super as he exited his flat. He was so excited he forgot to
lock the door after him.

4

The rats left Thaddie completely alone the rest of the night.

They ignored him the next morning, too, although Thad
caught glimpses of them here and there before he went out,
and that concerned him.

For a moment he wondered if he had hurt their feelings
by knocking them off Thrice's back so the guy could escape. But rats, Thad remembered, didn't seem to have any
feelings. Not enough of any kind people had to make any
difference, unless it was a wavery sorta loyalty that lasted

right up until a person—even another rat—made the mistake of taking them for granted.

So if they weren't hurt or pissed at him, what was wrong?

Ignoring them, he found a hotel room without the black X he put on the door to remind him the toilet was stinky-full, and went inside for his morning ablutions. He had to get some money today for food, not just because he was hungry and nearly broke again but because Robby and the others—in their current bad mood—had to be fed. When he got done up here, he'd pick out one of his best sweaters and pair of jeans to don before going to work. He had a neat new dodge he thought would go over better if he looked sharp.

Glad the old hotel had gotten in a supply of moist towelettes before closing down, Thaddie began to wash his face above the washbasin, automatically staring into the mirror.

Startled not by what he saw, but by what he didn't see, he reached for another towelette and, believing he must have gotten something in his eyes, scrubbed at them. Then he looked back at his reflection.

And that was the problem, because Thaddie's whole face and head were all fuzzy in the mirror.

Then, too, the boy thought, squinting over and over to clear his vision, his eyes were now his most noticeable feature and the whites of them were kind of reddish.

Thad shook his head at his reflection with some anger and more fear, his lips pressed together. The impression he had was that he suddenly looked different to himself, maybe older too, but definitely a little sick. "Damn old Thrice and Sweet Thing!" he cursed them aloud, turning from the basin and drying his face and hands. "Comin' in here where they don't belong and givin' me a cold!" His eyes even smarted some, he realized, suddenly frightened.

Being by yourself wasn't as terrible as Thaddie supposed

a lot of people imagined it was. Being by yourself if you
were sick, though—well, nobody else was going to come
bring him food or, worse by far to consider, medicine, if
he got *really* sick.

"If I had to change," he said aloud while he was going
back downstairs to the lobby, "why couldn't I have got
bigger?"

Two of the rats were messing around with some scrap
of garbage or maybe the deceased Rodge and peered, frozen, up the stairs as Thad headed down them.

They turned and ran.

Which wasn't their style around him, whom they knew
so well and might have believed was bringing food to them.
"What's goin' on?" Thad demanded, hands on hips.
"What the hell is *wrong* with you guys?"

He had his answer when Robby himself, hearing Thad's
commanding tone of voice, came scampering into view.

Below the teenage boy who remained on the stairs,
Robby, the pack leader, rolled on his back like a puppy sur-
rendering to its master or a fully grown dog, indicating his
sense of helplessness, absence of hostility and—worship.
The rat was quivering, trembling.

Robby's scared of me, Thaddeus Madison realized. *It's
like he's saying* I'm *the real leader of the pack!*

5

Sagging with tiredness, eager to get some rest before he
combed Enid Godby's phone book for Caroline's location,
Marshall stripped off his clothing as he crossed the loft.
The blood-stained shirt would go out with the trash but,
while the rest of his garb was salvageable, he left everything including his underwear where it landed. Possibly
some of Buddy's late friends or family members who'd

stopped by to see him wore clothes Marshall's size; he would have to check that out among those garments he had not yet worn or discarded. A Laundromat, happily, was just around the corner.

He poked around in the refrigerator awhile, found some cold meat on a saucer that seemed suitable for a snack. It was his all but invariable custom to have his biggest meal at dinner, when the sun had gone down, and he was usually in bed asleep at this early hour. But the day before had been a busy one, and often an upsetting one, and Marshall had never taken time to dine. Perhaps a bite now would chase his headache and ease the old soreness in his eyes. *If only you and our children were still here, sweet Deborah, he told his dead wife, I could still be the most peace-loving and civil of men.*

"Come, Marshall," he ordered himself, sitting naked on a chair in what had been the late Buddy's dining area. "Such pointless emotionalism will only make you weep again and exacerbate the vision problem." Relaxing, he nibbled quietly but hungrily at his snack and peeled away the nail instead of choosing to eat it. When finished, he would have many refrigerated and fastidiously labeled bottles of liquid with which to wash the brief meal down.

A combination of sleep, properly subdued lighting, and the very particular diet which Marshall forbade himself much of the time was all that would be needed to restore the usual acuity of his vision; he knew that. What he couldn't be certain about was the extent to which he had worsened the condition with experimentation over the years. The thing was, no physician could read more astutely or be more opportunistic than he, and, as certain chemical advances were made, he had procured them by any means possible and dosed himself.

Intriguingly enough, most of those modern potions had truly brought him comfort for some time before, unfailingly, the adverse reactions promised by science set in with a vengeance.

He had used Sectral, an acebutolol prescribed for high blood pressure and irregular heartbeat, and the solution had helped his eye problem until the expected anxiety and periodic confusion made Marshall drop it. The amiloride and hydrochlorothiazide mixture, Moduretic, had helped his vision by day but also brought mood swings and obliged him to wear sunglasses most of the time. Worse, when he had scratched a finger, he'd found it difficult to stop the bleeding except by sucking consistently on the wound. More or less reluctantly giving that one up, he'd experimented with eyedrops that were an advancement over solutions Marshall, as a very young man, had been urged to take: Digoxin had made a halo around most lighted objects, which Marshall thought beneficial due to the psychologically angelic inference—but when he read that it might lead to night blindness, he quit it entirely.

Oddly enough, he'd felt a real soothing of his eyes during his marriage to Deborah, when he began trying a chlordiazepoxide and clidinium combination. During that best of times he'd had little reason to go outside. Now, however, such drops capable of making one's eyes sensitive to sunlight were unthinkable to use; more business than ever before needed to be done during the day.

Now he would simply have to suffer his recurrent problem stoically and remind himself each time that he would soon be able to return to the peace and quiet of his own dwelling.

Along with, Marshall thought as he went back to the fridge and took a great gulp directly from a bottle labeled BUDDY, the inevitably coming, direct luxury of his own unique diet.

Marshall lowered the bottle without returning it to the refrigerator, making a face. For an instant he thought somebody had been in the loft and tampered with his food and drink. But then he saw the yellow hairs on the bottle where his mouth had been, and smiled. Bits of the souvenir mustache had come off—almost as if the former tenant were seeking some sort of reunification—and a hair or two had gotten into Marshall's mouth.

He started to replace the bottle in the fridge, mindful that only a few drops remained in that particular container, and an unexpected, quite sudden hammering on the door to the loft nearly made him drop and waste the rest of the irreplaceable liquid.

Livid as well as shaking minutely, Marshall strode across the floor and tore the door open. "Yes?" he demanded, glancing up.

A much taller, more powerfully built man stood just outside. The stranger wore an expression of astonishment, but for the moment Marshall neither knew why nor cared. "I-I'm Henry Campbell," the large man stammered. "I'm the one who collected the—"

"I know who you are," Marshall snapped. "What I don't know is what you want."

"Well, I *d-did* want to come in," Henry said hesitantly. He finished, lamely, "About your payments."

Marshall considered the request without really feeling any concern or, for that matter, curiosity. "Come in, then," he said, turning and gesturing for Campbell to follow him. "But I've been up all night and I need to catch a few winks before beginning the day."

Staring at Marshall's naked, retreating form, and halfway expecting to find other people present in the loft, Henry entered. After a pause he closed the door.

"I can't imagine you have any complaints about the way I've promptly brought down to you the outrageous sum you ask for the privilege of living in this hovel." Marshall annoyed by the intrusion, did not offer a chair. "Mayhap you

193

have come to tell me the payments have been reduced?''

Henry Campbell couldn't figure out where to direct his gaze. This scarcely courteous stranger, as muscular as himself but smaller and lighter, was offputting in his unabashed nudity. Just as discomfiting for Henry was the man's face, because something was wrong with it. A discreet fifteen feet from Marshall, he had the impression that bits of the unknown fellow's face were sloughing off and that his crookedly growing yellow mustache was—well, shedding. Then the possibility that the man possessed some dreadful disease occurred to the sensitized Campbell and, though he went no nearer, he was forcefully reminded of his own beliefs.

''I'm terribly sorry to have come at a bad time,'' Henry said. ''And, no, there's no price reduction—though I'm familiar with a number of agencies that can be of assistance to those who are . . .'' He sensed there was no way to complete his remark without infringing upon the stranger's privacy.

''To those who are—*what*?'' Marshall asked sharply. ''I am certainly not indigent or helpless.'' The headache that had begun after Miss Godby's death was back. He truly required rest now. ''I have sought nothing here but to be left alone. So, I repeat, Mr. Campbell: to those who are *what*?''

''To those who aren't Buddy!'' Campbell answered desperately, recalling why he'd gone up there. ''I don't wish to be rude, sir, but you aren't. You are definitely *not* Buddy!''

''Well, you have me there.'' Pleased they were getting down to it, Marshall smiled and glanced at himself. For the first time he realized he had donned no clothes before answering the rap at the door. ''I am indisputably not Buddy. *But*—Buddy knows I'm *here*.''

Henry relaxed somewhat, let his heavy shoulders sag.

The other man, after looking about, had found an apron and was tying it around his waist. For Campbell, it almost made this a domestic scene. "It's just that it would have been the correct thing to notify us you were minding Buddy's place while he was away." Henry sniffed, grew aware of what a strong room deodorizer the stranger used. It was nearly sickening. "There are certain rules, you see. Regulations."

Marshall's eyes blinked with pain. Unbidden, a distinct image of Crossland, the officious bureaucrat at the SoHo home, flashed through Marshall's mind. It was Crossland at his worst from Marshall's standpoint too, because the human bottleneck was *living* in the mental recollection. For precisely a count of three Marshall considered the ramifications of a new idea that occurred to him.

Then, without haste, he turned back to Henry Campbell. "But Buddy isn't 'away,' " Marshall told him. Feeling a pinch when the corners of his mouth turned up in a reflexive grin, he began to pull the residue of yellow hairs from his upper lip. "Gone, yes," Marshall explained. "Technically . . . not 'away.' "

Campbell observed what the unidentified interloper was doing, even grimaced when it appeared that a layer of gray skin came off with the mustache. But each person had his or her own lifestyle and that need not concern Henry, he decided. Pulling himself to his full and usually intimidating height, he took two steady, businesslike steps forward. "I believe it's my duty to take a look around the loft, sir."

"I suppose it is." Marshall stepped aside, bowed slightly, gave permission with a motion of his open left palm. "May I propose that you begin at the back and work your way forward?"

"Sounds quite proper," replied Henry, moderately warming to the man's show of cooperativeness. Yet other questions were forming in his mind as he drew level with the refrigerator, almost to the screen beyond it. He had become dimly aware he still had not gotten the stranger's name or any sort of explanation as to why he was there and Buddy was—gone.

Then he was anything but dimly aware of the staggering stench assailing his nostrils. Trying to stay as politic as possible under the circumstances but so revolted by the smell he momentarily couldn't walk around the screen, Henry noticed the refrigerator door wasn't tightly closed. Hesitantly, he glanced over his shoulder at the man whose face seemed to be . . . changing . . . with every bit of skin—makeup?—he peeled away. "Pardon me for pointing it out, but I believe something in there may be spoiling."

"Surely not." Marshall edged closer, as though to check, but neither opened nor closed the fridge.

"Well," Henry revised his polite suggestion, "may be going *bad*."

"I believe it's much too late for anything in there to go bad," Marshall said with the utmost equanimity. He smiled at the big man with shining, bloodshot eyes.

"Well, then," Henry said, reaching out an impulsive hand to tug the refrigerator door open, "it's just plain *dead*!"

The contents of the fridge were in full view as the dutiful little light went on.

"Now, that's an observation with which I can agree," Marshall said from beside Henry Campbell.

An entire segment of shelving had been removed from the refrigerator to make room for row after row of bottles, Henry saw. Bottles with labels pasted on them, each one bearing a message of hand-printed information and identification. He saw that in some instances people's names were the primary data on the tags; others, though, featured more mysterious intelligence: Male or female, friend of Buddy followed by two figures that could have represented an individual's approximate age, and, Henry thought wildly, the date when this—somewhat peculiar—stranger met the person. His increasingly anxious gaze scanned label after label, took in identifications of BUDDY'S SISTER, BUDDY'S UNCLE, BUDDY'S MOTHER.

Henry started to back up and hastily close the refrigerator door, but the other, the naked man, was too close to keep from running up against him. Clearing his throat, Henry used his index finger to point at no particular bottle filled with red liquid. "You sure do like your tomato juice!" he said heartily, possibly as nonjudgmentally as he'd ever managed during his sensitized existence.

Marshall's real brows rose and he nearly smiled. Instead, he said soothingly, "You haven't looked closely enough, Mr. Campbell." He waited for the other to recoil from the ugliness of his true face. When nothing like that happened, Marshall thrust his bare arm past Henry to indicate the all but drained bottle bearing Buddy's name itself on the label. "As I said, gone . . . but not forgotten."

"I *don't* understand," Henry said flatly. The words spilled from his mouth before he could stop them. They were actually a lie, of course.

Marshall shouldered him aside. "Look," he said, reaching into a lower level of the refrigerator. He showed Campbell one, then another package wrapped in butcher paper. Each had a hand-scribbled identifying label similar to those on the bottles. "Look!" Marshall directed his uninvited visitor, raising and exposing additional—and similar— packages of meat.

Henry's mouth opened, but he couldn't conceive what to say, and when the man in the apron caught his arm in an amazingly tight grip and half dragged him around to the far side of the refrigerator, knocking the screen away, there was definitely nothing Henry Campbell could imagine saying. *"Look!"* Marshall commanded.

197

All Henry could do was stare, smell the rotting odor that soared to his nose as Marshall Madison then kicked aside a new covering to show him the skeletal bones stacked waist-high on the floor, and wish he had written another letter to the editor instead of going up to the loft.

That the bones were human was unmistakable. Though most of the legs, arms, and hips had been picked clean, other portions of the species' anatomy had been ruled unfit by the man who had replaced Buddy, and drooped or sagged intact.

"I will have to take some of these away now," Marshall said, more a statement of intent or mental note for himself than a regretful comment, "If there is to be room for an oversize gentleman like you." He smiled, then jumped lightly, lithely, and easily locked his hands around Henry's throat. His thumbs were digging in, his heels pressing deeply in preparation for a single tremendous snap.

But in spite of the fact that Marshall hadn't meant to underestimate the strength of the much larger man, Campbell's defensive instincts brought both arms up at once, throwing Marshall to one side.

Then he was bolting for the door in stark terror.

His bulk combined with his prolonged physical indolence to keep Henry from summoning anywhere near the speed required to reach the door before Marshall was upon him.

Wielding a femur quickly snatched up from the bone pile, Marshall had crossed the loft floor with an alacrity that was virtually supernatural. When he brought the improvised weapon down on the back of Henry's skull, the fellow hit the floor instantly in a shower of fragmented bone—conscious but deeply stunned. Face on the floor, he saw ten or eleven inches in front of him a still-flopping scrap of recognizable human flesh that had come loose from the breaking bone.

"Jackals! Guarding your pusillanimous, paltry dominions!'' Marshall said from astride Henry's broad back, fingers scrabbling for purchase beneath the big man's chin. ''Horning in, *forcing* me to act—all of you, *obsessed* with your little wants—while I am left with my magnificent needs you shall never understand!''

Instead of merely breaking the interloper's neck as he had planned in his initial attack, Marshall planted his knees just so and then began pulling back on the head with his powerful fingers locked beneath Campbell's chin. It took longer that way, and it was harder; but the man had interrupted all his plans, spoiled his sleep, interrogated him as if he were a common criminal, and, worst of all, treated Marshall as if he might be as slow-thinking and cowardly as ''Henry Campbell'' himself! Simply reciting the litany of the fellow's bad manners and ignorant mistakes lent renewed strength and stamina to Marshall's task. *Fascinating*, he thought, *how far back the head can go before the light in the eyes dims! And how one can see the Adam's apple in the throat bob into view like fruit rising to the surface in a child's game . . .*

It wasn't till the light went out that Marshall remembered his detestation of dying and his admiration, even periodic yearning, for the death state.

When he was able to stop crying—staring Henry's face was as wet as if the fellow had drowned in his bathtub—it no longer seemed quite right to Marshall to deal with the man's remains as he had the other unbidden visitors to the loft. Because he knew where the fellow had lived, Marshall decided the proper thing was to leave the Campbell body where, while living, he had presumably spent his favorite hours.

It seemed a providential sign that he was behaving aright when Marshall had carried the hulk on one shoulder downstairs to the Campbell flat and found the door left open.

He arranged the huge, pale corpse in a chair at his computer, left one slowly stiffening hand lying on the keyboard.

Marshall went swiftly but wearily back up to his loft naked without knowing Henry's other hand was dangling the rather frilly apron Marshall himself had been wearing. *It must have snagged on his fingers while I was picking him up*, he realized after closing his own front door and noticing the apron's absence as well as his own nakedness.

Picturing the reaction of the authorities when they eventually found Campbell's body sent Marshall into gales of uncontrollable laughter. He knew he would definitely add *this* to his journal!

The unimaginative police would probably send out an all-points bulletin for a woman who had lost her apron—a woman seven feet tall weighing at least three hundred pounds! What other general description was possible once they had seen how poor Henry died, and what *else* had been done to him!

Chapter Nine

1

Camille succeeded in making herself awake earlier than she really liked to by setting her mind before going to sleep last night. It was a trick Jake didn't know about both because Camille never really believed any secret she had would be interesting to anybody else, and because her husband wasn't beyond using the knowledge for his own purposes. Because they included sexual intercourse, an activity Camille was always pleased to share with Jake at night, it seemed best to let him believe she unfailingly found it difficult to arise quickly in the morning.

Besides, however much Jake used to like telling her ebulliently that sex to start the day was *really* the "breakfast of champions," Camille's feeling was that sunlight revealed a great deal more about the defects of her anatomy than she was inclined to advertise! Of course, if she had told him what had crossed her mind one morning when

201

he'd caught her with her eyes open and then pounced good-humoredly on her like the Lone Ranger jumping on his horse—that they "might just as well do it under a spotlight"—Jake would've said that was the *best* idea she'd had in years!

Sounds from the first floor reassuring her that Jake and Caroline were downstairs having breakfast, Camille sat up, slipped her glasses on, blinked at the world with her smoky eyes, and went into the bathroom on tiptoe. Peeing hurriedly, she threw on yesterday's clothes and rushed downstairs with a single objective in mind—the one for which she had wound her mind last night like an alarm clock:

Catching Caroline for a little talk before she'd left for school. So long as Jake believed nothing was "coming down," as he put it, he would take off for work and a brief mother-daughter chat might clear up the mystery of Care's latest emotional upset. Regardless of what Caroline had said about their parental inability to "believe" something perfectly dreadful, Camille remembered the bewilderment and chaotic emotion of girlhood quite well. *Everything* loomed large and seemed too imposing to handle alone at the same time that a child wanted to feel she could dispense with Mom and Pop's outmoded advice.

Camille smiled enigmatically to herself on the stairs. Dads had their uses, they were nice for a daughter to have around. But it took the moms to understand the differences between the problems a young woman had that *couldn't* be easily solved and those that could. Fathers mixed them up, made them more complicated, then concentrated on the ones that were sort of for show or general complaint.

With Caroline still finishing breakfast at the table, Jake motioned Camille to the front door for a hasty stage-whispered comment: "I tried to draw the kid out on what she meant by saying her brother won't ever grow up. And that silly crap about our not being able to believe what was comin' down in that lunatic bastard's home." His earnest, honest face looked disbelieving and hurt. "Cammy, I couldn't get to first base with her!"

"That's why I got up early," she said calmly, and kissed him. She was so eager for him to leave her alone with Caroline, she accidentally bumped the back of his head on the doorframe. "You run along and see if the other drivers have scared anything up."

"Yeah, well"—Jake frowned, rubbing at the spot where she'd hurt him—"good luck." Camille had the door wide open and he was backing out. "But personally, I don't think you're gonna—"

"Tonight," Camille said vaguely, and closed the door in his face.

"What was all that about?" Care asked. Having finished her last spoon of oatmeal and reaching for her glass of milk to wash it down, she had heard bits and pieces of what her Pop was saying. "You guys don't need to be worrying so much about me. I'm fine."

"I know you are." Camille sat next to her at the table, rested her palm on the hand not lifting the milk glass. "Fathers don't know what it's like, getting periods and everything; they can try to be very nice, like your dad, but a few tears leave them all unglued." Camille paused to appraise how effectively her approach was working. "Of course, you said some pretty unusual things."

Caroline glanced up, seemed on the verge of speaking, then turned her face blank. "I have to get to school."

Camille took the girl's wrist, smiling widely to appear as unthreatening as humanly possible. "Honey," she said, carefully choosing her words, "you can tell me. You and Pop were watching that Frank Langella movie, and he was so—well, so fascinated by that young woman's blood. I was wondering, since you started and everything, if it was just sort of a bad reaction to . . . well, a man with that kind of sick mind at a time when you . . .'' Unable to find words to complete the thought, Camille let the remark stand on its own.

Care wrested her hand loose, looked embarrassed as she jumped up. "For goodness' sakes, Mom, the man playing the vampire is older than Pop!'' She darted her head forward to give Camille a quick kiss. "See you this evening.''

A wave of unexpected, nauseating terror for the child inundated Camille as Caroline turned. Too many girls all over America lately had been giving their parents fleeting kisses—see-you-later pecks that turned out to be the last kisses the parents ever received from them. Now it was beginning to appear very possible that this twelve-year-old's natural father might be the kind of man who made such sweet little farewells the *final* ones. Camille couldn't understand why she herself could not fully remember that, focus on the horror of the possibility and—and *do* something about it. Was Jake's life so much more brutally experienced that he could just *accept* the existence of such terrible people, or was it something he naturally recognized and something she could not, or wouldn't? *"Care?"*

Poised on the exact razor's edge of womanhood, Caroline glanced back expectantly from near the front door. At one and the same time she seemed to Camille to be extraordinarily like the lost little waif who had come into this house and captured their hearts, and a new category of feminine being who might be known only by strangers Camille had never seen. The thoughts raced through the adoptive mother's mind so swiftly she wasn't even detaining Care, holding her there in the house, very long. Jake sometimes said growlingly that young people "act like they invented sex, booze, doing a bunch of hairy-ass shit.'' Staring at Care, it was easy then to believe a person of her age was at least reinventing, redefining, certain things. And Camille very much wanted to hold the girl she accepted as her daughter there in the house until most of the things that would to some extent reinvent and redefine Caroline Spencer no longer could hurt her.

"You surely didn't mean your brother won't grow," she forced herself to say, "so does that mean you're afraid he might—die?"

"I have to go, Mom," Care said. Her lovely eyes said yes, but not just that.

"Caroline, why would you think Pop and I wouldn't believe anything you said about your birth father? Especially when we know he may already have harmed someone?" She believed she had spoken calmly, reasonably, and waited for the reply without realizing she was literally holding her breath.

Care stared back at her from a distance that seemed to grow, though the girl became no smaller. All the clues to what she might be thinking were the tears in her eyes. "I believed in the Easter bunny just as long as I could, Mom. And Santa Claus. Because that made you and Pop happy. Well, I don't *want* to believe what I know now is true, but I c-can't stop—'cause it is the truth." She yanked the front door open. "See, it would be easier for both of you t' believe in the Easter bunny again than what I know!"

The door didn't quite slam behind the girl.

For a long while Camille remained where she was, sitting at the dining table, fiddling with silverware, forcing herself to get used to the only new fact she could grasp: The three of them had made a wonderful family, life had become just about as good as it was going to be for them, and it was doubtful either she or Jake had known that—until now, when it was too late. The happy home she'd yearned for had actually *existed*, and Camille couldn't be positively sure she'd even noticed it!

An imperfect family of strangers was ruining it all, even if one of them was dead. Caroline's concern for her brother,

her love for Thaddie, was understandable at least, however much it might be . . . getting in the way. But Care's refusal to say more than she had about Madison, a crazed *killer*, was very hard to take. Why couldn't the girl trust them enough to hear what she believed she had seen, or experienced?

It was possible, Camille thought, anguished by the idea, that Caroline was experiencing divided loyalties and didn't actually possess some dark, impossible-to-believe secret at all. It was—however heartbreaking it was to consider, however understandable in the abstract—possible Caroline was *protecting* her first father.

If it proved that that was true, Camille realized with the bleakest emotions of her life, it would simply crush Jake.

And it wouldn't really do a lot for me, she thought.

2

With the boss out somewhere as usual, Lou Francenella was comfortably seated in Salty Dugan's tiny office when the phone rang. Because it was the line reserved for taxi business other than customer requests for cab pickups, Lou broke away from the poem he was writing, sighed and picked it up.

It was Timothy on the line, and old Lou knew right away why the driver was calling in. In addition to the fact that Lou regarded the much younger man as an anarchist because he always had his nose in the *Taxi Times* and argued politics at the drop of a hat, Timothy was neurotic as hell. He had the highest absenteeism Lou could remember noticing in all his years of driving a hack, and Air Willie had asked Lou once why he hadn't offered a ride to Jesus on the way to the Crucifixion.

"What is it today, Timmy?" Lou barked into the phone.

"Beriberi, typhoid, or just another case of the crabs?"

"Very amusing, Lou," the familiar voice said in his ear, coughing a little. "Just a little cold that I'd rather didn't develop into the flu or infect other people. Tell Salty if you see him."

"Jesus, Timmy," Lou said, letting his eyes twinkle because the cabbie couldn't see him, "I only hope the shock don't kill the poor bastard!" He took the phone away from his ear, grinning, reaching for a pencil to record the message.

"Don't hang up, you old groin rash!" Timothy said loudly. "And my name is 'Timothy' as you damn well know!" He coughed again. "Tell Jake I got a lead on that kid he's looking for. At least I think it might be him."

Lou screwed the telephone into his left shoulder, got his pencil ready above a pad of notepaper. "Where was this?" he asked.

Timothy explained his glimpse of a half-naked, running girl and his encounter with a clawed-up guy, gave the location to the older driver. "He said there was a young kid with pet rats or something hanging out in some old building down there, but he wouldn't show me which one. It's in Shit Row, of course, so most of 'em are closed up."

Nodding to himself, Lou grunted a sound at Timothy and hung up. He went back to his poem in progress, making a mental note to tell Jakey about it and also inform Salty Dugan about Timmy's newest absence. He had twisted a couple of lines of his poem around so he could use "lavender" instead of "purple," but now he needed a rhyme for the replacement word, one that made sense. The trick was to locate the word or words in his mind, not resort to the rhyming dictionary he carried everywhere, because that seemed like cheating. Even if he did resort to the book almost every time after he'd formed so many sounds on his pursed lips that he started to look like a senile man mumbling in his *own* mind's eye!

But now he couldn't concentrate for shit, thanks to the anarchist Irishman. Instead of testing syllables with his lips, Lou was recalling the way Sally Schindler'd shamed him, and Willie Crawfield had boasted how *he'd* find the homeless boy. Jesus, it wasn't that Lou Francenella didn't *care* about missing kids, didn't *want* to help! It was just that smart old geezers these days didn't go out on the damn streets and *ask* for trouble.

Lou put his pencil in his pocket. Willie wasn't the only one who'd acted like he could spot the boy, there'd been Pepe, Timothy—who'd already *gotten* a lead—and worst of all, Sal. An old broad, a transfer from another company, a *woman*!

Lou rubbed his hand over his bald head, put his poem and rhyming dictionary in his windbreaker pockets, and tore off the note he'd scribbled down for Jakey. The one with information about the possible location of the homeless kid.

"Cover this phone, Otis," he shouted as he left Dugan's little office and, shrugging into his jacket, made his way at his personal hurry-up speed toward the cab yard.

He forgot to leave another message for Jakey or one for Salty about Timothy's latest unscheduled day off until he'd left the building.

He also didn't notify the dispatcher about where he was going in his cab.

3

"So are you getting serious about this woman, Detective?" Kerrigan asked.

He'd asked the question so idly, Jesse Lewis was instantly put on alert and became as wary as if the officer had been a defense attorney and Jesse was in the witness chair. "What woman is that?"

Patrick Kerrigan blinked, the one indication that the officer realized he might have overstepped his bounds. "You know Jesse," he said coaxingly. He went on staring out the windshield as if there were something potentially unusual about traffic congestion in the Times Square area. "The woman you're seeing."

"Seeing?" Jesse repeated, looking straight ahead through the same windshield. "A *woman*? I see *many* women out there Kerrigan, if I look into the cabs or turn my head to check out the sidewalks: I see women of every age, color, and nationality, I see women from Elvaston, Illinois, and Cedar Rapids, Iowa, and Indianapolis, Indiana! I see tourists, and whores for every income, I see women slumming and—right over there, see her?—women in uniform!" He swiveled his head around to face Kerrigan, and snorted. "I see no woman out there I am getting serious about. No, I don't."

Pat made the tough turn onto Forty-second, got madder than he had before at Detective Jesse Lewis, and finally—in the smallest of ways—let it show. "What about the woman at the apartment? The one whose phone number you gave me?"

Lewis contrived to look devoid of expression as Kerrigan's gaze touched him. "What about her?"

Pat had to lean on both the horn and the brakes to keep from plowing into an oversize white man who stopped walking, for no obvious reason, two feet from the sidewalk. "Are you getting serious about this woman you're *banging*?" he demanded. Immediately, he wished he hadn't put it like that.

Jesse Lewis smiled briefly, covered it with the most self-righteous of expressions. "I don't see why a nice Irish-

Catholic boy like you would draw the conclusion—just because you know I was *vis-i-ting* a lady and took you into my confidence—that I was engaged in—well, in anything but *social* intercourse!''

Fuck you, Pat Kerrigan thought, but kept the suggestion to himself. He pulled the car over to the curb, sighed, and turned off the motor. ''I don't know either, Detective,'' he said, putting his left hand on the door release. ''Sorry if I got personal.'' He started to open the door, hesitated. ''I also don't know why you want to keep this whatever-it-is we're both assigned to on a strictly business basis, but I guess that's your call.''

Lewis saw Kerrigan had stopped the car in front of an adult movie house, knew Pat was paying a routine visit to a snitch who sometimes provided them with information of varying value. There was no need for him to accompany Kerrigan. He answered the young cop's implied question— ''We're partners, that's what 'it' is, but I don't know how much I trust you yet''—but Pat was already out of the car and swinging around the front to the sidewalk.

Shit, I have to cut this altar boy some slack! Jesse thought, slumping in the passenger seat and kicking the floorboard. Suddenly his head seemed to spin with the assortment of contradictions it was filled with: repeated confirmations of the assumptions he'd grown up with that white men couldn't be one hundred percent trusted because they hated his black ass even before they saw his face, and the ones from the truly sincere religions—Catholics, Baptists, Jews—were those who could never be full-fledged partners even if they wanted to be. Not-so-frequently repeated rejections of his assumption, down to and including a white Catholic woman who had said she loved him at just the moment Jesse'd fallen head over heels for her, then gotten the *fuck* out of that relationship before anything happened that couldn't decently be undone. Thinking about

Kerrigan now, the seeming offer of friendship, or at least an active partnership, made the detective wonder if he *had* ended that other relationship as "decently" as he'd told himself.

What the hell is Kerrigan's first name? Jesse wondered abruptly, turning his head to gaze out the side window.

—Just as a little white boy about nine or ten years old passed by the police vehicle, a pasty-faced but well-dressed kid who looked as if he hadn't slept or eaten in weeks. *I know that face*, Jesse thought, and it was like pushing a button on an internal machine.

Photos of all varieties began to whir, to click themselves before the memory-eye Lewis sometimes believed had contributed more to his getting the promotion to detective than any other factor or skill. Even as the small boy meandered on, occasionally glancing from side to side in the familiar manner of a thief looking for an easy mark, Jesse felt sure he'd find that cute but ill-looking face with the striking eyes and brows in his personal memory banks; after all, most of the mug shots he'd stuck in there belonged to adult males, so there weren't that many children to—

"The *Madison* kid?" Lewis asked himself aloud, sitting straight on the car seat and staring after the boy.

But the Model One Jesse Lewis Computer didn't have software that added years to a remembered face, and the little guy half a block ahead of him now looked as if he hadn't aged more than a couple of years since the photograph Jesse had found in the old file on Thaddeus Madison's deceased mother. Surely this was a different boy, maybe Jesse's going-on-forty memory was as fucked up as all his relationships.

One way to find out, he realized, and opened the door. If he slid over under the wheel, Kerrigan wouldn't know what had happened either to him or the car, so Jesse chose to go after the kid on foot to question him.

J. N. Williamson

Neither running nor quite jogging, definitely not strolling along, Lewis half hurried after the boy. Nine or ten paces along, it occurred to him that if this *was* the Madison child, his father, Marshall, might already have found him—or possibly Thaddeus was going, right now, to meet the killer. Perspiring slightly, Jesse eyeballed passersby, tried to ascertain if the kid was—in any sense—with anybody. The answer to that was no, definitely not, but it didn't mean Marshall Madison wasn't waiting for his son. And it didn't mean Madison wasn't *behind* Thaddeus, even Jesse himself. But there was no way to determine that; the sole description Jesse had of the murdering cocksucker was the one provided by the Kendall brat, and it was sheer horseshit.

I should've gotten Kerrigan, Jesse admitted, swearing at himself. He began to trot after the child, realizing he was nearly to the corner and knowing this intersection was always hell for both pedestrians and drivers. *Patrick, that's his first name,* the detective suddenly had it. *Irish, of course—like Pat Ewing of the Knicks! Patrick Kerrigan!*

Two men holding hands loomed in front of the boy Lewis wanted to talk with, and when he stopped and then started to swerve around them, he gave Jesse a chance to catch up. "Thaddeus Madison?" he said amiably enough, laying his hand on the boy's shoulder. "Detective Lewis. I want to ask you—"

Jesse found himself rocked against several passersby, wig-wagging his arms for balance and failing to get it, rebounding off a storefront with such force it half winded him. Shaken and astounded, embarrassed but unhurt, he regained his feet and saw—a good three-quarters of a block away—the quickly vanishing-point figure of a running boy.

Lewis was after him at once, making cuts around people on the street that most running backs would have admired. Several times before in his police career he'd had to pursue

212

suspects on foot and he'd caught up with all of them.

By the time Jesse had sprinted a complete block, the little boy he'd set out to catch was a dot on the crowded horizon. When he had paused to be sure the fleeing child had not turned into a side street or dashed through an open door, enough time had passed that he was no longer in Jesse's field of vision at all.

Lewis gaped where the boy had been and reassured himself it was because of his awe and appreciation of athletic prowess, not because he was unable to get his breath.

Heading back to the vehicle, pretending nobody had been watching, Jesse reminded himself of the fact that the evening papers and TV news would carry stories concerning the kid's father along with pictures of the two children he was looking for. Jesse and Kerrigan had taken care of that quite early that morning. That kind of coverage ought to turn up something.

I'm going to have to get serious about some woman, Pat, he practiced what he was going to tell his partner. *When little white boys can take me off my feet and beat my ass in broken-field running, it's time the ol' detective settled down.*

4

Why the hell was Cammy trying to hurry him out of the house this morning? He tried to dope it out while he was leaving Lefferts Avenue and swinging past Prospect Park, but Jake didn't understand. Unless, of course, Cammy had believed she could get Care's "unbelievable" secret out of her without the interference of a mere man, sweet Caroline's dumb old Pop.

The more he considered that idea, the better he liked it. Not *liked*, Jake corrected himself as he drove across the

213

bridge to Manhattan; he thought it made sense. Women today were the first ones to say guys all kept secrets, believed men thought themselves superior to every dame on earth, and lacked the sensitivity to hold back a fart in church. Then how come it was the ladies who huddled together in whispers and changed the subject whenever a guy showed up? How come it was dames who appeared in all the TV or newspaper ads in underwear Cammy wouldn't dream of putting on, chargin' men up when all they wanted was to watch a game or a flick in peace and quiet?

God, I hope she finds out what else is bugging Care, he thought, hammering his horn at some moron driving a good five miles under the limit. Not that having a blood father who was crazy as batshit and pulling the noses off people wasn't *enough*, f'chrissakes, Jake added loyally. Evidently the son of a bitch was trying after all these years to find Caroline and Thaddie, Jake could grudgingly give him that much, but—

A stark mental picture of the man—out of control, practically foaming at the mouth, wanting to rip people's faces off—took shape in Jake Spencer's mind, and it was just about the scariest thing he had ever experienced. Because Care, and Cammy, put in cameo appearances in the frightening image and Jake couldn't see himself there, protecting them.

For a half second tears clouded the cabbie's eyes and he had to knuckle them out. He realized that sometimes he lost sight of the fact this wasn't some hotshot from the old Heights who was planning to use The Law to get his children back, that it wasn't even a redneck runaway pappy with a hair up his ass. This guy Madison was literally a man who could walk into some place he'd never been before, talk to a perfect stranger, and—and *take his life away*. There were bullies Jake had known, shitheads who really *did* beat their wives and kids, other stupid guys who got a little loaded and picked fights. A male human being with arms, legs, a dick, and balls like Jake who could *intentionally* do something physical knowing the other person would die *forever* was more foreign than anyone he could imagine in the most backward countries on earth.

Someone like that could hurt us, any of us, and do it real bad, then not give a damn, Jake told himself firmly. If he thought it often enough, maybe he could get it, hold *onto* it.

Maybe he'd be smart enough, if the Madison murderer showed up at the Spencer house, to remember it—and be ready to kill. *First.*

Sweat poured out as if a big sponge were squeezed inside him. That couldn't be allowed to happen, Madison simply arriving at Jake's own home; it just couldn't. It was too much of a test for a normal guy to have to take. Taking the other man's life, first, would also mean ripping out a part of himself Jake had striven very hard to nurture until it was natural to him, and throwing it away. It would mean, too, that the very worst part of Jake, which he had convinced himself had never really existed, would have to be *recovered*—fast—and *allowed to function.* Then, when it was all over, he'd have to do something he imagined every decent man was afraid might be impossible:

He would need to go back immediately to being under complete self-control. Domestic and sensitive and tender. Loving. "A man with amnesia," he said aloud.

In midtown Manhattan he caught a glimpse of old Lou at the wheel of a hack, stopped at a red light and headed in the opposite direction to Jake's cab. But what was Lou doing out on a shift this early in the day?

Jake slapped his horn just sharply enough to make it a "hey, there" sound, saw Lou glance around, obviously recognizing the toot of the same make car. Jake wrestled his window down as Lou just looked in another direction entirely! "Yo!" Jake called, merely edging the cab forward as the lights changed. "Lou!"

But Lou drove on by without the slightest sign of acknowledgment.

Now, what the hell was *that* about, Jake mused, and where was *he* going?

5

He didn't know why he hadn't wanted to wave to Jakey except he might have had to stop a second and chat, and Lou Francenella didn't want to tell the guy where he was headed.

Lou'd gotten it into his head that he was going to be the one to locate the missing kid before his crazy, original old man did, and yakking with Jakey would obviously have meant the two of them following up on Tim's info.

Last night it had rained and the buildings and sidewalks down here, a stoned-man's throw from the Bowery, were as wet-faced as if they'd stepped out of a shower and couldn't find a towel. Lou thought that was a little poetic, but the facts were that washing everything you could see in this part of the city wouldn't scrub away the sin or blood or loss. It just turned things oily, like old coins that should've been retired years before. Timmy, he paid too much attention to how his body felt—crap, a man could listen to what was happening in his guts all day and swear he heard Bad Things growing—but he was right in calling the area Shit Row. What a place for any boy to try to grow up! Even if the kid Jakey wanted to find didn't have something wrong with him physically, he could do nothing but get bigger here, Lou figured. Growing up was what went on inside a person and you didn't see the result with your eyes.

Lou found the intersection Timmy had identified and started a slow drive down the street some clawed-up guy had come from, according to Timothy. Movie bad guys used to call this "casing the joint" or something, Lou recalled, smiling tightly to himself. Well, it was right up Louis Albert Francenella's alley, because getting old had taught him a thing or two: When you couldn't find the get-up-and-go you once had, you stayed put and thought things out so you didn't waste energy when you finally got it in gear. Timmy reported a half-naked babe runnin' past his cab, moving fast, said he sorta sidled forward for a few seconds, and then the bloody fella younger than Tim had come runnin' out into the street. Considering the fact that New York City wasn't exactly overflowing with athletic girls, especially ones who were so scared they didn't take time to button up, she probably hadn't run very far. When you added to that how fear made a person breathe faster than normally, that the young guy had also been scared, *and* that something had clawed at him so much he wasn't really *chasing* the girl—he was running away too—it made real good sense that neither of 'em had come far.

So that, Lou told himself smugly, meant he shouldn't have exactly a huge problem in figuring out the most logical place for a small kid to hole up. Or, for that matter, for two older kids to go either to turn on or play a little game of Hide the Weinie.

It turned out to be a boarded-up and ratty old hotel no more than two-thirds of a block from the intersection where Timmy spotted both the girl and the guy. Lou knew the hotel was the place with every wary, observant, hard-boiled lump of hard-won experience in his just-starting-to-stoop-some old body. He knew it because he knew the city, people, he had been a horny teenager looking for some mischief, and because most poets were intuitive, good or bad poetry aside.

217

Down here there wasn't a lot of traffic, and driving most of the way around the block until he could park the hack both legally and far enough from the lobby of the used-up hotel so nobody inside the place was able to notice him was easy. "Duck soup," Lou muttered, climbing out of the vehicle and, after a moment's pause, leaving it unlocked. With any luck he'd collect the kid and be back at the cab in four, five minutes. Hell, he didn't even see anybody on the sidewalks at all. "Duck soup," he said with the cheerful grimness of manner most people saw in him and instinctively walked around the side of the hotel, completely ignoring the boarded-up front doors.

Nothing but a failed, deserted store across the street from where he stood. Perfect cover for a boy who wanted to get into and out of the hotel without being noticed. "Where's the entrance to your hidey-hole, son?" Lou asked with only his lips—

And saw a window with a missing pane just about large enough for a human being to squeeze through. Of course, a piece of cardboard or something—maybe an old box or carton—was pulled up against the space. Any bright kid would think of that.

Grinning, Lou tapped the cardboard with one blunt, hard finger. It fell away.

Now there was nothing in the window. *Except me, in another minute*, Lou thought, and began squirming through.

6

Arising for the rest of the day, Marshall felt refreshed, revitalized, renewed! He couldn't remember feeling so fit and eager to get to work at an important project in months, perhaps years!

By the time he had bounded to his bare feet on the loft

floor and was beginning to get dressed, two names were again on his lips—*Caroline; Thaddie*—but not with the shadowfall merger of wistful loneliness and raging frustration that had been his lot so long. Now, *now* he tasted the syllables of his offsprings' names with reawakened hope and a sense of his old poised but unstoppable certitude.

At his best, Marshall reminded himself as he donned a floor-length dressing gown he considered most becoming, his was a self-confidence to which he was richly entitled. Not only was there a buoyant and buoying appreciation of personal invulnerability if it were not absolutely justified in all the circumstances of life that was itself a shield from most social attacks; there was also the moral conviction he took from the knowledge that *these children were his*! Even if he had generously admitted to an occasional failure to imagine himself in another man's boots, what drove him so relentlessly now was a matter of unarguable fact, not to mention rightness: *His* seed had impregnated beloved, beautiful, fatally narrow-minded Deborah—twice, not once!—and a father possessed both an obligation and a prerogative to have his children with him.

And so I shall, Marshall swore, preparing himself for the task of first locating his daughter.

Placing several kinds of pens, a yellow highlighting instrument, and two pencils on the table beside the telephone that once had been Buddy's, Marshall then made a cup of hot tea and carried it, along with Enid Godby's personal directory, to the chair in front of the table. Sitting, he arranged the dressing gown comfortably and attractively around his legs, smoothed back his hair, and picked up the name-and-address book without haste. It was quite true that young Thaddeus required his presence as soon as possible, but rushing matters tended to create errors of judgment. Besides, it was hard to break habits of long standing, and Marshall was rarely obliged to hurry. The peculiar quality of his life and custom, he realized, had given him that much at least.

Marshall sipped his tea, made a mental note to discover if such a noisy and populous city had one or two stores nearby with the taste to import the better teas. Deborah had handled such minor refinements of life for him; eventually he'd simply have to look into these questions himself.

Of course, after he had brought the children to live properly with him, all three of them would stay very little longer in New York City or even the United States. Without sweet Deborah, it was time for him to revisit his roots—and for Thaddeus and Caroline to be introduced to them.

Marshall opened the thin little Godby directory to the letter A, planning to work his way through the entries—in terms of scanning them for clues about Caroline's devious, sneak-thief substitute father and their whereabouts—without leafing through the book. That was what virtually everyone he had ever known would do, of course; glance briefly at all the pages in the unreasoning hope that a clue would spring straight up at them and supply a paragraph of detailed information suitable to *Encyclopedia Brittanica*! No such belief in "luck" for the methodical, learned, patient gentleman. That which was most desirable was always, in Marshall's experience, hardest to obtain. More time was lost forever by attempting to save it than by controlling one's impulsive temptations.

Ironic, humanly sad, and a bit maddening that he was likely to locate Caroline before Thaddie. Not that he would value her less in the long run than he would the boy; but the vital bond first formed in the family was with bright, handsome, similar-to-him Thaddeus. He had little doubt Caroline would know where the boy was or at any rate that the adoptive parents would know. People today were unconsciously cruel as well as inclined to make the most grievous mistakes, but Marshall could not imagine a brother separated from a sister on any lasting basis because of some governing body's ruling or incompetence.

Sad, too, if minimally encouraging, to discover relatively few personal entries in dear Enid's little book. Oh, there were telephone numbers or addresses for the lady's bank, a grocery that delivered, a bookstore, and a church by the time Marshall arrived at the letter D, but—no people to speak of! Marshall sighed, shook his head, sipped more quickly cooling tea. What was it men and women these days did for anything not linked to earning an income or indulging their rather bizarre appetites? During his marriage he had become cognizant of the fact that few people either read or wrote many letters, thereby depriving themselves of two of the great and usually inexpensive pleasures the world offered them. Did they not marry, have families as he had, remain in contact with one another even if they permitted themselves to exist in cultural squalor?

For the first time it began to seem possible to Marshall that the old woman whose pained and worthless life he had ended with such *panache* and mercy might not have made a record of the adopted parent's residence or phone number after all. He saw the name of a female employee of the Internal Revenue Service (under *I,J*), that of a physician in the M's, a crossed-out female name under *R* with Miss Godby's minute note: *Deceased.* By now, in fact, he was leafing through the directory pages simply because some of them were blank. Panic and the first sign of impotent fury welled up in Marshall's breast—

And then he heard the distinctive beeping sounds of sirens outside the building and went to the loft window to see what was transpiring.

Two police vehicles, an ambulance, and a fourth vehicle Marshall could not identify were stopping at the curb and a mixture of uniformed policemen and men in plainclothes was streaming into the building.

For only the smallest part of an instant Marshall flattened his body against a wall so he would not be seen, and cursed himself for not having repaired his mask.

Defending himself against or exterminating them was one thing—probably two from their viewpoint, he corrected himself—but being seen without a mask in broad daylight was and would be forever unthinkable. Unless, or course, the extermination was inevitable.

When he belatedly remembered all he had done to Henry Campbell last night, and that the big man's body remained at a desk in his lower apartment, Marshall relaxed. He became a typical spectator at one of contemporary society's most common and yet intriguing live-action scenes. An onlooker, unscathed by another's agony, while law-enforcement personnel cleaned up the mess.

There was something oddly quieting, reassuring, about watching what was happening down below and knowing one had—what was the modern phrase?—dodged the bullet oneself. Possibly it was linked with a superstition that had become broad-based, the idea that lightning struck only once in the same place. To the onlooker it was possible, Marshall thought reflectively, to believe a death occurring in the same building, block, or town, even in one's own professional circle or general age group, acted as a personal inoculation against similar mishap or tragedy. *How wonderful*, he pondered the fact, *to be the next lightning bolt! Here I stand, as invincible and unnoticed as clouds not yet filled with thunder, knowing I can prove their simple superstitions wrong . . . whenever I choose to strike!*

Time passed and his patience was rewarded. Strong men, clearly grunting with the effort, brought out the huge but petty remains of Henry Campbell in a bulging body bag. Of course, Marshall realized, the unmarked vehicle must have been from the coroner's office. And one of the men in plain clothes was surely the detective in charge of the investigation. Marshall pressed his face to the window like a child wanting to see everything in a candy shop and miss nothing. One such man, black, approaching middle age, seemed to be telling others what to do; he was Marshall's candidate for chief investigator, and Marshall found it difficult not to giggle like a boy when he remembered the apron clutched in Henry's fingers! "What do you think of that, Sherlock Holmes?" Marshall asked aloud, lips moving against the window. "What fine deductions can you make from the corpse of a giant missing a layer or two of his facial tissue, a cheery woman's apron dangling from his hand!"

The detective turned his own face up suddenly, as if sensing someone else's gaze on him!

Marshall leapt away from the window, panting slightly, uncertain if he had been glimpsed. Swiftly, he collected the souvenir left by his latest caller along with a deep-red mustache that was the gift of another visitor whose name escaped him, and ran to the mirror near his bed, far into the loft. Adhesive and makeup were close by, and it was a matter of seconds to replace the discarded mask that had heretofore served him so well. *I could have a career as a makeup artist now*, Marshall thought while he tidied up the covering concealing the remnants of his—actually, Buddy's—earlier callers.

When he peered again from his window, he saw that all the authorities' vehicles had left. Everything was back to normal. Life would continue, as it always did, the way Marshall Madison ordered it.

Back at the telephone with a fresh cup of tea, he moved ahead methodically from R to S. There, staring into Enid Godby's little book—immobile, mesmerized, almost not daring to breathe—Marshall saw it.

The name, Spencer, a telephone number—and a tiny check mark. In red.

Marshall flipped through the rest of the personal directory, returned to the letter A and once more studied all the letters and pages preceding S.

No one but the female who was listed as deceased had received a special notation from the old lady but *Spencer*! No one else had been given a check mark! No one else's name, phone number, or address had been the recipient of the special emphasis afforded by the color red!

And how singularly appropriate that was, Marshall realized with jubilation, partly because this truly was going to be a red-letter day!

Marshall stroked the pen he had removed from dear Enid's house as a souvenir, certain it was the very implement she had used to append the confirming check mark. Perhaps he should not have stolen it, he knew that—but for most of his life red had always been his favorite color!

"Fret not, sweet and adorable Caroline," he cried, standing for a moment and spreading his arms wide to the gray, autumnal day behind the windows of the loft. "Fret not, Thaddeus, blood of my blood. Your Father is on his way!"

7

Still grinning, Lou Francenella crammed his aging body through the missing pane in the window, got his upper half into the murky shadows of the abandoned hotel, and hesitated, deciding to let his vision adjust.

It was also a pause to get his breath. Doing this was like crawling on all fours down the aisle of a movie theater, he decided—which would by God get your kisser slapped pretty good if you pulled a stunt like that in the old movie house he'd gone to in the Bronx as a boy! *Jeez, I'm all fired up over this*, he marveled. Well, age didn't amount to a row of beans when you got down to it, long as a guy had his health! So maybe it'd been a mistake sitting around on his fat arse, kiddin' himself that he was actually a wonderful poet who just hadn't found his métier yet. He was a *damn* good versifier, he wouldn't back down from *that* even if nobody'd bought a poem by Louis Francenella yet, but there were still pretty *excitin'* things to do if you got yourself involved.

Gradually able to discern the dimensions of a lobby to his right, Lou started to push himself the rest of the way through the window. And nothing happened.

Grin gone, Lou frowned. What the hell was he doin' down in Shit Row trying t' help some little homeless kid even Jakey hadn't met? The awareness of how ridiculous he must look from outside the old hotel turned to a sharp concern for the fat arse he'd sat around on. Jesus, he was vulnerable as all get-out if some prevert happened by—it'd be wham, bam, thank you, *buddy* if he didn't haul it inside in a minute! Then the thought of who or what might *already* be in the hotel occurred to Lou, and, panicking for a second, he began wiggling through with all his remaining might.

To his mild surprise, the panic worked and he found himself rolling head and shoulders onto the hotel floor. One uncontrolled foot and leg collided with a fake potted plant, knocking it on its side with a clatter loud enough to wake the dead; and old Lou sat up fast, arms raised and hands fisted in a defensive boxer's stance. Somewhere in the building noise sounded like a half-dozen tap-dancers on speed, then gave way to yawning silence seemingly meant to make the listener yawn as well.

Lou didn't yawn but, chalking the sound up to imagination or the fact that the joint was a wreck, tugged himself to his feet and brushed at both the front and seat of his work pants. *Jesus, Mary and Joseph*, he thought, limping a bit as he headed toward the lobby, *I prob'ly look like I live in this dump!* Last time *he* went barging off on some gawdamn fool's errand. Poets wrote gawdamn poetry!

"Kid!" he called, hand cupped a round his mouth. "Where are ya"—Lou paused to remember the name of the boy he was looking for—"Thaddie? C'mon out, nobody's gonna hurt yuz."

No answer and, by now Lou figured that was how it would be. Crap that started out with surprises, started tough, remained that way to the end. A man who lived a long while knew *that*.

To his right, Lou saw, was the place where the concierge put the fancy customer's clothes and shit. So's they wouldn't have t' *hold* it till their fancy rooms was ready.

But why was the little room positively *filled* with clothing? This hotel had been boarded up since gawdamn Woodrow Wilson was president from the look of it!

He ambled over to take a closer look, realized after taking just a brief gander at the garments that they were pretty new and obviously belonged to a boy. *Well, Lou*, the old cabbie told himself with a proud grin, *you've done it again!*

The rats, led by Robbie, were too afraid of their new human leader not to protect Thaddie's things in his absence.

Lou didn't see so much as one of the vermin before they were grinning at him. From below, then from waist level, then face-to-face, and finally, from up and over.

He didn't even have the time to realize how right he'd been about crap that began surprisingly and toughly stayed just that way to the end.

8

The phone was ringing like crazy when Caroline got home from school.

Where Mom might be was a question answered by Camille herself, calling down from upstairs when she heard the girl unlocking the front door and dropping her books on a table. "Answer that, honey, will you?" Mom asked. "I'm taking a bath and it's been ringing on and off for twenty minutes."

Care sighed hugely—hopefully enough for it to reach Mom's ears—and called back that she'd do it. Sometimes answering the phone was a big mistake because Caroline knew both bill collectors and phone salespeople tended to make the last big push of the day late in the afternoon. She supposed it was because they hoped to get the dads who'd worked an early shift or the moms who'd gone to lunch earlier with their pals. Whichever it was, Care hated to be rude to people—or give bad news to her folks—and she wasn't a very good liar.

She switched on the TV, turned it so she could see, before going to the jangling phone. She hadn't turned up the volume a lot because Mom yelled at her about that; just enough so maybe the person on the other end of the call would believe her if she said she couldn't understand what they were saying and asked 'em to call back.

" 'Lo," Caroline said as tentatively as possible.

Pause. "Is this the Spencer residence?"

Caroline paused too. A picture on television told about a murder, then the anchor lady was saying something about two children.

The girl would not know later if she paused because of what she was seeing or dimly hearing on TV or because of the voice coming through the telephone line into her ear, and her memory.

"Yes, it is," Care said. Her own voice seemed to come from a greater distance than the others she was hearing. It was coming—just like that of the man on the phone—from a distance measured by time. Confused, vaguely frightened, she said, "May I ask who's c-calling, please?"

"Such good manners in one so young!" exclaimed the caller. "You *are . . . so . . .* young, aren't you?" The man gave off tremendous tensions, yet he was also trying to sound *nice*, Care realized. "Do you still loathe the crass and the coarse, as I taught you? You prefer—you *desire*—the rarefied, the refined?"

Caroline wished she'd left the TV volume down; she also wished she'd turned it up till it was screaming. She wished many things, then wanted none of them. She couldn't speak, couldn't answer.

"This is my Caroline," said Father. It was not a question. "*Isn't* it?"

Care spun her body around and it matched what her mind was doing. *Father will find us 'cause he can do just about anything he wants*, another remembered voice promised her in the cells of a memory sheathed by every good, bad, and in between layer of time. Helpless, nodding because . . . the man . . . was at least partly right, she concentrated fiercely on what the television screen was showing and what the audio was saying. *And there was her bro Thaddie's face*, just the way she had last seen him!

"Where are you, my pretty, my own?" Father whispered. "Tell me where you live."

With Pop and Mom, she thought at once, opened her mouth slightly to say the words, feared they would hurt him.

"Car-o-line," Father's voice sang, "you aren't being polite now. You must *tell* me. Darling girl, we shall be together again, you, Thaddeus, I. Tell Father where you are living. You must."

The TV screen showed a red backdrop. Against it *Caroline saw her own face* from years ago, centuries, eons—lifetimes in the past! Her pale face—then hers and her bro's too—whites on red. *Reds and whites!*

"My Caroline, say the words, simply say your location—and I shall get you very, very quickly." He sounded more impatient, almost angry like he'd gotten at Mama that time. *"Tell me!"*

"You chose Thaddie!" Caroline said, beginning to cry. "Not me!"

She hung the phone very carefully back where it belonged, disconnecting them, and sank to her knees on the floor of her home. Her head and shoulders went forward and she stayed that way.

Part Three

Child of Twilight

"Death will not see me flinch; the heart is bold
That pain has made incapable of pain."

—Dorothy Parker, *Testament*

Chapter Ten

1

After getting safely away from the police detective, the street-smart Thaddie was too wary to try the daring con he'd planned to use for getting some money. What really worried the boy was the fact that the cop appeared to recognize him and also knew his name. Since Thad had almost no acquaintances and definitely no friends except maybe the rats, and he couldn't even remember the last time he'd told anyone his last name, the whole thing with the detective was serious reason for alarm.

Was that all real detectives had to do these days, he wondered as he retraced his steps up the street to the hotel—search for street kids who looked like little boys and hadn't even messed around with drugs or whoring? The one thing pleasant about the way this dumb day was going, aside from reacting fast enough to keep from being arrested, was the discovery of a talent Thaddie hadn't even known he possessed.

The ability to run so rapidly that that ol' policeman was left eating his dust!

In spite of the way he was going on feeling lousy, Thad was delighted with what he had done because knowing he could positively *cream* a fully grown man in a race meant that he had another way to stay alive in the city. Until then, everything he'd tried just to get food and keep out of danger had been based on outsmarting people, conning 'em one way or another on the basis of how small and cute he looked. Now—especially if he was starting to look older and maybe might begin to grow again—there was the neat knowledge that he could probably outrun most guys!

Except the combination of believing he should be extra careful today with some cop on his ass, and feeling kind of winded, nearly used up after his burst of physical exertion, left Thaddie with a rotten choice: Going home without anything to eat at a time when Robby and the others were treating him all weird, or just ripping off some food from a shop.

Before, Thad had been proud of the way he divided his activities into finding a mark who almost deserved gettin' stolen from, and then paying money for what he took to the hotel. Buying it, like anybody else.

Too tired and a little confused to know anything better to do, he'd stolen some untended sandwich buns and beef jerky, then smiled boyishly at the lady cashier and departed the deli—dawdling, as if he had just been looking around— with the packages under his shirt.

He couldn't remember feeling really dishonest before, as he approached the broken window he used as an entrance to the hotel, but he supposed he could get used to it if he had to steal things a lot. He wondered what Father would have said if he knew about his emotions and wasn't sure.

234

Mama, he remembered with a twinge of guilt, would certainly have been disappointed in him.

The cardboard he stuck in the window every time he entered or left the building was *gone*. Thad stood gazing at the gaping hole, more alert than he had been all day. It was possible the thing had just fallen down, of course; it was easier to stick it in place from inside the hotel than to draw it back to the window while he was outside. Or one of the rats might have brushed against it.

Or somebody could be in there who didn't belong. Maybe Thrice, Thaddie thought—waiting to jump him as he was climbing through.

Well, there was no other way the boy knew to get in, and this was the only place he had to call home, so what to do next was the easiest tough decision in the world.

Keeping his head up as much as possible, he popped his small body through the window, then regained his feet with a nimble swiftness that surprised Thad. Was this out-of-the-blue series of modifications developing inside him what adults meant by "going through puberty"?

Retrieving the buns and beef jerky he had thrown in before beginning his climb, Thaddie found his vision adjusting to the darker interior of the hotel much sooner than it usually did. Crazy, he thought, but he almost imagined he saw things more clearly in there and he even felt somewhat better.

But that stuff wouldn't protect him from being clobbered by a big guy's fist or blown away if someone armed was in here, and decided to take a potshot at him. Or slip out from behind something when he had gone by, and slit his throat.

Making less noise even than Robby and the pack unless they really wanted to stalk something, Thaddie kept going until he'd taken two steps into the lobby. There he stopped, his nose picking up the scent of rat—and, Thaddie realized, something else. This was also a surprise to him because the distinctive odor of the pack was all over the deserted hotel and the boy had long since gotten used to it. For a moment he believed another one of the rodents had died, maybe bloodily, but that didn't make sense either, since he had watched them tear other rats to shreds and the stink of their fresh spilled blood was also not unfamiliar to him.

Thad froze into a slightly crouched position, squinted across the lobby with all the big and small windows well boarded so that precious little light filtered through—and had to summon his best self-control to keep from jumping and making a loud noise.

By exercising the effort in this shadowy place, really trying hard to do it, he was able to make out the chairs, sofas, and registration desk in all their detail—

Except it was as if his eyesight had flipflopped and he was seeing the objects as extremely clear *photographic negatives*! For a second—it didn't last—Thaddie was seeing the world in its starkness as *black* on *white*! It might be the way some animals—maybe the rats—saw life.

And before his vision changed back again, the bewildered young teenager recognized a faint but discernible trail of blood droplets leading from where he kept his clothing, behind him at this moment, to a lobby chair with the back to him.

He realized, when he regained his normal, full-color vision the tiny reddish stains in the carpeting were blood and knew they were recent; they would look nearly brown when they were dried.

To end his growing sensation of tension and imminent terror, Thaddie ran to the center of the lobby without trying to stay quiet, then spun around to see what was sitting in the big leather chair.

A bald old man had his eyes wide open, staring straight at Thaddie.

Except that wasn't entirely true, because only one of the eyes was in the old man's face. Where the left one belonged was a splash of redness like an angry summer sun. For a fraction of a second, because the man was sitting up straight and one arm and hand were on the armrest of the chair, Thad thought the old guy was alive, probably another detective come to arrest him or, at least, make him leave the hotel.

Then he noticed a book lying under a dangling hand—it had a hard word in the title, ''RHYMING''—and he also saw stuff in addition to the missing eye that was wrong about the man. One ear was missing. About a million claw-and-bite marks on the other side of his face and neck. So the old bald guy was dead, Thaddie finally understood that much. Chunks were gone out of him here and there.

Then Robby's head suddenly came poking itself out of the dead man's windbreaker as if the rat was just emerging from a hole and a tunnel eaten from the center of the man's chest! *I wonder if he* did *do that*, Thad wondered, but didn't want to go near enough to check it out. Other members of the pack came into view, following Robby, one from the man's sleeve, another from behind the guy's back—the body slumped a bit then—and another from one of his pants legs. A few other rats who had been elsewhere in the lobby, playing or maybe having some snacks, scampered back into the still tableau before Thad and danced proprietorially on the dead guy's lap.

And finally the boy got it, understood most of what had happened. The man had invaded the hotel, probably messed with some of Thad's stuff, and Thaddie's pets had protected everything by gang-killing the old guy.

Then they'd acted like a lot of little kids trying to get better allowances from their folks, dragged the body into the lobby, and . . . well, arranged it in a chair where Thaddeus Madison couldn't possibly miss seeing it.

The leather chair with the corpse was within a yard of where Thaddie's feet were whenever he slept on the lobby sofa at night.

It was a wonderful tribute, the boy realized, wondering what to do with the old man. Really and truly, from a rat's standpoint, it couldn't be any nicer to anyone—definitely not even another rat. Shit, they hadn't eaten *much* of it. They'd been more considerate and thoughtful than Thurman and Rhonda Tinsdale, and Mack Kendall, and the fat dude with all the doughnuts, and Sweet Thing and Thrice—and practic'ly *everyone* Thaddie'd ever known (*since Mama*, he reminded himself, and Care, and—maybe Father). The rats never yelled at him or hit him, they'd shared crap with him, they'd never run off or disappeared forever (unless somebody in the pack killed 'em)—they'd had the control of themselves to be as nice as *rats* could, even with the biggest meal in front of them they'd ever had and with him out of the hotel awhile . . .

What was Robby doing? He'd hopped down from the chair after coming out of the old guy's jacket and making sure the rest of the pack was there, and now he was walking—not running or stalking, but walking like a pet dog—slowly toward Thaddie with his head sort of lowered. His long tail was neither out straight nor curled beneath his body, just lightly dragging the lobby floor, making it real clear he wasn't attacking.

No, not attacking. Thaddie stared down, the start of a thought that Robby was actually cute in his own way dying as if somebody'd blown it to bits with a bomb. Robby was definitely not attacking.

He was bringing something to Thaddie.

Just like he'd brought part of Rodge, the rat they'd killed up on the roof that time.

Carefully, Robby was gripping the ''something'' in his

mouth as he raised his head to regard Thad. It was dripping
red.

2

If there were words Jesse Lewis and the other cops in Homicide hated more than "crime wave," they were probably
"serial killer." The first two words might just refer to a
bunch of white-collar stiffs passing bad checks or ripping
off old folks with cheapjack repair jobs on their roofs or
driveways. These days, of course, neither the fucking media
nor much of anyone else bothered to get particularly excited
about hearing the words unless people were dying. But
even then, more often than not, "crime wave" meant some
blown-brained junkies shooting liquor store owners or fast-
food clerks; and when you came down to it, not that many
New Yorkers owned liquor stores or worked fry vats before
they paused to cover the cash register.

Besides, most of the restaurant people who were wasted
were young. Jesse didn't mean that city dwellers from thirty
to seventy didn't give a damn about kids but that they, like
the store owners who were held up, fitted a smaller dem-
ographic category—the sort that excluded every *other* variety of job holder in New York.

The words "serial killer" carried right along with them
the unavoidable implication that *anyone*—meaning to the
citizen reading the newspaper or watching the six o'clock
news that they, too, might be included—could be mowed
down. That no one, necessarily, would be safe again until
the serial killer was caught and locked up.

Jesse Lewis wouldn't normally even permit himself to
remember the *other* word that brought panic through the
borough like a mothering ocean wave. "Terrorist." If the
word even occurred to him, it came to the detective in a

whisper with the same hushed sibilance as cancer, AIDS, castration, and his personal death. He never, *ever* wanted to have the responsibility for apprehending one of . . . them.

Looking down at the body of the nice old lady named Enid Godby, however, told Detective Lewis he might very well be hearing the words "serial killer" hurled at him by reporters in the media and sooner or later his own boss.

It seemed to Jesse, straightening up after examining the newest murder victim, he was seeing the handiwork once more of the crazy prick named Madison—

And that he'd already seen that nauseating work earlier on this very same day. When he and Kerrigan—*Pat (Ewing) Kerrigan*, Jesse amended his reflections—answered the call about the dead super. "The dead super who really *was* damn near as tall as Ewing," Jesse said under his breath.

"Same guy?" Patrick asked softly. He meant "same suspect." The officer was once more warming toward Lewis now that the latter was trying to be more communicative. "You think?"

Jesse didn't nod a reply but flashed a wide-eyed glance in Kerrigan's direction. "Let us say that I'm inclined to think *about* that possibility, Pat."

"Well, we know this lady used to have the same job Crossland had." The younger detective sounded as if he were proving the case aloud to Jesse, or trying to. He shrugged his broad shoulders. "Makes sense Madison got her address from the home in SoHo and came here to see if Ms. Godby knew where the kids were."

And did she, Pat? Lewis mused. *Did the son of a bitch learn where they are*? "What could Mr. Henry Campbell, deceased, have to do with the Madison children?" he asked instead. "Or do you *exclude* the gent with the apron and maybe look for some homophobic connection, in that case?"

"Can we take this now, Detective Lewis?" inquired one

of the coroner's people, body bag at the ready.

Jesse looked away from the man. "You may remove the deceased woman," he said with the mildest of reproachful tones.

"Gee, Jesse," Pat picked up the question. "I don't see *how* to connect Campbell."

"For the interesting murderer, Patrick," Lewis murmured, "style can be as important as substance." He pressed his fingers on his back, above the hips, arched. *That little white boy must've been part* deer! "We must bring our style, *our* artistry, to match and finally surpass his own."

Kerrigan gave him a sharp, very nearly amused look and seemed on the verge of a crack. "Do we have a connection, Jesse?"

"Enid Godby's throat was throttled, fast, her neck was broken—yet he placed her body on the floor, even remembered to arrange her skirt properly." Jesse's brows rose. "I'd bet my badge there are—no other marks on her. And Henry Campbell was—"

"Sitting at his computer in a chair!" Pat finished for him. "Probably killed somewhere else, but—well—'arranged' as you said, at his desk! And probably not molested."

"Excellent." Lewis permitted himself a warm smile. A thought occurred "Imagine carrying Mr. Campbell, especially after he became dead weight."

Kerrigan did.

Jesse went back to imagining what Marshall Madison *wanted* with his children, exactly. He had been wondering that for some time.

It was almost as dreadful a speculation as the words "serial killer" and "terrorist." Now that he thought about it a moment, the detective realized, Madison—in a very real way—was both.

And more, he added to himself without knowing precisely what he meant.

3

All day, in Jake's view, was weird. Everything he did, the fares he picked up and the places where he was obliged to take them, seemed to exist under some dark or peculiar cloud. Except that was only the way most people put it, Jake realized; for him it was more like a wet sponge containing something unpleasant or disgusting hanging over his head.

He'd told himself it was just because of how ol' Lou sort of gave him the finger by pretending he didn't see Jake in his cab or hear him tottling the horn. Nobody could convince him Lou hadn't realized he was there because the crusty old S.O.B. never missed a trick. The guy could probably tell one cab from another by the sound of the motor, maybe the horn. So Jake had wanted to find out what Lou's problem was, and all Otis had been able to tell him was that Francenella said to cover the phone and went chargin' out of the place as if he was going to pick up some rich fare who made a habit of leaving five-hundred-dollar tips.

Noticing Timothy hadn't checked in—which he always did unless he was feeling sick again—Jake had buzzed the Irisher's home phone but failed to make contact with the guy. Since Timothy played company politics like a champion and he knew he had to phone in if he was takin' a leave day, it seemed likely to Jake that Lou'd gotten that call even if the old man hadn't left a note about it. But what that had to do with Lou bookin' out of the joint like he had a fire in his pants, Jake had no idea. All it did was keep the day's start on the same weird note where it had begun.

By midafternoon Jake was sure something shitty was coming down. He didn't consider himself a superstitious man and disliked allowing bad feelings to ride herd on him, but you also had to be truthful with yourself. Of course, he had reasons to have a lot on his mind these days thanks to Caroline's murderous original old man and the mysterious crap even she had been laying on them lately.

Nothing changed the tenor of the day or made Jake doubt the potential accuracy of his doomsday mood when he finally got home to Lefferts Avenue and, looking toward his house, shuddered all the way down to his feet. There was no one including Cammy whom he would have dreamed of mentioning it to; but seeing their home in fall shadows slipping up the walls like someone painting the house upside down—seeing how *still* it looked, just the way it would be someday when nobody lived there anymore—scared him more than he could remember being frightened. Some homes, he knew, were always like that; walking into them would be saying hi to trouble, heartbreak; worse. But *their* house had always had hope in it, and love, and the good beliefs. Right up until then.

Care wasn't waiting to greet him with a hug and a big hello when he unlocked the door and went in.

Cammy was hurrying belatedly toward the door to open it for him, and one look at the face he loved so much confirmed everything he'd felt the whole lousy day.

For a second he didn't even notice their daughter was behind his wife, she was so quiet, almost hiding back there like some stranger who wasn't sure she was welcome.

"The police are sure it's—him," Cammy said, not even kissing or touching Jake. She didn't have to explain whom she meant. "Care saw it on TV." She hesitated as if she had a great deal more to say but might be afraid to get it said. "I just had the radio on and he also k-killed that nice Enid Godby."

243

"Jesus." Jake felt his eyes filling. "I'm so sorry to hear it."

"Jacob," Cammy said as she took his hands, "Care wants to tell us now. About . . . things."

Jake noticed the girl had sort of come around her mom but stood somehow apart from both of them now, her eyes red from crying and carrying a message he'd seen in them before. It was the you'll-never-be-able-to-believe-me look, and it tore his heart out. He nodded, got her to come over so he could give her a one-arm hug.

I'll try, baby, he thought as they all wandered to chairs like people looking for the right seating arrangement at an execution. *I promise I'll try with all my heart.*

4

The commotion in the center of the lobby was awful, the worst thing Thaddie had ever heard in his life, he believed.

Bowing his head against the few garments he had hung on hangers, he recalled other sounds—some of them words people had spoken—that were worse to hear. His mother on the final night of her life, when she'd barricaded the door of the bedroom to keep Father out, those terrible things she'd said all because of what she had *thought* Father did to him, and he hadn't been old enough to understand her—then the things she said when Father got home and Mama . . . died. Those were worse sounds. In a way, so were those things Father really *had* told him about in the bathroom, and the sounds they'd made together. However loving Father'd been, *they* were worse. Because they'd changed all their lives around forever.

Isn't it funny how it took what the rats are doing to make me remember the way it was? Thad thought while he searched for the oblong white box containing his new shoes. *First time I ever remembered all of it.*

It was even kind-of funny (though he knew that wasn't the right word for it, since he almost never laughed and he *sure* wasn't laughing now) how it had taken him until the time he saw that girl Sweet Thing nearly naked, and wanted to do stuff to her, to understand what Mama had thought Father was doing to him. 'Cause that *wasn't* the way it had been, who in the world would want to have sex with his own little boy!

Thad found the box with the shoes, brought it down, glanced over his shoulder to see if Robby and the others were paying any attention to him. He shivered at what he saw, licked his dry lips; started putting on the never-before-worn shoes as quietly as he had ever done anything. The noise the rats were making was pretty high up on the list of awful, he was sure of that.

What had happened was that after he'd refused to take the part of the old man Robby had gotten for him, the pack had rejected the food Thaddie'd brought for *them*. He guessed now he had never seen anything like the gleaming in Robby's eyes or the way Robby had stood at Thad's feet, staring up at him. The big rat had kept on looking straight at Thaddie while he used his nimble front paws to begin poking the bloody organ into his own fang-lined mouth. It hadn't actually been defiance, mostly, Thaddie saw; it was two other things adding up to that: You're dumb because you're turning down food I'm friend enough to give away, and, maybe you're bigger and stronger, but you aren't *smart* enough to be our leader and didn't you notice there are more of us than *you*?

So from Robby's standpoint as a rodent, he was taking back his role as leader without even needing to kill for it.

Yet. But the entire pack was in the biggest feeding frenzy Thaddie'd ever seen or heard. He knew they could be like crazy children when they got going and find it hard to stop, so he had gotten an idea how to outwit them and wait, if he was very lucky, till they calmed down again.

With cops outside looking for him, he didn't believe he should go back out until he had to, and besides, all that was happening today was makin' him feel woozy, sort of out of it. But he had no guarantee that Robby wouldn't get it in his smart little head to sneak after him while Thaddie was sleeping and make sure the human wouldn't try to become boss again (not that he'd ever wanted the darn job!). And now the rats were getting a chance to decide how much they *liked* the taste of people.

Even if they hate it and throw up the old man, Thaddie thought, new shoes laced and tiptoeing more quietly than he'd ever moved in his life toward the stairs, *I'll never sleep in that lobby again*. There were blood and guts everywhere.

And just the smell of them made him feel—real funny.

The idea he'd had was to change his regular shoes for this pair that might have the smell of some clerk or manufacturer on them but certainly wouldn't have much of his own scent, 'cause he'd never had them on. So he'd been very, very careful not to touch their soles and, even if Robby or some other rat finally figured it out, maybe he could be safely locked in one of the still livable rooms on another floor of the hotel.

They weren't actually safe, any of 'em, the place was so old, Thaddie knew. But even the worst room would be better than being out in the open with all those rats, sound asleep.

It was pitch dark in the hotel hallways, the floorboards were pretty rotten in places, and it was a time when Thaddie wished he could almost see in the dark as he had once already. Now, though, he felt really sick at his stomach and needed to wolf down the buns and beef jerky he'd taken. The food sounded awful, but a guy on his own had to be smart and do what was best just to keep alive. As for the spooky atmosphere of the hotel at night, it was just something he'd have to put up with.

Not many rooms remained that Thaddie could imagine using for anything at all, and it crossed his mind he might have to think about moving if Robby didn't kill him and he didn't die from whatever was makin' him so sick. Alone in one room that looked fairly safe, first bolting the door and then checking out the windows to be sure they were locked—the pack could easily get at him from the fire escape, even if they had to crawl along a ledge—the boy sat on the floor with his back to the door and ripped his packages open with his teeth.

Out of the blue he started thinking about Mack Kendall. He wondered if the tub had ever gone to a good foster home, if there was such a thing. He thought about Rhonda and Thurman Tinsdale. He hated to admit it, but he guessed they weren't the worst things in his life.

He thought about Sis. Good ol' Care. *Gosh*, he hoped she was okay! When he tried he could nearly remember what she looked like, but of course she prob'ly didn't look like that now. If she was lucky at all, she was growin' up. . . .

Mama. Her nice, pretty face came into view in his thoughts like magic, and he smiled. Well, *she* hadn't changed, 'cause she was dead. That was one thing about dying: You might just be a memory but, so long as they buried you, you always looked the same way to folks who remembered you. He was almost like Mother himself, he guessed . . . except maybe nobody remembered him at all. Except for the rats. Thaddie made himself eat more food, for energy.

Father had said he'd come get him and Care, but Father—well, Father was also like him in a way 'cause neither one of them would have changed, hardly at all. More dimly than a distant echo, Thaddie recalled Father saying that about the two of them, in the bathroom that time.

So prob'ly it didn't matter if he'd decided he actually wanted to be like Father. Because he just was.

And it also didn't matter if he changed his mind about bein' like Father, who'd forgotten the big promise he made to Care and him.

Thaddie didn't know if he fell asleep or passed out and might be dying, and that wouldn't have mattered to him either.

5

They had gravitated to the dining room for this most important of family discussions, not because of any conscious decision but because, Caroline imagined, sitting around the table let them be as close to one another as they could be without standing up. Even the most comfortable rooms elsewhere in a home had well-spaced chairs, mostly, and whenever three people perched on a couch to have a talk, it got really awkward. The two on the ends had to say things around the one in the middle, and *that* person had to speak to the others while sort of staring straight into their noses!

Sitting across from or next to each other at a dining room table let everyone have just enough space; and besides, here you could have mugs of hot chocolate which Mom brought in along with a big pitcher of it for refills.

The bad part, Care realized, was that this setting made her think about lots of good times with Father and Mother when she was just a little kid.

There was also the part that Pop and Mom expected her to tell them the many secrets about her first parents, secrets she had kept even from herself most of the time since that original family simply ended. Almost as though a huge bomb had fallen out of the sky and, without killing every member, had dispersed everybody and—and turned them all into mutants, like in the sci-fi movies she and Pop often watched together.

Nobody was pushing her to start talking (though her handsome Pop looked like he might just explode if she didn't begin), but it was harder to do than anything Caroline could recall. She realized she was messing with the salt and pepper shakers instead of sipping the hot chocolate and saw that there was a weird sorta reason for that: Because of how Father had turned out and Mother had killed herself— she still believed with all her heart Father hadn't murdered Mother, no matter what others believed—Care's first family was like the pepper shaker. Most folks didn't like pepper as much as salt and they just kept it around in case they forgot what it tasted like or wanted something different.

And *this* family, well, it definitely belonged in the salt shaker. Most people liked it and didn't mind if it was around all the time. Maybe it didn't have the spice of her first parents' smart conversations, all those intellectual things Father and Mother used to discuss and wanted to teach her bro and her, but salt was *regular*.

But now, even if she'd tried harder than everything to fit into the salt shaker, what she *had been* might somehow sprinkle her out to be blown away, and Thaddie didn't seem to be *anywhere*. She loved Mom and Pop one hundred percent—truly—but it was like they nearly believed she should just plain *hate* Father now, as well as put herself first instead of Thaddie, and Care didn't think she could do those things. Not for anyone.

"I don't remember Miss Godby much," she said for openers, "but I'm sure sorry she died."

"She didn't just die, I think," Pop said from her left. She was sitting between them at the head of the table. "I think she got a little help."

"Jacob, *shh!*" Mom said from Care's right. "Go ahead, honey."

She squeezed her eyes shut for a moment. "I know Father probably killed her, *and* the man who got her job, and maybe others too. He's trying to *find us*—Thaddie and me."

"I hope he's not earning his living as a bill collector," Jake growled. He raised his palm. "Sorry, kid. I know this is tough for you."

"Pop," Caroline said, eyes wide and looking straight into his eyes, "you *don't know how hard* it is." She stopped for a breath, wished there were some other way to tell the story to them. And knew there wasn't. "And h-how much I have to say."

"We're right here," Camille said tenderly. "We'll listen to every word."

"There was something Father—my first father—said not very long after he did what he did to Thaddie," Care began anew, ignoring the glances exchanged by Jake and Camille. "What he told my first mother while Thaddie and I were with them at the table. He said, 'You cannot take my children and hide with them, because you know *I will find* all of you.' And then he said, 'And you cannot turn me in, not only because they can't hold me but because I am a man no longer in time, no longer of this world.' He added, 'That is why I made my world here, with you, Thaddeus, and Caroline. Everyone must have a world.' "

Jake said, "Gawd, he was crazier than—" and clamped his jaws together. He wriggled his fingers to show he'd try not to interrupt again.

"He wasn't through, Pop," Care said. "He went on. 'Whatever you believe I have done or what I am, Deborah, you know I do *not* lie to my family. Therefore, you could never be so cruel as to deny me that world for all time.' " Care swallowed hard. "That's why she arranged for s-someone to come get us, and then committed suicide. I think it was the c-closest she could come to a decision that would be best for everybody.''

Camille nodded although she did not understand at all, then refilled her adopted daughter's mug. ''We don't really understand what he meant, darling.''

''Father—Marshall Madison—has a real serious illness.'' Care sipped hot chocolate, felt grateful for the warmth it gave her inside. ''He thinks he's awfully ugly, and deformed.'' She blinked. ''Not many people but us ever saw him the way he looks.''

''*Is* he?'' Jake asked. As he did so, it occurred to him that Madison seemed to have killed everyone who might have caught a glimpse of him since he began searching for Caroline and Thaddie. That meant the police probably didn't even have a description of him. ''Is he ugly, *awful* to look at?''

''No,'' Care answered, her tone so sad it made her folks' hearts heavy to hear it. She was peering down, to hide the tears. ''He has something called 'Body Dismorphic Disorder'; I've read about it in a psychology book at the library.''

Shit, Jake thought, *if he really is crazy, they'll never lock the bastard up for good.* But he kept his mouth shut.

''See,'' Caroline went on eagerly, ''the reason I know he didn't kill my b-birth mother is because she was the only grown-up who ever made him believe she thought he looked nice. And . . . and Thaddie and me, we almost never saw anyone but each other, Father, and Mother! So he knew *we* could l-love him, because we didn't know other men Father would've believed were handsome. He looked *normal* to *us!*''

Care's Mom let her mouth drop open in surprise. The surprise was for the tears she felt in her smoky eyes, tears for a human being as miserably unhappy as Marshall Madison must be. "Every mirror must have been terrible for him," she said.

Care nodded. "When I was little, the only mirror in the house was in my mother's compact. He tried to write during the day, but the money came from Mother's job. Just about the only time Father ever went out was at night. When it was *dark*."

Jake was absorbed in a consideration of what Caroline had said, but he couldn't let himself feel any sympathy, even if the son of a bitch *was* sick, for a man who slaughtered people to get his own way. This crap just made Madison *more* dangerous—except, Jake thought suddenly, it might make him sound like *something else*, too. Something even farther out than a bastard who went around murdering innocent people to get his own way.

"I haven't told you everything yet." Care wiped hot chocolate from her upper lip with a napkin, suddenly wanted to tell the rest of it so she would never need to go through this ordeal again. "I know now Father didn't do *any* . . . sexual abuse . . . to Thaddie in the bathroom. But Mother couldn't understand, I think, or wouldn't believe what *really* happened." She took a deep breath, looked from her Mom to her Pop. "My first Father *did* kind of attack my bro though, and I'm afraid he *did* sorta—infect Thaddie."

"Well, Jesus, honey," Pop exploded, confused, frightened, and appalled by what he was learning, "he infected Thaddie with what? *Ugliness?*"

The phone in the dining room rang so piercingly it was as if the caller mentally willed it to make them jump. Relieved to have a change of mood, Jake leapt up and grabbed it, said a curt "Yeah" into the mouthpiece.

An expressive and mellifluous baritone said into Jake's ear, "*You!*" It was somehow an accusation, a sneer, and a curse. "*You*, the insidious, despicable poacher of other men's offspring—the emasculated opportunist who de-spoils the homes of adoring parents at the time of their greatest grief and travail!''

Jake was caught so completely unprepared, he could not instantly reply. But he knew without question who was on the other end of the phone line.

"*Speak*, you child stealer!" Marshall roared. "You *do* have my girl and boy—*don't* you?"

"I have one child," Jake said at last, "and she's mine, you murderous son of a bitch!"

"Tell me where you are so I may come *destroy* you," Marshall said tightly. "And claim my own!"

"No, baby," Jake said, aware now that Cammy and Care were staring at him and knew whom he was talking to. "Tell me where *you* are—if an ugly creep who preys on old women has the *balls* t' do it—and I'll come meet you, man to man!"

Silence. For an instant Jake believed the connection was broken. It was not.

"Oh-h-h, you should not have said that to me, Mr. Spen-cer," Marshall sang. "But it is fascinating to be aware of the fact when another man makes the most *fatal* mistake of his lifetime."

6

The main reason Sally Schindler was usually so hard on the adults she met was so she could always go soft on the subject of kids.

Sal knew that—she'd worked it out in her own mind during the long drives with passengers who preferred si-lence to chitchat with the driver—and wouldn't have apol-ogized for it if anyone else had ever figured it out. The way she saw it, her job and her life itself were filled with adults, the majority of whom were obvious assholes, the rest of them, particularly men—simply not so obvious about it. She couldn't possibly get away from men and women because the city was full of them and because, dammit, she was an adult herself! Sally was stuck with assholes, would be to the day she died and then afterward—since she firmly believed in an afterlife—she'd still be stuck with herself. That was the breaks.

But kids were another matter. There weren't any in her family for the good reason that Sal *had* no family, and if she ever really had been a kid herself, she either didn't remember much about it or she'd screwed that up too, just like everything else she had ever done—except for becoming a good cabdriver. Deep inside, Sal realized that girls and boys were only going to be adults too, after they'd grown up; but since she wasn't related to them, she never had to see the start of creeping assholery come over good kids.

Besides, you probably had to like *something* you saw in life if you hoped to make it into a decent afterlife, so kids were it for Sally Schindler.

She'd go to the wall for them if the opportunity ever arose.

Which was why she had put her money where her mouth was when Jake Spencer amazed her by being one of the few guys she'd known who seemed to give a genuine damn about children. (Sayings like that were funny, she noted, heading downtown. People were already putting their mouths in too many unsanitary places these days without putting money in them!) Twenty years ago—*horseshit*, Sal, she corrected herself, *it would take at least thirty-five*—she could've gone for a fella like Jake.

Shortly after he had left the cab company today, puzzled because old Lou hadn't nodded or anything when Jake spotted him another hack, Sally had wondered why Timothy didn't seem to have called in and where Francenella was headed before his shift even started. She buzzed Timothy at his house and found that he had phoned in, leaving messages about his onrushing flu—and the news that he might have gotten a line on the whereabouts of the missing little boy. "That old grouch Lou may have gone out to use *your* info to locate the kid," she'd told Timothy. "I'll bet a sawbuck he's tryin' to steal your thunder, Timmy!"

Which was exactly what Sal herself then decided to do just as soon as she got her cab! F'chrissakes, *she* was the one who had *wanted* to help Jake Spencer, the one who'd talked all the limp dicks into looking for Thaddie Whatsit! Lou and the rest, shitcrap, they'd all looked down on her because she had come over from Yellow—as if she were a fucking *spy* or somethin'!

Following the directions Timothy'd given Francenella, Sally easily arrived at the same intersection as Lou and had drawn the same conclusion: The place where little Thaddie had holed up was probably within a couple of blocks.

And it was the right neighborhood for it too, Sal realized. No incoming mayor was ever going to be able to say New York's problems could be solved during his administration as long as blights like this existed. Any tourist who'd made the mistake of driving into the city and didn't know where he or she was going could see areas like this and discover real fast that Manhattan didn't have the right any longer to set itself up as America's greatest metropolis.

And anyone who got out and walked around, she thought as she noticed a car parked in the shadows just ahead when she made a sweep around the block, might as well wear a bull's-eye on their back or chest.

. . . Not just a car sitting there, looking abandoned. One of their *own* taxis . . .

Sally got out of her cab just long enough to try the door, find it was unlocked, and be sure no one was in it. For a sec she'd been afraid ol' Lou might have had a heart attack or something. But the hack was empty, and that meant the old fart had climbed out and very possibly gone—somewhere— to see if he could find Thaddie's pad.

Sal got back into her hack, slammed the door, and began to take another, closer look at the buildings within easy walking distance of the old guy's cab. One thing sure, Lou was a pro, he'd been on the job even longer than she had, and he wouldn't ditch his wheels without having *some* reason for doing it.

Her watching eyes focused on a wreck of a hotel she hadn't noticed the first time past the line of crumbling buildings, and when she saw motion—up a story or two— she braked the cab to check it out.

A parade of catsize, furry beasts—*Ogod, rats!* Sally realized—was making its way along a ledge.

The rodents in the lead had stopped outside one window as if they were trying to figure out how to get in.

Sal drove off with squealing tires, hoping the noise might startle one or two of them enough to fall off the ledge. *What if the boy's in there?* she wondered, heading for a phone to tell both Jake and the black cop she'd seen on TV that Thaddie Madison might be there.

7

Jake had never been a man who was easily scared, or so he adamantly believed. Not for himself, he would have said, meaning not in terms of the chance of him being physically harmed. He knew it was true that most men including him could be scared shitless by the threats of such things as loss of income or home and family, maiming, blindness, insanity, or Alzheimer's, plus the quirks an individual guy had (and was entitled to, in Jake's view) about heights, bugs, tight places, and crap like that. But those scary things weren't what a man *meant* by saying he wasn't easily frightened, because most guys would just pick up the pieces and gut it out with some of those things while the rest of them weren't supposed to become real threats till you were really *old*.

And the majority of men, including Jake, didn't get exactly *spooked* by most bad things that could happen to their loved ones—well, unless it *was* a kid—because they turned those worst horrors of all over to God and Jesus, Mom or the wife, and maybe to a doctor or some hotshot organization guys never heard of until the time of need developed, and then they just collapsed. Fear couldn't get you if you'd been taken out of the game and were certain the most nightmarish events were already taking place.

But no man had ever told Jake he would destroy him or reacted to a perfectly justified insult by saying Jake had made a positively *fatal* mistake.

His own next reaction was the urge to slam the phone down, go think it over or discuss what to do with Cammy; but he knew that hanging up might just get him, his wife, and their daughter literally *stalked*—as if by a feral animal crawling through the underbrush, unseen—and he guessed that what really *did* frighten him was not even *seeing* death coming. A guy had some sort of right to one good *swing* at the son of a bitch!

"Do you know, sir," the voice in Jake's ear suddenly cooed, "where my son Thaddeus may be?"

This change in Madison's approach startled Jake but also revived his courage. "I suppose he's on the streets, thanks to you." He turned his head slightly, lowered his voice, conscious of Care's open-eyed scrutiny. "Couldn't you wring that information from the old woman you killed?"

"I treated her in every fashion as a gentleman would." Then a different kind of threat, more sinister than the others, appeared to creep chillingly into Marshall Madison's voice. "For your sake, Mr. Spencer, you had better be able to say the same about my Caroline."

"Who the hell are *you* to say such shit to me!" Jake exploded. "Whatever happens to that poor son of yours, Madison, you better have one thing clear: Care's mine and my wife's. From *here on out*, ya bast'd!"

Marshall chuckled. "My, do I detect a *Brooklyn* accent? Careless of you to let me narrow the chase, Spencer—but you're *new* to this, aren't you? As you're new to the truth about . . . bloodlines." He paused for full effect. "Caroline will return to me ultimately, regardless of what you wish to believe. Just as it is with Thaddie, she will be mine forever. In the dear fullness of time, she *will* choose me, *not you!*"

"You're wrong, Madison." Jake found his hand, clutching the telephone, trembling. "Just as wrong as you're evil."

"Don't tell me, please, that I'll fry in hell. Its minions will have to catch me first." Madison laughed and it would nearly have been engaging in other circumstances. "Before this enjoyable chat is over, sir, I must point out that Thaddeus's earliest reunion with me is, beyond all dispute, in *his* best interest. If you know where I may find him, I beg of you to tell me."

Jake, surprising himself, also laughed. "Only somebody as crazy as you are would believe Thaddie might be better off with you."

"*Ask Caroline,*" hissed the voice over the phone. The intonation froze Jake in place. "Unless she has been completely driven from her senses by you . . . people . . . she will know that I would *not* lie about such a matter, and that I *am* speaking the truth." He cleared his throat. "I shall contact you again, very soon. You also have my word on *that*."

A loud clicking sound was replaced by a buzz, and the end of the conversation—to Jake—was very much like awakening from a nightmare. Trying to keep his voice steady, he turned back to his family, faked a chuckle. "Care, you'd never believe what the guy told me! He said you'd know he wouldn't lie about, well, Thaddie's health and yours. And he said your brother really *needs* him now and that you'll *agree* with him!"

Caroline turned pale. She started to cry, not loudly but with tears blurring her pretty eyes and dropping to her cheeks. "I s-said I was afraid he'd infected Thaddie, remember?" Her face contorted into a grimace of terrible unhappiness, and Camille reached out to hug her. "Then he m-must have *done* it, Pop—'cause Father *wouldn't lie* about us."

Jake simply *stared* at her.

It was Camille this time who asked, in a whisper the standing Jake barely heard, "Infected him with *what?*"

Jake once more observed the you-won't-believe-me look on Caroline's worried young face and knew, now, he would believe her. He sank into his chair at the dining table, and he didn't have to wait long to hear her secret at last:

Care squeezed both their hands and said it. "My birth father is a *vampire*."

Chapter Eleven

1

For Camille Spencer, Caroline's announcement was perhaps the most unexpected statement she had heard, quite apart from the question of believing it or not—and it was also perhaps the saddest to hear.

Because Camille had imagined she stood ready to accept anything at all this girl she loved with her whole heart might say. Humanlike, she had run through a dozen or more ideas that might explain what Care had on her mind. It had seemed to her that she'd covered every possibility and thereby prepared herself to believe Caroline's secret unquestioningly.

Later, in private, of course, it would be her maternal duty to seize upon the admission or disclosure, then endeavor to find the kernel of fact in it that would prove her loyalty to Care; and finally—as necessary—set about to rearrange the fantastic, child-based distortions of reality. Camille felt it was what every mother did, or should do, in the face of dreadful things troubling a child. It was how mothers enabled their daughters to piece themselves together and go on, and it made mothers feel good again about everything.

There was nothing whatsoever in Camille's tidy corner of what was actual in life to permit her such well-intended rationalization. She knew she could not seize this disclosure at all without being soiled everywhere, would not be able to seek *any* kernels of fact. To her this was not a distortion of reality born in a young person's mind, because even momentarily *considering* such an announcement—"my birth father is a *vampire*"—was tantamount to a grown-up trying to believe in Santa Claus, or the Good Fairy.

Cammy was so stunned, she could neither remember Care's use of the same examples or do more than continue to hug her while the maternal fingertips patted Caroline's quivering shoulder with the meaningless regularity of a metronome.

Jake thought first of the *Dracula* film he and Care had been idly watching, the image of an actor's mouth looming—abnormally long teeth shining like snow—above an actress's bared throat. Jesus, how many flicks about that guy had they made? How many times had poor Lucy been bitten? It was kind of like going to the dentist in reverse. You leaned back in the chair and he showed you *his* teeth, instead.

But if what Caroline and that damn Madison were saying was true, *this* vampire dentist gave you anesthetic you never came out of. Or if you did, maybe lousy teeth and a bad overbite weren't very important problems in your life anymore.

Okay, yeah, I can believe it, Jake decided. *I can believe it for my kid because the bastard still needs to be killed or locked up for good.* He swallowed the rest of his lukewarm hot chocolate and patted Care's hand. If it took a crucifix or a stake, he could play Van Helsing in order to take care of his only kid. Screw the rest of the details. The guy he had just talked to on the phone *was* a monster; a *thing*.

Jake sat back in his chair, pretending to have heard Caroline's disclosure without the astonishment he had really felt, messed with the rubber band keeping his shoulder-length brown hair in a makeshift ponytail. "Okay, let's make everything as clear as possible for your old Pop and Mom." He watched Care turn her head slightly to see his expression, and rejoiced that some of the tension *had* left her. "You said your bro really needs this Madison now, because Thad's infected, and that 'Father' wouldn't lie about you guys. My impression was that vampires either, well, tore out somebody's throats, or didn't. If that's not what happened and your first old man isn't really a pervert, what *did* happen?"

Caroline, Camille noticed, wore the same kind of expression she did when she was trying to discuss any topic that embarrassed her. It was the incongruity of that—the little girl who once had peed her bed, who hadn't wanted to say she had the runs, who eventually reddened when Camille tried to warn her about her first period—looking just as flustered and hesitant in describing her birth father's *vampire* attack—that finally convinced Camille of this awful, *other* reality.

"After my first mother, Deborah, caught Father with Thaddie," Caroline said, "they got to talkin' about it at dinner. Sometimes like Thaddie and I weren't even there." She was speaking so softly, both her folks had to lean closer to understand her words. "So then Father had to explain about himself. For a long, long while after that, I just couldn't r-remember it. I didn't *want* to, I guess."

"Sure," Jake said. And, "Go on, darling," Camille said.

"He went and got the big book he was always writing in and read parts of it to all of us," Care continued. "I think I wanted to believe it was all pretend stuff—fiction—and that's how I . . . forgot so much. But that's *not* what he said it was.'' She swallowed hard, coughed. "He said he was very, very old but he didn't change because of how he'd been—*eternalized*—when he was young.

Jake had to say the word aloud to be sure he'd heard what he thought he had. "Eternalized?''

Caroline's chin bobbed. "It meant 'being turned completely into a vampire.' And the person who was already one always had the choice of doing that and not killing anybody, 'assisting another mere mortal to live throughout time'—I remember that's how Father put it.'' Her gaze darted from one to the other of her adoptive parents' nearly incredulous faces. "Or killing them. And this was really a big choice to make, a special one, because it's very hard to kill a vampire, so you had to be sure the person you did it to was someone you'd *want* to have around for hundreds of years.''

"I can buy that,'' Jake said. But his head was beginning to ache. "The other guy would know your secret—what you were too.'' He frowned, fought back against the voice inside him that was insisting he was discussing impossibilities as if they were real. "I guess it *would* be just about the closest family of—of all the people on earth!''

Caroline brightened. Her expression was one of admiration for Jake. "That's just what Father—well, *he*—said, Pop! You're as smart as he *ever* was!''

The girl's praise created bewildering ambivalence in Jake. He knew she meant it as one of the highest compliments she'd ever paid anyone. But she was also comparing him with—because the facts of Marshall Madison's most recent actions could not be altered—a cold-blooded killer.

"Well, that was what made him do what he did to my bro,'' Care went on. "He said everything he could think of to make my other mother understand that he just wanted to have his family with him, *always*—because he loved Thaddie and me so much. It *was* a compliment to us, I think; even if he made Thaddeus first, he *meant* to do me too."

"He sneaked around behind Deborah's back," Jake interrupted, almost making it an angry snarl. "If he was doin' his kids such a favor, why would a father have to do it *that* way?"

"I guess Deborah didn't know," Camille added, sounding dubious about it, "what kind of man her husband was?"

"No!" Caroline exclaimed. "She *didn't*—not till he was telling all of us. I don't believe she believed him either. I think she thought he'd just g-gone crazy because of the disease that made him imagine he was ugly." She turned to Jake. "And he was smart enough to know she wouldn't understand, *that's* why he sneaked."

Maybe he did *just go crazy*, Jake thought but kept it to himself. "Okay. So if Madison vampirized Thaddie—and that's *all* he did to him—why is the kid so sick now that he 'needs' the creep? Especially if your big brother is going to live forever anyway?"

"That's just *it*, Pop," Care answered hastily, eyes enormous with the strain of persuading both her folks to believe and understand her. "Thaddie isn't a vampire *yet!* Don't you *get* it?"

Jake held her intense gaze with difficulty, and sighed. "No, honeybun, I don't. Maybe I'm not as smart as Madison after all. But if Thad's not something like that yet, why in God's name would we wanta help Madison get his teeth into the kid again?"

"Pop, Mom," Caroline said, this time grabbing their hands, "eternalizing someone is a *process*. Like—a series of shots. Shots you can't start taking unless you're gonna get them *all*. Just one, and it'll make you real *sick* eventually.''

''Perhaps a doctor could help your brother,'' Camille offered.

Caroline drew herself up straight in the chair at the end of the table, closed her eyes, and concentrated—did everything in her power to make the situation clear to them.

''Think about any movies or stories about people who get turned into vampires,'' she said, ''get turned into them *all* the way.'' Care was speaking more carefully and maturely than they had ever heard her speak. After the long period of blocked memory, it was as if she had fully assimilated the past and could still see aspects of it by way of a grainy but detailed film running through her mind. ''Vampires have problems with sunlight, they hate looking into mirrors, and sometimes they must have human blood. I don't know how often, but . . . Marshall . . . made himself go a long time without.'' She paused, a fine line appearing between her lowered brows. ''Otherwise they can seem mostly like regular people. Now: What did I leave out?'' Her eyes opened. The tears were back but it *was* a question.

Jake and Camille admitted apologetically that they just didn't know. But the girl clearly wanted something else from them.

''It isn't only that vampires don't *die*,'' Caroline said, ''*it's that they don't get old and die!*''

Jake stared at her, still not quite getting it.

Camille, as a mother, did understand. ''Oh, dear God,'' she whispered.

''At whatever age they're bitten by a vampire at *all*,'' Caroline said, squeezing their hands as hard as she could, ''they *stop getting any older*. So my brother . . .''

Jake got it now as Care's voice trailed into silence. ''So your brother, after just the one bite, *can't* grow up?'' The muscles of his stomach tightened; he felt nauseated and cold all over. "Poor little Thaddie can *never* be an adult, right? Yet his body and his mind were programmed by nature and are sayin' he also *can't stay* a boy!" He was suddenly afraid he'd begin crying any second. "That it?"

Caroline jumped up to throw herself into her dad's arms, already weeping. "Father turned my big brother into *nothing*, Pop. B-but if he finishes that awful *series* of bites, he'll at least be *alive!*"

Camille forced herself to accept the rest of the equation:
And if he wasn't allowed to become a complete monster—a vampire—an innocent child would be dead.

2

Thaddie awakened, still sprawled on the floor of the dark hotel room with his back against the door, feeling eyes looking fitfully at him.

They were the eyes of the once-favored rat, Robby, whose gift he had spurned.

And the other members of the pack were also peering in from the ledge outside the room, their sleekly muscled bodies grouped around the rat who had clearly taken back his leadership—and intended to keep it this time.

Under other circumstances, regardless of how scary they were in their staring silence, they might have stayed out there all night without the occupant—Thaddie, in this case—really needing to fear them. But everything in the old building had gone untended and unreplaced since long before Thaddie Madison went there to live. The glass in the window was both cracked and loose-fitting enough that a somewhat rested Thaddie heard and felt the whistling autumnal wind—and a sudden concerted assault on the window would definitely break it or drive it, in shards, back into the hotel room. Robby needed to prove his right to leadership, he had no choice but to accept the risk of being badly cut if—*no*, Thaddie thought, *when*—he was ready to begin hammering on the pane.

Of course there was the one fact Robby probably wasn't smart enough to know, and that was the teenager's human intelligence. Thad knew without question Robby had deployed some members of the pack to a post outside the door of the room—in the unlit corridor—so the boy was not going just to open the door and run. Until Robby realized that *wasn't* going to happen, and started leading the rats on the ledge in a determined attack on the weakened windowpane, Thaddie was safe.

Which wouldn't be long, because Robby was prob'ly the brightest rat Thaddie'd ever known. All the time the boy had judged and studied the rodents, the beasts—especially Robby—had done the same with him.

Besides, it was getting too cold in there; and besides, also, Thad was starting to feel humiliated, really shamed by the way his own health, the cop chasing him, and the rats who once had been his to command were pushing him around. The longer he looked back at the creatures on the other side of the window across the way—glared into Robby's furtively shrewd, eager little eyes—the madder he was getting.

That was when the amazing thing happened a second time!

Just as he'd done it once before, Thaddie was able to see the animals on the ledge without color—in white on black, like a photograph negative—but now with terrifically greater clarity than he'd ever seen *anything* before! Even the few objects in the bare room, the outline of the closed door (with the ominous absolute silence gathered behind it), and the jagged crack in the window glass leapt into astounding sharpness of detail! He could almost see the rats' skeletons!

I am Father's son, Thaddeus Madison thought. Yet it was very nearly as if some secondary force had seized control of his mind, twisted it until the thought was produced in the first person.

But it's true I am, and didn't I once think that was the greatest thing in the world to be? Thad asked of himself. At least he *believed* it was his question, his challenge; getting to a crouch on the hotel floor, he sensed how little control he had in judging the difference. *But does it matter?* came another thought. *Remember when it seemed wonderful*—remember *it, Thaddeus!*

He did so, mentally pushing aside the partition, drawing the memory into focus with the identical white-and-black clarity of his current, special vision. *My son and I will live together through eternity,* Father said, and used the same voice Thad had believed now to be his own. *We shall be special people, my progeny and I joined only by your sister—and those whom the two of you choose when you are ready, as I have chosen you.*

Then the man had crouched as Thaddie was now, himself, but naked as the small boy had been, warned him "it" would hurt, a little—

And Father had bitten him. And *he* had—only after pleading—bitten Father! They had taken each other's blood—and lapped at the wounds in their necks like dogs lapping water from their bowls! And it *had* seemed special somehow, a privilege to be chosen—

Till Mother opened the bathroom door and saw them enfolded in the clinging embrace.

Thad climbed to his feet steadily, holding to the long-banished memories. Memories Mother had made sound dirty, forbidden. Yet it hadn't been sex—and it *had* been too, Thad admitted for the first time—it had been Father's first step toward his little boy's—

"Eternalization," Thad said aloud, seeing the rats freeze

when they heard him speak. Yes, *eternalization* was what Father had begun to do to him, *for* him.

Thaddeus knew then there was but one other word to explain what Father had done, what he was—and *what Thaddeus himself must be*.

He laughed at the staring vermin. Ignorant, audacious beasts! Absurd to fear such ridiculous little creatures.

Absurd to be afraid, Thaddeus thought, parting his lips as he smiled, of *anything* at all!

3

After hanging up following the conversation with the nearly illiterate cretin in Brooklyn, Marshall was obliged to do battle with his own outrage—a fury that, lacking a focal point on which to release its pent-up power, turned familiarly inward on him.

Injustice was not new to him—scarcely that, scarcely a surprise even with those conditions which he clearly had every right to direct to his advantage—but he had never in all his many years expected to be called vile names by the man who had taken Marshall's *own* flesh and blood! Somehow, in spite of the practical manner in which he had tracked the trail of his politically kidnapped son and daughter, he had never really *believed* that the man holding Caroline would refuse to divulge as small a thing as his *address* so that the child could be properly placed once more in her real parent's arms!

Knowing he needed to regain his self-control and devise some ruse that would drag Jake Spencer's location out of him—perhaps a proposed compact, a meeting on neutral ground, possibly even some kind of trade—Marshall had said he would call back. Now was definitely the time for the *closest reasoning*, the *most astute idea-generation*, yet all he felt like doing was pacing.

Or, of course, to satisfy his own meager and infrequent personal desires, the gratification of the flesh that could be his only by one means: That which he had denied himself since, it seemed, the last living being who had cared about the all but omnipresent damned Buddy had visited the loft. All that remained of those unfortunate callers—apart from mere morsels of skin and bone—was quickly losing its liquid flavor and, far worse, its essential nourishment.

And that imbecile in Brooklyn, of *all* places, could not even know that poor, young Thaddeus, who had not been permitted the opportunity to complete his eternalization and consequently did not even know what would save him, was bound to die horribly unless Marshall's beloved daughter was effective in convincing Jake Spencer! Caroline, whom Marshall hadn't even had the chance to *begin* saving from a life of abysmal human ordinariness and who could lose her life to anything from childhood disease, an automobile accident, a venereal complaint, childbirth, one of the common fatal diseases, or old age! *Damn*, the Spencers were preventing the girl from becoming immunized against the killing potential latent in practically everything!

Couldn't *someone* simply knock at the door of the loft in order for him to balance the scales a *mite*, a *smidgin*? Glancing wildly around, Marshall saw nothing fundamentally worthless or large enough to be worthy of one ameliorating, violent action except the bony remains of dear Buddy's friends and family members beneath the covering on the opposite side of the refrigerator.

He drew back one foot and leg, then placed a thunderously accurate kick in the center of the pile closest to him. For a moment the air was filled with white or bloodied projectiles of many sizes. Arms struck the distant loft wall, skeletal fingers becoming separated and soaring like penny rockets. Legs still attached to the hipbones came apart in collisions, some shattering like bone China, others caroming off the floor and appearing momentarily to be gifted anew with the ability to walk.

Had it *always* been like this for people such as he? The world had made his kind a leper, a nomadic wanderer with no place to settle down safely for long, merely because of differences other people—those with brief, curtailed lives—were too envious to try to understand. Called *kathakanos* on Crete, their heads were severed and boiled in vinegar! Rumanians excised the heart of the *strigoiul*, cut it in half, then drove nails through their heads! In Serbia jealous citizens severed the *vlkoslak's* toes before pounding a nail into the neck—well, at least some self-righteous citizens were being exposed for what they were! In Macedonia oil was poured on a *vryolakas* and yet another nail used to inflict agony or embarrassment, this one through the navel! All the romantic Irish did to vampires—whom they called *deargdul*—was leave stones on the grave, and Bulgarians actually used wild roses in the hope of chaining a *krvoijac* to his place of burial! Where *that* one had come from, Marshall thought as he paced, waving a disgusted arm, he hadn't the faintest idea!

But even the more pleasant notion of being entwined by roses if he ever chose to expire could not really mollify or calm him because he needed to find Thaddeus or at least Caroline now, and he could not think what approach to use when next he telephoned Jacob Spencer. Marshall considered getting some more money, riding to Brooklyn in a taxi, and combing the streets; but Caroline *would* have grown, unlike little Thadeus, and he might not even recognize her at once—or Jake Spencer might very well keep her inside his house! It appeared hopeless, even if kicking the bony remains had taken the edge off his fury, and in addition to the ongoing location problem, he was probably not in full command of his powers. Without question he required—

Someone rapped loudly, quite forcefully, on the door.

Startled but smiling with anticipation, new mask in place, Marshall hurried to open it.

Two men, not one, were waiting. Each of them was exhibiting something pinned inside a billfold.

"Sorry to disturb you at such a late hour," one of them said, a severe-looking black-skinned gentleman, "but it's about a murder. Possibly you heard the sirens when we were here to investigate?"

"We're looking for any information we can get," said the other, taller man. He was clearly attempting to see around Marshall into the apartment. White, he was also bulkier, younger. "May we come in? We're talking with all the tenants."

For a long moment Marshall considered the suggestion quite seriously. Indeed, he welcomed it.

Ultimately, however, he knew he had no time for self-indulgence. The return call to Spencer should be made soon. "Alas, I'm afraid not. I am—"

"Sir," the first officer interjected, "there's an outside chance the dead man was in some way connected with a missing child. A small boy who may be in danger." He indicated Marshall's dressing gown. "Unless you put that on pretty quickly, you were up anyway."

For Marshall, the man's little deduction was unneeded. "A missing *child* . . . in danger" was sufficient to interest him.

"Forgive my hesitation," he murmured, stepping away from the door. "Please. Come in."

Both policemen were already inside before Marshall remembered the human bones he had left strewn, by his violent kick, all over the far end of the flat.

4

While Pop and Mom talked about what to do now that they seemed to believe her and knew that Thaddie was in terrible danger, Care went to the rec room to sit alone, toying nervously with the locket Mother had given her so long ago. Care heard little that her adoptive mother was saying, but every now and then Pop's voice rose nearly to a yell when his feelings got the better of him.

To some extent Caroline understood why they—especially Pop—were upset. A lot of what the Spencers had done to help her live a normal life had to do with the way they'd shown her love and expected, gradually, to be loved back; but that wasn't all. They had taught her the difference between right and wrong, and Care herself had been bright enough to figure out that she was happier and really got more out of life by *trying* to be good. Now they thought— specially Pop—it should be easy for her to sort-of leave both Thaddie's and Father's fate up to God, or somebody else. What they didn't wanta think about was how much she *still* loved them both, how she could tell them Father was being truthful—she'd seen the look on Pop's face, like she'd betrayed him or something—and how she absolutely *wouldn't* let her big bro die if it was up to her!

Sitting there in the neat rec room where they'd all had such nice times, not even bothering to turn on a light, Care felt sorta abandoned. She hadn't felt like that since Thaddie was sent away from Miss Godby's home to live with foster parents and she'd had the impression that all of life was painted either red or white—not black and white, like her wonderful folks wanted it to be: red both for the blood her first mother shed when she killed herself and for the anger she guessed she had always seen in Father and, a lot of times, in Pop. White not so much for innocence but for how *pale* people got when they were awf'ly scared, or *very* mad.

Care had learned to like reading books, especially biographies. She'd hoped she would learn more about people, why they did some of the things they did. She had noticed many of the old movies she and Pop saw together were based on stories by a man named Poe, so she'd borrowed an old book from the library called *Israfel: The Life and Times of Edgar Allan Poe* by a guy named Hervey Allen. Reading it, she thought she'd found out why Mr. Poe wrote so many sad or spooky things.

The writer's wife, who was real young, named Virginia, had tuberculosis, they were terribly poor, and Virginia was dying. Well, Edgar climbed a cherry tree and started throwing cherries down to his wife. She was wearing white and caught them in her lap, and both Virginia and Mr. Poe were having a good time.

Then Edgar looked down from the tree, ready to drop some more cherries—Caroline had memorized this part— ''into the bright red pile already gathered in Virginia's apron, when white and crimson suddenly became one in the tide which leaped from her lips.'' Care nodded, wept again a little in the dark rec room just thinking about it. Reds and whites, 'way back in 1846. Innocent, loving folks having a nice time with innocent cherries—then the blood, poor pale Virginia, the sadness, and, Caroline felt sure, the anger of the young writer over losing everything he had.

Thaddie, to her, was like both young Edgar and—pale, dying Virginia. Was it always going to be like this whenever folks were happy?

A tiny part of Care sorta wanted to tell her birth dad where they lived—*shout* it to him when he called next time—because, just like Pop and Mom, he would never,

ever hurt her—not like everyone else thought "hurt" meant. He'd just do what he had done to her bro, only he would do it often enough that she *never* got sick, exactly; and then she, Thaddie, and Father would live forever! Caroline switched on the TV with Pop's gadget, just to have a little light, opened the locket to squint down at—at Mother Deborah's lovely face, and to ask her: Was it actually *that* bad being alive for the rest of time and learning things from Father, learning 'em with Thaddie and herself?

Deborah Madison just went on smiling—as unchanged in the small photograph she once placed in the locket and gave her daughter as any vampire—but, in a way, the two mothers Care had known whispered answers in her ear: Deborah was already in Heaven. Mom and Pop would go there someday, and, if she stayed alive, Caroline would never see them again. A time would come when she remembered her handsome Pop even less clearly than she could picture Marshall and Deborah Madison and the life they'd all led. Her folks' religion—Care's now—taught that people who were good and believed in Jesus lived forever anyway—and being good didn't mean, *couldn't* mean, killing other folks for their blood.

The hard parts were that Thaddie had been a good boy when Care saw him last—she believed he still was too, she truly believed that!—and that she just *couldn't* do anything to hurt Father, because he'd never done anything to hurt *her!*

Concentrating on the open locket, Care almost didn't hear the phone ringing again.

And just when it did, she'd been amazed to see *Father's face* in the side of the locket where there'd never been a photograph of him for years and years! *His* face, smiling, *beaming* up at her! The face he'd hated more than any other 'cause of his sickness, one of the three faces Care had once loved more than any others in the world! It wasn't clear or

275

easy to see like Mother's, and Caroline sensed nobody else could even have known it was there; but she knew, she saw his intelligent eyes gleaming and his smile widening . . . and he was whispering her name, *Caroline, my own sweet Caroline*, with his moving lips! And Father was asking her a *question* too, he wanted to know where she—

Pop's voice snapped out "Hello!" from the other room, and Care, without closing the treasured memento, carefully slipped it into a pocket of her jeans. Then she jumped up, her head spinning, and ran out to see who was on the phone. And what would happen next.

"Yeah, go ahead, Sal," Pop was saying, motioning with his fingers and hand for someone to get him a pencil and pad of paper. Both disappointed and relieved it wasn't Father phoning, Care gave him her pencil and pointed to the pad Pop was somehow overlooking on the little stand with the phone. "You think Lou went in there alone and he never came out?"

Caroline and Camille both saw the odd look in Jake's eyes, caught the way he was trying to indicate there was big news without actually speaking to them. Daughter and wife asked, in unison and in whisper, *"Thaddie?"*

"Well, I kind of wish you'd just called me, Sal," Jake continued mysteriously. He was scribbling something on the notepad and Care, peeking, saw it was an address or location! "Sure, you did the right thing, Sally. Gawd, I really appreciate you workin' so hard—Timothy and Lou too. And I hope nothing's happened to ol' Lou." Pop listened another moment, then asked, "Can you let me have your number in case I need ya?" And he scribbled figures on another page of notepaper.

Hanging up, Jake turned to the other members of his family in an obvious state of ambivalence neither Care nor Cammy associated with him at all.

"Maybe—*maybe*—my friends at the company have located Thaddie,'' he said slowly. His wife, having listened intently to what he was saying to Sally Schindler, just nodded. His daughter made a cheering sort of sound which Jake cut off with a head shake. ''I'm afraid there's more to it than that, that Lou Francenella may have gotten . . . hurt . . . in the same place. So we're gonna have to move *real* fast, but you need to know the rest of it. I don't know what the best thing is t'do.''

Care recognized yet another expression she'd never seen on her Pop's face, and she was frightened all over again.

5

''Why would you think the death of the unfortunate Mr. Campbell, in this building, was connected with the—ah, little street boy you're looking for?'' Doing his best to prevent the two policemen from advancing deeper into his loft apartment, Marshall had planted his feet firmly just inside the front door. Arms akimbo, he regretted the appearance of rudeness given by his failure even to offer the gentlemen seats. But as much as he would have enjoyed a half hour of intellectual banter, and personally benefited from killing them and then wastefully draining every drop of their blood, there was the welfare of his children to consider. He widened his eyes, raised both eyebrows—or those of the victim from whom he had removed them. ''Surely you don't think Henry was some kind of pervert who took advantage of . . . what did you say the child's name was?''

Jesse Lewis shook his head dismissingly. ''We have nothing like that to believe, sir.'' He tried to get a firm fix on what this fancy dude in the robe actually looked like, but the lighting in this loft was sparse, made pockets of darkness not only in the parts of the place Jesse could see but in people's faces. *This* bird, though, might have looked odd in daylight; his face appeared to have different colors, and his brows didn't seem to gibe with the rest of his mug. "But there've been a number of murders lately that could be the work of a single killer, so we want to see if Henry Campbell's death fits in."

Pat Kerrigan, notebook flipped open and pen in hand, said, "What did you say your name is, sir?"

"Alas, Campbell was only the man to whom I paid my rent," Marshall told Lewis. "I *left* it for him. There was no relationship with the gentleman." He glanced from Jesse to Pat, returned his gaze to the detective. "I confess to a soft spot for children; your reference to the homeless boy is what piqued my interest at this late hour, as you know. If you care to give me his name, perhaps I could make inquiries of my own."

Jesse backed up a few feet, leaned one hand on the loft door. He gave the appearance of relaxation and weariness simultaneously. "I think I said he was 'missing,' sir, not 'homeless.' But you're right, nevertheless. May we have *your* name for our records, Mr.—Mr.—?"

Marshall rarely watched television, did not know his name had been mentioned on news reports that day, and almost answered. But this shorter, darker officer was scarcely audible now that he had stepped back, Marshall had automatically stepped nearer when Jesse spoke, and Marshall—turning his head to the left to be certain—saw that the younger and taller policemen had stayed where he was. What *could* he be *writing* in his notebook? "I don't even know *your* names, Officers," he said not quite accusingly. "And I still do not understand why you chose to interview me, first among the tenants in this building, at such an ungodly hour."

"Quiet desperation to find ourselves a very . . . ungodly . . . killer," Jesse said, speaking so quietly Marshall edged forward an additional step to hear. "You see, a lady cab driver told us tonight she had seen some unusual activity around a closed-up old hotel called the Eventide down on Jerseyside." Lewis studied their host in the somewhat different lighting at the door, became aware that there was something familiar about the man—and something that stank. "Another taxi driver may be missing, and this Ms. Schindler thinks he and the boy we're looking for may be inside the hotel." Jesse's prided memory for faces, even ones that looked tricked out in makeup, began backing up to retrieve a certain description: one he himself had concocted when the chubby kid, Kendall, had given them a *phony* description. "We're going over there when we leave here."

Marshall again glanced to his left. But he didn't see the second detective, that way, and Marshall wouldn't be able to see what the fellow was doing—or where he was—unless he turned completely around. Now, what the black officer was saying tended to confuse Marshall's customarily logical, linear passage of thought. Was it possible he was so lucky that this pair of law enforcement people had dropped by and virtually handed Thaddeus to him?

"Well, I certainly don't *object* to telling you my name," Marshall said with a show of straight-arrow-citizen honesty. "I am—"

"*Jesse*," said the second, white officer. The voice was tight as a violin string.

Marshall turned, saw that Pat Kerrigan had gotten almost to the refrigerator before stopping. The man was looking toward him and his superior officer, but he was pointing. Indicating the wide assortment of scattered bones Marshall, in his pique, had kicked from the concealing coverlet.

Both Marshall and Lewis were walking back quickly to join Pat. "Just what the hell are those, sir?" Jesse asked from a careful pace behind Marshall.

"I'm an amateur archeologist," Marshall answered at once, "just back from a dig."

"I don't think so, sir," Kerrigan said, picking up an ankle with a bit of the heel of a foot still attached. He was making the most disapproving sort of face and something between his fingers was jingling. "Unless you got real lucky and found a past society that manufactured charm bracelets."

Marshall smiled. It was the kind he'd often used successfully for the reason that it reflected his sense of invulnerability and his appreciation of badinage. "Not all the bones are from the dig," he said lightly. "I see that one of the little prosthetics I make as a hobby got mixed in with the *genuine* article. I use them for artistic comparison, you see."

The man behind Marshall made a sound the vampire, without turning to see and spoiling the fun, felt sure was the freeing of a firearm from its holster. "That's Detective Second Class Kerrigan and I'm Detective Lewis, sir." The voice hesitated. "Would I be wrong in placing a pretty large wager that your name is . . . *Madison?*"

In spite of his icy poise, Marshall glanced abruptly back at Jesse.

Looking straight ahead again, he saw Detective Second Class Kerrigan jumping slightly, getting a hand on something hanging from the ceiling, and tugging at it. For an instant it appeared Pat wouldn't be able to bring down the entire leg because Marshall's kick at the bone pile had been so powerful the naked toes were embedded in the ceiling.

Kerrigan, though, was young, tough, and determined. With a grimace, he rested the nearly intact leg on the palms of his hands and came close to shoving it into Marshall's face. The big toe, he observed with small pride, had remained stuck in the ceiling. "You want to try again, Mr. Madison, or shall I just read you your rights immediately?"

"Well, well," Marshall said amiably. "I *tried*."

He snatched the leg from Pat's hands and struck the Irishman on the side of the jaw, felling him on the spot. Kerrigan lifted his head off the floor, stared wall-eyed at them, and died.

The police .38 in Jesse Lewis's hand roared twice, the bullets entering Marshall's back at point-blank range. Their combined force drove him forward, stumbling, one of them grazing his spine and causing him the first real physical pain in more than one hundred years.

Jesse, revolver readied but himself readier to provide first aid to a dying man, put one hand and arm down.

Marshall wasn't *there!* Moving faster than Lewis had believed anyone could move, Marshall was at the detective's side, nearly behind him! With nothing in his hands now, the vampire groped for Jesse's wrist, closed his fingers around it, and merely *pulled* on the arm. The agony was severe as the arm became dislocated, but Marshall was only beginning.

As Lewis strove to liberate himself from the other man's grasp, tried simultaneously to hit Madison with his still-functioning left fist, he realized Marshall had released the wrist and was digging his fingers—*burrowing* them, they felt as if all ten digits were sinking into his flesh—into the tops of his shoulders on either side of his neck. Now Madison's face was close to Jesse's, except—it *wasn't* his face, Jesse saw that even in his growing pain! Intending to smash Madison at the base of the nose, Lewis summoned his strength, brought up his left arm—

And when Marshall moved his head back the fraction of an inch, Jesse's hand had smeared off most of the vampire's mask. To the detective's surprise, Madison's grip on him slipped, an expression of true horror appeared on his most ordinary of real faces, and Jesse drove his knee into the creature's groin.

Except it did not land solidly, and Madison's lightning-quick reflexes brought his own hands up under Lewis's knee—and *flipped*.

Jesse, half-stunned, saw to his amazement that the murderer had *thrown* him—sliding—all the way to where he ended up beside the bleeding, dead Pat Kerrigan. He started to roll, knowing what would happen—

But Marshall Madison was atop him first, the anguished, even deeply offended face inches above Jesse's face. It wasn't even possible to wiggle, and Madison's knee was pinning down Lewis's only working arm.

"I should have liked to thank you for pointing my way to my beloved son, but you and your companion weren't good guests," Marshall said. "All I can do to express my appreciation, sir, is allow your *blood* to live somewhat longer . . . in *my* body."

Without awaiting comment, Marshall opened his jaws more widely than he had had the chance or reason to do for a long while—stared in Jesse Lewis's eyes until it was anatomically impossible to see them—and chewed his way through the detective's flesh and jugular vein. The blood pumping up into his mouth overwhelmed almost all his practical and fastidious reasons for the prolonged abstinence. To some extent it was like coming home to Marshall, a reminder of why he went on existing—

And why it was any parent's obligation and duty to bring such an opportunity for exquisite fulfillment beyond all description to his offspring! He'd had regrets, a few; but this was his only reason to live, his special curse, his *way*.

At once sucking and munching to keep from spilling the *soupçon* of a drop or tasty bite as he held his head back, Marshall patted the dead detective's still chest with something—distantly—like affection, and stood.

Afoot, towering above tragic death, staring down at the motionless, still-seeping bodies, Marshall pressed his palms together in a clasp of euphoria. The power trickled through his body in the old familiar way, reinvigorating and restoring his tissues, his unconquerable might.

I must take the time to be polite, he thought, suddenly running like a flash toward the telephone. *I promised to call Jake Spencer back, and I shall.*

But now—ah, *now*—when he spoke with the idiot, he would know that their encounter would occur only after Thaddeus and he were again together! Father and son, off to save the fair damsel—*what* could be more romantic than that!

That was when Marshall finally thought of a way by which he might be able to find darling Caroline's location without needing to coax it from the child stealer.

When his idea proved to work, Marshall could not properly cry his sympathetic tears for the brave men he had slain because he kept bursting into howls of hilarity. Perhaps—at last—he was fully himself again!

6

Jake explained the problem he saw in the idea of going, himself, to try to get Thaddie out of the deserted hotel—and, if Sal Schindler were right in her assumption, rescuing old Lou as well. There was the fact of Lou's disappearance itself, which made it sound as it someone or something overpowered the old poet of the wheels. "For all I know," Jake said as calmly as possible, "some creep is holding the kid there against his will and knocked Lou off when he tried to help Thaddie. I'm willing to stick my neck out, but what's the point if he's armed? He may have already taken Lou out."

He watched Cammy mull over what he was saying and decided he was probably right. But Caroline was another matter entirely; all she wanted just then was to be safely reunited with her brother.

What he hadn't told them about was the rats Sal had observed trying to get into the hotel room or his fear that they could be rabid and might have killed both the boy and old Lou. He knew Care well enough to realize she'd insist on going with him, and knew himself well enough to know he might let her—the situation was that important to her.

Yet he sure as hell didn't want Care to be put at risk, or, for that matter, to be along if Thaddie had been killed by the fucking vermin and partly eaten.

Jake also hadn't commented on the fact that Sal said she had notified the police, who were much better equipped to tackle problems this tough. Shit, they were probably headed for the old hotel already, might even be there by now!

But the rest of it was that he had a working man's distrust of most authority figures, especially if they needed to tread lightly and remember that a small boy—and maybe a pretty decent old man—could be in the middle of this.

And Jake himself had *promised* both Caroline and poor Enid Godby to be personally involved in locating Thaddeus Madison *and* bringing him to safety. The problem there, much as it pained Jake to think about it, was that the kid had been on his own and on the streets longer than most boys could be without becoming pretty badly warped. If he'd remembered what his old man said to him the way Caroline did, and if he wasn't physically ill but believed *he* was actually a vampire—regardless of whether Care's and Marshall Madison's stories were a fact or not—Thaddie was very possibly a weird little creep by now. It might not be kind to think of him like that, but Jake's responsibility was to Care, first and foremost. Who could say what he might do if he *was* still alive and realized his sister had been well cared for and loved all the years he *hadn't* been?

"I don't want you to risk being hurt," Cammy said when

he had paused to think. Her gaze shot to Caroline and it was clear she really meant "you and Care."

The pretty girl who was just beginning to embark on the journey to adulthood regarded Jake with the most anguished, divided expression he'd ever seen. The division, he sensed, even if he couldn't have expressed it in words, was one of loyalties. Her lips parted as though she meant to speak, and she said nothing. It was the time Jake Spencer once had dreaded to the roots of his soul back when Caroline was new with them, had another last name, and he had feared the child he loved might someday have to make a choice between the man who had fathered her and the man who was, in the truest sense, her father now.

I always wondered who she'd choose, Jake thought, searching either for a smile to give her or a few words to speak and remove the burden from her heart. He'd never wondered long, just as he hadn't ever spent much time trying to choose between dying of a stroke, heart attack, or cancer.

The phone rang and the caller simultaneously forced the issue and, in a fashion none of them could ever have predicted, prevented the majority of them from needing to make many truly startling choices.

"Mr. Spencer," the male voice said in Jake's ear, "*I* kept my word and got in touch with you again."

"That's sure as hell a gold star and two new Brownie merit badges for you, Madison," Jake said, nodding to Care and Cammy to establish that it was Marshall.

"I should adore a further exchange of barbs," Madison went on, something about him sounding different now to Jake, "but I have time only to tell you there's been a change in my plans."

"Yeah? You're gonna give me your address, right?"

Marshall—freezing Jake to the spot by doing so— seemed almost to giggle, then to follow that sound with something very much like a sob. "Forgive me if my emotions appear to be shifting rather wildly, sir," he said. "But you see, they *are!*"

"Are you drunk or what, Madison?" Jake demanded.

"Ah, Mr. Spencer," Marshall sang, "I am intoxicated by life—that is all. Entranced by its unceasing fountain of delightful surprises flowing within easy access to all who cherish it so *much!*" He paused as if to regain his dignity of manner. "I mentioned a change of plan. Put bluntly, you need not tell me where you dwell. I had visitors after we spoke. They were good enough to enable me to return to the proper next step in restoring my family: Saving the life and the sanity of my firstborn child."

"You *know* where Thaddie is?" Jake asked, both startled and dismayed.

"The police officers investigating a sudden demise here in my building received a reliable tidbit of information from some female taxi driver," Marshall said. Once more he laughed; this time it was a snicker. "My, it *has* been an informative and entertaining hour for me, sir! Now I shall bid you a good night, for I have much to do. Kindly inform my daughter that her brother and I will be with her soon. Unfortunately, common sense dictates I dare not tell *you* the hour of my arrival—but soon, Mr. Spencer, *soon.*"

Jake shouted, "Wait!" and thought frantically how he could keep the creep on the line long enough to learn where he was. The possibility of the killer showing up in Brooklyn at their home was surely the most alarming one of his life. "How did you find out where we live? I'd be surprised if the cops told ya."

"They weren't that cooperative, no," Marshall answered with a chuckle. "But I warn you, when I've explained my deductive prowess, you may be as embarrassed as I was. Brace yourself, sir!" He drew in a deep breath. "Replenished by a most satisfying midnight snack, I looked up your

name in the Brooklyn phone directory—having discerned
your *charming* accent—and there, too, I found your address
on Lefferts Avenue. Of course, it matched the telephone
number I acquired from poor Enid Godby!''

Jake heard a detonation of uproarious laughter just before
Madison broke the connection. He slumped down in his
chair at the table, too confused and, suddenly, tired to want
to conceal all he'd heard, but also unsure what he ought to
say with Caroline avidly listening. Madison's open comments about the police visit, his weird amusement (or high),
his reference to a "midnight snack" suggested those cops
wouldn't be around to rescue Thaddie or, Jake figured, anybody else. Ever.

For the first time it dawned totally on Jake that the madman pursuing his child and her older brother very likely
was a vampire—at least something with supernatural abilities—strength too, probably. Caroline also said he was
truthful, and Jake believed he was; at least to the degree of
following through on his threats. If the weird bastard said
he was eventually coming to Brooklyn to try to take Care
away, he meant it. Knowing that canceled out the fact that
Jake knew diddly-squat about how to fight vampires except
for what he'd seen while he was yawning his way through
late movies with Caroline.

*If he's going out right now to pick up the boy and turn
him into one more* thing *as evil as he/himself is, and I don't
try to stop him,* Jake thought, *then guys like me may not
have the right even to try to protect our own kids.*

Ignoring the anxiously waiting faces of his family, Jake
glanced down at Sally Schindler's phone number and dialed
it. "Sal?" he said. "Jake Spencer. The killer's headin' for
that hotel to get his kid, and the cops aren't gonna be there.
Can I get a little help?"

He smiled at her answer, nodded, said, "Thanks," and
hung up.

"Find us a cross or crucifix, and a Bible—anything else religious," he said to Cammy, glad to feel decisive again. "I don't know whether that movie crap works, but I don't think Madison is gonna stand still while we drive a stake through his heart." He watched Camille rise without a question, run from the room. Jake kissed Care on the forehead. "Get your coat on, kid. We're gonna go try to find your bro—and bring him home!"

Caroline moved even more swiftly than her Mom.

7

By the time Thaddie was on the roof of the hotel, standing beneath the stars and only dimly aware of how chilly it was getting, he had no clear memory of what he had done to the rats to keep from being killed in their attack—except, of course, for killing *them*.

Most of what he remembered about it now was that Robby had reacted to his speaking aloud by using his strong animal body and those of the three rats with him to crash through the glass and come skittering across the floor at him. But he had surprised them all by charging at *them*, scooping Robby up, and killing him—in some way Thad didn't recall. Without remembering a single detail, he knew he'd even opened the hotel room door to let the others in, slammed it shut, and slaughtered every last one of his "pets"—any ol' way he could and sometimes with the cornered rodents swarming over him like enormous bees with clawed toes.

He understood now he'd triumphed over the beasts because he had not only accepted the fact that he was like Father but admitted that Father was a vampire. Just like Thad had been told that night in the bathroom by Father, he'd found himself changed in whole *lots* of ways—not just in the way he saw things differently. He had been very strong, very fast. Powerful.

Now the amazing powers he'd had were gone again, Thaddie didn't know how to get them back, and he saw that Robby and the others had clawed and bitten him dozens of places in his small body before they died. Standing in one place made the filthy roof bright with blood at his feet, and he didn't feel very good anywhere.

He'd also felt lonely; that was why he had gone up to the roof again. He supposed the Eventide Hotel had itself been dead when he came there to live, but now everything *inside it* was dead—from the two rats he had sort of befriended and all the rest of the rodents to the bald old man sitting in the lobby chair. *Prob'ly just his skeleton now*, Thaddie thought, reminding himself of the food fight and feast the vermin had enjoyed after he'd rejected Robby's offer to share.

So he had climbed up here to keep from being one of the dead things inside the hotel—at least he could see the stars now, or the occasional cars below him in the street— and to look one last time for Father.

I'm like Father, but I don't know how to do all the stuff he does, Thaddie reflected, shivering as the autumn wind picked up. It seemed likely that Marshall Madison could do thousands of amazing things, because just the temporary changes in the boy's own vision and his strength suggested as much. *Right now I don't even know how to stay alive, Thaddie thought*.

He sank to his knees beside the two- or three-foot-high protecting wall running all around the old roof, partly to diminish the effect of the biting wind, partly because he was feeling a little sleepy. To stay conscious, he began trying to remember the details he'd heard about vampires ever since he was real little. Maybe there'd be a clue in that stuff, maybe there was another neat thing he could do to be strong again, to be special.

To live at least till he grew up, even if Father's pledge that they would live forever didn't look very good to Thaddie right then.

Chapter Twelve

1

Marshall wanted to leave the loft the moment he broke off talking with the child-usurping Spencer on the telephone, but certain things he saw out of the corner of his eye made him pause, impatient and irritable, to consider the little practicalities of his busy life.

First he removed his already-soiled dressing gown—the two bullet holes in it probably had ruined the garment, damn those detectives' eyes!—and, naked, swept up the strewn and shattered bones. His wounded back remained sore; a nice bath would have helped. Only time for basics like getting dressed.

Then he added the policemen's remains to the somewhat disorderly pile under the coverlet, replaced the screen, and glanced around to see what else should be done before he departed.

He clapped a palm again his forehead in self-disgust. He

had very nearly left without a *mask*! Detective Lewis had torn the old one from Marshall's face, and, locating it, he realized only a portion of it could be salvaged.

Marshall went back to the bone pile beneath the coverlet and, working more speedily and less selectively than usual, used bits of his more recent acquisitions to accomplish something like an adequate replacement mask. Donning it consumed another few hectic and costly minutes.

Finally, because he definitely planned to go to Brooklyn later that night and fully restore his family, he emptied one of the bottles in his refrigerator at a gulp, washed it thoroughly, and—when he had dressed—slipped it into a breast pocket of his suit jacket.

I don't want to waste a drop of you, Jake Spencer, he thought, patting the pocket. *Perhaps I can recall a few ancient ceremonies to prolong your agony even on the other side of life.*

Until the instant when he was appraising the appearance of the loft—experience certainly had taught him one could never be sure when modern visitors would drop by—Marshall had meant simply to walk to the hotel where little Thaddeus so direly needed him. Because his early boyhood had been rather sheltered, if marked by genteel poverty, and automobiles had been nought but the whimsical prophecy of dreamers and crackpots, he had never fallen into the habit of considering any transport, first, by horse and carriage. By the same token, he was also old-fashioned enough to think that any desirable location in a present city was both within walking distance and clearly marked by street name and family names or address numbers conveniently posted for the properly invited visitor.

In New York, Marshall remembered with growing annoyance, it would be easy to believe that the extermination of all taxi drivers would render common mobility an impossibility!

Carefully locking the loft door, Marshall rushed down the steps and began jogging toward a street more apt to be prowled by cab drivers in quest of a late-night passenger. *Be of good cheer, Thaddeus, Caroline*, he thought—*Father is on his way at last!*

It was not the first time he had wished fervently the old myths about his kind were one hundred percent true. No vampire he had ever known had the ability to become a bat or any other winged creature, and fly. In fact, he could not transform himself by command or mere wish into anything else at all, and in most circumstances he was content to be nothing more than what he was:

An exceedingly intelligent, well-informed, charming (when masked) and witty, compassionate but logical man who adored his loved ones, would do anything whatsoever for their welfare, and *could* take virtually any action toward that end. And, of course, a father who customarily would *never* leave his offspring to fend for themselves without his guidance, aid, and comfort because there were very few ways by which he would *ever* die. Finally (he completed his mental notations), he was that rarest of parents who meant it completely when he said his life would not be worth living without his children. The lack of that insight into his admirable character explained why so many mortals had had to perish these past weeks; none of the deaths was remotely his fault. Bloodlines were everything to a fellow such as he.

He hoped with all his heart that Jake Spencer and any mate the man might have would be the final ones to die at his hands because, in his opinion, they failed to grasp the nature of a complete and completing parental love.

"Taxi!" he called, rushing out into the street when he saw such a vehicle approaching. If necessary, he would hurl himself in front of it, then force the driver to take him to the Eventide Hotel. God help any passengers in the taxi before him! "TAXI!"

2

"I know it's late, dammit, Timothy, listen up!"

Timothy listened, up and over and in. The tip he had provided was probably right on the button, but the boy they had been looking for might be in danger and old Lou hadn't shown up, his cab was abandoned. Lou would no more abandon his cab if he could do anything about it than he'd stop writing abominable poetry and calling Timothy "Timmy."

"It looks like the cops got waylaid," Sal rattled in his ear, "and Jake is on his way to try to save the kid. But the killer who's in all the news will probably be there too. Can you get on the horn and tell some of the other drivers you know?"

"It's done," Timothy promised, trying to pull on his pants while he talked into the phone. He'd called most of 'em at one time or another on behalf of issues discussed in the *Taxi Times*. "Be careful what you do, Sal—watch that pretty neck of yours."

" 'Pretty neck,' huh?" Sal repeated, chuckling hoarsely. "You really *are* an 'Irisher' like ol' Lou said, aren't ya?"

3

Even if his passengers this time were the people he loved most, Jake had never driven from Brooklyn into the city so fast. He had no way to know how far Madison had to go from his place, and that was the main reason he'd asked Sal Schindler to get involved. Now he wondered if he'd done the right thing, because Madison was mad as a hatter, regardless of what else the S.O.B. might be, and even Jake didn't dare imagine how he'd handle the killer if it came down to a fight over Thaddie. He'd just wing it if that happened.

And Care, Jake realized, checking her out where she sat in the backseat—perched on it, actually, except when his quicker stops and turns threw her off balance—well, he should've been a stricter pop. It was obvious Madison's primary interest was in the son, the male; crazy as it was, the madman seemed to be old-fashioned enough to think sons were somehow more special than daughters. Or maybe, it was just that Madison had already screwed around with poor Thaddie's mind and, Jake guessed, his body, enough that the kids' original father yearned for god-damn *seconds!* But he wanted Care too, and now Jake wished to God he hadn't brought her with them.

He also wished he hadn't automatically let Cammy come along; but this was how it was with the three of them, they did everything they could together and, deep inside, he supposed he didn't really love Caroline more than Cammy did. He guessed he was just more open with it, more emotional or something.

Camille was using the seat belt, sitting as stiffly and passively as possible, saying no more than she had to because it would not have been possible to say all the things she might wish to say if this ride were the last one they took together. She had what Jake had suggested they bring in her purse and, whether the holy artifact and Book would be any direct help in dealing with this terrible man they were rushing to confront, their presence in her bag brought Camille warmth and solace. Jake was so overwrought, he hadn't even thought to turn on the taxi's heater—or maybe it was broken—but that was all right. She would not try again to decide what manner of being Marshall Madison might be. He was evil, and a part of Camille yearned to beg Jake to turn around and drive . . . anywhere else.

Care was wondering what her bro would be like now, if he'd missed her at all, and trying to believe he was okay. Any negative thought about Thaddie could not be allowed in. She also wondered if she was going to see Father again after all this time, if he truly wanted her back, and what she would say to him. In a way, even the clearest memories of him that she'd unearthed from the remembering part of a small girl's mind—however clearly she'd heard his kind but authoritative voice or had seen the face she once loved as much as Pop's—were no different from recollections she had of the first books she'd read or the first motion pictures she'd seen. Those, too, she remembered in a part of her that belonged to someone who sorta didn't exist anymore. So was the love she thought she felt for Father nothing deeper than the love she remembered for the residents of Pooh Corner, or Oz, or for the Muppets and Mickey Mouse?

Care pulled her locket, left open, from her jeans pocket. When Pop wasn't looking toward her in the rearview mirror, she waited till streetlamps and headlights provided illumination and studied the two sections of a locket that seemed, now, older and sadder than anything Care could remember. Getting it out of her pocket, she had snapped the hinge, the two halves were scarcely linked any longer, and Mother—Mother Deborah—might have been a face in some antique album. No, not that. Caroline had all good memories about Mother, except at the last. It was mostly that she now looked to Care as if she were smiling a good-bye, and had on her lips the words "It's all right."

Care froze, tremored. Father's face did not appear magically in the second half of the locket any longer, but she believed that instant *something* was there. Nothing to be seen with her eyes, but a trace or shadow that called to her, wanted to welcome her, through the old locket. *A trace of something that wished to use her as Thaddie had been used!*

Before Care could change her mind she rolled the window down and dropped the memento into the streets for the New York traffic to crush into nothingness.

You won't get me back with your tricks, Caroline thought fiercely. Maybe some other way or some other time, she swore to herself, glad for the chilly breeze from the open window. *Not* like that. Love couldn't be allowed to just take or tell what to do.

Pop suddenly swore, braked the cab enough that Care's attention was snapped forward so she could stare between him and Mom through the windshield. "What the hell is going on?" Pop asked nobody in particular, continuing to slow the taxi. "We're almost where we wanta go but what's with all the traffic at this time of night in an area like this?"

Caroline and Camille both saw the lines of automobiles converging at the intersection just ahead of their car and had no answer for Jake. Merely their shared apprehension.

4

"How much farther is it?" Things were going wrong, he knew it. His powers were restored and he sensed a change, a grievous loss somewhere.

The taxi driver who liked to be called "Air Willie" peered at his passenger by way of the review. He was a funny-looking dude but he sure didn't look like *much*. Well, it was Sal's show from Willie's viewpoint, and it was no big problem doin' what she'd asked: Taking his sweet time in bringing any passengers who wanted to go there to the shit-ass Eventide neighborhood. Maybe it *would* help the little boy. "Had t' take a detour, sir."

"I'll double your fare if you get me there within three minutes," Marshall said, trying to keep from shouting at the man—or simply killing him and seizing the cab.

"Wooooo-*eee*, sir, that'd make close to twenty dollar!" Air Willie jived him, hiding a big sarcastic grin behind one hand. Maybe the mothafucker thought he'd sell out little boys for goddamn peanuts! "I sho will git my ol' ass in gear."

Two seconds later Willie saw the tail end of what Jake Spencer had seen, and beamed with pride at the sight.

It looked like half the taxis in New York had formed their own parade! On duty or off, with or without passengers, drivers from their company and at least two others Air Willie identified had responded to Sal Schindler's call—and maybe Timothy's, since the Irish cat was really into protecting cabbies and their rights—for help. Help for a little boy they didn't know, and one of their own. It was a positively *glorious* parade!

And damned if it didn't look like William H. Crawford had the bad ass guest of honor sittin' on the backseat of his own hack!

He still doesn't look like much, Willie thought, starting to wonder if he couldn't take this weird-looking man himself—

And then realized he would have to stop, along with all the other drivers, around a block from Jerseyside and the Eventide Hotel. Now what the fuck was goin' on?

5

The line of traffic—it looked like nothing but taxis to Jake—came to a complete stop. He knew they were a block to a block and a half from their destination, so Jake got out, ready either to raise hell if there was no good reason for the post-midnight backup or, if necessary, to leave Care and Cammy where they'd be halfway safe and just run the rest of the way to the deserted hotel alone.

Because it was a misty night and the vehicles' lights were creating more glare than illumination for anybody on foot, Jake trotted toward the intersection with a chip automatically on his shoulder and a combination of wisecracks and obscene commands on his lips. There'd better be a goddamn semi or garbage truck jackknifed right in the middle of the fucking street, he thought, or he was gonna give 'em a big piece of—

"Sal!" Jake interrupted his own Manhattan melody, astonished to see the tough-minded woman cabdriver in the middle of half a dozen male hacks, clearly snapping instructions and gesturing with both hands. "I'm glad t' see you but what's comin' down?" he demanded.

Sal hefted a monkey wrench from the trunk of her cab, tapped it on her palm. "I'll tell ya what *isn't* comin' down, Jake," she said, looking grim and ferociously determined. "Any little boys at the hands of some gawdamn gutless murderers—or any old farts like Lou, if he's still okay." She gave Jake a flirting wink, patted the back of her perpetually blond hair. "And no sensitive hunks like you are gonna get fucked over by some limp-dick asshole who can get his jollies only from *hoitin'* folks!"

Looking admiringly around now that his vision was adjusting to the glare, Jake realized what Sally Schindler was doing and, glancing with a grin back up the line of cabs, he motioned to Cammy and Care to join him. Without asking, Jake knew Timothy, at home sick, had been the guy primarily responsible for contacting so many of their fellow drivers so fast.

Though he, Sal, and a few other cabbies were gathered

here, a block or so from the hotel, many more were ringing the whole block on which the Eventide was located. Even as Cammy and Care rejoined him and Jake put his arms around them, other drivers were pulling their hacks out of line, making U-turns when necessary, and rushing to provide further protection for the small boy in the hotel. Even a vampire, Jake decided, might have second thoughts about doing his thing in full sight of so many ordinary, decent human beings.

"What's going on, Jacob?" Cammy asked after a nod to Sal and the other couple of drivers she vaguely recognized.

"Well, honey," Jake said with pride, knowing he'd never again feel like shit because his family wasn't from a snazzy area like his wife's, "these are all my friends. Yours, and Care's." He gave them each a brief kiss and got them headed toward the corner. "They're gonna see to it we go save Thaddie, and also a gent named Lou, if we can possibly do it—without interference from any creeps who never knew how *lucky* they were!"

And within a quarter of a block the assembled drivers began to form a human corridor for the Spencers. Jake sensed the heightened feeling of security emitted by his wife and daughter as drivers, male and female, fell into step behind them the moment the three of them passed by. These were the people a helluva lot of New Yorkers told jokes or swore about, but they were also the men and women out-of-towners usually depended upon to find any of the places boasted about by the mayor, and he was happy to be one of them. In a way he wasn't even surprised to learn they were one big fraternity, just the way Timothy liked to—

Jake saw a cab stopped on Jerseyside, the back door opening; a man in a suit climbed out. The hack was near the corner and also close to Jake, Cammy and Care as they walked on. It took Jake a second to recall that some of the drivers had been on duty and realize that the man leaning back in—apparently to pay the driver—must be a passenger. He felt neurotic getting uptight but, he told himself, anyone might get the wind up at a time like this. They kept walking, urged forward by the growing mass of humanity at their backs, and drew almost abreast of the man who had gotten out of the parked taxi. As he had done every cab length of the caravan, Jake tried to get a gander at the cabbie's face and give him a wave of appreciation.

At the instant Jake recognized Air Willie and saw the necklace of blood below the man's chin, Care stopped in her tracks, pointing to the passenger starting to turn in their direction.

"Father," she said in a tense breath, and neither she nor anyone else could ever have decided if she was actually calling out to Marshall Madison.

6

Marshall blotted his lips with a handkerchief, put it back in his pocket. It had not occurred to him he might be recognized. But part of his makeup and mask had come off when he'd guessed what the taxi drivers were up to and felt obliged to force his own cabbie to edge nearer to the corner. Ripping out the fellow's throat had been a necessity to keep the brave man from fighting back and making a scene.

With the tears in his eyes from what he'd just done, Marshall stared through the cab lights and, though he knew it was her, he was unable to see Caroline clearly. Of *course* they had known one another instantly; it proved the bond they shared! It wasn't just the voice he had heard on the phone but the inflection in his darling's voice the night

Deborah took her life, and a portion of his own loving heart.

"Come to Father," he said, his own inflection midway between a coo and a command. Paying literally no heed to the many people on the street, he spread his arms invitingly and smiled, blinking his eyes to clear them.

Jake felt the electric tension Care gave off and instantly started toward the killer.

Before he or Marshall Madison could act or Care was obliged to make a decision, Sal Schindler—followed by at least nine or ten of the huskier male cabbies—stepped in front of the whole Spencer family. All of them crossed their arms except Sal, who held her wrench low with both hands tightly grasping it. A driver inside his cab switched on a spotlight he had added to his rig to read addresses late at night and pinned Marshall in its beam.

Marshal blinked but laughed. "Hasn't Jake Spencer told you who and what I am?" he demanded of them. "Do you fancy all of you *combined* can keep a father from his only daughter?" He took a step away from the taxi he'd used, and his snort of derision made the cordon of drivers edge back, marginally closer to the Spencers. "Where are you, Mr. Spencer? Are you such an unmanly swine that you must hide with a *female child*?"

Knowing normal men, Sal swung her wrench back just far enough to catch Jake with a slight blow to the groin. "Your obligation's to the two kids," she said sharply, "not to what I hit!"

"This lady's right, Madison," Jake shouted. He nevertheless shoved himself among the front line of people protecting Care and Camille. "*I'm* going to find your boy, not you—and get him all the help he needs to keep from turnin' into something like you!"

"You're an imbecile who raves of impossibilities," Marshall said. He saw his adversary now clearly, sneered at a man no more imposing than Jake Spencer challenging his paternal rights. "Only *I* can save him, Spencer. Only *I* can keep my daughter alive for an eternity. Come, darling Caroline—we shall fetch Thaddeus and begin our new lives!"

Irish Timothy and black Otis, late in getting there, materialized behind Jake and between him and his family. "Give the word, buddy," Timothy said, "and we'll take over from here."

"The daughter you fathered was separated from her brother," Jake yelled at Marshall, ignoring Sal, Timothy, the rest of them. "She *suffered*, Madison—because of *your* goddamn needs! She has a good life now, man, can't you understand that? Are you too fucking weird to understand that Care wouldn't *want* to be with a father who already hurt his own son so badly he may be *dying*?"

For the first time the expression on Marshall's partly unmasked face changed. It seemed to Jake that he sagged slightly, didn't take a backward step but caved in a little, might even have shown a flicker of sad understanding in his eyes and face. "It is possible you are correct about Caroline, though we have not heard from her, have we? You people may or may not have ruined my plans for the three of us." Marshall drew himself erect. "Concerning my son, however, you are hideously mistaken. Believe me. Unless I treat him, that entrancing little fellow will surely die."

"He won't!" Jake argued. "We'll—"

"Oh, yes," Marshall said, nodding. "He will die agonizingly—and quite mad." He turned his head, blinking against the lights. "Who will tell me where the hotel in question is—who will assist me in *saving his child's life?*"

All but forgotten once more, Care pulled away from Camille. She burst through the cordon until she stood equidistant from both Jake and the others, and Father. "*I* can speak for me," she said quietly but forthrightly. "You can all hear what I have to say."

Horrified, Jake took a single pace, intending to grab her arm, to pull her back. But Marshall did the same—and both fathers left their arms outstretched, not touching Care for fear of what they could inadvertently do to her.

Arms at her sides, Caroline looked up at the man who had fathered her. "Take off the rest of that silly mask first," she said. "I want to see you like I remember, Father. Please."

Marshall swiveled his head, reminded of how many strangers were suddenly staring at him. The wind, there on the street corner, was stronger; he thought he saw white flakes swirling in the air between his daughter and him—and he was afraid. Tears once more stood in his eyes, but they were, he knew, truly for him. He used his fingernails to claw off the last remnant of his disguise in spite of his condition.

"You're still so good looking," Care said with a satisfied smile. Then she drew in a new breath. "Father, you never harmed any one of us at home. Till you got sick, and did what you did to Thaddie. But you really did it to *all* of us. You know that, Father, you *have* to know it—because you're the smartest man I ever saw."

Marshall could not hold her gaze. Glancing away, he saw blood on his fingers from the cabdriver he had killed. The red stains against the new snowflakes dancing before him made him hide his hands in the pockets of his suit coat. "I *loved* each one of you," he said simply. No other words occurred to him.

"We loved you too," Caroline said. "Part of us always will. Father"—she groped behind her for Jake's hand, and it was there at once—"now I love my new parents." She turned her head to smile at Camille. "They love me too. *Please.*" She put up a hand to touch Marshall's cheek and began to cry. "Please, be my good, *kind* Father—the one I loved so. Be that way again for Thaddie, me—and Mother."

He tried to focus his logical mind, to concentrate. Thaddeus was near, he knew, but exactly *where* was knowledge he did not possess. The driver of his cab had only followed the others to this location, and none of these people would tell him. Meanwhile, Marshall knew, Thaddie was dying, might already be gone, or mad. Even if he could kill so many people without their sheer weight bringing him down, there was not—for the only time Marshall Madison could remember for more than a century—enough time.

And he could never tear out their throats or strangle them with Caroline watching. He could never hurt *her* in any way.

Marshall put his right hand deeper into his pocket and drew out the empty bottle into which he had planned to collect Jake Spencer's blood.

Before anyone realized what he was going to do, Marshall raised his arm to let his jacket sleeve fall back, exposing his right wrist and a part of the forearm.

"All intelligent creatures must love," he told Caroline, and took a long, slow step to the rear. Away from her and her new family and many friends. "That is what *I* learned from my wife Deborah and my two children."

"Father," Care said, becoming alarmed.

"But if they cannot love, and be loved in return— entirely understood and accepted—then their choice is between acts of creativity and acts of destruction." Marshall tilted his head back. For a second only the whites of his eyes showed. "I no longer know the difference."

Lifting his arm, opening his mouth, he sank his fangs deep into his wrist, then savagely rent it until he was able to capture the outpouring of blood in the bottle clutched in his other hand.

As Camille grabbed Caroline and held tight, Jake rushed forward, horrified but trying to help. The vampire was sinking to his knees on the street, his whole even-featured face the purest shade of white Jake had seen.

But Madison was holding the bottle with his blood aloft, pressing it into Jake's hand. *"To save Thaddeus!"* he cried, resisting the cabdriver's effort to wrap the mangled wrist in his own handkerchief. *"Swear to your God you'll use it?"* he begged.

Before Jake could say a word in reply, Marshall slumped on the sidewalk in the fetal position, his dead face grinning at Jake as if he had, somehow, won after all.

7

One of the drivers Jake hadn't noticed at the intersection, a long-legged man named Pepe, showed up in his cab, horn-blasting a path in order to reach Jake, Sal, and the others. "There's a kid up on the roof of the hotel!" he shouted through his open window. "Hop in and I'll getcha there, *fast!*"

The three Spencers, maternal Sal, and heavyset Otis wedged their way into the cab at once and Timothy, really too sick to have reported to work, clung to the open rear door with only his toes inside the vehicle. Immediately Jake remembered Pepe's rep for driving from point to point faster than any other cabbie in the company, and Pepe didn't let his name suffer: Instead of turning around, he *backed* around the block and all the way to the front of the boarded-up Eventide Hotel without once taking his foot from the accelerator!

Jumping out the door before Pepe's hack had stopped quivering, Jake wondered why he was still clutching the sticky bottle Marshall Madison had given him. Sweet

Christ, had the S.O.B. thought he was going to *inject* it into the boy's neck or just give it to him to *drink?*

"I'll hold it," Camille said, seeing his expression. She had a tissue in her palm and, avoiding Jake's questioning glance, took the container of blood—with great care.

"Look!" Caroline cried, pointing. "Look up *there!*"

Everyone including the other drivers who had run the last half block or so heard Care's shriek, and stared where she was pointing.

They saw a boy who did not appear taller than an eight- or nine-year old, his eyes as big as saucers, standing behind a low railing on the roof of the unlit and dilapidated old hotel. Because of whistling winds blowing occasional gusts of powdery snow in a variety of directions, the boy sometimes seemed to vanish before their eyes. Each time he reappeared, Care and her family detected more about him: His now-filthy clothes, ripped in a dozen places or more; the deep scratches and splotches of blood, some of the wounds still running; the way his footing looked unsteady on the roof, whether because of his injuries, some unknown sickness, or ice they could not see from the ground; and— occasionally, but not often—his expressive young face.

Several of the male drivers had rushed to the entrance of the hotel and were trying to tear away the boards, break the doors down. "He can barely stand up," Sal said, whispering.

"His *face,*" Camille said, "he doesn't know what's happening . . . who we are."

"Bro!" Caroline shouted loudly, running as close as she could in the hope Thaddie would see her. "It's *Care*, Thaddie—come on down!" But he'd disappeared again.

Abruptly the wind velocity dropped and Thad's head and shoulders again popped up, directly above his sister. "Where's Father?" he called, the words just loud enough to tell those beneath him that he was reacting to Care. "I want *Father*!"

But no one knew how to answer him.

"Thaddie," Care finally called back, "you can come live with Pop and Mom and me. It's *nice,* bro you'll like it. B- but Father—" Staring the long distance up, Caroline searched for words no one has ever found for loving use at such a moment. "Father's dead, Thaddie—but *I'm* not, *you're* not—so come on down!"

Camille placed the bottle of Marshall Madison's blood in Jake's hand. He took it without hesitation, edged a step or two forward. "We know you don't feel good, son, that you feel funny and weak." Slowly, carefully, he raised the bottle full of redness as high into the air as he was able to reach. "Your dad *came for you*, boy, he really did. He wanted you to have this. Come down to the lobby, help us open the doors, and—and maybe it'll make you fine again, so you can come and live with your sister and us." Jake saw the boy's expression, swallowed hard. "It's . . . *Father's* blood."

Thaddie immediately climbed up on the roof's railing, wobbled. For an instant it was as if he were the magic-believing small boy he'd never been allowed to be—or maybe, because he thought now he was like his father, he imagined he could swoop down and seize the blood, flying just like the vampires of movies and myth. Perhaps he wished to die; perhaps he wanted to bear his sister off with him in the crook of one frail arm and soar with her to a land where mothers were really mothers, fathers were really fathers, and children—for a while, at least—simply could *be.*

Thaddie shot his arms out before him, dived from the roof of the hotel, and—just for the tiniest part of a second—it almost appeared that Thaddeus Madison might actually fly.

Epilogue

Child of Dawn

For quite awhile, two members of the Spencer family had more nightmares—the kind one awakens from with every detail exceedingly clear and haunting—than usual.

For nearly two years, Caroline Spencer did not dream at all and slept quite poorly. She went to a psychologist, had frequent talks with ministers both Jake and Camille wanted her to see, and talked about the last day of her biological father's and brother's lives mostly with Mom. Pop was there, but he finally admitted that he was deeply regretful that he had offered Marshall Madison's blood to confused and dying Thaddeus. When he broke down at last and wept, told them how he felt responsible for "what happened to that kid," Caroline was not remotely reminded of the way Father had so frequently wept.

After Care said something like that to Pop and told both

her folks how much she loved them, they sent out for pizza and had a party. Jake was okay then.

Caroline had an awful nightmare one more time, during her senior year of high school. Pop and Mom came running into her room to comfort her, terribly worried, and gently asked her to tell them about it.

"I dreamed I was going to flunk two subjects and not graduate on time!" Care wailed. And it took her a whole minute to understand why they had dissolved into tears and were taking turns hugging her, and giggling.

But Care flunked nothing and, one evening early in May, she asked Camille and Jake to buy her a dress for graduation.

"Do you have any idea what sort of dress you want?" Mom asked.

"Yeah," Pop said from his place at the dining table, "just remember your old man isn't made of money." He pointed at her with his fork. "And it's definitely *not* gonna be one of those dresses cut down to your belly button, got me?"

Care grinned with pleased embarrassment and called him silly.

Then she turned to her mother to answer her question. "I saw just what I want in the mall last weekend, and it really wasn't expensive." She hesitated, peered at each of them with her lively eyes dancing. "It's neat, and pretty—and it's a white dress with tasteful polka-dots. *Red* polka-dots."

"Red and white?" Camille said, almost but not quite making a face. "It sounds just a little gaudy, but I suppose . . ."

Then she saw Jake's happy face, and Caroline's, and got it.

"Y'know," Pop said, "I think maybe we can just swing it." He reached out for their hands, squeezed them. "You always did have good taste, Care. And so did *we*!"

WHEN SHADOWS FALL

BRIAN SCOTT SMITH

Martin doesn't believe his aunt's death is an accident, and he and a couple of buddies are determined to find the truth. But when he starts sneaking around the house of his aunt's new "friends," he never expects to witness a blood-drenched satanic ritual. But he does see it, and more important, the witches see him!

Suddenly Martin is in a horrifying race for his life. He has to stop the witches before they stop him for good. And he has to do it before Halloween night, the night of the final sacrifice, the night when the demons of hell will be unleashed on the Earth, the night when shadows fall.

___4313-0 $4.99 US/$5.99 CAN

DRAWN TO THE GRAVE — MARY ANN MITCHELL

"A tight, taut dark fantasy with surprising plot twists and a lot of spooky atmosphere."
—Ed Gorman

Beverly thinks that she has found something special with Carl, until she realizes that he has stolen from her. But he doesn't just steal her money and her property—he steals her very life. Suddenly she is helpless and alone, able only to watch in growing despair as her flesh begins to decay and each day transforms her more and more into a corpse—a corpse without the release of death.

But Beverly is not truly alone, for Carl is always nearby, watching her and waiting. He knows that soon he will need another unknowing victim, another beautiful woman he can seduce...and destroy. And when lovely young Megan walks into his web, he knows he has found his next lover. For what can possibly go wrong with his plan, a plan he has practiced to perfection so many times before?

___4290-8 $4.99 US/$5.99 CAN

Dorchester Publishing Co., Inc.
P.O. Box 6640
Wayne, PA 19087-8640

Please add $1.75 for shipping and handling for the first book and $.50 for each book thereafter. NY, NYC, and PA residents, please add appropriate sales tax. No cash, stamps, or C.O.D.s. All orders shipped within 6 weeks via postal service book rate. Canadian orders require $2.00 extra postage and must be paid in U.S. dollars through a U.S. banking facility.

Name_____
Address_____
City_____ State_____ Zip_____
I have enclosed $_____ in payment for the checked book(s).
Payment <u>must</u> accompany all orders. ❑ Please send a free catalog.

HOWL-O-WEEN
Gary L. Holleman

Evil lurks on Halloween night....

H ear the demons wail in the night,
O ut of terror and out of fright,
W erewolves, witch doctors, and zombies too
L urk in the dark and wait for you.
O ther scary creatures dwell
W here they can drag you off to hell.
E vil waits for black midnight
E nchanting with magic and dark voodoo,
N ow Halloween has cast its spell.

__4083-2 $4.99 US/$5.99 CAN

Dorchester Publishing Co., Inc.
P.O. Box 6640
Wayne, PA 19087-8640

Please add $1.75 for shipping and handling for the first book and
$.50 for each book thereafter. NY, NYC, and PA residents,
please add appropriate sales tax. No cash, stamps, or C.O.D.s. All
orders shipped within 6 weeks via postal service book rate.
Canadian orders require $2.00 extra postage and must be paid in
U.S. dollars through a U.S. banking facility.

Name_____
Address_____
City_____State_____Zip_____
I have enclosed $_____ in payment for the checked book(s).
Payment <u>must</u> accompany all orders. ❑ Please send a free catalog.

Elizabeth Massie
Sineater

According to legend, the sineater is a dark and mysterious figure of the night, condemned to live alone in the woods, who devours food from the chests of the dead to absorb their sins into his own soul. To look upon the face of the sineater is to see the face of all the evil he has eaten. But in a small Virginia town, the order is broken. With the violated taboo comes a rash of horrifying events. But does the evil emanate from the sineater...or from an even darker force?

___4407-2 $5.99 US/$6.99 CAN

SHADOWS

Kimberly Rangel

WHERE TERROR RULES...

In the distant past, in a far-off land, the spell is cast, damning the family to an eternity of blood hunger. Over countless centuries, in the dark of night, they are doomed to assume the shape of savage beasts, deadly black panthers driven by a maddening fever to quench their unspeakable thirst. Then Selene DeMarco finds herself the last female of her line, and she has to mate with a descendent of the man who has plunged her family into the endless agony.

_4054-9 $4.99 US/$5.99 CAN

THE TAKING

DONALD BEMAN

What could Sean McDonald possibly have done to deserve what is happening to him? He was a happy man with a beautiful family, a fine job, good friends and dreams of becoming a writer. Now bit by bit, his life is crumbling. Everything and everyone he values is disappearing. Or is it being taken from him? Someone or something is determined to break Sean, to crush his mind and spirit. A malicious, evil force is driving him to the very brink of insanity. But why him?

_4202-9 $4.99 US/$5.99 CAN

CHARLES WILSON

NIGHTWATCHER

"A striking book. Quite an achievement."
—Los Angeles Times

The staff of the state hospital for the criminally insane in Davis County, Mississippi, has seen a lot in their time—but nothing like the savage killing of Judith Salter, one of their nurses. And with three escaped inmates on the loose, there is no telling which of them is the butcher—or who the next victim will be. Even worse, as the danger and terror grow apace, the only eyewitness to the nurse's death—a psychopathic mass murderer—begins to reveal a fearsome agenda of his own.

___4275-4 $4.99 US/$5.99 CAN

Cold Blue Midnight

Ed Gorman

In Indiana the condemned die at midnight—killers like Peter Tapley, a twisted man who lives in his mother's shadow and takes his hatred out on trusting young women. Six years after Tapley's execution, his ex-wife Jill is trying to live down his crimes. But somewhere in the chilly nights someone won't let her forget. Someone who still blames her for her husband's hideous deeds. Someone who plans to make her pay . . . in blood.

___4417-X $4.99 US/$5.99 CAN

Dorchester Publishing Co., Inc.
P.O. Box 6640
Wayne, PA 19087-8640

Please add $1.75 for shipping and handling for the first book and $.50 for each book thereafter. NY, NYC, and PA residents, please add appropriate sales tax. No cash, stamps, or C.O.D.s. All orders shipped within 6 weeks via postal service book rate. Canadian orders require $2.00 extra postage and must be paid in U.S. dollars through a U.S. banking facility.

Name_____
Address_____
City_____State_____Zip_____
I have enclosed $_____ in payment for the checked book(s).
Payment <u>must</u> accompany all orders. ❑ Please send a free catalog.
          CHECK OUT OUR WEBSITE! www.dorchesterpub.com

WHEN FIRST WE DECEIVE

CHARLES WILSON

"With his taut tales and fast words, Wilson will be around for a long time."
—John Grisham

When a young police lieutenant in a sleepy Mississippi-coast town responds to a routine prowler call one night, he isn't expecting to find the handiwork of a killer. But his grisly discovery is just the beginning of a horrible nightmare...a nightmare that may kill him and his wife.

___4401-3 $4.50 US/$5.50 CAN